D0985074

Other novels in the EVE Universe

EVE: The Empyrean Age
EVE: The Burning Life

TEMPLAR ONE

Tony Gonzales

GOLLANCZ
LONDON

First published in Great Britain in 2012 by Gollancz
An imprint of the Orion Publishing Group
Orion House, 5 Upper St Martin's Lane, London WC2H 9EA
An Hachette UK Company

A CIP catalogue record for this book is available
from the British Library

ISBN 978 0 575 09020 0 (Cased)
ISBN 978 0 575 09021 7 (Trade Paperback)

1 3 5 7 9 10 8 6 4 2

Typeset by Input Data Services Ltd,
Bridgwater, Somerset

Printed in Great Britain by
CPI Group (UK) Ltd, Croydon, CR0 4YY

The Orion Publishing Group's policy is to use papers that
are natural, renewable and recyclable products and
made from wood grown in sustainable forests. The logging
and manufacturing processes are expected to conform to
the environmental regulations of the country of origin.

This book is dedicated to the DUST 514 team:
Never let anyone tell you the odds

Additional material available
at www.gollancz.co.uk

PART I

Madness

1

GENESIS REGION – EVE CONSTELLATION
THE NEW EDEN SYSTEM

>>SIGNIFICANCE MISSION LOG ENTRY
>>BEGIN RECORDING

Given the confines of my exile, insanity is surprisingly fleeting.

From the murky depths of madness, reality churns and boils over my head, a great distance away. Like a pair of entangled protons, my actions seem hopelessly enslaved to a new consciousness that many, including my old self, would consider repulsive or depraved. Yet at some point the mind accepts that whatever is happening, the person drowning can't possibly be me, and that someone or *something* else entirely has been writing these log entries – treating them like unwanted feedback, mere static interfering with the perfectly arranged experiment.

The drone I mutilated is barely functional, though its companions are more concerned with my well-being. In fact, they were indifferent as I ripped into this creature's innards with primordial barbarity. Instead of defending their brother, they took action to protect me from myself when it became clear that physical pain was no obstacle to my rage. My hands, pulped and broken, were tended by medical drones as others held me still. A mesmerizing ooze of cybernetic entrails mixed with my own blood coated the floor; I was absolutely captivated. It was a welcome reprieve from the unbearable ennui of this wretched life.

But my fascination eventually ran its course. The deep, jagged laceration gouged into the drone's faceplate inspires a strong desire to do the same to myself, if only these infernal machines would allow me. For a short while, I was feeling productive, satisfied that it was better to create a disfigured monster than to not create anything at all. At least, such was the logic that justified reaching for that wrench in the first place.

The destitute thing now drags itself through the ship, searching in vain for parts that can only be had from fellow drones, who are unwilling to donate them. I note with subtle amusement that it is searching for a *solution* rather than just accepting an outcome without question, which vaguely resembles my own determination to understand the means through which this exile is sustained.

It stands to reason that the machine's search for answers gives it something to live for. Science has always provided answers for me, not the pathetic faith that my deceased colleague Aulus Gord would have insisted upon. Her Majesty Jamyl would agree, if only she could do so without killing me first.

Equally disconcerting is that I needed to be carried back to my cabin following hours of intense, soul-crushing mourning. The person I used to be was dead, and I felt obliged to grieve. At first the drones offered 'comfort,' as defined by the AI architect who thought to impart his own rubbish notions of empathy into these machines. Then they insisted on drugs, concerned that their inexorable mandate to protect me was in jeopardy. Clearly, I was a danger to myself. If these drones knew such a thing as hope, they might wish their orders would be lifted someday so they could give me the violent end I deserve.

I suppose none of this matters now, as there is little chance that anyone will ever find these logs. That I still adhere to the Imperial regulatory protocol of maintaining them, even when they are largely the same from day to day, speaks volumes about my decaying state of mind. So here it is:

The *Significance* is holding position dangerously close to the EVE

Gate, whose quantum turbulence remains markedly elevated. Tachyon emissions from this massive defect remain steady; several dozen traces of parallel universes pass through the ship every second. All systems are functioning normally, save for the drone I nearly destroyed.

No experiments are in progress. No surveillance probes are due to return for maintenance. No further progress has been made in determining the reason why I am protected from my tormentor here.

Empyreans continue to proliferate in numbers and power. The war has claimed more lives than any empire has the means to track.

We are all EVE's bastard children. And I, Dr Marcus Jror, am the worst of them.

>>END RECORDING

2

DOMAIN REGION – THRONE WORLDS CONSTELLATION
THE HEDION SYSTEM
IMPERIAL CORRECTIONS PENITENTIARY (ICP) 89
SOVEREIGNTY OF THE AMARR EMPIRE

Deep within the orbital fortress of ICP 89, rows of entombed prisoners lined the curved walls of a vast chamber, spiraling upward in perfect rows like larvae on the inside of a giant hive. Not unlike a capsuleer, these inmates were suspended in a viscous gel that kept their immobilized flesh sanitized and nourished. All external references and sensory information was controlled by brain-interface dreamcast technology under the direction of mind wardens, whose task was to enforce the sentences handed down by judges.

Convicts were kept in persistent REM sleep to ensure that the memories of reconditioning would be firmly entrenched in their new life. Psychologists working alongside the mind wardens assisted in the rehabilitation by walking directly into the consciousness of inmates, placing them in the virtual role of their victims and forcing them to suffer vivid re-creations of their own transgressions for as long as it took for the 'Reclaiming' to be complete.

Regardless of their crimes, the souls who ended up here had asked for forgiveness, or – in the case of those whose ethnicity was anything but True Amarr – were compelled to do so by a merciful judge. Such was to prepare them for a return to society, and Imperial technology would ensure that their transition would be seamless.

Many of those who completed their sentences were welcomed back with open arms. As their beloved Empress once declared, wayward children must be corrected from time to time, and once they emerge from holding, they are considered forgiven souls, fully reclaimed, any dues owed to society paid in full.

But sometimes, the imprisoned have no home to return to. The record of their arrival at ICP 89 was the only proof of their existence, and for one very special inmate, this too would be removed from the archives. Lord Victor Eliade, Empress Jamyl's closest advisor, had been seeking individuals orphaned from the universe for a unique reclamation program – one that would be tested for the first time on inmate 487980- A.

Somewhere else in New Eden there were records stating that his name was Vince Barabin, last reported to be aboard the privateer salvage vessel *Retford*, which was destroyed in the T-IPZB system three years ago.

VINCE WAS DEEP IN PRAYER, gazing upon a surreal shoreline glimmering in the soft light of twin moons. Gentle waves lapped against his ankles as he breathed in the fresh sea air of virtual reality, contemplating his favorite verse of the Scriptures:

> *All things were created by the Divine, and so the glory of our faith is inherent to us all;*
> *When thine heart shines with the Light, thou shalt know no hardship;*
> *When thine actions are in Light's name, thou art immortal.*
>
> —*The Book of Trials*, 2:1

When he learned those words, his mind was carried throughout the regions of the Empire, through clusters of stars surrounded by beautiful worlds and wonders whose memory often brought tears to his eyes. In his wildest dreams – those few that he could recall since emerging from Reclaiming – he never grasped how New Eden could be such a vast and breathtaking creation.

Yet he was saddened as well. The faith firmly established that the universe was created for True Amarr, which he was not. The other races of New Eden were descendants of the impure, tracing back to lineages tainted by the Demon on worlds that Amarr could not save. For those blemished peoples, the inescapable test of their existence in this domain was finding the will to return home. Though Vince could never be True Amarr, the Empire would welcome him if he embraced the faith. This act – gathering all the wayward children of New Eden into the blessed shelter of Amarr – was known as the Reclaiming. Though his Caldari roots were long forgotten, Vince wanted nothing more than to become True.

Though he could no longer remember his crime, he knew his incarceration was deserved. But he no longer thought of himself as imprisoned, and he had learned to see the world in a new light. That meant his journey to spiritual redemption was nearly complete. He might have arrived there already if not for the distraction of a recurring dream. Something about a small ship, with a crew he once cared about, and of losing them all to circumstances he could have averted if only he had found the courage to do so.

These visions, the priests explained, revealed a deep fear of failing a test of faith – an encouraging sign that demonstrated that he was eager to prove himself. They warned that he must be prepared to seize the opportunity when it arrived. His indiscretions as a wayward child had led him to the blessed gates of Amarr. He would accomplish more than he ever dreamed possible and do so in the name of something righteous and good.

It is so much more than a faith, Vince thought, turning away from the sea. *It is a code of honor and a way of life.*

As he walked along the beach, he saw another set of footprints forming. An apparition emerged: the fog of light that always preceded the appearance of a priest.

He froze when he realized who it was.

'Faith be with you,' Empress Jamyl said.

Already collapsed in the sand, Vince was terrified. 'My Empress, I should not be in your presence. . . .'

She knelt before him, placing both hands on his shoulders. Vince shuddered, keeping his head down.

'Rise,' the Empress said. 'Don't be afraid. Walk with me. . . .'

He paused before taking the virtual hand of Empress Jamyl I, the supreme ruler of the Amarr Empire and the very manifestation of divinity itself. Standing slowly, he fought an overwhelming urge to look directly upon her. He did not feel worthy of such a privilege.

Gently pulling his hand, she led him down the beach.

'I grew up on these shores,' she remarked. 'I loved the tranquility, the peace, the wonder of all those stars above. . . . When I was young, the palace guards let me wander about, wherever I wanted. I was never in any danger. There are times when I miss that innocence, of not having a care in the world. . . .'

As the first rays of dawn reached out from the horizon, Vince could see structures forming ahead. Farther inland, he could make out the beginnings of a majestic skyline; a solitary spire rose high above the other buildings.

'Is this Xerah?' he asked, still not looking directly at her.

'Yes,' she answered. 'This is how my beloved city was three years ago, on the morning of June tenth.'

People were starting the day, which promised to be a gorgeous one. Vendors opened doors to shops along a boardwalk as a group of teens ran across the beach, surfboards tucked under their arms. Deeper behind the beachfront, hovertrams arrived at platforms to take passengers inland, and Reclaimed laborers worked alongside drones building a new park on the waterfront.

There was no evidence of police or anything that could exert force anywhere that Vince could see.

'They lived in such wonderful times,' Empress Jamyl continued, saddened. Vince turned as her voice trailed away. More angelic than he ever imagined, he watched as she set her gaze on the sky.

'Sadly, in their bliss, they had become naïve. . . .'

A flash of light followed by a deep explosion startled Vince; a ball of fire was rising from deep within the city. Military drones streaked overhead, coming from beyond the sea, flying so low their engines nearly deafened him. Antiaircraft fire rose up from inland as the sound of nearby screams and panic filled the air; a second beam lanced down from space, reducing a city block to ashes.

And then the sky darkened as thousands of dropships converged on the city like a swarm of insects.

When Vince turned to look where the surfers were, he saw their corpses washing up on the sand just ahead.

'The Minmatar did this?' he asked, knowing the answer.

She didn't answer him directly.

'My people were brave ... every last one defiant until the end.'

With a wave of her hand, the imagery changed. The magnificent city that had welcomed the day was now smoldering ruins. Smoke rose from the shells of wrecked buildings; the great ancient spire that dominated the skyline was toppled in half. The staccato of isolated pockets of gunfire carried over the landscape; the muffled thuds of explosions broke through the crash of waves near where they were standing. Bodies were strewn among the rubble and in the streets as combat MTACs marched through the ruined avenues, their ominous metallic steps echoing throughout the metropolis. Though it was midday, the sky was dark, blotted from the plumes of uncontrollable fires.

'This is the Xerah I returned to,' she said bitterly. 'The invaders were vanquished. But this was no victory.'

Vince was fixating on the dead surfers. As their lifeless forms were turned over by waves, he could feel anger building within him. It felt strangely familiar, almost soothing. Though he was peripherally aware that this was only a dream, he was nearly overtaken by the urge to fight.

'It was just the end of the beginning,' she said, letting go of his hand. 'Do you know how many Paladins I've sent to die since this day? How many soldiers use what happened here as inspiration to fight on distant worlds?'

'I would fight and die along with them,' Vince said. 'Even knowing the outcome, I would do it. That's my redemption.'

She turned to face him. 'Is that what our faith tells you?'

'That's what my *heart* tells me. Our faith tells me this is what I was meant for.'

'To give your life for Amarr?'

'Yes.'

She approached and circled him slowly, studying him. He kept his eyes straight ahead.

'That is not your destiny,' she said. 'You will defend the Paladins you would die among . . . '

Vince could hear his own heart beating.

'. . . for I shall make you an angel among us, a warrior that can never fall.'

Her eyes were full of passion.

'So much blood has been spilled defending our faith, our culture, and our way of life . . . so many fall at the hands of empyreans,' she said. 'Though their souls live on, we deprive them of precious time here, in *this* life, which is unique in every way and so crucial in preparing us for the journey beyond.'

Again, she placed her hands on his shoulders; he knelt before her.

'We must protect them. And to do so, you must become immortal as well. . . .'

What Vince didn't know was that his physical body had long since been removed from its holding area in ICP 89. While his mind walked on the virtual beach, his body was already being accosted by medical drones, which pierced and disassembled his flesh with startling precision. His blood was drained and replaced with an infusion of synthetic bioplasma crawling with nanites. His spinal cord was augmented to interface with cybernetic technology. Some of his bones were replaced with light alloys that were nearly unbreakable. Those that were not replaced were encased in a fullerene nanomesh to render them twice as strong. Tendons and muscles were augmented to become hyper-efficient and optimized for powerful contractions that could be controlled with infinite precision. By the time the transformation completed, Vince would be something more than just human.

As he knelt in the virtual sand, the base of his skull was removed so his brain stem could be implanted with a neuro-interface socket.

Vince looked up at the divine image of his Empress.

'I need you to defend our way of life,' she continued. 'There are those who are determined to harm us, and they cannot be reasoned with. They will not stop, not ever, and the bloodshed will continue unless we strike the fear of God into their hearts. You will become the first Templar – an immortal holy warrior of Amarr – on equal footing with True Amarr and, by virtue of your actions, even greater still.'

She looked past him, toward the ruins of her homeworld.

'This is how you will serve us,' she whispered. 'This is the redemption you seek.'

3

THE FORGE REGION – ETSALA CONSTELLATION
THE VASALA SYSTEM – PLANET V, MOON 15
ISHUKONE CORPORATE FACTORY – TEMPORARY HQ
SOVEREIGNTY OF THE CALDARI STATE

A fleet of Ishukone warships emerged from warp just outside of their headquarters station, turning in unison to align with the hangar bay. The untrained eye might have suspected these menacing vessels just returned from the Gallente Federation border. In truth, they were escorting their CEO on routine business, who never traveled anywhere without bringing intimidating firepower with him. He flew at the front of the pack, inside the pod of a Raven-class battleship, immortal and powerful – but by no means impervious to harm.

Ishukone Chief Executive Officer Mens Reppola, one of the most influential figures in all civilization, had withstood the pressures of being responsible for 300 million people fairly well.

He was building a formidable legacy, having successfully guided Ishukone through one of the most tumultuous periods in Caldari State history. Two years ago, the assassination of his predecessor and close friend, Otro Gariushi, had left the mega-corporation on the brink of financial default, and with it, the very high probability that many of Ishukone's labor commitments would shift to purely military obligations under the dictatorship of State Executor Tibus Heth.

Leaderless for months, the mega-corporation lost hundreds of thousands of lives. Workers were activated for military service and sent to die anonymously in the ongoing war with the Gallente Federation. For Mens, who was running the security arm of Ishukone at the time, this was a senseless disaster he knew Otro would have never allowed. With the support of investors, Mens bet his entire personal fortune on taking an ownership stake in Ishukone. The strong-arm tactic impressed the Board of Directors, which, like Mens, was growing weary of the direction in which Heth was leading the Caldari State.

Mens worked tirelessly to salvage the fortunes of Ishukone. He swam against the populist tide of those who believed in Heth's vision of a centralized economy. He redirected the mega-corporation's focus from heavy industry to research and development. He recalled Ishukone-supplied troops and equipment from a war he felt served no good purpose for the State, let alone his mega-corporation.

And he did it all with a brave face. Ishukone today was in a better state than it was three years ago. It had, despite Heth's near-constant efforts to sabotage Mens, finally turned back into a profitable corporation.

By all accounts, Mens should have been proud. But all victories come at a price. In truth, his success was killing him, and for those who knew him best, it seemed like a matter of time before the weight of Ishukone would crush him completely.

'LORIN, I TOLD YOU I can't be there,' Mens snapped, briefly losing his concentration. 'It tears my heart out, but if you knew what we were discussing—'

'*Your* heart? What do you think it's doing to hers?' snapped his wife. 'You *need* to hear what she has to say in person. For God's sake, Mens! She's that close to walking away from you for good!'

A lapse in concentration made the 99,000-tonne vessel at his command veer to port. Mens quickly corrected the Raven-class battleship's course, but not before his cruiser escorts turned high and wide to avoid a collision.

'*What am I supposed to do,*' he seethed. 'I can't be in two bloody places at once—'

He stopped himself too late.

'Ah . . . I'm sorry; I didn't mean to say that. . . .'

Mens ignored the inquiries from his escorts, asking if he was alright.

'No, I understand perfectly,' she said. 'You can't be here to look after us yourself. Why bother when you can just hire muscle and tech? You're more obsessed with protecting yourself from a *ghost* than you are with spending time with us. Face it, Mens: Ishukone is more precious than your own family.'

He throttled back the warship just outside the station's bay doors, halting the entire flotilla in his wake. A staggering amount of money had been spent developing an elite counterintelligence unit for Ishukone. The team's primary purpose was preventing Heth's Provists – the political enforcers of his government party, the Caldari Providence Directorate (CPD) – from infiltrating the organization. But they had halted dead in their tracks many attempts of espionage from their corporate rivals as well.

Ishukone had become a black box to the rest of New Eden. Secretly, its prime directive had become a ceaseless search for a man known only as the Broker. By far, there was no graver threat to the mega-corporation's security. The Broker was responsible for the murder of Otro Gariushi and had made threats against Otro's sister, Mila, as well. Mens Reppola was the only man who knew where Mila was, and that made him a target.

The Broker's tireless vendetta against Ishukone was because Otro had the audacity to defy him. The Amarr Empire used a mutating virus called Vitoc to control its legions of Minmatar slaves, and Otro Gariushi gained possession of an antidote called Insorum. This drug was priceless: The Empire would pay any price to squash it from existence. The Broker offered a king's ransom in exchange for the formula, but Otro refused to sell it, and the decision cost him his life. But even that wasn't enough for the Broker, who vowed to strike down everything else dear to him as well.

There had been no trace of the Broker in years. If it were any other man, there would be enough forensic evidence to convince any police agency that he was indeed dead. But that was exactly what the Broker wanted his hunters to believe. He could be anyone and, thanks to cloning technology, several people at once. Worst of all, he had the patience of immortality. When the time was right – even if it was decades from now – he was bound to strike.

Since Otro's death, Mens had placed a barrier around his family, literally surrounding them with so much physical and technical firepower that even a State-sponsored military effort would have trouble penetrating it. And even then, it might not be enough. The strain of being surrounded at all times by weapons and prying eyes was reaching critical mass. It was a maddening paradox, because the more evident the security measures, the less secure everyone felt. Yet it was all that Mens could do to protect his family, and it was more than anyone else could provide. But it was still a life of fear, which for Lorin Reppola meant it was hardly a life at all.

'That's not true, and you know—' he started to tell her.

'Prove it,' she interrupted. 'Your daughter needs the assurance that her father is going to be there when she needs him most. *This is one of those times*. You can't hire someone else for this.'

Harbor Control hailed the ship with a direct broadcast: 'Commander, you're cleared to approach. Is everything alright?'

Mens ignored it.

'Lorin, please—'

'Show us you're not a selfish bastard,' she said.

Before he could get another word in, the comm signal terminated.

THERE WERE NO CHAIRS in this conference room, and the counter-intelligence team gathered around the chest-high table. Because his time was allocated in exact quantities to his many responsibilities, Mens felt that meeting areas had no reason to be comfortable. Time was precious, and both he and his closest lieutenants shouldered enormous burdens.

Whenever they met, everyone stayed on their feet. By these virtues, meetings were necessarily prompt, short, and directly to the point.

Under normal circumstances, it would have been extremely uncharacteristic for Mens to arrive two minutes late.

'The Citadel,' he said, strolling to the head of the room. 'Tell me what happened there.'

Counterintelligence Chief Anton Markov spoke first.

'Pursuant to the passage of TRUST by the CPD, Heth has deployed Provists to each of the mega-corporations to perform detailed audits of financial and military assets. Despite our refusal to participate, Provists appeared at our station in Korama demanding access to classified datacores. When the techs refused, the Provists threatened them, and security was called in. In the resulting scuffle, one of our guards was killed.'

'In our own facility?' Mens erupted.

'Yes, sir. The guard's neck was broken in the fight. Ishukone Watch arrested all Provists and wants to bring a capital murder charge on the one responsible – with your approval. The CPD already warned us not to do that.'

TRUST stood for Transparency for Unity and Strength, a controversial bit of legislation passed by Heth requiring more disclosure from mega-corporations about their activities. On the surface, the act was beneficial to investors and equitable for State-controlled institutions such as the Caldari Navy, which relied on corporate funding. Most people believed it was just the continuation of Heth's unsubtle efforts to consolidate his grip on power.

'Of course they did,' Mens fumed. 'So what'd they threaten us with now?'

Anton paused, as if caught off guard by the question. 'Sir, I—'

'He doesn't know,' muttered Ralirashi Okimo, the Chief Technical Officer of Ishukone, a grave look on his face. 'I'm sorry to be the one to tell you this, but the State Science Academy has formally revoked your daughter's enrollment, citing our lack of participation in the TRUST Act.'

The words nearly took the air out of his lungs.

So that's what she wanted to tell me, Mens thought.

'They made a scene of it: Bastards literally pulled her right out of class, in front of everyone. The same exclusion criterion will likely be applied retroactively to all Ishukone residents,' Ralirashi continued.

'Heth is using the example of your daughter to send a warning to others.'

I'm losing my family for this, Mens thought, lost in a trance as he stood among colleagues who were helpless to do anything except avoid looking at him directly. *The only thing that I could give her to make up for my absence in her life was that institution, where the best minds of Caldari science and culture had gone. She'd opened that door by herself, using her own smarts and work ethic. All I had to do was hold it open for her.*

Instead, I slammed it in her face. For Ishukone's sake.

It started like a siren approaching from far away: rage, swelling within Mens Reppola.

'The CPD will use this as leverage to free their Provists and force our compliance with TRUST,' Anton continued. 'Thousands of Ishukone civilians are enrolled in programs there. Strategically speaking, they're taking tomorrow's intellectual capital away from us. As of now, the press is unaware of these events.'

Tibus Heth. Going after my own family.

'Mens ... ' Ralirashi urged. The two had been close friends for years. 'There's no wrong answer here.'

The words of his own wife haunted him: *Show us you're not a selfish bastard.*

'Charge them,' Mens said quietly. 'All of them. They'll face a judge here, in Ishukone courts. Unless they've been bribed, our magistrates will convict them. Post heavy security around the holding location, including extra warships. Send a very clear message that we're not taking this any longer.'

'And the press?' Anton nodded.

'When the story breaks, tell them our version of the truth. But leave my daughter's name out of it.'

'Yes, sir.'

'Meeting adjourned,' Mens declared, leaning on the table with his knuckles. 'Keep me informed of the CPD's reaction.'

As the room cleared, Ralirashi was the last to exit. Mens took him gently by the arm and pulled him off to the side. His other hand activated a discreet ECM (electronic countermeasure) device.

Nothing electronic, including the room's own surveillance system, would be able to record their conversation.

'I need a ship,' he said. 'A fast and stealthy one.'

Ralirashi never made eye contact. 'When?'

'As soon as you can.'

The engineer glanced at his datapad. 'There's a convoy leaving here in an hour. Take a shuttle to Sigma-Two, in the unfinished deck level. Construction drones will see you aboard. Don't be gone longer than six hours.'

'Thank you,' Mens said, releasing his grip.

'She doesn't need that damn school,' Ralirashi added. 'I'll teach her myself everything she needs to succeed.'

'I know. But enough is enough. I need to let an old friend know what I plan to do.'

Mens considered letting his wife know that he would be delayed, then thought better of it.

What would be the point now? he thought.

Ralirashi stole a glance at him before hurrying away.

'Tell her that *this* old friend says hello.'

AS THE CHIEF EXECUTIVE OFFICER of a Caldari mega-corporation, keeping a low profile was almost impossible. Those responsible for the safety of Mens Reppola knew his whereabouts and itinerary at all times, positioning armed escorts and sentry technology well ahead of his arrival. Sneaking away from this security detail was a daft notion, unless aided by the freakishly intelligent and resourceful mind of Ralirashi Okimo.

Station camera footage would show that the Ishukone CEO retired to his quarters to sleep shortly after their meeting, leaving instructions with colleagues and guards that he was not to be disturbed. Medical AI systems monitoring his health would indicate that he was sleeping soundly, without the assistance of meds. For added measure, the AI would recommend that he be left in that state for a minimum of six hours to help alleviate evidence of acute psychological stress in his biorhythm.

Of course, all of this data was bogus. The unfinished hangar of

Sigma-Two was taking an unusually long time to complete – tight budgets being what they were – which left it manned entirely by drones, whose memories would be erased after loading the starship capsule containing Mens Reppola into a Wolf-class assault frigate and equipping it with a cloaking device. When he returned later, this ship and all evidence of its existence would be disassembled and recycled into scrap.

The convoy itself, twenty ships long, was comprised entirely of Minmatar- constructed vessels, a popular choice for freight companies doing business with the mega-corporation, given the attractive cost and performance of its haulers. Mens would leave with that convoy as an escort, broadcasting an IDENT signature that registered him as a noncapsuleer. Upon arrival at the next port of entry, Mens would set course alone on a dangerous journey some forty star systems away to the Geminate Region.

Hidden there among the searing stellar winds of the Mjolnir Nebula, he would find Mila Gariushi, and inform her in person of his intent to leave Ishukone for good.

4

BLACK RISE REGION – KURALA CONSTELLATION
THE PRISM SYSTEM – PLANET VI: LIMA PEARL
SOVEREIGNTY: CONTESTED

Killing human beings was effortless for Federation Navy Captain Korvin Lears.

As with all capsuleers, the warship wired directly into the neural pathways of his brain responded like a natural extension of his physical self. Every aspect of the vessel's vast capabilities, from the warp engines to its lethal arsenal, was controlled by the will of a single pilot. Quantum computers aboard the ship – in this case, a Myrmidon-class battlecruiser – worked in perfect harmony with the cybernetic implants in Captain Lears's brain, processing massive amounts of information instantaneously and freeing his will to focus on the decision of the moment – which in this instance was the complete obliteration of a Caldari battleship.

Some of the fiercest fighting between the Gallente Federation and Caldari State was in the Black Rise Region. The conflict here, as with most of the fighting elsewhere in the Empyrean War, made few headlines in the densest populations of Empire space. The 'losec' regions – constellations surrounding the periphery of high-security space – were sparsely populated before the war began. Composed mostly of isolated colonies, the habitable worlds of these systems were still being developed by the corporations of nation-states, each of which shared a vested interest in hiding the true cost – in both credits and blood – of their operations.

The war in space was dominated by the capsuleers, and their power over mortals was staggering. There were no enforceable treaties in Black Rise, nor conventions regulating the treatment of prisoners. The conflict was testing the limits of human decency, and every government was complicit in its abominations, whether as direct participants or simply in looking away from these affairs entirely.

Captain Lears, a decorated veteran of the war and regional specialist for operations in Black Rise, was currently fighting alongside Federation warships from the Placid Naval Forces Command in a pitched battle against elements of the Caldari Navy. Acting on intelligence provided by covert scout patrols, the Federation intercepted terra-ops warships attempting to land mechanized infantry beneath the orbital defenses of Lima Pearl, the sixth planet of the system. Though outnumbered, the terra-ops ships were fighting valiantly against impossible odds. As drones and fighters weaved through packs of battlecruisers exchanging fire, Korvin was oblivious to the scale of violence surrounding him.

His concentration instead focused on the plasma bolts of his own railguns as they burned deeper into the Caldari battleship. Part of his hyper-awareness was tracking information that was utterly nonessential: He was counting the number of lifeboats ejecting from the disintegrating vessel, and comparing that figure with the typical crew complement for that ship class.

The target began breaking apart, splitting in two before exploding violently. When the bluish white blossom dissipated, a tumbling mausoleum of charred, twisted metal was all that remained. Korvin fixated on the wreck, adding his count to a running tally that he'd been keeping since the war began.

Then the mausoleum began calling out to him.

Whispering. Murmuring. He couldn't bring himself to turn away from it.

'Gunfighter One-Six, new primaries are stuck in the bubble at mark two.'

The voice of the theater commander was loud and crisp, but

Korvin didn't acknowledge him. His own camera drones were still focused on the wreckage as the other Federation vessels turned toward the remaining Caldari. An inhibitor field made it impossible for the ships to escape, as their propulsion engines were crippled by gravimetric interference. They would barely be able to defend themselves.

'Weapons free,' the commander continued. 'Destroy all remaining targets.'

But Korvin wasn't listening. Images of corpses filled his vision as the camera resolution was amplified. The audio converters of his ship interface were functioning perfectly, but all he could hear was what sounded like a room full of people, where many conversations were happening at once.

A voice rang out from the distance: 'Gunfighter One-Six, do you copy?'

The conversations were getting louder. Sinister things were being spoken. A resonance of evil arrested the senses of Korvin Lears as his mind focused on one floating corpse in particular. The skin of its face and scalp had been burned completely off.

A voice from another pilot in the squadron rang out: 'Commander, two bogies are Badger-class transports. Scans reveal persons of interest on board.'

Korvin's trance was almost broken by the word *transports*. They were unarmed most of the time, relying on escorts for protection. For terra-ops ships, some of that cargo could be troops, but there would almost certainly be civilians on board. The sensors of the Myrmidon conveyed that its escorts had already been destroyed.

The sound of the voices was beginning to hurt his ears. A wicked shout jolted him. And the corpse, Korvin swore, was smiling at him.

'Copy, Gunfighter One-One,' the commander said. 'Engage the transports and report.'

All the voices screamed at once, while the corpse just stared its frozen, skinless cackle through Korvin's soul. He writhed inside the pod containment fluid, convulsing as though his demons were locked inside of there with him.

Another Federation pilot answered the call of duty.

'Roger; two Badgers locked down, engaging.'

Korvin saw the first volley of plasma charges slam into the target, taking its shields down on impact.

'Gunfighter One-Six, what's your status?'

A second volley ruptured its hull. A single lifeboat ejected. The corpse kept laughing.

'One-Six, are you alright?'

He could hear the captain of the transport begging for mercy right before it exploded, and suddenly the voices in Korvin's mind silenced.

It had all become perfectly clear to him now.

'No,' he mumbled, directing the Myrmidon's gun turrets toward the other vessels in his squadron. 'I'm not alright.'

Before the commander could answer, he locked his weapon systems on the lead Federation warship and opened fire.

'Lears, what the hell are you doing?'

The second Caldari transport, already crippled from Federation plasma fire, began ejecting lifeboats. One more volley would destroy it for certain.

Korvin placed a second stream of concentrated railgun fire on the lead Federation ship. Its shields buckled, and the rounds detonated against its plate armor.

'Friendly fire, cease fire!' the pilot exclaimed, taking evasive maneuvers. 'Command, I'm under attack from a friendly! What the hell is going on?'

Korvin locked the other three Federation warships while tracking the number of lifeboats ejecting from the remaining transport. If one more got free, he could safely assume that he had saved at least 90 percent of the passengers on board.

'Shut your weapons down!' the commander shouted. 'That's an order!'

With a thought, the Myrmidon's railguns spit volleys at each of the remaining Federation ships, disrupting their attack run. Elation swept through Korvin as the last lifeboat rocketed away from the crippled transport, which by now had only a skeleton crew or even just its brave captain left behind.

'Captain Lears! Shut your engines down right now!'

He was at peace with himself.

Any moment now, his own comrades would retaliate with lethal force for his inexcusable betrayal. But he was immortal. When his ship was destroyed, he would awaken in a cloning vat at a Federation Navy base, surrounded by armed guards with orders to escort him directly to a court-martial and charges of treason.

'Don't let that son of a bitch escape!' the commander shouted.

His bliss was replaced with miserable clarity. The plasma blasts streaked across space for him, and he reflexively took action to secure his survival.

He saw one last escape pod eject from the battered transport.

Do some good with this chance, Korvin thought, focusing on the tiny craft as it sped away. *Make it worth what I just sacrificed.*

With a clear conscience, an uncertain future, and a heavy heart, Captain Lears warped away as bolts of plasma converged on the empty space behind him.

5

ESSENCE REGION – VIERES CONSTELLATION
THE LADISTIER SYSTEM – PLANET IV, MOON 4: RÉNEALT
PRESIDENTIAL BUREAU STATION
SOVEREIGNTY OF THE GALLENTE FEDERATION

The spacious apartment of former President Souro Foiritan was furnished with an aristocratic decor, fitting for an accomplished politician. Collections of lavish gifts presented by the bourgeois and elite power brokers of New Eden were arranged with artistic precision throughout the flat. They were the relics of a storied career at the highest level of government, a career that had come to an abrupt and humiliating halt.

Souro preferred to keep the place dark, which was how he found it upon returning from a day of meetings with academia. But sitting comfortably inside was the man who had replaced him, along with his security drones.

'Good evening,' President Jacus Roden said. 'You don't return my calls.'

Souro glared at him.

'My datapad discards junk messages,' he said. 'You'll be hearing from my lawyers about this—'

'Before you say another word,' Jacus interrupted, placing his own datapad on the table. 'Just watch.'

A volumetric projection of two men materialized in the living room. One was of President Roden. The other was Federation Grand Admiral Anteson Ranchel.

'HOW MANY HAVE WE LOST?' President Roden asked.

'One mechanized division and three engineering battalions,' Admiral Ranchel replied.

'Which is how many soldiers?'

'Twenty thousand, give or take a few hundred.'

'"Give or take," Admiral?'

'I'm sorry, Mr President. I've become numb to statistics.'

'This many dead because of one capsuleer attack?'

'He had help on the surface, probably Dragonaurs.'

'So terra-ops for Villasen are terminated?'

'I'm afraid so, sir.'

'How many colonists are still down there?'

'About ten thousand in three separate outposts. They're spread out by hundreds of kilometers, all of it impassable by ground and with limited comms between them. We think our forward teams made it to one of the settlements, but . . . '

'Go on.'

'Once Caldari Navy SPECFOR or Dragonaurs sweep through, it's over.'

'No prisoners will be taken?'

'Not likely, sir. No.'

President Roden shifted uncomfortably in his seat.

'And, of course, we'd treat them in kind,' he said.

'That's right,' Admiral Ranchel said indifferently.

'How are we supposed to win hearts and minds with those tactics?'

'We lost hearts and minds a million casualties ago,' the Admiral said. 'The colonists don't care who's winning in space. They're tired of being shot or tortured for saying the wrong thing to the uniform of the week.'

'I'm sure our soldiers aren't shooting anyone they're not supposed to,' President Roden said, narrowing his eyes. 'Right, Admiral?'

'We do what we can.'

'Well that's not good enough, now is it?'

'No, sir, it isn't. The point is, it'll take months to replace the bodies we lost in that engagement. We won't be able to put boots on the ground there for a long time.'

'That's unacceptable.'

'On that we agree.'

'I'm disappointed you admit it with so little remorse. Do you have anything else to report?'

'A Navy capsuleer with Placid Command fired on his own squadron, then managed to escape following fleet orders to neutralize him. His whereabouts are currently unknown.'

'Unknown.'

'The capsuleer's name was Korvin Lears.'

President Roden tilted his head.

'Was it?' he asked.

'You know him?'

'Who doesn't, Admiral?'

'Captain Lears had just participated in a terra-ops interdiction mission over Lima Pearl when he became unresponsive and attacked Federation warships. He was attempting to save the crew of a Caldari transport, and he succeeded.'

'Who was on that ship?'

'Several officers and a contingent of civilian engineers.'

'Civilians were on board?'

'Yes, sir.'

'And he was ordered to shoot them down anyway?'

'Given the profile of ranked personnel on board, the civilians were deemed expendable.'

'Do you think he was attempting to save the civilians or the officers?'

'It doesn't matter,' the Admiral said, raising his voice slightly. 'Captain Lears will be charged with treason if and when his clone awakens in our custody. Sir.'

'You didn't answer the question.'

'I beg to differ.'

'Ah. So killing civilians is a valid tactic in our military doctrine now?'

'In those circumstances, yes. Disobeying orders and firing on fellow pilots is not.'

'He was disobeying an order to attack *civilians*—'

'He was once a close associate of Alexander Noir, *sir*. The worst traitor in our history. He should have never been allowed in a ship to begin with.'

'Is he responsible for any Federation fatalities?'

'What difference does it make? A jury will decide his guilt or innocence.'

'I know the rules of our courts, *Admiral*.'

'With all due respect, *Mr President*, I don't think you do.'

THE PROJECTION WITHDREW BACK into the datapad. President Roden leaned forward to scoop the device off the table as his host unleashed a low whistle.

'Stress brings out the worst in everyone,' Souro mused. 'I've heard about your disagreements before, but that outburst . . . I don't know what to say.'

President Roden pushed the tumbler offered by Souro's maid off to the side.

'Oh? What else have you heard?'

'The usual,' Souro said smugly. 'Mostly that you're a ruthless son of a bitch who doesn't know how to connect with people. Nothing you don't already know, I'm sure.'

The man elected to replace Souro Foiritan as President of the Gallente Federation was a capsuleer. The founder and former CEO of the mega-corporation Roden Shipyards emerged from a reclusive retirement to run for the presidency after Foiritan stepped down on his own accord – or so he insisted. A host of national setbacks followed by the loss of Caldari Prime when the war began dismantled the popularity that Foiritan spent nearly a decade cultivating. For all his impressive contributions to the Federation, both to its culture and as a nation, he was remembered most for failing to engage the most powerful class of human beings in history: the immortal capsuleers, or 'empyreans.' The voters demanded change, and when a Federation capsuleer emerged as the front-running candidate, they eagerly offered their support and proved more than willing to overlook a past that was anything but pristine.

Jacus Roden was strikingly different from the charismatic, good-looking Foiritan. At first glance, he was a much older man; his head was shaved, and he was shorter than average, with a slight build. He walked deliberately, as though moving too fast would break something. But his cybernetic augmentations – at least the ones that were obvious – gave him a haunting appearance. His eyes were his most visible and striking modification: The irises were emerald green, capable of emitting light that some believed was tied to his emotions, while the conjunctiva was laced with microcircuitry. Separate lines of metal trim ran along each jawbone, beginning below the ear and ending where his sharp chin began. With the right lighting conditions, Jacus Roden's head looked like a greenish skull.

No one knew what those eyes could see – only that they weren't the ones he was born with.

'It doesn't have to be this way,' Jacus said calmly. 'Granted, I could find what I'm looking for elsewhere. But I would much rather hear it from you.'

'What if I'm not interested in discussing it?' Souro muttered, jutting his chin toward the two intimidating sentry drones standing at the door. 'You plan on coercing it out of me?'

'Now, Souro, let's act civilized,' Jacus said. 'You should speak like the man who brought greatness to the Federation. If only for a short while.'

'I don't have anything to say to you,' the ex-President growled, downing his tumbler in a single gulp. 'Which means you have no reason to be here.'

Jacus leaned back in the chair, crossing one leg over the other. 'You know, we were all good men once—'

Souro stifled a laugh, then composed himself.

'— but all men, being human, are fallible creatures,' Jacus continued. His green eyes brightened ever so slightly. 'A man betrays the Federation, and just like that a great enlightenment ends. Souro, as President you allowed the first public execution in centuries, giving in to the mob's thirst for blood. I'm no saint. But I don't have that failure on my conscience.'

Jacus was referencing the capture, trial, and brutal public execution of former Grand Admiral Advent Etturer, who sold the secrets of the Federation's border defense network that had enabled the Caldari Navy to invade the Luminaire system. The resulting occupation of Caldari Prime, right in the heart of the Federation capital system, persisted to this day, with millions of Gallenteans remaining trapped in quarantined sections of the planet.

Souro Foiritan spoke through gritted teeth.

'What did you come here for, *rodent*?'

'Tell me, how many lives did you destroy during your career?' Jacus asked. 'I'm a politician now. . . . That practically makes us brothers. Do we not act in the best interests of the Federation? To be fair, it's only natural to find places where self-interests intersect with . . . *national* priorities. So there are no more *truly* good men left, assuming any ever existed at all. These ugly times bring out the worst in us. Only the lesser evils remain. And you, dear friend, are no more or less evil than I.'

Souro feigned the most polite tone that his anger would allow.

'How can I help you, President Roden?' he asked.

'That's better,' Jacus said, leaning back and clasping his hands before him. 'We can disagree and still be civil. Now, I would like to hear, in your own words, why you believe Admiral Ranchel is, and I quote, "numb" to the catastrophic loss of Gallentean life.'

'Because he's insulating himself from reality,' Souro muttered, refilling his own tumbler. 'All of us are.'

'The reality of facing the consequences of your own decisions?' Jacus asked.

'Capsuleers have become more powerful than anyone anticipated,' Souro said, pausing to take another sip. 'The toll they've taken on human life is too astounding to believe.'

Jacus unclasped his hands, narrowing his eyes.

'Difficult to trust them, I know,' he said.

'They're an abomination,' Souro sneered. 'Present company excluded, of course.'

'Of course. Yet the people voted one to be their President.'

'So they did. Not long after they burned a man to death for treason.'

'Democracy is indifferent to the hypocrisy of its own people.'

'Which *people* are you referring to?' Souro scoffed, downing more of the potent drink. 'Those lucky enough to live in secure space are the biggest hypocrites of all. For them, this war is peripheral: It doesn't affect their lives in the slightest, and the goddamn corporations are happy to keep it that way. If they knew what we know—'

'Nothing would change,' Jacus interrupted. 'As you say, all the wealth here insulates people from caring too much.'

'That won't last forever.'

'No, not without curbing the body count,' Roden said, leaning forward, 'or without a technical breakthrough to smash the stalemate.'

'Aha – so *that's* why you've come here,' Souro said. 'You were right to say you could have learned all this elsewhere. Like from your own Intelligence Director.'

'I need both sides of the story, and I have neither the time nor patience to play politics,' Jacus replied drily. 'Advancements in drone tech were available while you were still in office. Why weren't they deployed?'

Souro laughed.

'Your Grand Admiral is insolent, and you don't trust your own cabinet,' he said, leaning back. 'What do you need to do to earn some respect? Visit old Presidents for advice?'

'Charming,' Jacus said. 'Please answer the question.'

Souro was surprised at his own urge to do so.

'Every AI that we've ever experimented with can be compromised – even those produced by Roden Shipyards. I doubt that's changed since I left.'

The eyes began to glow again. Jacus gave the truth agent in Souro's whiskey more time to do its work.

'Tragically, our efforts to cut losses in this war haven't been very effective,' Jacus said. 'But I'm sure there are other options in the vault we haven't tried.'

'Oh, there are a few things,' Souro slurred, now feeling the effects of the drink. 'Dark, nasty stuff . . .'

'I just want to know about one,' Jacus said, more deliberately than usual. 'A classified Navy program called "The Cain Directive."'

'"Cain . . ."' Souro's eyes closed, and his head fell back into the chair as though in a meditative trance.

Jacus studied his prey intently. 'Please tell me about that one, Souro.'

The former President was now completely anesthetized. Though unconscious, his motor skills, audio processing, recall, and cognitive abilities were responsive. He spoke slowly but clearly – and would remain pleasantly agreeable for the rest of their conversation.

'The Navy floated several proposals for creating supersoldiers,' Souro started. 'Most were like the Caldari model: They combined elements of cloning and cybernetic engineering. Some proof-of-concepts became elite fighting units, but not in any widespread capacity.'

'Why not?' Jacus asked.

'Because attrition is still costly,' Souro said.

'You mean from the expense of producing the soldier?'

'No,' Souro said, as some drool began trickling from the corner of his mouth. 'It's losing experience that hurts. You can't replace the knowledge that dies with a veteran soldier quickly. But there was another idea.'

Jacus stood and began gently dabbing Souro's face with a handkerchief.

'Please go on,' Jacus encouraged.

'One group wanted funding to apply immortal-capsuleer technology to soldiers.'

'Interesting,' Jacus noted. 'What happened to the idea?'

'No one thought it could work,' Souro said. 'The equipment that supports cognitive-state transfers would have to be miniaturized. Then you need cybernetic tech that preserves a soldier's memory. And all of this would need to happen in an uncontrolled Battlefield environment.'

Jacus reflected a moment. On starships, the capsule is what

managed state transfers of a capsuleer's mind at the point of destruction. When the protective pod was breached, a snapshot of the pilot's brain was taken and transferred into a clone using entangled communication systems. But it was supported by a huge interstellar infrastructure network based on stations and stargates.

'Our best people couldn't figure this out,' Souro said. 'Then there were ethical constraints.'

'How so?'

'Testing new technology on humans, even if it passed survivability assurance in AI constructs, wasn't something I was comfortable with,' Souro said. 'I didn't see anything promising enough to justify it, so I canceled the program. Creating an immortal soldier was beyond our capabilities. It probably still is.'

'Do you know if anyone else is pursuing this?' Jacus asked.

'We know the Caldari aren't,' Souro answered. 'Tibus Heth allegedly scoffed at the idea of immortal soldiers. We're fairly certain the Minmatar have tried and failed. But we don't know about the Amarr Empire. We haven't been able to see inside there since the Elders' attack.'

'Very well,' Jacus said. The ex-President's maid, who had been in the employ of Roden Shipyards as a spy for much longer than as a maid for Souro Foiritan, quietly left the room. Per Jacus's request, no one on that station would ever see her again. The sentry drones allowed her to pass, all the while maintaining their active jamming of the recording equipment in the room. The memory of the apartment's AI would be deleted and replaced with video of Souro drinking himself to sleep. He would awaken later with no recollection of the encounter and find a letter of resignation from his maid.

'I have just a few more questions for you,' Jacus said, making sure that Souro was comfortable. 'Does the Broker have this technology?'

'We don't think so. He operates by making multiple copies of himself and manually pushing situational-state information to a central repository, presumably the original copy.'

'Are you certain?'

'No. You never can be with him.'

'But you think he's dead?'
'There's plenty of evidence to suggest as much.'
'If he's still alive, do you think he would actively pursue this tech?'
'Without question.'

6

HEIMATAR REGION – HED CONSTELLATION
AMAMAKE SYSTEM – PLANET II: PIKE'S LANDING
CORE FREEDOM COLONY
SOVEREIGNTY OF THE MINMATAR REPUBLIC

At long last, the night mercifully surrendered to dawn. A grayish white fog began to snake its way through the rocky terrain like blood seeping from an old wound. The surviving Minmatar Valklear soldiers defending Core Freedom removed their night-vision equipment to see the unenhanced wickedness in its true light: columns of smoke rising from craters as shattered war machines and mutilated corpses littered the barren landscape. The Valklears had stopped the Amarr attackers within sight of their objective, but only barely.

Weary to the bone, the Valklears who could still stand began the 'mercy and salvage' part of their mission: collecting weapons, unspent ammunition, incapacitated drones, reusable cybernetic limbs or organs from fallen soldiers, and any functional mechanical parts that remained. With no reliable support from the Republic Fleet, every last bit of scrap was precious for the colony, and anything salvageable would be given to the city engineers for reprocessing.

Given the dire lack of supplies, the 'mercy' component of the mission was the unconditional execution and harvesting of any surviving enemy soldiers, including officers. They were worth more dead to the Minmatars than alive.

Surveying the battlefield from a gunship was General Vlad Kintreb, who at 160 years of age had been a soldier for more than a century. Though he had experienced far worse, he knew that for many of his troops, this had almost certainly been the longest night of their lives.

He ordered the pilot to set the craft down amid the carnage. Two MTACs and a squad of commandos rushed ahead to secure the landing site, as several Valklears looked on with blank, dazed expressions.

The General was going downrange, they muttered, to check upon his children in the field.

VLAD KINTREB STILL WALKED under his own power, although most of the bones in his legs were reconstructed from titanium. The usual mineral-scented air reeked of explosives and ionized gas. He breathed the familiar stench deeply, ignoring the rush of past battles roaring through his memory.

Behind him, the bodyguards kept their distance, while the deep metallic impact of towering combat MTACs flanked either side of him. The chicken-legged walkers, 'Spearstrike' assault variants of Minmatar design, were now a salvaged patchwork of gold and brown armor plates. Minmatar cannons hung beneath weapon pylons lined with Amarr guidance systems. Vlad grunted at the sight of them. Like the rest of his garrison, there was a time when these magnificent vehicles were intact.

Pausing over a disemboweled corpse, he reached down to turn the remnants of its severed torso over. The stub of a spine, charred black from an explosion that detached the pelvis, drew his attention. Unfazed by the gore that fell away from exit wounds behind the rib cage, he ran his fingers up the bone, then inspected the skull and jaw.

'Kameiras,' he growled, shaking his head.

For General Kintreb, the irony was sickening. Kintreb's knowledge of human anatomy was developed in classrooms and raw battlefield experience. He could tell just from looking at bones what he was dealing with. His Valklears had defended the colony from the Amarr elite infantry known as Kameiras, who were entirely of Minmatar origin. Genetically, Minmatar tribal ethnicities tended to be taller and more physically robust than the True Amarr. But the Kameiras were bred from the best physical specimens of slaves in the Amarr Empire to become holy warriors. Eligible children were placed in a conditioning program so optimized that by the age of nineteen, they were as strong and powerful as was humanly possible without the aid of cybernetic augmentation.

The Kameiras were a significant investment for the Empire and were the best infantrymen they had – arguably more reliable than even their own Paladins.

Vlad stood slowly, ignoring the tinge of pain in his lower back. Distant, muted explosions rumbled through the landscape, and more gunships roared overhead. Somewhere in the mountains beyond, Valklears were cleaning up the last pockets of stragglers who still had the strength to fight back.

General Kintreb brushed the grime off his gloves, glancing back toward the outer fortifications. From a kilometer away, a great complex dominated the entire horizon. Deep behind its walls were antiship defenses to which the colony population – and the division of troops left defending it – owed their lives. If not for them, they would have been vaporized by orbital bombardments ages ago.

The infrastructure at Core Freedom was immensely valuable. Covering nearly five hundred square kilometers, a conglomerate of industrial outposts provided access to the massive resource deposits of Pike's Landing. Ore extractors, processors, and an alloy-smelting plant provided the nucleus of what was once a thriving industrial hub for the entire system. Central to all this was the colony's most prized possession: its space elevator, the only one on the planet. With its six sky cables tethered to the orbiting industrial megacomplex high above, massive amounts of material could be transported offworld at a rate that dwarfed the lift capacity of even the largest dropships.

With its mineral wealth and developed surface infrastructure, the

Empire coveted Core Freedom. But getting ships into position to direct pinpoint orbital strikes was impossible because of its deadly antiship missile batteries. All ranged ordnance attacks were vulnerable to point defenses and shields. The only way to take the colony and its infrastructure intact was to land troops well beyond the perimeter and unleash a frontal assault, disabling the planetary defenses and then letting the guns in space impose their will on the targets below.

Last night, Amarr launched a ferocious assault with their best troops leading the charge, and nearly succeeded in breaching the last line of ground defenses before the outer walls. Stretched too thin by the conflict raging closer to their homeworlds, the Republic Fleet couldn't afford to divert resources to the frontier, and reinforcements would've been easily shot out of space by capsuleers loyal to the Empress. In fact, very little of the equipment available for General Kintreb's troops was original-issue gear. Most of them deployed with Amarr weapons, all scavenged from prior battles.

Unless something drastic changed, the General knew that they couldn't hold the colony for much longer. Pleading to the Republic Fleet for help – even to Sanmatar Shakor himself – would do him no good, as there were countless other generals, on other Minmatar frontier worlds, all begging for the same.

Shadowed by men and machines, General Kintreb continued his walk, slowly making his way toward a fallen Valklear lying upright against the wall of a shallow crater. Peering over the ledge, he found another scene of defaced humanity: the corpses of two soldiers, one Valklear, the other Kameira, sprawled opposite each other. The Valklear corpse – whose IDENT tag he recognized – was decapitated. The Kameira was on his back, with a charred blast hole in place of where his heart should have been. A white-hot microblade was still clutched and active in his hand.

General Kintreb imagined the men holding this position were surprised by the crazed Kameira, who – with no ammunition remaining – was determined to fight to the end. Several laaknyds – voracious scavenging insects accidentally introduced to the planet's ecosystem – had already begun partaking of the decaying corpses. One emerged from the chest wound of the fallen Kameira, its serrated pincers full of flesh. Before long, there would be many more of them.

Vlad knelt before the upright Valklear, in whom the laaknyds showed no interest, and knew he was still alive.

He gently removed the mask and night-vision scope. Wide, unfocused eyes appeared.

Behind him, his bodyguards readied their aim on the soldier that Vlad was determined to help.

A rifle lay across his lap, which Vlad slowly lifted and set aside. An inspection followed: short, irregular breaths, rapid pulse, some scarring on the armor, but no breaches.

This was neuro-trauma. PSYKLAD munitions were reportedly used ahead of the assault. Any soldier who was unprotected could hallucinate to the point of self-destructive insanity.

General Kintreb didn't care about the danger.

'State your name and rank,' he ordered.

His eyes blinked, but did nothing else. The upper torso of the closest MTAC swiveled slowly; the turret beneath its cockpit rotated toward them.

Vlad placed a hand on the Valklear's shoulder.

'Let's just start with your name.'

Another blink; a tremor ran through the soldier's hands.

'I'm sorry about your squadmate,' Vlad continued. 'But you have to get to your feet.'

Laaknyds were approaching the corpses in groups now, segregating themselves into tasks. Some continued their gory excavation, passing fresh meat to couriers that scampered back toward the nest. The larger bulls took up sentry positions, forming a protective cordon around the carcasses. Several laaknyds were facing General Kintreb and his fallen soldier, their raised pincers warning them not to tamper with their meal.

'Stay with me,' Vlad said, gripping both shoulders. 'We've got to go, *now*—'

The movement was too sudden. The soldier lunged forward and clamped onto the General's neck, pulling him inward. Vlad sensed that this was either panic or a delusional plea for help, but that no longer mattered, as the MTAC – the only protective unit with a clear line of fire – unleashed a single cannon round with a disabled fuse.

Vlad felt warm blood splash across his face, and the grip around his neck released. His pulse accelerated out of anger, not surprise. The round entered the man's shoulder, exited through his upper back, and burrowed into several meters of volcanic rock. The soldier's arm had been shorn clean off, scattering the insects as it came to rest near the protective cordon.

'Send medics to my position,' Vlad ordered.

The body armor was doing its part to save the Valklear's life, releasing biofoam around the wound and injecting the man with adrenaline to keep him from slipping into shock. Vlad tore a medpack off the man's kit and removed more biofoam packets, stuffing them into the open wounds.

A beat-up air sled arrived within seconds. Two medics quickly jumped out, hoisting the unconscious soldier into its flatbed.

'Neuro-trauma, possible PSYKLAD ordnance,' Vlad grumbled. 'Wipe his memory before he wakes up.'

The medic quickly saluted. 'Yes, sir.'

A moment later, they were gone.

General Kintreb didn't acknowledge the MTAC pilot who fired the shot, nor the bodyguards who eased off their weapons in relief. Instead, he glared at the laaknyds, several of which were taking test nibbles of the severed arm.

Help from the Republic wasn't coming. The blood coursing down his face was evidence of that. Their survival was not likely. It was time to break some long-standing principles.

'Commander Bishop,' Vlad muttered.

The voice was loud and clear. 'Yes, sir?'

'Mordu's Legion,' Vlad said, wiping some blood off his cheeks. The sun was higher now, and the insects were working quickly to get back into their nest for shelter. 'Make the call.'

'Wilco.'

More gunshots sounded in the distance.

Someone once said that pride was the mask of one's faults, Vlad thought.

The insects were eating around the Valklear Special Forces patch.

Well, here's my ugly face for all to see.

CONCORD

7

GENESIS REGION – SANCTUM CONSTELLATION
THE YULAI SYSTEM – INNER CIRCLE TRIBUNAL STATION
SOVEREIGNTY OF THE CONCORD ASSEMBLY

The mercurial figures of CONCORD's Inner Circle gathered under conditions that hardly seemed adequate for all the power at their fingertips. Gone were the days when they met in ostentatious settings surrounded by absurdly lavish comforts. The 'new' meeting location was supposed to be temporary, and its appearance and function remained just as haphazard as when it was hastily assembled three years earlier.

The Empyrean War began with the near-total destruction of their previous meeting place – a station once thought indestructible – and like so many others who lived through those historic events, these leaders would never be the same.

No one spoke as the members took their seats. The only sound was the whir of electronic motors as probes descended from fragile gantries and inserted into the neuro-interface sockets in their skulls.

'Tashin, what do you have?' Inner Circle Director Irhes Angireh demanded.

'The evidence you were looking for,' he answered, though his mouth didn't move. A blur of volumetric projections depicting personnel dossiers, security footage from research facilities, and classified incident files began taking shape before the circular arrangement of seats. 'We have confirmation that all four nations are directly funding or researching immortal soldier technology.'

'Even the Caldari?' Irhes asked. 'I thought Heth wasn't interested.'

'He said he doesn't *believe* in the program,' Tashin corrected. 'But he's still funding corporations who do.'

'Which ones?' Irhes asked.

'Wiyrkomi and Sukuuvestaa,' Tashin answered. 'Heth is playing them against each other. Neither has made any real progress.'

'So who's winning this race?' Irhes asked.

'The Amarrians,' Esoutte Denaert hissed. 'They'll have prototypes ready in a year, maybe two at most.'

'Heth is bluffing,' Tashin commented. 'Who *wouldn't* want the tech? No one wants to admit the urgency, but it's plainly obvious.'

'Here's urgency for you,' Esoutte said. Lists of soldiers – millions of them – were streaming before her. They were compiled KIA lists from several national armies. 'Most never made it to a battlefield before they died.'

'We've said it a thousand times,' Irhes said. 'Why rush down this path even faster by bringing immortality to soldiers? It doesn't make sense—'

'No, *you've* said it a thousand times,' Tashin scoffed, annoyed at the Director's outburst. 'It makes perfect sense. Look at the casualty figures. War is ugly business. It isn't our place to judge how nations wage it, so long as the means doesn't interfere with *our* charter.'

'This is about cost,' Esoutte said, as schematics of human soldiers, with and without cybernetic augmentations, flickered through the air. 'The Caldari are the best at fielding armies quickly. Every citizen is trained and can be brought to fighting shape in a matter of weeks, but it's still hugely expensive.'

More figures displayed the development cost per soldier, including arms, augmentation, conditioning, and training. Tashin was about to begin a lengthy presentation.

'The other nations don't have the luxury of mandatory conscription, so their costs are even higher—'

'What does this have to do with anything?' Irhes exclaimed.

Tashin, though immobilized at the neck, managed to twitch.

'I'm merely pointing out that there's good reason for them to be developing immortal technology, and that it's probably not the evil superpower excuse you're looking for as grounds to interfere.'

Irhes would hear none of it.

'What about the human cost?' she demanded. 'Did you even think about what could happen if empyrean technology was passed on to soldiers? Of the power it would give the nation that owned it? Have you completely forgotten what our mandate is?'

The imagery became a mottle of red – a conditioned response that Tashin, like the other members of the Inner Circle, had trained himself to perform as a means of masking what he was really thinking. Instead of revealing his anger toward the Speaker for belittling him, Tashin willed himself to display the CONCORD Mandate in rather sarcastic fashion across the room:

To protect the right of civilizations to grow and prosper;
To preserve the surviving sovereignties of the Dark Ages;
To serve justice to those immortals who abuse the privilege of everlasting life;
To safeguard the mortals of worlds from dangers which originate in space;
To prevent empyrean technology from causing the destruction of humanity.

'Brilliant,' Irhes sneered. 'But do you understand what that actually means?'

'Perfectly,' Tashin said. 'And I still maintain that the evolution of empyrean technology is *inevitable*, and you're naïve to suggest it can be prevented.'

'I'm with Irhes on this,' Tatoh Okkamon interjected. 'Immortal soldiers have one purpose, and the consequences of abuse are unthinkable. I support any measures presented to put a stop to it.'

'Now just wait a moment,' Esoutte pleaded. 'We can't interfere with the sovereign rights of nations to defend themselves!'

'We can where it concerns the governance of immortals,' Irhes growled.

'Immortal soldiers would absolve the living from ever having to wage war,' Tashin said. 'It's the ultimate deterrent.'

'Which is precisely why we have to stop it from developing in the first place,' Irhes demanded. 'Whoever wins this race can wage *any* war *perpetually.* That is a nightmare scenario, and I'm astonished it even needs to be stated.'

'I agree we should stop the tech from developing,' Tatoh said. 'The question is *how.* The moment the assembly nations even suspect we're opposed to it, they'll accelerate their research programs – or worse, transfer them to the outer regions.'

'Then our jurisdiction must expand,' Irhes told them.

The images projected by the other members abruptly dropped as the implications of her statement took hold. Mordu's Legion, the Intaki Syndicate, the Khanid Kingdom, and several other sovereignties that operated well outside the boundaries of the four primary empires appeared.

'You're not serious,' the astounded Tashin said. 'You can't enforce this. They'll kill you for trying.'

'Where is this obsession coming from?' Esoutte asked. 'This almost seems personal.'

The sound of the Director's voice was loudest over the area where Tashin and Esoutte were sitting.

'There's nothing personal in recognizing that we're at a crossroads in history,' she thundered. 'We've seen what empyreans are capable of. If it wasn't for us, we might have lost every mortal in existence. *This is exactly why CONCORD was created in the first place.* It's *our* responsibility to make sure that never happens!'

'Irhes,' Tashin said somberly. 'I know their power grew faster than any of us imagined. I was in Yulai when the Elders attacked. I was scared for my life. But this isn't the answer.'

'I disagree,' Tatoh said. 'We have to try. The threat is real; the mandate is clear.'

Tara Rushi had yet to speak, though it was clear from the projections floating above her that she was weighing both arguments carefully. All matters trivial and historic were decided in

CONCORD by a simple majority vote, and she had become the tiebreaker in this crucial moment.

'*If* we were to proceed,' Tashin asked, 'how do you propose we put a stop to it?'

'We use THANATOS,' Irhes said confidently.

'Three of them are already searching for the Broker,' Tatoh said.

'We'll create a fourth. One for this explicit purpose. To do whatever is necessary to convince the empires to cease their efforts, and if necessary, sabotage their research outright.'

Tara finally spoke.

'The Joves would have never allowed this,' she said.

'The Joves are dead.' Irhes scowled.

'I see,' Tara said. 'Then I shall abstain but give my vote to you, Speaker. Since you seem to know what's best for us all.'

PART II

Absentia

>>CONCORD/DED Datastack 13AoB: 'Preliminary Report: The Apocrypha Event'

>>Owner: AI Construct Argos-1

>>For Inner Circle, Select Members of the DED and CONCORD

>>EYES ONLY

>>Summary

On 10 March, YC 111, ten star systems in the New Eden cluster were struck by a previously unrecorded stellar event called a 'mass sequence CME anomaly.' The cataclysm killed over 190 million people, the bulk of whom resided in the underground cities of Seyllin I. The events appear to have been caused by the detonation of separate stockpiles of isogen-5, which is a highly volatile, naturally occurring mineral found only in the proximity of Class-O stars. Immediately following these explosions, concentrated waves of plasma emanating from the local sun dissipated throughout affected systems along a focused magnetic field, obliterating everything in their paths.

Although each system affected by the catastrophe was host to a Class-O star, there is no obvious pattern to their locations. However, each system was struck by identical events simultaneously, despite their physical separation by many light-years.

Shortly after the event took place, numerous spacetime topological point-defects, or 'wormholes' as they are more commonly called, began appearing throughout New Eden, also with random frequency and distribution. To this point, the only naturally occurring wormhole in the entire cluster was the EVE Gate, which collapsed thousands of years ago. These new defects, literally tears in the fabric of spacetime, were found to be stable enough to allow the passage of starships. Despite warnings that the egress point of these defects was unknown and that their stability was likely temporary, many empyreans began traveling through.

All ships entering these defects were transported to uncharted regions of space outside the New Eden cluster. The nearest recognizable objects to onboard navigation systems were quasars, the oldest and most distant celestial objects in the known universe. If not for fluid router technology, these ships would have been completely isolated from 'known space' and lost.

Wormhole space, or 'w-space,' as it soon came to be known, was also permeated with defects, all of which were unstable. As of now, there are hundreds of recorded instances in which wormholes have collapsed behind passing ships. Remarkably, most of these ships were able to navigate back to New Eden space by scanning down and then entering other defects. Although their destinations were unknown, enough traversals eventually led back to random reentry points in the New Eden cluster.

As detailed later in this report, the odds of these newly discovered defects all coincidentally pointing back to the New Eden cluster are extremely small.

>>The Sleeper Civilization

Pilots entering w-space have reported encounters with the automated defenses of an ancient and presumably extinct race of humans known as the Sleepers. While they are believed to be of Jove descent, very little is known about them. What is known, however, is that they were extremely advanced, having mastered all present 'foundation' space-faring and biomedical technologies thousands of years ago. But discovery of their reach across the universe – specifically, their consistent appearance in w-space systems – was completely unprecedented.

The 'Apocrypha Event,' as this series of anomalies has been called, had the immediate political effect of temporarily distracting the empires from the Empyrean War. Despite the risks, capsuleers began migrating to w-space for two primary reasons: to harvest valuable resources for sale and consumption in New Eden, and to recover Sleeper technology.

The first Sleeper artifact returned to New Eden possessed unique properties never before observed in applied-materials science. It was manufactured from fullerene-based polymorphic alloys capable of being adapted instantaneously to almost any engineering application. For example, two separate samples of the alloy – each of which has the same tensile strength as tritanium construction alloy – could be fused into one seamless sample by applying uniform high-voltage current through both specimens. Reversing the charge and the magnetic polarity of the sample breaks it into the original components.

Overnight, demand for this new technology spawned a multi-billion- credit industry for Sleeper salvage, which in turn supported the emergence of a new class of warships called 'strategic cruisers.' To clarify, ships are built to fill specific roles in naval warfare. In classical starship engineering, hulls are designed around core subsystems, such as weapons, propulsion, and power plant. Under this traditional methodology, the ship can perform only one role effectively. But those constructed using polymorphic alloys can be adapted to fill dozens of roles, since major subsystems can be swapped without compromising hull integrity.

CONCORD has privately warned governments against using the technology because it is not fully understood. For example, we are unable to determine how these alloys are created. All attempts to synthesize them have failed. Yet every strategic cruiser that has ever been built is using material salvaged directly from Sleeper artifacts. One retrieved sample suggests that the fullerene alloy was conceived for computing purposes, not structural engineering. Without understanding its origins or application, we are either underutilizing a potent new technology, at best, or exposing ourselves to unimaginable risks, at worst.

By and large, the empires have heeded our warning. The

capsuleers, however, have not. Their interest in Sleeper tech continues unabated, and for the time being, ungoverned.

>>Mass Sequence CME Anomaly

All stars eject plasma during the main sequence stage of their lifespans over ranges, durations, and frequencies that vary with the age and type of star. Such 'stellar flares' produce a stream of supercharged particles called 'proton storms,' the speed of which is determined by the strength of the flare event itself. Storm speeds approaching the speed of light are rare among Class-G and smaller stars, although the spin rate of the star can create stronger magnetic fields and, thus, more powerful events. But they are fairly common in Class-M stars and higher.

Stellar flares produce radiation across the entire electromagnetic spectrum, ranging from radio waves to gamma rays. The most powerful ones produce coronal mass ejections, or CMEs, where actual stellar material is cast off from the star and hurled into space. In the case of a Class-G star, the average mass and speed of ejected material is 1.6×10^{15} g at 500 km/s. A CME usually begins with a preacceleration phase in an intense magnetic field above the star's surface, typically along the equator but also above 'sunspots,' whose appearance varies with the star's natural cycle. Plasma accretes and then enters a postacceleration phase as trapped particles are accelerated quickly along closed magnetic field lines. Upon reaching critical volume and speeds, the plasma overwhelms the field and escapes into space. For a Class-G star, the typical force released by this event is the equivalent of a billion megaton nuclear bombs.

>>The Seyllin Star

The Seyllin system is host to a potent but otherwise unremarkable Class-O star, whose solar weather activity was monitored by a network of Federation satellites collectively known as 'Cassandra.' At approximately 1100 hours local on 10 March, YC 111, the last telemetry received from this network revealed several anomalies:

- that a drastic and unexpected shift in magnetic activity in the solar atmosphere had occurred;
- that this field shift was oriented in the same plane and direction as the planet Seyllin I;
- that an abnormally large solar prominence, or preacceleration CME event, filled this field almost instantly;
- that a separate, powerful gamma-ray burst was detected away from the star but inside the orbit of Seyllin I and along the same plane as both the planet and the solar prominence.

Less than ten minutes after Cassandra went off-line, the side of Seyllin I facing the sun was struck by the largest proton storm ever recorded. A megadose of gamma and X-rays destroyed installations as deep as thirty meters below the surface, flash-ionizing the air supply and igniting every surface within. Although the night side of the planet was somewhat shielded and thus spared the full brunt of the blast, the storm was still powerful enough to destroy the electrical grids supplying the underground cities of Loadcore and Southern Cross. If Seyllin I had an atmosphere to start with, it would have been vaporized entirely or blasted away into space.

Several hours later, the ejected coronal mass – traveling at speeds approaching one-quarter the speed of light and estimated to be orders of magnitude more massive than an average Class-G event – slammed into the planet with enough force to break it apart, completely reshaping the world into molten rock and metal. The colonists who survived the initial radiation blast perished in the cataclysm that followed. Survivors who were evacuated from the system before the CME arrived suffered disfiguring burns and the immediate onset of aggressive forms of cancer. Of the millions who were killed, the vast majority were Federation citizens.

In all, ten New Eden star systems – each with Class-O or Class-B blue stars – were struck with stellar anomalies identical to what occurred at Seyllin, all at the same time. Of the systems where solar weather data was recoverable, each one recorded identical anomalies: an unspeakably powerful magnetic shift and accelerated CME event with the local sun, along with the simultaneous, isolated detonation of concentrated gamma radiation from a location between the system's innermost planet and the sun itself.

Of these affected systems, T-IPZ provided us with the most clues as to the cause.

>>T-IPZ and the Terrans

System T-IPZ was classified as a vital point of interest in the eyes-only investigation of Empress Jamyl's 'Xerah Effect' superweapon, named after the city above which the weapon was used with devastating effect against a Minmatar Elder navy task force. T-IPZ was under THANATOS surveillance at the time of the Apocrypha Event and reported identical solar anomalies before disappearing: Like Seyllin I, the innermost planet of T-IPZ was destroyed, and a gamma burst was traced back toward the vicinity of an ancient Terran station orbiting the same planet.

The station, whose origins predate the closure of the EVE Gate by 14,000 years, was a location where an extremely rare and volatile mineral known as isogen-5 was stockpiled. This mineral exists only in the presence of blue-star systems, and loses its volatile properties when removed from its original locale. Isogen-5 possesses unique gravitonic properties whose behavior is not understood; its scarcity and hostile native environment make it difficult to study.

It is not known why the Terrans were stockpiling the material. Before its destruction, THANATOS discovered that drones manufactured autonomously within the station possessed the technology to move the material from its source to the station; conventional ships cannot even approach it. Later, it was discovered that the same technology that protects these drones is used in the Xerah Effect weapon housing, which requires the mineral as a primer to fire.

But most importantly, THANATOS observed that the low-orbit area where the weapon was fired remains symptomatic of dark-matter collisions observable just outside the event horizon of black holes; cross-brane gravitonic distortions in normal timespace still resonate at both this site and the former site of the Terran station obliterated during the Apocrypha Event.

Subsequent THANATOS units confirmed that all ten

Apocrypha locations contain the same postevent trace residue of an isogen-5 detonation, all of which were presumably large enough to cause the immense gamma bursts recorded at each site.

>>Argos-1 Conclusion

Given these observable events, we summarize our findings as follows:

- *The isogen-5 stockpiles were entangled – either the detonators or the material itself.* No other explanation can account for simultaneous events across multiple star systems.
- *The purpose of the stockpile was to draw an energy yield from the sun that isogen-5 by itself could not reach to achieve some kind of critical mass.* The Terrans had the means to transport the material anywhere they wished. There is no discernable reason why they would need a structure so large and close to the star, except for the explicit purpose of amassing concentrations large enough to interact with the star.
- *The energy expenditure was intended to be destructive.* The lack of Terran structures anywhere else in the system, in addition to their placement in environmentally hostile locations near Class-O stars, suggests that they were built with the intent to eventually destroy them.
- *It is probable that the Terrans were constructing an interstellar transit system similar to but much more advanced than our own stargate transit system.* The postevent gravitonic residue, isogen-5 properties, placement near massive objects like Class-O stars, resulting topological point defects, and consistent presence of Sleeper colonies in w-space suggest that the Terrans already had jump technology but were attempting to harness natural forces to achieve a similar result.
- *The transit system was either incomplete when the event occurred or was detonated incorrectly, or we do not yet understand how to use it.* What appears to empyreans as random wormhole activity may in fact follow a pattern, but no such analysis has been attempted.

*

The New Eden's leading authority on Sleepers was Dr Marcus Jror, former chief scientist to Amarrian Holder Falek Grange. His whereabouts are currently unknown. He has been designated a Tier-1 surveillance target for THANATOS, pending acquisition of any information that could lead to his discovery.

>>END 13AOB

9

GEMINATE REGION – F-ZNNG CONSTELLATION
SYSTEM UBX-CC – THE MJOLNIR NEBULA
INSORUM PRODUCTION FACTORY

Mila's hands moved with the precise control of a surgeon, delicately placing a microservo the size of a grain of sand into position. The circuitry beneath the patient's thorax was fully exposed, an anatomical maze of wires, chips, and synthetic muscle fibers bathed in the glow of overhead operating lights. Behind her mask, she allowed herself to breathe only when the component clicked ever so slightly into place. The margin of error was little more than a hair's breadth; the slightest change in the angle of the tools at her fingertips would undo a painstaking effort that had required hours of focused concentration.

'A brilliant performance,' the drone patient commended. 'You have the skills of a machine, albeit a slow one.'

She accepted the smug directness of her AI companion as a compliment. It had been three years and counting since her last physical interaction with a human being.

A large insectlike drone with a triangular-shaped head and large dark eyes on each side emerged from the shadows and offered the thorax plate cover for the patient. Smaller drones clinging to walls and ceilings looked on with curiosity that seemed eerily genuine.

'You can finish up,' Mila said, setting the tools down. The sadness in her voice was apparent, and several drones began nudging against her legs like sympathetic pets. Every mechanical creature in the factory was part of the same collective AI. Though they each differed in appearance and function, they all responded to the same name: VILAMO, who was programmed to protect her at all times. Mila developed a friendship with them, and together they sought to learn all they could about the cruel universe she left behind.

The insect drone affixed the thorax plating in seconds. When the patient lifted itself off the gurney, all the drones suddenly turned toward the door, their multifaceted eyes changing from a greenish blue hue to deep red.

Mila tensed up.

'An unregistered Wolf-class frigate just emerged from warp outside the perimeter,' VILAMO announced. 'The ship has been immobilized.'

'Who's the pilot?' Mila breathed.

'IDENT scans indicate that he is the Ishukone CEO Mens Reppola.'

Mila felt an emotional surge flush her cheeks. The antennae of a smaller drone swiveled in her direction, registering the sudden change in her biorhythm.

'We cannot verify unless we take him into quarantine,' VILAMO cautioned. 'Shall we proceed?'

'*Yes*,' Mila exclaimed, trying to calm herself. 'God, yes!'

'Careful,' VILAMO warned. 'Our foe wears many disguises.'

IT WAS A HELLISH PLACE to find an old friend.

Searing hot gusts of stellar dust and gas pummeled Mens's ship as it was approached by tentacled drones the size of battleships, seemingly impervious to the turbulence of the Mjolnir Nebula. The facility had changed significantly since Mens brought Mila Gariushi here years ago; the structures had not only grown but evolved into distinctly organic shapes. As his ship was embraced and hauled into something that resembled an insect hive, Mens noticed gill-like serrations on its metallic surface that moved and undulated with the chaotic current. VILAMO appeared to be harnessing the energy of the nebula itself, using its adaptive intelligence to find a way to thrive in this hostile environment.

But hospitality to strangers wasn't one of the AI's strengths.

Once Mens was removed from his pod, a pair of menacing spider drones, each bearing pincers as long as a man's arm, gathered his carcass off the grating as he retched containment fluid from his lungs. They warned him that blood was going to be drawn for genetic analysis, with or without his consent.

Fortunately for Mens, he passed their test.

The last time he saw Mila in person was in the harrowing moments following the death of her brother. It had been Otro's final wish that Mens rush her to this forsaken sanctuary, which he and his good friend Ralirashi Okimo had built in complete secrecy. As the senior officers of Ishukone, they had made many enemies over the years. The construction was prescient of them, for now it was sheltering Mila from both the Broker and Tibus Heth. These two were responsible for Otro's murder, plus hundreds of thousands more in one of the worst atrocities in history.

Where, exactly, Otro had acquired the technology to build it all remained a mystery. Eerily similar to rogue drones, these machines could assess, learn, and adapt to all conditions necessary to serve their primary purpose. From this hidden lair, Mila was able to follow the events of the past three years from afar and to search for ways to track down her brother's killer. Despite her isolation and absence from the spotlight, there was little that Mila didn't know about Caldari affairs – especially about the mega-corporations.

She never stopped grieving for Otro. But her pain had given way to a cold, ruthless determination to set things right in Ishukone. This was a rare instance – personal revenge and the greater good aligning. Vengeance was not just for her but for the entire Caldari State.

Mila stared at her trusted, beloved friend with whom she shared countless memories. They – Otro, Rali, Mens, and a select few others from their inner circle – were a family in all but name. Their bond was unbreakable. Besides Rali, no one understood her better than Mens Reppola.

It was overwhelmingly good to see him again.

'I could kill you for coming here,' she started.

Mens nearly smiled.

'This was the only way,' he said. 'We took the necessary precautions.'

'Did Rali approve of this?'

Mens gave her a thoughtful look.

'He never said one way or the other.'

Mila had dimmed the room before he arrived. She couldn't be certain of how she would react to seeing someone – anyone – after such prolonged solitude.

Let alone him.

She was hopeful at first, then apprehensive, that the answer to her next question was what her irrational heart wanted to hear.

'Why have you come here?'

Mens reminded himself that several hundred million Ishukone civilians were counting on his honesty.

So, for that matter, was his family.

'I'm stepping down,' he said, with more conviction than he truly felt. 'I came here to tell you in person.'

Silence prevailed. Spider drones gathered at the door behind him, and the smaller specimens huddled beside her.

The sadness on her face crushed him.

'Have you told this to anyone else?' she finally asked.

Mens shook his head.

'Ishukone is destroying me,' he stammered. 'Your brother was a much stronger man than I.'

She forced herself to smile.

'He would disagree with that.'

'I've prepared a list of possible successors,' Mens continued, eyes glassing over with pain. 'Rali will assume executive command until you present your recommendation to the board.'

He took a deep breath, and hung his head.

'I'm sorry.'

Mila told herself to focus.

'I know Heth threatened your family,' she started. 'He's a coward. He recognizes that you're a danger to him.'

'Look at me,' Mens said, regaining his composure. 'Do I look dangerous to you?'

'You've always been hard on yourself,' she said. 'I won't bother telling you how much Ishukone needs you, or how much respect you've earned among your peers and the people you lead. So you tell me . . . what can I do to convince you to stay with us?'

He gave her an incredulous look, as if she should know the answer already.

'*Help me* run Ishukone,' he said.

'You know I can't do that,' she answered. 'Not yet.'

'We can't run from the Broker forever,' Mens said, remembering the exchange with his wife. 'At some point we have to take a stand!'

'Forever is exactly what he has that you and I don't,' Mila answered. 'Until we know for certain what's become of him, this is the way things have to be.'

Mens exhaled forcefully.

'Heth has unchallenged support,' he said. 'It's just a matter of time before all the cards fall.'

It was true. Clever politics had turned the other mega-corporations against Ishukone, isolating them from the spoils of war and the resultant economic windfall. Mens fought bitterly to keep Ishukone out of a conflict that his predecessor would never have endorsed. What he never counted on was the Caldari State faring so well in the fight. Entire systems had been taken from the Federation; their armed forces were among the most feared in New Eden; and Caldari flags still flew over the ancestral homeworld of their origin. Even those who had opposed the war from the beginning could no longer argue that it was costly. In fact, the Caldari State had profited handsomely from it.

Tibus Heth remembered exactly who had and who hadn't offered their support, back when the outcome was less certain.

Ishukone was now the unpatriotic, undeserving, uninspiring example of 'restrained' Caldari politics that the State could do without – a 180-degree turnaround from years earlier, when it was Ishukone setting the example for everyone else. Otro Gariushi died trying to prevent a war he believed would be the State's undoing. Instead, it had become a shining example of how unrealized the State's potential really was.

The mega-corporations smelled blood. Ishukone still owned considerable assets and territory that would hold its value no matter who took possession of them. Mens Reppola was out of Heth's circle, and it was just a matter of time before the dogs attacked.

'Mila,' he said. 'We're *that* close to losing everything. You're better at this game than I am. The CEOs would listen to you—'

'I can't return,' she answered forcefully. 'Until I learn how to destroy him, this is where I hold the line.'

Mens deflated.

'I've given Ishukone *everything*,' he said. 'They're going after my family now, and I can't do a goddamn thing about it *without your help*!'

In a rapid unison of metallic clicks, the two spider drones advanced to within a meter of where he was sitting before the echo of his shout subsided. But he was unfazed: This was passion he could no longer repress.

'I'm sorry for raising my voice,' he said. 'I shouldn't have come here.'

'There is another way,' Mila said quietly. A moment of clarity struck, as her mind sought solutions to the impossible. 'It's so risky that I'd almost rather not share what it is.'

'What risk is greater than doing nothing?' he asked.

'Mens,' she said softly. 'These are the highest stakes in the game. If you go down this path and fall, no one can help you.'

'We've taken big risks before,' Mens replied. 'And I'm almost out of things to lose.'

Mila took a deep breath before saying a name:

'Oiritsuu.'

Mens frowned.

'*Haatakan* Oiritsuu?' he asked. 'The ex-Kaalakiota CEO? She's practically Heth's pet—'

'That's only what the cluster thinks of her. I *know* this woman. Otro and I once considered her the most dangerous person in New Eden. Heth was right to go after her first, but he should've killed her instead. He thinks he can keep her on a leash while exploiting her intellect. *Nothing* that woman does is an accident. Trust me. If the media says she's willingly orchestrating deals on Heth's behalf, you can be certain they benefit her personal agenda in ways no else but her can know.'

'What agenda is that?'

'The same as mine: to remove Heth from power.'

'So a mutual enemy makes us allies.'

'A very deceitful ally. But she knows of something that can protect Ishukone from Heth. Who knows what she'll ask for in return. That's the risk.'

'What is it?'

Mila paused for a moment.

'Heth's spies learned that the Amarr have found a way to use empyrean technology for infantry applications. They think they're close to testing the first human prototypes of immortal soldiers.'

'That's impossible.'

'I thought so, too. But if you knew how many agents died to bring Heth that information, you might reconsider.'

Mens felt his stomach turn over.

'The Amarr have acquired a decisive edge in modern warfare, and Oiritsuu knows where to find it,' Mila continued. 'The same technology that keeps you impervious to harm in space can now do the same on a surface battlefield.'

Mens shook his head.

'Heth would be developing it himself if he knew—'

'He found out by *accident*,' Mila interrupted. 'He was more interested in the superweapon Empress Jamyl used to vaporize the Minmatars at Mekhios. Instead, his agents stumbled across this. But the fool still doesn't think he needs it; he believes too much in the Caldari military instead.'

'Are you saying Heth had a chance to get this technology and *passed*?'

'More likely is that he thought it wasn't worth the cost of trying to steal it,' she answered. 'Mens, this is how you protect Ishukone from the mega-corporations and the Provists. Whoever owns that technology will dictate the terms of all negotiations … forever.'

'You're certain she knows how to get it?' he asked.

'These drones are capable creatures,' she said. 'VILAMO has been watching her for a long time. Rali designed him well. If you trust him, then you should trust the information that his creation is providing.'

Mens considered this. He had to assume the information was accurate. But not knowing what Haatakan Oiritsuu would ask for in return was something else entirely. And there was no way to know if the information she offered was actionable. That was the greatest risk by far.

But the reward would place Ishukone in an absolute position of power. It would forcibly restore détente with the mega-corporations, which was exactly what they needed. Then, and only then, could he conscionably relieve himself of duty, leaving his successor in a much more stable position than the one he had inherited.

Now, Mens felt almost euphoric. He had come here seeking a way out, and Mila had unfailingly delivered.

'Haatakan is not someone to cross,' she warned. 'You *must* honor the terms of any agreement you reach. Exiled or not, she was once the most powerful CEO in the Caldari State. Don't underestimate what she's capable of.'

'I won't.'

'Then I'll arrange for her to contact you. Don't try it yourself: Heth will know immediately.'

'Understood.'

An awkward silence passed. Mens stood; Mila did the same.

'Thank you,' he said finally, extending his hand.

Mila closed her eyes as she took it. When they gripped, she felt a warm sensation rush through her chest and neck.

She desperately hoped he felt the same.

The drones exited quietly, satisfied there was no danger.

For Mila, the warmth of holding someone dear so close, after spending so much time alone, was overpowering.

Mens was a married man. But this was the way things should be.

Her eyes still closed, their lips found each other's.

A perfect storm of emotions engulfed them, an irrepressible urge for physical contact and a desperate need for intimate understanding. They had come a long way to find each other.

It was tragic and wonderful, morally reprehensible yet physically divine. And it was, without question, the most passionate lovemaking that either had ever known.

10

PURE BLIND REGION – MDM8-J CONSTELLATION
SYSTEM X47L-Q

Korvin Lears never felt so alive.

Adrift in space, his senses registered only that he was the pilot of a Myrmidon-class battlecruiser with no crew on board. The ship's greenish gray hull was laced with dozens of symmetric cavities, all the lifeboats and escape pods that once filled them long since jettisoned. The 250mm railguns bristling along either side of the vessel's stout midline were useless, their ammunition depleted as he fought through harm's way into an endless expanse of nothingness.

As a traitor to his nation, there was no Gallente port to return to. He was a kill target for any Caldari warship that chanced upon him. And then an eternity of imprisonment awaited.

The empathy that Korvin felt for his victims was never stronger than right now. He could see them all – women, children, old and young – in the star fields and nebulas of his travels, haunting him as his soul searched for a *solution*, of which death, of all things, was not one.

Korvin would have it no other way. The only way to escape was to redeem his worth, to somehow make right all the wrongs of his privileged life and begin a legacy that was noble and worthwhile.

The only question was how.

*

THE MLW *MORSE* WAS a retrofitted Drake-class battlecruiser with two of its turret bays removed to accommodate a dropship hangar. The warship was capable of launching and retrieving Panther-class or smaller gunships, allowing it to participate in limited terra-ops, typically with lightly armed away-teams numbering no more than eight to twelve soldiers per sortie.

But the *Morse* had some teeth as well – six heavy missile bays, to be exact. Capable of filling space with inordinate amounts of destruction, the Drake was a formidably armed marvel of Caldari engineering, which was, in the words of its present owner and captain, 'largely under-utilized.'

As with all vessels belonging to the mercenary faction known as Mordu's Legion, the *Morse* had deployment orders more befitting a peacekeeping force – albeit, a decidedly preferential one. Founded by veterans of the first Caldari-Gallente War, the Legion was a refuge from the political arm of the two warring nations, offering open borders and a safe haven to those ethnicities displaced by the conflict. To accept Mordu's offer of amnesty was to reject the governments of both nations, or else face charges of treason. Trespassers, spies, and would-be vigilantes looking to settle old scores were executed by firing squad and sent back to their respective nations in flag-draped caskets for proper military burial – a morbid tradition courtesy of the Legion's harrowed war veterans.

What started as a small colony had grown into an empire in its own right. Today, the Legion's population numbered in the millions, having amassed enough technology and resources over the years to become entirely self-sufficient. As a fugitive on the run from the Lai Dai mega-corporation, Captain Jonas Varitec not only found a home with the Legion but prospered among them. Highly regarded by pilots and mercenaries alike, he had assembled a talented group of officers who trusted him completely – even if their own eccentricities made for a dysfunctional bridge at times.

THE *MORSE* WAS CURRENTLY forty kilometers off the UR-E6o system stargate. They were on a recon patrol, reporting on ships passing through the Pure Blind region. If anything hostile was spotted, there was heavy cavalry on standby to deal with it.

It was obligatory duty on behalf of the Legion. But 'babysitting' stargates was tedious, especially since ship traffic in these remote constellations was light. As such, the *Morse* crew was bored.

'So I'm lying there, pretending I'm still asleep—' Miles said.

Jonas rolled his eyes, leaning toward the telemetry projection to his left. 'Oh boy, here we go ... ' Despite a reputation as a talented helmsman, Engineering First Officer Miles Lacey often told irritating and largely bogus tales of various social conquests to help pass the time during patrols. A former native of Arcurio and a Caldari Navy deserter, Miles was – in the opinion of the female personnel on board – a bright, socially inept, and rather unattractive Deteis specimen who used his hands too much when he talked.

'— and instead of just grabbing her clothes and leaving, I hear her sneak into the bathroom.' Seeking refuge from the incoming fable, Jonas called on his weapons officer.

'Blake, is there anything out there?'

'No gate activity, no new contacts,' she answered, shaking her head. The Gallente native had bright red hair cut rather harshly over her emerald eyes. At twenty-two years old, she was the youngest officer on board – although most of the crew knew better than to remind her of that. 'I think I've heard this stupid story before.'

'But she's in there for, like, a half hour, and I don't hear any water running!' Miles continued.

Although the *Morse* was more than five hundred meters from bow to stern, the bridge was buried deep within the ship in a cramped space, shaped like an octagon. Jonas sat at the center on a platform facing three viewscreens. The captain's chair was elevated slightly above the stations where Miles and Blake sat on each side of him. The three could operate most of the ship's main functions from here, while presiding over a crew of about 150, a third of which was devoted to maintaining the dropship hangar and away-team accommodations toward the rear of the vessel. This was where the fourth command officer of the ship spent most of his time – a mercenary of Mannar ancestry who answered only to the name *Mack*.

'Why don't you tell Mack this one; I'm sure he'd love to hear it,'

Jonas grumbled, raising other displays at his bridge controls.

'So I just *have* to find out what she's doing in there, because I'm getting all hot and bothered just thinking about it—'

'You know you're sick in the head, right?' Jonas snapped. 'There are cures for this kind of shit.'

'Oh, I'm not interested in any remedies, sir,' the young engineer said, without breaking stride. 'So I sneak over there, and just when I'm about to reach the door—'

'— your mom walks out?' Blake sneered.

Jonas was about to start laughing when the viewscreens brightened and the massive stargate suddenly came alive. It was the first ship to come through in hours.

Blake and Miles exchanged glances and then settled into professional mode.

'Well,' Jonas muttered, 'here comes a welcome change of subject. . . .'

KORVIN SAW THE DRAKE parked high above the gate and froze. Icy, lead tentacles spread across the pit of his stomach as fear took hold of him. Of all the gates he'd jumped through since his act of betrayal, the reflex became automatic: Align the ship with the nearest celestial navigational reference and warp toward it. Get the hell out of harm's way as quickly as possible.

But he knew the Drake was a Mordu's Legion ship. There was a chance. It all depended on how rational its captain was . . . and how insane Korvin would have to be to trust him.

JONAS'S EYES WENT as wide as saucers.

'Fed Navy battlecruiser!' Blake warned. 'Capsuleer pilot!'

'Engines primed, we're ready to warp out!' Miles said. 'Captain?'

The Myrmidon was the Federation answer to the Drake; a heavy battlecruiser that mixed drones and railguns to match the firepower of the Caldari missile boat. It would be a fair fight, except this ship was piloted by an immortal who could react faster and smarter than the *Morse* crew could – and take huge risks without fear of losing his life.

But Jonas had an instinct here that, like all gut feelings, had no logical explanation.

'Put the shield hardeners up,' he said quietly.

'*Captain?*' both officers said in stereo.

'Just do it. And sound battle stations.'

HE DIDN'T RUN, Korvin thought. *But there still isn't enough information to assess intent.*

Korvin raised his own hardeners. The ship's active sensors began emitting while his targeting computers calculated a firing solution.

'HE'S LOCKING US UP,' Blake warned. 'Track in five seconds.'

'Return the favor,' Jonas said, rubbing his chin. Something was bothering him about the ship's appearance. 'Give me an optical scan, ten times magnification, please.'

Miles was visibly sweating as his fingers danced on volumetric controls. The Myrmidon's rack of 250mm railguns filled the screen; each turret was already pointing toward them.

Jonas panned the camera downward, noticed all the missing ejection plates, and felt better about his instincts.

'He's got us,' Blake said, sounding exasperated. 'Transversal is zero; firing solution is optimal. Neither of us can possibly miss. Now what?'

'Now,' Jonas stated, 'we find out what's on his mind.'

'HI,' THE DRAKE CAPTAIN BEGAN. 'Name's Jonas Varitec, captain of the Mordu's Legion warship *Morse*. Since we've both dropped our shorts, I thought we should pillow-talk a little.'

Korvin was unaccustomed to this. He could actually feel anxiety moving in waves up and down his spine – fear of living, fear of dying. Fear of what to say next to this curiously calm Drake captain.

For a mortal, this guy has a pair.

'So tell me ... what's a Federation Navy capsuleer doing all the way out here?'

An honest query, or a setup question. No way to be sure.

Korvin's only remaining weapons were drones, and they wouldn't be able to break through the Drake's shields before getting picked off.

But it was the only way to be sure.

'HE'S LAUNCHING DRONES!' Blake yelped. 'Five Tech-two Hammer heads!'

Jonas didn't flinch.

'Are they orbiting him or vectoring on us?'

'*Orbiting*, sir.'

'Turn the hardeners off.'

'*What?*'

'HOLD IT THERE, BUDDY,' the Drake captain warned. 'That's not what I want.'

He lowered his defenses. An act of trust.

'I'm pretty sure that's not what *you* want either,' he continued. 'You're not the first broken man to wander through here.'

Korvin felt relief wash over him like a tsunami.

Redemption.

'Look,' the Drake captain said. 'I don't know what you're running from. I don't want to know. But you've got sanctuary here as long as you leave it behind. There's no turning back. You understand?'

Tears forcibly gushed from Korvin's eyes, mixing with the neuro-embryonic containment fluid surrounding him.

'Just follow me. We'll take you all the way in.'

'BLAKE,' JONAS COMMANDED, 'let HQ know that we're bringing a capsuleer back with us. We're taking him to see the old man: He's got this thing about meeting all the ex-Navy guys directly. Ask them to have the escorts back off; we don't want to spook our guest.'

She nodded, still bewildered. The Myrmidon had already taken position alongside them, its defenses lowered and drones withdrawn.

'Okay.'

'Miles, kindly take us to Five-Zee. Fastest route possible, please.'

The engineer turned suddenly to face the *Morse* captain.

'How the hell did you know he wasn't going to attack us?'

'Because I know capsuleers,' Jonas growled. 'He's just human like the rest of us. There's no way he wandered out here looking for a fight. That ship isn't crewed, and I'll bet there's no ammo left for those rails.'

'Pretty ballsy to stare down a cappy like that,' Blake remarked.

'Yeah, well,' Jones muttered as the ship's warp engines activated, 'sympathy has got me into trouble before.'

11

PURE BLIND REGION – MDM8-J CONSTELLATION
SYSTEM 5ZXX-K – PLANET V, MOON 17
MORDU'S LEGION HQ STATION

The 'old man' that the *Morse* crew was taking Korvin Lears to see was the legendary Muryia Mordu. He had many faces – all of them aged – depending on who you were. There were very different sides of the iconic man who founded the Legion.

If you were a member of the Legion, you were treated with all the reverence of family. Mordu was a patriarch who cared deeply for those who placed their trust in him. Whether a civilian or former Navy Admiral, it wasn't uncommon for the man to greet you with an embrace and the sincerest inquiry about the welfare of you and your loved ones.

He wore the most eccentric attire imaginable in support or jest of ambiguous Caldari and Gallente national holidays, sports teams, unusual anniversaries, or sometimes, for no discernable reason whatsoever. While no one dared to offer counsel on his fashion sense, some guessed that his flair was merely a reflection of his mood; it was always a good day for the Legion when his outfit made children giggle.

When meeting with a head of state, renowned scientist, or other figures considered highly competent in their field, he was quick to discover gaps in their expertise. Mordu devoured knowledge, and his intellect was respected internationally, if not always favorably. But there was universal consensus that creating a modern nation-state – as he had done almost single-handedly – required the kind of genius that emerged but once in a generation.

But he was known for his dark side as well. Sooner or later, adversaries of Mordu found themselves staring down the barrel of a gun. Betrayal was inexcusable to Mordu, and as a matter of professionalism, he often personally ensured that loose ends in the Legion were cut to make that point perfectly clear.

As a former Brigadier General in the Caldari Navy, Mordu was no stranger to violence. The Legion survived for years as a mercenary enterprise alone, though its biggest client by far was the Navy. Unfortunately, Mordu never thought much of Tibus Heth, strongly objecting to his bigotry and swift rise to power. He was already distancing the Legion from Navy affairs when the siege of Caldari Prime enraged Mordu so much that he placed a bounty on the dictator's head.

The Legion's outstanding contracts with the State, worth billions of credits, were promptly terminated.

Business, however, remained brisk. The ongoing Minmatar – Amarr conflict provided a trove of contracts for the Legion's services, and though the affairs of mercenaries were invariably dark by nature, their reputation for honoring agreements while navigating the complications of international rules of engagement was nearly pristine.

He was thus very surprised to learn that CONCORD had dispatched a representative of their Inner Circle to see him. After all, Mordu's Legion fell well outside their jurisdiction, and the two factions had never dealt with each other in any capacity before.

Surprise gave way to anger when it was revealed that this 'representative' used deceit to board the station, illegal technology to infiltrate restricted areas, and brute force to incapacitate the guards assigned to watch the office in which he now sat.

MORDU SAW THE WORLD through an augmented reality display superimposed onto his vision. The data was generated by the station

AI and routed to cybernetic implants in his brain. Despite her disarmingly attractive looks, the AI warned him that the intruder's biorhythm was abnormal, and that passive jamming technology was masking her true capabilities.

She was fit but not physically overbearing, with blue eyes, cropped jet-black hair, and pale, baby-smooth skin. Mordu had heard that CONCORD was hatching custom-grown clones for special missions. These hybrids were biological anomalies with remapped arteries, dense muscle structures, faster-than- normal resting heart rates, and perfectly symmetrical vein patterns in their retinas, among other oddities.

The AI posited that the woman sitting in front of Mordu was broadcasting prerecorded biometric telemetry. Even though scans showed a beating heart pumping blood through veins and lungs inhaling and exhaling air, nothing about her was normal.

But she wasn't a capsuleer – at least not one that he'd ever seen. There was no implant over the brain stem, and the scanners didn't detect a shred of inorganic material, metal or otherwise. She looked to be a hybrid between Caldari and Gallente ethnicities, a soft beauty that could appear harmlessly meek or stone-cold cruel.

Mordu was deeply furious.

'Before you say anything,' he said, standing in the doorway. 'There's a very good chance you won't leave this station alive.'

She smiled pleasantly, as though he'd commented on the weather.

'Threatening a CONCORD official is a felony, Mr Mordu,' she said.

'Not here, it isn't,' Mordu growled. 'But falsification of ship registration and assault are felonies as defined by Legion law. I'd be concerned if I were you.'

'My actions were regrettable but necessary to keep my identity as a representative of CONCORD secret. Victims were paid considerable compensation for their troubles. I hope you understand.'

Mordu's office was rigged with a variety of self-defense apparatuses, not the least of which included a pair of retractable 20mm railguns in the ceiling, designed to shred men and machine. It wouldn't take much more than a thought to transform this woman into a chunky puddle.

But for the intimidation factor, security drones and armed guards were now standing behind him.

'There will be consequences for your actions regardless,' Mordu warned. 'Now tell me why you're here.'

His guest showed no sign of being intimidated at all.

'The Inner Council sent me to ask for your assistance.'

'Really,' Mordu said, crossing his arms. 'What a first impression you're making.'

She raised her hand for silence.

'Please listen.'

Glaring for a moment, Mordu strode purposefully across the office and sat before her. The guards standing at the entrance raised their weapons and took aim.

'I'm listening.'

The woman now had a pleading expression that was unnerving.

'The Empyrean War has endangered the human race,' she started. 'We have learned that member nations of CONCORD are aggressively researching infantry applications of capsuleer science. The first nation to acquire this technology could wage a war without risk to itself. We cannot let this happen. We are working directly with national authorities to dissuade them from proceeding.'

She paused, studying Mordu for a reaction and finding only a hard stare. She continued her plea.

'The charter formalizing the existence of CONCORD sanctions the mandate by which we are sworn to act. To uphold our mission, we have passed legislation expressly forbidding research that advances capsuleer technology.'

Mordu narrowed his eyes.

'We have never interfered with your affairs, nor passed judgment on the activities that sustain you. But we need your help. Between the personnel you offer refuge to, and the work you perform on their behalf, the Legion is uniquely positioned to report on the activities of the Caldari State and the Gallente Federation—'

'That isn't accurate,' Mordu interrupted. 'While it's true that we offer amnesty to refugees from both nations, we ceased all business with the Caldari Navy once Tibus Heth put a titan over Caldari Prime. We blacklisted the Federation Navy after their Grand Admiral was executed for treason. Espionage is not one of the services that we provide. There is nothing we can or will do for CONCORD.'

The woman continued as though begging the much older man to be reasonable.

'I respectfully disagree, sir,' she said. 'As mercenaries, you have profited from the suffering of others in the war. But rather than ask you to spill more blood, we'll pay you for information that prevents more from being shed. If your operatives passively discover leads about the development of capsuleer technology, we'll reward you for that information. If you're open to contracts for active investigation, we'll pay double your rates. Mr Mordu, this contract is worth your while, and it will benefit the whole of humanity itself!'

'Tempting,' Mordu sneered. 'And if I refuse?'

'That will be disappointing,' the woman said, her expression turning from hope to sadness. 'But let me make this perfectly clear: If we learn that Mordu's Legion is withholding information from us about capsuleer research, well . . . the Inner Circle doesn't want that to happen.'

'Did I just hear correctly that CONCORD is threatening Mordu's Legion?'

'All you heard was the strength of our convictions and a generous offer to help us honor a mandate that protects humankind.'

'I see. Is that everything you came here to tell me?'

'Yes.'

'Then there's nothing left to do here,' Mordu said, turning toward the guards in the room. 'Please see her back to her ship. If she tries anything, kill her.'

The woman rose slowly, without ever taking her cobalt-blue eyes from Mordu's.

'The datapad confiscated upon my arrival contains information on how to contact us,' she said. 'You may keep it. There are contract propositions that explain what we're looking for and instructions for how to find it. Should you decide to accept our offer, you'll find it quite useful.'

'Noted,' Mordu said as guards surrounded her. 'Now I have a question for you.'

'Of course,' she said, clasping her hands behind her back.

'I don't believe I got your name.'

'My name is Tatiana Czar.'

'"Czar,"' Mordu repeated, feeding the query to the AI. No information was returned. 'I've never heard that surname before.'

Tatiana surveyed the room as a prod from the glowing barrel of a vowrtech pushed her along.

'It's Khanid,' she said on her way out. 'From the old commoner's dialect.'

'"Commoner," right,' Mordu warned. 'I hate liars, Ms Czar. Don't ever come back here.'

ALONE IN HIS OFFICE, Mordu took a moment to reflect.

Tatiana Czar – whatever she was – was escorted to the hangar entrance several levels down and left without incident. The guards who had been roughed up by the unassuming visitor voluntarily transferred the 'compensation' delivered by CONCORD to the Legion's treasury – a gesture that Mordu expected and appreciated. The ship she arrived in was an unremarkable Tristan-class frigate with Interbus tags; no one had expected a CONCORD representative to disembark. The datapad she left behind contained the proper encryption keys for all the levels leading to Mordu's office, even though these were changed daily.

Mordu clenched his fist and rapped the desk lightly.

There was a security breach, and it needed to be found quickly. CONCORD was playing a dangerous game, and before he could retaliate, he needed to understand how they had compromised him so easily.

Then the words of Tatiana Czar returned to him.

She was right: Immortal soldiers would have a devastating impact on humanity, especially if one nation alone possessed them. But if his operatives discovered the tech first, it would be he – and not

CONCORD – who would decide what should be done about it.

For now, it was time to move on to other matters: The *Morse* had just arrived with a capsuleer in tow. Mordu was impressed with the incident report: The encounter had been handled well by its captain, Jonas Varitec. The man was ready for higher-profile assignments, and Mordu intended to reward his competence by sending him to evaluate a contract opportunity in the Amamake system. The Minmatar had appealed directly to the Legion for assistance in their war against the Amarr Empire. If Jonas accepted the work, he'd be entitled to a percentage of any contracts awarded there. He was sure the captain would leap at the opportunity.

The damaged Federation Navy Myrmidon was latched to its berth in the hangar, and Mordu could see the pod gantry extracting the capsule from its hull. He very much wanted to meet the immortal floating inside of it.

TATIANA CZAR WATCHED HER Legion escorts peel off as she approached the X-70MU stargate. They probably assumed that the capsuleers who patrolled this area would almost certainly detect and attack the vessel. She expected as much.

But her death would only be an annoyance at worst.

12

GENESIS REGION – EVE CONSTELLATION
THE NEW EDEN SYSTEM

>>SIGNIFICANCE MISSION LOG ENTRY
>>BEGIN RECORDING

Is there anything more tragic than the corruption of genius? It seems criminal that the essence of what one *is* and how one should *think* could be determined by a societal devotion to a *meme*, a *belief*, and a *cause*.

Let's say the *meme* is the Amarr conviction that the Divine and the Empress are one and the same; that the *belief* is that an all-powerful God has chosen Amarr to rule all things; and that the *cause* is the holy crusade to convert all of humanity to this faith.

Now imagine that Empress Jamyl is the embodiment of all these things and that this figure is loved not so much for her divinity – though there are plenty who believe such rubbish – but for the *idea* of what she stands for: a savior born to lead an underachieving nation fractured by a human, and thus imperfect, royal caste.

The sheer power of the public's devotion to this myth has aligned billions of people under one banner. Would it not crush their hearts to learn that she admits the burden is too great for her to bear, that she knows she cannot possibly live up to the expectation of such blind adoration, and that she is wise enough to accept that doing good must sometimes come at the cost of doing great evil?

And because of this, one swears allegiance to her, unconditionally, no matter what the consequences.

Spare no pity on such a fool.

I once considered myself wise to the ways of the universe – a man of science, resolutely guided by the moral code of Amarr.

Today I remain a disciple of science and devoted to the absolute destruction of the Amarr Faith and, so tragically, the Empress who presides over it.

I imagine this admission begs the question: What does it take to turn someone so violently away from his convictions?

To answer this, I shall start by playing back a memory to my attentive audience of drones, who very much wish that I would sleep, rather than continue to torture myself.

>>MEMORY PLAYBACK: LOG 313

>>NEURO- MIMETIC FOOTAGE ENGAGED: JROR, MARCUS, DR.

>>LOCATION: W-SPACE

>>NEAREST CELESTIAL REF.: QUASAR J142847

>>313.10

... Long-range visual inspection of the discovery reveals a symmetric central hub encircled by a secondary concentric hull. Eight superstructures aligned with crossing spokes emerge perpendicular to the primary disk, which measures almost 6.5 kilometers in diameter. The structure is at least twelve thousand years old, but remarkably, still appears to be generating power.

The task force dispatched from the Matriarch Citadel has arrived and is approaching cautiously. Several heavy drones of unknown origin are orbiting the structure. Each is nearly as large as a battleship – probably sentinels, programmed to drive away intruders. ...

>>313.16

... We are suffering catastrophic losses. The AI behind these machines is extremely advanced, and our ships have no reliable countermeasures for their weapons. The drones are using beam technology we've never encountered before, carving our cruisers to pieces with ease.

Space is littered with tumbling wrecks and dead servicemen; the drones are even attacking ejected lifeboats. They are savage things, cruel and remorseless.

The fleet commander wants to pull his forces back, but even if I could allow it, they are still doomed. The Sleepers have blanketed the area with gravimetric jamming . . . the engines of our ships are now crippled. . . .

>>313.25

. . . Drones stopped their attack the moment she arrived. There is no discernable reason why they should have. The Archangel Guardians are with her, but neither she nor her escorts ever fired a weapon.

She apologizes for not coming to our aid sooner but sounds weak and confused. I hope she has the strength to maintain control long enough for us to complete the mission.

On my command, three dropships are launched. Each is carrying a dozen heavily armed men. Their task is to board the Sleeper structure, and I am to accompany them.

The sentinel drones are circling again, much faster than before. Their weapons are still primed. But they allow the dropships to pass, seemingly against their will. . . .

>>313.28

. . . These commandos are well trained and supported by drone tech of their own. But we don't know what to expect once we're inside. Given what we've just seen, I doubt it will be enough.

Scouting ahead of us, the first two teams are unable to find suitable landing spots, and their attempts to use shaped charges for a controlled breach all fail.

I was about to report failure when the bottom center of the hub dilated like an iris.

Our pilot informs that the other two teams will board first. We watch in silence as they slowly ascend into the aperture, which appears capable of opening much wider.

The fleet commander advises us to hurry. Reinforcements are unavailable, he explains, as the wormhole through which we entered is highly unstable and in imminent danger of collapse. . . .

>>313.41

. . . The air is too thin to breathe without survival suits. Commandos cautiously move out as the dropship's sensors blanket the area in search of movement. Finding none, they signal for me to come down while others prepare my equipment for transport.

I am terrified to discover that this place is instantly familiar.

There is a distinctly organic appearance to the interior; huge spiral designs resembling Fibonacci sequences flow seamlessly into other patterns stretching as far as I can see, covering the entire hangar.

Taken all at once, this place seems eerily alive.

The forward teams discover stranger patterns emerging from corridor floors and blending into bulkheads. A soldier remarks that some of them appear to be moving.

I hear a shout, followed by gunfire. . . .

>>313.49

. . . The attackers have no weapons. They are not wearing masks.

Their eyes are completely black – no whites in them at all.

Errant beam fire nearly kills me. A rifle barrel is punched through a man's chest. Another man's skull is crushed by his own detached helmet.

Blood splatters across my mask, making it difficult to see.

An explosion knocks me to the floor. There is absolute silence, and I am surrounded by death. . . .

>>313.60

. . . My wounds are serious, but Empress Jamyl urges me to press on. Only six of us survived, but the attackers are dead. Miraculously, my equipment is still intact.

Pain roars through my back when I try to walk. . . .

*

>>313.83

... We discover a massive circular concourse lined with sealed containers. Each holds a specimen in cryogenic storage.

The commandos are struggling to load the dead onto the hover-sled. Nine of these Sleeper aberrations managed to kill thirty armed men with their bare hands.

We do not know if or when more will awaken. But my orders are explicit.

The nearest subject is cryogenically frozen but attached to a cybernetic implant coupler that extends from the brain stem into what outwardly appears like a solid block of metal. Mass-spectrometer analysis reveals that the material is a hybrid composition of metallofullerenes – individual germanium and palladium atoms suspended within a carbon icosahedron fullerene. A third material, possibly a molecular alloy, is also present but cannot be identified.

This block extends directly into the bulkhead, which appears to be made of the same material. Very low voltage electrical activity is present.

The bizarre anatomy and physical composition of the subject makes it impossible to determine if revival is possible. Subject weighs 68 kilograms and would stand 175 centimeters tall. Its sex is indeterminate.

Genetic analysis of the attackers is complete, and two of my suspicions are confirmed with absolute certainty: The Sleepers are human, and the Joves are their descendants.

The soldiers want to execute as many frozen specimens as they can for 'precautionary measures.' Inwardly, I admit to wanting to do the same. But there are probably hundreds, if not thousands, more. Unless we can get them all at once, there is no point.

Better to just leave this cursed place as quickly as possible. ...

>>313.115

... Cutting away the entire pod – including a segment of the attached bulkhead – depletes six plasma torches and takes nearly three hours.

By the end I can barely stand from the pain, and the notion of being surrounded by dormant killers is driving us all to the point of madness. . . .

>>313.131

. . . Every Sleeper corpse, including the cryogenically preserved one, is now safely aboard the *Significance*.

Empress Jamyl and her Archangels depart in silence. For my own safety, I am instructed to return to the New Eden system and begin my research.

As I prepare the *Significance* for warp, a fireball blossoms on the Sleeper structure. It seems the fleet commander couldn't resist the urge to exact his revenge.

His actions will cost him his life, as my ship is the last to exit before the wormhole collapses. . . .

>>STOP MEMORY PLAYBACK

>>RESUME LOG 743

It was the brain that Empress Jamyl was after.

After thousands of years of evolution, the Sleepers decided that four lobes weren't enough to meet their cognitive-processing needs. Among other changes, this civilization reengineered themselves to add a fifth lobe to the cerebral cortex, combining and enhancing the functions of the thalamus and hippocampus. The extra gray matter was integrated with a curious slab of material encapsulating the brain stem and extending to an implant cavity that penetrated the skull, very similar to the neuro-interface socket that capsuleers use to communicate with machines today.

Even with the assistance of the most advanced AI available to science, it took years to model the anatomy and inferred biochemistry.

In summary, the Sleeper brain was refactored to route memories to a solid-state recorder. Therein was a feat of supreme biotechnical advancement: a fullerene-based quantum computer embedded within the brain, which can continuously record the memory of consciousness. This device is integral to the anatomy, which can retrieve information from quantum storage faster than it can from organic brain matter.

The fifth lobe incorporated a densely packed cluster of neurons that branched into a neural network extending to every region of the brain. With the state recorder and its complementary anatomy, it was possible to enable full memory-only consciousness transfers without the overhead of transmitting massive volumes of state information, such as neuron configurations and firing sequences.

It differed wildly from capsuleer technology, which relies on a huge, cluster-wide infrastructure of receiving and assimilation stations to support the cumbersome transfer of state data. With Sleepers, it was possible that only a fractional volume of differential information would be needed to move a person's essence to another clone, *if* that clone shared this brain anatomy, and depending on the storage capacity of the implant itself.

What was remarkable was that the gene needed to grow this fifth lobe from an embryo was present in the specimen's DNA but switched off. Like some grotesque mutation, the brain would develop with four truncated lobes and a cavity where the thalamus and hippocampus should be. At some point, a live test subject must have been raised with the gene switched on so that the growth pattern of the fifth lobe could be recorded and used as a template to assemble the organ from raw biomass later on.

Which meant that this subject – and probably all the others in the Sleeper station – were clones, identical copies artificially grown in vats not too different from those used in clone production today, with the cerebral implant added during the appropriate phase of gestation.

All it needed was the memories of a real person to give it life.

I STRUGGLED TO UNDERSTAND why the Sleepers did this to themselves. The savagery of their attack haunted me, yet in hindsight, I could almost sense they were fighting for their lives – just doing what living things do when cornered. It was possible they were just automated husks, no different from the sentinel drones that attacked our ships. Examining their remains yielded no clues on how long they had been awake for. But hundreds of dormant specimens were still there, perhaps awaiting the transfer of a consciousness more than twelve thousand years old.

Or maybe there was a consciousness already embedded within them. My devotion to the mission forced me to suppress that possibility. But the idea persisted. The will to live is so powerful in nature; life *always* tries to find a way.

Empress Jamyl decreed that Amarr must have the technology to produce an immortal army, and I was charged with delivering it. She wanted an unstoppable crusade to spread our faith and end the war. This was necessary, so her thinking went, for the greater good of humanity. And, as with many other dark secrets buried within her, she knew exactly where to find the technology to make this crusade possible.

AFTER ENOUGH SPECIMENS had been harvested and analyzed, a clone design for the first immortal soldiers using original Sleeper technology finally emerged. Slaves and war prisoners of all races – except True Amarr, of course – were brought here as test subjects, each with a freshly installed neuro-interface socket to facilitate the extraction of their consciousness for installation into these new clones.

Early test subjects died in writhing agony, caused by everything from incorrectly mapped neural pathways to runaway autoimmune responses. Some held on to consciousness just long enough to beg for death and then slipped away. Others awoke the equivalent of cripples or lunatics or just empty husks with no memory or cognitive capacity at all. The lucky ones never opened their eyes at all.

Unfortunately, but not surprisingly, science prevailed. The first poor soul to survive the refined process was a Caldari criminal, wanted by the Lai Dai mega-corporation for a crime undeserving of this punishment. The transfer of his essence into the new clone design was seamless; he was now a soldier with no equal. He had become immortal, and like the Sleeper origins of his new brain, only barely qualified as human.

To keep the research secret, the remaining original test subjects, though perfectly healthy, were liquefied, sorted, and added to my growing collection of biomass, a soupy sludge of amino acids, stem cells, proteins, and organic molecules destined to be recycled into another potential crusader.

With the transfer process now 'perfected,' a very impatient Empress Jamyl sent twelve of her most devoted Paladins to undergo the transformation to immortal holy warriors – volunteers, this time.

I could only imagine the sales pitch.

Any other man might feel proud of this accomplishment. Were I not trapped here, I might celebrate this great leap for Amarr by flying the *Significance* into the nearest star.

>>END RECORDING

13

GENESIS REGION – EVE CONSTELLATION
THE NEW EDEN SYSTEM

>>SIGNIFICANCE MISSION LOG ENTRY
>>BEGIN RECORDING

Even with the benefit of hindsight, there is little I could have changed.

Lord Falek Grange was the master architect of my shameful life, and he did his ruthless work with Empress Jamyl by his side. Combined, they became the object of my devotion in the most extreme sense; I was absolute and unconditional in my commitment to them.

As far as influences go, my parents did little to prepare me for the cruelty of the universe. The gift of my natural intellect was amusing to them, at best a topic of idle chatter among their aristocratic peers. As the only son of wealthy Holders, I was entitled to the same lavish lifestyle that was the birthright of generations before me. When I was eight years of age, I realized that I was born into an elite, homogeneous theocratic caste, with no means of exceeding its boundaries. Even if I was born a complete imbecile, I would still be entitled to this opulent, mundane lifestyle.

This terrified me, and I became determined to prove that intelligence still served some functional purpose in the world.

My insatiable appetite for knowledge only intensified as I absorbed volumes of information from virtual academic constructs. Yet my parents failed to grasp that I sought a *context*, any context, for an application of my skills. I desperately needed a chance to assemble everything I learned into a masterpiece worthy of genuine praise rather than subtle patronization.

At the core, I was just a child who wanted to please his parents.

My frustration was not unnoticed. As with any Holder residence, our estate was tended by slaves, and many were devout caretakers with whom I spent more time than with my mother or father. They were an attentive audience that made my naïve and admittedly egotistical self feel appreciated. I was convinced they were genuinely impressed with my advancement and natural gift. I began to confide in them, sharing in the few childhood delights that an under-privileged child might consider normal: rolling in the grass with pet slavers, playing hide-and-seek across the manicured grounds of our home, running with reckless abandon through local fairs while under the watchful eye of Paladins.

They provided comfort when I admitted to feeling unloved by my parents, holding me tight as I cried, promising not to tell anyone of my tears.

With this newfound intimacy came innocent trust, and they began asking questions that I was more than happy to answer. I saw no harm in explaining how biometric security systems could be bypassed or how the glaive collars around their necks could be disabled or how to hack the estate's datacore or how to fabricate a decryption key that would grant access to restricted areas of the grounds. I relished the sensation of triumph with every conquered challenge, basking in the adulation that my companions returned, eager to prove to them again and again how much potential I had for scientific greatness.

They were my only friends.

I loved them all. And I knew they loved me as well.

One night, I was escorted to my quarters for bed. I remembered hearing that it would be overcast and triple new moons; the sky would be black as satin, a good night to hide under the covers in fear of imaginary monsters lurking outside. My parents made their customary visit, gave the obligatory kiss on my cheek, and said something disingenuous. As they left, the slaves followed. The last one out – her name was Sasha – paused and looked my way. I thought her eyes were glistening; there was a sadness about her. Just as I thought to ask her what was wrong, she left, gently closing the door.

I fell asleep wondering if I had done something to disappoint her.

After a fitful sleep, the sound of my mother gasping in shock shook me out of bed. My father, his voice cracking and desperate, was upset as well, pleading in earnest with angry men. Throwing open the door, I emerged from my room and saw a transformed world before me: A dozen armed Paladins were inside the foyer; my slave companions were being led through the front entrance, their hands cuffed behind their backs. I ran after them, ignoring the warnings of strangers, dashed through the front entrance, and froze.

Sasha's corpse was splayed across the steps, her crimson blood contrasting brightly with the marble upon which she fell. Her hand – the same soft, reassuring flesh that had touched my heart – was gripped around the stock of a rifle. Two more companions were nearby, facedown and contorted in gruesome ways; several dead slavers – I recognized the protective animals by their pet names – lay riddled with blast marks.

Later I would learn that Holders in the estate bordering ours, some ten kilometers away, had been murdered by slaves who had somehow broken free of their glaive collars. The running gun battle that ensued resulted in multiple fatalities, as the rogue slaves possessed intimate knowledge of Paladin response tactics and terrain. It was a suicide mission, the investigators explained. There was no way for the slaves to escape the district, let alone the planet. Their goal was just to spill as much Amarr blood as possible before their own inevitable demise.

Investigators further concluded that Sasha died protecting my estate, turning on the slaves who wanted to kill my parents during the rampage, and likely myself as well. The pursuing Paladins, unable or uninterested in determining her motives, shot her to death anyway, ending the night of terror.

A crude but effective decryption device made of salvaged household electronics was found among the deceased slaves. It didn't take the most sophisticated detective work to determine its origins.

I was made to sit with Paladins, high priests, and detectives alongside my parents in a theocratic court to explain my actions. I told them that it just never occurred to me that the information I divulged could be used to do harm. That was the honest truth, if not a pathetic one. I thought 'slaves' were perfectly content with their role in society. I believed them to be utterly incapable of hurting anyone.

Through tears that flowed more for confusion than despair, I declared that it just seemed illogical that knowledge or science could be used to commit acts of evil. Nor, I added, was this lesson apparent in what little of the faith I had been exposed to. I regretted admitting this immediately; the judges and priests shook their heads, their faces impassive, not at all empathizing with my plea. I could sense the deepest shame welling up in my parents at my ignorance.

When asked about my relationship with Sasha, I answered that she was more caring toward me than my own mother was, which earned me a vicious slap from my father. The Paladins reacted forcefully, instructing him not to do that again. But the pain spreading across my jaw triggered a realization, something that ripped apart the veil of my innocence. In that moment, two burning hatreds were born: One was for my parents, whose unforgivable detachment I blamed for this tragedy.

The other was for slaves themselves. I would eventually harness this emotion into a zero-tolerance policy for even the mildest of indiscretions and hold them accountable to the most extreme interpretation of our faith. Administering punishment was therefore a convenient alignment of inner rage with the religious justification to become a sadist. That I didn't really believe in God at all was irrelevant, provided no one else knew.

And so at last, here was my masterpiece. I had finally achieved the recognition I sought, though I had not a single friend in all the world to share it with.

The magistrates and priests recessed briefly to discuss my fate. I was left to sit with my parents.

'How could you do this?' my father demanded. My mother said nothing, her face puffy and red from grief – not for the trauma I was enduring, I was convinced, but for the embarrassment I had wrought on the family name.

'Because I didn't know any better,' I admitted.

'That's unacceptable!' he bellowed, grabbing my arm. 'I *raised* you to know better!'

The same Paladins who earlier warned him not to get physical stepped forward. I gave my father the coldest stare I could.

'I was raised by slaves. Not by you.'

They were the last words I ever spoke to him.

As the magistrates returned to take their seats, I felt as though I were in free fall, at the total and complete mercy of immutable laws of physics, and that I would be banished to the cellar of some reliquary and forced to memorize every word of the Scriptures until a bishop declared my soul purged of sin.

But instead, a miracle of sorts happened.

They declared that I was innocent of conspiracy, concurring that I had been the victim of a cunning plot of sabotage. I was, after all, only a child, and thus emotionally unprepared to see through such an elaborate and deceitful scheme. However, I was found guilty of the juvenile misdemeanor charge of negligence, of which the sentencing guidelines were entirely contextual and discretionary. It wasn't uncommon for a slave child or even a non-Holder Amarrian to be given a flesh-ripping shock-lash or two, depending on the infraction.

My punishment was to take an aptitude test on the spot, with no preparation.

While the courtroom watched, mathematical challenges and scientific queries materialized in the space before me, and immediately my mind shut everything else out. I was in my element now, completely at peace and oblivious to my surroundings. I quickly and flawlessly worked through one problem after the next. I finally had a chance to show the world what I was capable of.

I don't know how long I was standing there. But the sound of the chief magistrate declaring 'Enough!' snapped me back to reality.

The results showed what I knew all along – that I was different–and that, in the magistrate's view, I wasn't realizing my full potential while under the misguidance of my parents.

I was to be sent to Amarr's elite institution for applied sciences, the Royal Amarr Institute, and given advanced placement in a special program for the development of intellectually gifted children. We would each be assigned a personal mentor – each a former graduate of the program itself and very much accomplished in a specialized scientific field.

The magistrate further explained that the mentor assigned to me was a prominent scientist poised to earn a seat on one of the most powerful institutions of the Empire – the Theology Council, the Empire's highest court. They said that he was revered with the utmost respect by both academia and the church alike – an extremely rare combination in modern times – and that I should consider myself blessed to be under his tutelage.

But my parents gasped as though I'd been sentenced to death. Despite my misgivings toward them, I was frightened by the passion of their response. My father protested furiously and my mother begged for mercy. I remember them being restrained by guards as the magistrate ordered them to be silent. He then stamped the verdict, sealing my fate. Court was adjourned, and the Paladins informed us that a courier would visit our estate to take me to the Emrayur system within thirty-six hours.

It wasn't until I was aboard the dropship lifting upward from my homeworld that I learned that the name of my mentor was Lord Falek Grange. At just eight years of age, that meant nothing to me, except that the name of the Holders who were murdered because of my ignorance was Lord Talhur Grange, his wife Miko, and one of their sons, Hathim.

My greatest influence was about to become a man who lost his entire family as a direct consequence of my personal ambition.

>>END RECORDING

14

CITADEL REGION – AREKIN CONSTELLATION
THE AHYNADA SYSTEM – PLANET IV: KRYSKOS MAR
BLACKBOURN CITY – VALOMER DISTRICT ACADEMY
SOVEREIGNTY OF THE CALDARI STATE

Thirty Years Ago

'Don't you quit on me, Barabin,' the instructor barked. 'The State needs you to be strong.'

Vince thought his lungs were going to burst. His legs kept kicking through the brutally chilled water while his burning arms struggled to keep his MK25 Gauss rifle over his head. Surrounded by other teenaged cadets fighting to stay afloat, Vince felt as though acid were pumping through his veins, and every fiber of his being was begging to quit.

The class was enduring the mandatory basic military training imposed by the State, comprised of vigorous physical conditioning, weapons and tactics training, and regimented academic learning. Nearing the end of their standard education, these students would graduate directly into military or mega-corporate assignments, depending on their best competencies. But this had been an especially bad week for Vince: The extra minutes tacked on to their water-survival class were due to his failure to come prepared, unable to work through a simple differential equation that could have been solved had he performed last evening's assignments.

As per the Caldari way, the entire class would pay for his indiscretion, regardless of having a very good excuse.

'Whose State is this?' the instructor bellowed.

'Our State!' the class screamed back.

'Whose?'

'Ours!'

'Louder, dammit!'

'Our State!'

The cadence sounded more like desperation than conviction. Everyone was suffering; the air was filled with the sounds of anguished grunts and wheezes as the cadets continued to tread water, and Vince knew it was his fault.

His classmates would get retribution for this, of course – almost certainly during the walk home from the academy. Then his father would ridicule him again, and depending on how much he'd had to drink, likely challenge him to a fight. And Vince would have to let him win, because his father refused to lose, no matter what. Struggling to find the right balance between making an acceptable effort and allowing a victory with minimal damage was a delicate, if traumatizing, affair. And then Vince would be unable to sleep, living in fear of the next encounter, and lately, just the thought of facing another day.

In fact, he couldn't remember the last time he'd slept soundly at all.

'When you don't prepare, people die,' the instructor said, staring down at Vince from the pool's edge. 'Every soldier is the difference between winning and losing, between living and dying!'

His arms started to fail him; the lactic acid buildup in his muscles was starting to overpower his will.

'Sixty more seconds,' the instructor taunted. 'All you have to do is tread for another minute. You think you can do that?'

'Yes, ma'am. . . .'

'I can't hear you!'

There wasn't enough air in his lungs to answer back. Vince thought of his sister Téa, and his arms straightened out for a moment. He didn't want to let her down by becoming a failure. She always tried to protect him from Father's fits of senseless anger, and for that he owed her dearly.

'Speak up, cadet!'

But the fatigue was clouding his senses, and suddenly it no longer seemed rational or even possible to keep the rifle upright. The answer to his suffering was so easy. His classmates would beat him later for quitting. But that experience couldn't possibly outlast the suffering he was enduring now.

The resounding splash of defeat was unmistakable; the weapon fell to the bottom of the pool as Vince kicked toward the edge, his arms nearly useless.

The instructor's reaction was predictably one of extreme disgust, and she took her wrath out on those cadets who continued their struggle, while Vince watched, shivering uncontrollably.

A LATE-SPRING STORM CARRYING MOISTURE from the warmer northern climates was grinding its way down the coast; a white coating of snow spotted with bits of grime and ash already bathed most of the city in a postindustrial glow. Several hundred thousand Caldari called this port city home, but during the day more than twice that number were within its borders. Operated by the Wiyrkomi mega-corporation, this particular district linked much of the southern hemisphere's industrial base with space elevator access several hundred kilometers to the north. The city was constructed around the deepwater port and massive rail-transfer yards; most of the surrounding buildings were six-story apartments with a central downtown area that included the academy, business spaces, and all of the supporting municipal structures.

Téa was waiting nervously for Vince a block away from the academy, following his strict instructions that they not be seen leaving the grounds together.

Hearing the sound of footsteps padding in the snow, she peered down the street and saw Vince jogging toward her. His uniform had been pulled on hastily; he had left in a hurry.

'You should go home a different way,' he panted. 'I really screwed up this time.'

She was a full year younger than him but the same height. 'No way. If Dad notices that we came home separately, he'll know something's wrong.'

'They'll all be waiting for me,' Vince said, looking around nervously. 'Harris, the squad captain, all those guys. I deserve whatever they throw at me.'

'No you don't. Dad does. He's the reason why you're struggling.'

Vince looked at his sister. She was the only person he cared about, or could trust, for that matter.

'Téa, I don't want to go home.'

'I don't either, Vince. But we don't have anywhere else to go.'

'Anywhere is better than this,' he said, trying to catch his breath. 'We should just run away. Maybe stow aboard a freighter heading back across the bay, or one of the maglevs heading north. . . .'

'Yeah, and then what?' Téa interrupted. 'We have no money. We have no support, no friends anywhere else. And when we're caught, the State will just send us to boarding dorms – if we're lucky.'

'God, I really miss Mom,' Vince said. His fatigue was making him especially vulnerable to emotions. 'Now more than ever.'

'There's no such thing as God,' Téa snorted. 'It's just you and me, and we're on our own.'

A shout called out from the alley. It sounded like the voice of Harris.

'Vince, we should go before they catch up.'

'It's too late for that,' he answered, trembling from fear. He curled his fingers into fists, his breath coming out in small puffs of vapor that dissipated in the cold. 'I guess the upside is that everyone coming after me is just as tired as I am. Téa, please go. I don't want you to see this.'

The sounds of several voices, much closer this time, echoed down the snow-covered street.

'I'm not leaving you,' she said. 'And if I do, it'll be to get help.'

Harris emerged from the alley corner, flanked on either side by two classmates, a boy and a girl.

'Barabin, you pussy,' he growled. 'I'm calling you out!'

Vince squared up to him. 'I know I messed up, and I'm sorry.'

'Sorry isn't gonna cut it, you lazy *prick*,' Harris said, shoving Vince on the shoulder. Harris was much taller and heavier.

Téa stepped in between them.

'Leave him alone! You have no idea what he's going through!'

'Yeah, it figures he'd hide behind his sister,' Harris growled, getting right in her face. 'Look, I don't care what he's going through. Vince let his squad down *twice* today. We paid for it, we're sick of it, and as squad leader it's my job to make sure it stops. Now step aside or else—'

The whine of an approaching municipal street cleaner – a big treaded vehicle that cleared and melted snow for civilian traffic – provided just enough of a distraction for Téa to launch her shin toward the older cadet's groin.

It caught just enough soft matter to stun him.

As Harris hunched over, Vince leapt toward the other cadet, colliding with him at the waist and driving him into the snow. The female companion lunged at Téa and dropped her with a well-trained jab-cross-elbow combo. The blows opened a deep cut on Téa's chin, and she lay woozy on her back, surrounded by bright droplets of crimson.

'You'll stay down if you know what's good for you,' the cadet growled. Téa tried to get to her feet, but a swift kick to her stomach stopped her.

Vince was too preoccupied grappling with the other cadet to help, and just when it seemed he might be able to wrestle free of his attacker's grip, a powerful punch came from nowhere and stunned him.

Forcefully heaved to his feet, he was thrown face-first into the side of a building, spun back around, and pummeled by Harris.

Bleeding from his nose and mouth, Vince fell to his knees. His ribs were so sore it hurt to breathe.

'It's for your own good,' Harris said, spitting. 'Get help, get with the program, or get the fuck out. Either way, stop dragging the rest of us through the mud with your personal problems.'

Vince said nothing, his eyes trying to blink away the pain. It was snowing harder now, and the only sound he was remotely aware of was the street cleaner, which was closer now.

'And you,' Harris said to Téa, who was now sitting up, clutching her chin. 'You've got spirit, I'll give you that. But no one likes a cheap shot.'

He kicked a boot's worth of snow into her face, and as the tiny bits of ice stung her skin, for the first time in Vince's young life, something long dormant and very dark thrashed free of its chains. The imagery of Harris abusing his sister – the blatant disrespect, utter lack of compassion, and cowardly act to someone who was clearly weaker and disabled – reminded him so very much of the man he feared and loathed the most in life.

Finding a reservoir of untapped energy, he waited until his three classmates walked past before launching his strike. Feeling no pain, he rose to his feet quickly but stayed crouched and took long strides toward his target to close the distance as stealthily as possible.

When he was at the fringe of their detection range, he summoned all his strength into a full-blown sprint, nearly slipping as he propelled himself forward.

He had achieved the element of surprise: The three cadets were not expecting another attack. Vince was acting on instincts fueled by a primal, remorseless rage; at no point was he fully aware of what he was doing.

The first cadet reflexively crouched, bracing for another attempted tackle. Instead, he was met with a savage knee to the face, opening deep cuts above and below one eye. He collapsed on the sidewalk, covering his injury, blinded, and terrified that the damage was much worse than it felt.

Vince was peripherally aware that the street cleaner was very close now and that his sister was trying to tell him something.

Ducking beneath a punch from Harris, he countered with a punch to the larger man's ribs, then a second when he sensed the first had winded him.

The female cadet was too stunned to do anything but watch.

Vince unleashed a furious punch to Harris's nose; it shattered in spectacular bloody fashion. The cadet staggered backward toward the curb, his back facing the street.

Then Vince followed with a kick to his chest, knocking Harris into the street and directly into the path of the oncoming street cleaner.

DOMAIN REGION – PARUD CONSTELLATION
PENIRGMAN SYSTEM – PLANET VI: CLAVELON
SOVEREIGNTY OF THE AMARR EMPIRE

Present Day

Vince noticed a falcon soaring far overheard and saw it so clearly that he could count the number of feathers in its tail. He also knew its exact range, heading, and speed, and if he chose to, could use any of the weapons arranged in front of him to blast it out of the sky with a single shot.

Instead, he was fascinated by the creature's beauty, and committed its image to memory for study later on.

Before Empress Jamyl walked away from Vince on the battered shores of Xerah, she left him in the care of a priestess that he was to address as Instructor Muros. Her objective was to guide him from virtual imprisonment into a new reality. If he could remember anything of his past, he would marvel at his elite physical prowess, such as the ability to run without tiring, lift great weights with startling ease, and react with almost preternatural quickness to any threat.

For all he knew, these things were as natural to him as they were to everyone else, and this was exactly what Instructor Muros wanted him to believe.

Vince no longer felt as though he were cast in a dreamscape. Instead, he was overwhelmed by his physical senses; every detail of his surroundings seemed amplified and relevant. He felt anxious all the time, especially after mental and physical training exercises, concerned that there was still more to learn, or something vital that he was missing. It was an obsession with thoroughness, Instructor

Muros explained. The desire to serve Amarr had become manifest in his soul; it was an eagerness to please the Empress and perform the work of God, and he was encouraged to embrace it with all his might.

Vince accepted this as truth, and made sure it was always at the forefront of his conscience.

He and Instructor Muros were alone at a nondescript Imperial Armaments training facility. From this elevated vantage, their location seemed isolated: There were no traces of civilization for as far as the eye could see. Only midlands vegetation and the occasional roaming herd of wild livestock grazing on distant prairies dotted the land. The facility itself featured a small barracks and firing range; if not for the raised searchlights, it would appear the place had been abandoned long ago.

'Do you know what these are?' Instructor Muros asked, pointing toward a rifle rack.

'I do,' he answered. 'But . . . I'm not sure how I know it. I've never actually *seen* any of them before.'

Arrayed before him were plasma rifles, arc cannons, various explosives, and electronics, all of which he could explain the inner workings of in intimate detail, down to the smallest nuance. Yet he was certain he had never studied weapons before.

'Your new mind was created with this knowledge,' she explained. Like Vince, she had a presence about her that was unnatural. Her skin was pale; grayish blue veins appeared beneath the skin around her jaw and temple. She had a fighter's build – long, athletic limbs; a tight, muscular core; and broad shoulders.

'Your body was made to use those weapons. Pick up the plasma rifle.'

Vince did so and was immediately surprised. He knew it should have been extremely heavy, but instead it felt light, almost comfortable.

'Look downrange,' she said. 'Fire at the targets.'

Fifty meters away, a narrow stone target sprung up from the ground. In one fluid motion, Vince raised the rifle, deactivated the safety, and pulled the trigger. The muzzle exploded violently;

the force of the recoil drove hard into his shoulder, which somehow had the strength to absorb the enormous impact.

A glowing pockmark the size of a man's fist tore through the stone target, and Vince's ears were ringing from the weapon's report.

'Very good,' she said. 'As you can see, the basic muscle memory for handling this weapon has been set for you. There isn't a single unmodified human alive who can fire that rifle accurately. Try it again – this time at multiple targets and with full automatic enabled.'

Vince's thumb instinctively switched a lever from its semiauto to full position. Several targets popped up at various ranges one after the other; he answered by squeezing off quick successions of bursts. Some hit, sending chunks of exploding rock hurling through the air; others missed the mark, angering him. He could feel immense heat radiating off the weapon and wondered how he wasn't burned. As the clip ran out of charges, a coolant flushed through the barrel, making a whining relief sound.

'Your aim will improve with time and practice,' she said. 'Perfect marksmanship cannot be completely burned in during the neural mapping sequence.'

She began pouring a glass of water.

'Put the weapon down and drink this,' she ordered, setting it next to the weapon rack.

As Vince went to take the glass, it shattered in his hand.

'This is something you'll need to learn,' she said, pouring another glass. 'Your skin was damaged while firing that rifle. But the nanotech in your bloodstream was able to dull the pain and make repairs as you continued firing. Learning to control your transition between environments quickly – moving from plus-human strength, to just human – will take some time. Now put that combat vest on.'

Vince knew the vest was inordinately heavy, but it proved easy for him to wear.

'Those plasma rounds cut through stone so easily,' he remarked.

'Yes,' she answered. 'Your vest has a layer of depleted uranium and active magnetic shielding to assist in diffusing plasma munitions. Most conventional weapons can't penetrate it.'

She removed another rifle from the rack.

'This one, on the other hand, can. . . .'

Vince had barely slipped the armored vest on when the instructor pointed the weapon at him. Before he fully realized what was happening, the muzzle discharged, and pain ripped through his lower abdomen.

'Why . . . ?' he stammered, reeling backward.

She answered by firing a second time, roughly in the same area of his stomach. Vince dropped to his knees, covering the wound; deep red blood with spots of silver began seeping through his hands.

'It's part of your training,' she said, leaning the smoking rifle over her shoulder. 'You may be immortal, but you'll still feel pain. These are the horrors you must endure to defend our faith. Now, stand up.'

Vince could feel something strange happening in his abdomen. The pain had eased somewhat; patches of numbness and tingling surrounded the wound. Somehow, despite the damage, he rose to his feet.

'Now man your rifle and shoot the targets downrange!' she ordered.

The bleeding was slowing down much faster than it should have. He hurried to the mount, grabbed another weapon, and began firing.

As he did, she began screaming in his ear.

'I have no need to run you into the ground, no need to improve your conditioning, no need to teach you how to fly a dropship or command a tank. Your body and mind know how to do these things better than any mortal!'

Target after target exploded downrange; the *hiss* of coolant flushing the barrel indicated his clip was depleted.

'Reload!' she hollered. Vince felt tightness in his abdomen, with mild discomfort – or was it just awkwardness – at the extreme range of his torso as he twisted to aim for different targets.

He slammed another clip home like he'd been doing it for years.

'You're wounded, but the nanotech in your bloodstream can bridge structural defects quickly, sealing off internal bleeding before it can incapacitate you,' she said. 'They'll also attempt to repair damaged tissue, starting with ligaments and working to muscle. Blessed as those micromachines are, they are finite! Whenever you take damage, their number depletes. If you keep getting shot up, they won't be able to hold you together.'

She pointed toward a thick, cylindrical vial on the table. Again, he was intimately familiar with what it was, despite having never actually seen one.

'Inject yourself with it,' she ordered.

Vince instinctively stabbed himself in the exposed flesh around the broken armor. Three high-gauge needles punctured his flesh, and a rush of nanites, painkillers, and adrenaline flooded his veins. It was so exhilarating that he gasped desperately, as though coming up for air from the bottom of the sea.

The pain vanished, and the bleeding stopped completely. The wound was gory, but he felt energized.

'One more lesson remains,' she said. A large armored vehicle with oversized wheels was approaching. It stopped next to the weapon rack, right in front of the firing range.

'I want you to cross the range and touch the wall on the far side,' she said. 'That's fifty meters of space. You must hit the armed targets before they can harm you.'

Vince scanned the range. It was wide open, with no cover to duck behind.

It was a suicide run.

'Listen closely,' she said. 'The will to live . . . the instinct to preserve one's self, is as old as nature. But as a Templar, you must learn to dismiss self-preservation *for life*, and instead preserve yourself *for the holy mandate*, a task that *only* the immortal can accomplish. You must accept on faith that you *will* live to fight another day, no matter what happens. You have no reason to fear *anything*. Do you understand?'

Vince nodded.

'Now, *go*!'

Vince leapt onto the range, weapon held out in front as he strode. His foot had barely impacted the dirt when the first target emerged; he caught it with two rounds. At thirty meters several more targets popped up at once – and two were armed.

Vince only had time to blast one of them before he was blinded by a mist of his own blood. Knocked off to one side, he struggled to bring the gun around to return fire, when a second burst caught him square in the chest and leg; he fell onto his back. His anguish was desperate; he felt rage and fear as he attempted to pull himself forward . . .

. . . and then shock as another round punctured his back.

He could feel the life pulling away from his body; he did not have the strength to inject more nanites, nor would they do any good if he could.

Vince was aware of only one absolute in these final moments: Despite his faith, his strong desire to serve the Empress, and everything the instructor had told him, *he did not want to die*, and this terror was maddeningly familiar to some echo of his past. . . .

. . . And then for a moment, just the briefest, most horrible moment, he saw an apocalyptic vision of beings with jet-black eyes and a dark, ancient symbol that struck the greatest fear he had ever known into his soul.

He screamed – and then realized he was upright. Breathing hard, he looked around frantically, then reached toward his abdomen.

There were no wounds. He stepped forward only to realize he had been standing in what appeared to be like a vertical casket. Others were neatly arranged alongside, and when he looked inside them, he saw inert copies of himself staring back at him.

A door opened; the gunnery range was outside. A corpse lay strewn in the dirt just thirty meters downrange. He realized he was standing inside the armored vehicle that arrived just a few moments ago.

Vince staggered into the daylight, still reeling from his vision, and walked straight toward the corpse. He stared at his own gory remnants and remembered with perfect clarity how he had died.

Instructor Muros joined his side.

'Is this real?' Vince asked.

'Yes,' she answered. 'You are immortal.'

'Where did I come from before this?'

'You were born to us this way,' she said. 'In the service of Amarr and our Holy Empress. We rescued you from death, and in return you devoted yourself to our faith. Tell me your creed.'

'I am a Templar,' Vince said, mouthing the words from implanted memory, even though he remained shaken. 'I am eternally devoted to our faith; I am the holy sword of the righteous, and I will defend Amarr will all my might.'

'Remember, all living things were born from dust,' Instructor Muros said. 'But now, you can never return there.'

15

DOMAIN REGION – MADDAM CONSTELLATION
THE SARUM PRIME SYSTEM – PLANET III: MEKHIOS
CITY OF XERAH
SOVEREIGNTY OF THE AMARR EMPIRE

Twelve Years Ago

Heir Mekioth Sarum, ruler of the Sarum House and former Grand Admiral of the Imperial Navy, lay dying within the walls of his own palace. At nearly 180 years of age, not even the wondrous technologies of the day could save his life, for these advances could not overcome the simple fact that the will to live had left him. To make the outcome absolutely certain, he had all his life-sustaining implants removed and his clones destroyed. It was now just a matter of time.

Surrounding his withering shell were various diagnostic machines and their metallic caretakers. The house physician stood solemnly nearby as slaves tended to the heir's bodily needs. Holders and priests prowled the antechambers; only a select few were allowed such privileged access to the palace grounds, let alone to the place where Mekioth Sarum would breathe his last. The moment seemed woefully unbecoming for a scene that in the mind of most Amarrians should have been a divine spectacle complete with choirs of angels and the radiance of heaven itself. An unprecedented shift in power was about to take place, as the heir of one of Amarr's five holy houses was soon to pass his sanctioned right of Imperial ascension on to the next chosen heir.

Instead, the atmosphere reeked poignantly of anticipation rather than piety or sorrow.

When Jamyl Sarum – just fifteen years of age – appeared in the doorway, the room fell silent. This slight young lady hardly looked the part of an heir apparent to an interstellar kingdom. Accompanied by her mother, Anla, she approached her father for what could possibly be the last time. Lord Falek Grange, the youngest and most influential Holder in the room, was speaking with the physician and caught her eye. He bowed his courtesy and then stepped out of sight without a word.

The rest of the occupants, recognizing the moment for what it was, did the same.

Confident they were alone, Jamyl approached her father's bed wishing she felt only sadness. Toxic emotions assaulted her as she took one painful step after the next, dreading the moment so much that bile crept up her throat. She was fearful for the things he would say. She was frustrated that their time together had been so devoid of meaning, and bitter that he was always hateful toward her, no matter how hard she tried to love him.

Anla had warned her daughter this was going to be difficult, but Jamyl insisted it was the right thing to do.

Her father's yellow eyes found hers while she struggled to find the words.

'Why did you come here?' he hissed.

'To be by your side,' Jamyl said, trying to mean it. 'To offer comfort, if you would be willing to accept it.'

'Comfort?' he scoffed. 'You came here to see it yourself, didn't you? That's a good little heiress . . . make certain I'm out of your way before claiming victory.'

'Father, please . . . ' Jamyl said. 'I just want to wish you well in the afterlife and let you know you'll always be with me—'

Mekioth coughed violently, spitting up across the space in front of him.

'Is it not clear that God hates me, you stupid child?' he hissed. 'Your whore of a mother should have told you that by now.'

'Mekioth, you bastard . . . ' Anla started.

'Anla, my dear – I have to know something before I die: Are there any more heirs festering in that rotten cunt of yours?'

'She will carry the burden of your tainted name,' Anla growled. 'Your legacy is the Battle of Vak'Atioth, and mark my words, if my daughter claims glory for Amarr, it will be by erasing your existence from history!'

'Then tell this unwanted child the truth!' Mekioth wheezed. 'Have you prepared her? Does she know how to lead armies and rule an empire? *Then show her!* Show her to follow your example, you conniving wench!'

It was too much. Jamyl turned and began walking out.

'That's it – turn your back to me! You should have never been born, you hear? Only I can speak for Amarr! I alone! Not you, not ever—'

He broke into wheezes and coughs laced with droplets of blood. Anla followed her daughter out as slaves rushed back to assist the dying heir.

Lord Falek Grange, who remained hidden, watched as mother and daughter left, and thanked God that Mekioth would soon be dead.

THEY WERE IN THE PALACE GARDENS, where the most exotic species of flora from every corner of the Empire were displayed in breath-taking arrangements, lavished by ornate sculptures carved from precious metals and stone. The air smelled of perfume and the sea, which you could hear from across the great courtyard and over the walls beyond.

This place seemed as good as any to confront some hard truths about destiny. Jamyl stopped and whirled around abruptly.

'What did he mean by "truth"?' she demanded.

Anla took a deep breath.

'The truth is that if he had his way, you would have never been born.'

She paused a moment to let that sink in.

'You were artificially conceived,' Anla continued. 'My ovum was fertilized with genes selected from his DNA. You are a Sarum: The lineage of great leaders runs through your veins, but Mekioth is no more your father than a stranger.'

It was becoming increasingly difficult for Anla to speak.

'I had to keep my pregnancy a secret, because if he knew, he would have killed us both.'

Jamyl threw her hands in the air in disgust. 'Now you're lying to make another point—'

'You have no idea what that man was capable of,' Anla interrupted. 'None at all. But, thank God, you had powerful allies. When they found out I was with child, they vowed to protect us from him. And the way they did it was by proclaiming the news to our people. The word spread quickly – even the other houses sent their congratulations. When your father found out, he was beset by unspeakable rage. But he couldn't harm us, because the people of House Sarum adored you before you were even born. They hailed him for producing an heiress. They saved you, Jamyl. Not even an heir could stand up to their will.'

'Stop. . . .' Jamyl interrupted. 'Just tell me why . . . how . . . what did he want?'

'What else, but the throne,' Anla said. 'Emperor Heideran is hundreds of years old; he doesn't have much longer, and Mekioth thought he would live to see it happen. He has been posturing to seize power for most of his life. A child would complicate those plans: He wanted no more competition than he already faced from the other houses. His selfishness was so great that he would place our lineage in peril by not producing an heir, violating the most sacred codes of our—'

'Glorious,' Jamyl spit. 'So I was conceived to give this house the heir my own father thought he would never need.'

'Jamyl, I wanted a daughter,' Anla pleaded. 'I wanted *you.* To be your mother, to have a wonderful life together. But in this palace, what I wanted was irrelevant. Leaving House Sarum without an heir was a greater shame than Mekioth's infamous failure at Vak'Atioth, and that is why I was able to conceive you at all. Lord Falek Grange arranged for everything; you have him to thank for your life. As for Mekioth Sarum, his bitter words betray the jealousy he feels. You have bested him already.'

'This isn't a contest!' Jamyl said angrily. 'He'd rather die than live without the throne?'

'Men like him never let go of their ambitions, even when they can no longer be reached.'

Jamyl was beside herself. 'He's been dead to me for a long time.'

'Power corrupts all but the strongest among us,' Anla said. 'Our name reaches back more than a thousand years. Every army that has ever served Amarr has been led by a Sarum. We have an *unfathomable* responsibility, to this house and to Amarr. Your father believed he would be Emperor because, for a time, so many wanted him to be. That moment passed him by. It now belongs to you.'

'Then I choose to pass it on to someone else.'

'We do not get to choose. We are Sarums. This is our destiny.'

'*I don't want it*. And you can't force me to take it.'

'You're right: I can't. But your people can. And they will.'

'My people? You mean the ones disgraced by that ... bastard up there?'

'Don't speak to me about disgrace. I'm married to the man who gave Amarr the most humiliating defeat in her history. The man who emboldened an entire race to revolt against us ... whose failures shook the foundations of everything we believed in.'

'Mother, I don't believe in those things. I don't believe in this faith, and my father's failure to win the love of his own daughter is proof of its hypocrisy.'

'If that is what you believe, so be it. The test of faith is different for us all.'

Jamyl rolled her eyes. 'Oh, these primitive traditions! What kind of God is so insecure that he needs to "test" people's faith in him? It's absurd!'

'You can choose what you want to believe, Jamyl. But you cannot choose the beliefs of our people.'

'I don't want this life! I'm here not for an act of love but for an obligation to myth!'

'Jamyl, you are here for the greatest love there is!' Anla pleaded. 'For all its abuses and distortions of meaning, people need *something* to believe in. They want to believe in *you*. The thought of you sustains them in their difficult lives. They find strength in believing that one day, a Sarum will be Empress. What greater love is there?'

The garden was beautiful, but Jamyl was fixated on the palace walls beyond it.

'I hate this place,' she said. 'I hate everything about it. I feel trapped here, no better off than the slaves. I'd rather endure the hardships of a commoner than be imprisoned here.'

Her mother smiled.

'Every Sarum that has ever ruled this house has said the exact same thing,' Anla said. 'Except one. And he will be dead very soon.'

DOMAIN REGION – THRONE WORLDS CONSTELLATION
THE AMARR SYSTEM – PLANET ORIS
EMPEROR FAMILY ACADEMY STATION
SOVEREIGNTY OF THE AMARR EMPIRE

Present Day

Concentrating with almost superhuman focus, Lord Victor Eliade, Captain of Arms for the Imperial Navy, gathered his thoughts carefully. Although the implants made it easier to hold such undivided attention, the extended duration of this session and the countless others since the ascension of Empress Jamyl were taxing him nearly to the breaking point. Thoughts were supposed to be the most private possession a man could have. But now, in his service to Amarr, even this inner sanctum belonged to her. The burden of having to audit every thought as it formed in the mind would drive lesser men to madness.

For years, Empress Jamyl was suspended in clone stasis at the Matriarch Citadel. In the plot engineered by Lord Grange to fake her death, her brain-state information was sent there after the Succession Trials. But instead of reanimating her, the AI safeguarding her essence began rebuilding her clone, changing its anatomy and performing biotechnical augmentations that no one believed were possible. Even Lord Grange was helpless to stop it, for fear of killing her. All they could do was watch and pray she would awaken.

When she finally did, she was blessed with divine powers, able to enter the minds of followers and hear their thoughts from across the cosmos. She had knowledge of wondrous things that were hidden from the rest of the universe. But there were dark moments as well. From time to time, she would speak in unknown dialects, harming herself and those around her in fits of supernatural rage. Something sinister was trapped within her, and Victor wondered if that was the price of being able to glimpse God.

According to Scripture, every True Amarr must face a trial of faith. Victor believed that hers was to become the living embodiment of the eternal battle between good and evil. As the link between this world and the everlasting, her burden was necessary to learn the true nature of man. And now that she learned to control the evil within her – as all men must – Empress Jamyl was at last fit to rule.

Victor accepted this without hesitation, as did her followers and guardians from the Matriarch Citadel, all of whom now formed her Imperial court.

She promised that she would never willfully breach their minds again. But her word, precious as it was, didn't make it any less unnerving that such a violation was even possible at all.

Victor was no longer the man he used to be. The otherworldly struggle taking place within Empress Jamyl was being waged right before his eyes; he was witness to things that no living soul has any right to see. Yet as her captain, he shared in her burden and in her commitment to break the grip of evil on humankind.

The Templars would achieve that. He was sure of it.

There were now thirteen prototypes ready for a live deployment. Their capabilities were impressive and frightening at once: These living, breathing immortal beings could become the army that would end all wars; they were the soldiers of the apocalypse.

An end to killing was within reach. Everything they had sacrificed, everything that Empress Jamyl had fought for, would be vindicated. At last, the Amarr Empire could lead New Eden to a new age of universal peace and prosperity.

Studying the report of their final evaluations, Victor tried to see only the data that would validate his hope in the Templars. Yet something else was there, a blemish that could be nothing or the deceitful face of something malignant. In fact, all the scientists assigned to the Templar development program saw this as well. And the root of it was essentially alien technology – these Sleeper implants – which were still not fully understood.

The simple truth was that each of these soldiers described experiencing a vision at the point of death during their training. By itself, this wasn't unusual.

It was that all thirteen described the *same* vision.

Lord Victor forced himself to regard the matter as materially insignificant and unworthy of delaying their deployment any further.

SHE WAS WAITING FOR HIM in the palace reliquary.

It was there, surrounded by tokens from Amarr's glorious past – weapons wielded by ancient generals on battlefields where faith reclaimed wayward peoples; parchments from antiquity sealing the transition of entire nations to the Holy Empire's embrace – that history would be made once again.

'My lady,' he said, bowing. The Empress was staring at relics from Vak'Atioth – fragments of singed, golden-hued starship armor believed to have been from the battleship captained by Admiral Faus Akredon, the field commander of that doomed fleet.

It took all of Victor's concentration not to regard the historical and very personal implications to her.

'Is the crusade that will bear my name upon us?' she asked.

'Yes, Your Majesty,' he answered. 'The first Templars are ready.'

Exhaling deeply, she turned to face him. Though she remained beautiful, her inner struggle was taking its toll.

'I pity them, Victor. Their suffering will be unimaginable.'

'Sacrifice of and for the noble, my lady,' he said.

'We only presume our actions are noble,' she answered, reaching out to touch the armor.

'Their sacrifice will bring an end to bloodshed,' he said.

'If that happens, it could be there is no blood left to spill,' she said, turning away from the relics. 'And we immortals are all that remain.'

Lord Victor took a moment to let her reflect before speaking again.

'There is a Minmatar colony in the Amamake system,' he started. 'The planet is called Pike's Landing. We've lost more than twelve thousand soldiers trying to reclaim it. We believe this is the ideal proving ground for the Templars.'

Empress Jamyl turned back toward the relics of Vak'Atioth.

'The performance of the prototypes has been flawless,' Victor continued. 'With some diversionary support from conventional forces, we think they can take the surface outposts intact.'

'I feel a kinship with these Templars,' Jamyl said. 'We understand what sacrifice means. All but one are True Amarr?'

'That is correct, my lady,' Victor answered. 'The Caldari specimen was the first successful application of the technology. But insofar as skills and ability go, he is identical to the rest.'

'I hope he suffers the most.'

Victor stood motionless as she looked over her shoulder toward him.

'Is there anything else I should know before I consent to this?'

'No, my lady.'

'Then so be it. The word is given, Victor. Unleash your Templars, and may God have mercy on us all.'

16

PURE BLIND REGION – MDM8-J CONSTELLATION
SYSTEM 5ZXX-K – PLANET V, MOON 17
MORDU'S LEGION HQ STATION

'Let's be clear about something,' Mordu started. He was wearing an imitation Amarr bishop's miter; a patch haphazardly sewn on bore the word *Fun* with a line drawn through it. Nonsensical insignia dominated by sad faces and the word *Sinner!* adorned the priest's robes on his shoulders.

'We do things a little differently than what you're used to.'

Korvin Lears stared blankly at his new benefactor and began wondering just what he had gotten himself into.

'You're part of the family now,' the old man continued. 'Just about anything you could possibly need, we can provide. And when your family calls for help, you have to be there. *I mean that.*'

The former Federation pilot considered this and thought better of speaking just yet.

'We're both here because of corporate-sponsored fratricide,' Mordu continued, walking to a small bar in his office. He produced two tumblers made of either crystal or diamond, Korvin couldn't tell which, except for the fact they were very expensive.

'See, my generation was able to convince yours that this war of ethnicities was justified ... and we fell for it. Politicians love the naïve. You're probably hearing voices, right?'

'I'm sorry?' Korvin asked, taken aback.

Mordu hadn't turned around and was inspecting a bottle of spirits that appeared very old.

'Murder enough people and eventually they start talking back to you,' he said, pouring the amber-colored beverage. 'At least, that was my experience. It starts with whispers, and then the occasional shout. You hear conversations, but not clearly enough to discern spoken words. You see them from the corner of your eye, turn and find nothing but thin air. Does any of that sound familiar?'

Mordu turned around, holding two tumblers of hard grain alcohol. Whether he chose to admit such or not, Korvin certainly knew those voices, and for a moment the visage of charred corpses and frozen death masks swirled before him once again.

His eyes glassed over.

Mordu set the tumbler in front of him. 'You'll be right at home with us.'

Korvin stared at the glass, reflecting on what he had left behind by coming here. He had no true friends left in the Federation, just passing acquaintances who kept their distance. The typical bonding between soldiers during war eluded him throughout his service, and the absence of meaningful camaraderie hurt more than he realized. In his isolation, he found refuge only by immersing deeper into his craft – his gift for piloting weapons of mass destruction.

The only people he loved were his parents, and now they were living in shame.

Immortal or not, Korvin found very little reason to live.

'To our many victims,' Mordu said, raising his glass. 'May we honor their lives and those who will fall to our hands tomorrow.'

Korvin frowned.

'What do you mean by that?'

Mordu took a sip, never breaking eye contact.

'We're in the mercenary business,' he said. 'This haven for schizophrenic ex-patriots is funded by doing what soldiers do best. The Legion exists because war is an inevitable condition of man, and though not everyone has the stomach to wage it, most people agree that it's a necessary evil.'

Mordu smiled at the perplexed expression on his guest's face.

'What did you think this was – free housing? Every man needs to earn his keep somehow.'

Korvin stared at his drink. 'I came here to get away from war, I didn't even realize I was—'

'We do what presidents, dictators, kings, CEOs, cultists, and assorted vermin don't have the balls or the means to accomplish themselves,' Mordu continued. 'That is the market we serve. It has existed for as long as civilization. And while we provide a sanctuary for those burdened by the killing they've done for the wrong reasons, we will demand that you kill for the right ones.'

'The "right ones"?' Korvin asked. 'So then we're still playing the role of God here—'

'Only I get to play God,' Mordu said, patting his own chest. 'Me. I make those choices so you don't have to.'

'Why would anyone trust you to make them?'

'Because I trust myself to make those calls better than Jacus Roden or Tibus Heth.'

'That's not saying much.'

Mordu narrowed his eyes as he took another sip. Korvin left his untouched.

'There are such things as just wars, Lears. And I do my best to make sure the Legion fights in them. Once I had to put down a Federation admiral who was abusing his power as a provider of "security" in a losec colony. The following week I authorized the assassination of a Caldari general who was stealing troop provisions and selling them to the black market.'

The old man adjusted his miter and smiled.

'Did that "black market" happen to have any Legion customers?' Korvin asked.

'Mercenaries are nourished by the spoils of war,' Mordu answered, downing the rest of the drink in one gulp. 'The fact that civilians died in both ops was unfortunate, but it's my personal judgment that mankind benefited with both men eliminated.'

'Means justifying the ends and all that,' Korvin said. 'Looks like I've found another uniform telling me who to point a gun at. You're dressed for a costume party and drinking whiskey. You've given me every reason to trust your judgment intimately—'

'Don't ask me to explain the calculus of my morality,' Mordu said. 'Just trust that I do my homework carefully and that no decision to use force is casual.'

'I suppose you manage every Legion contract, then,' Korvin asked, 'and that you get enough business to support this little empire?'

'That's right,' Mordu answered. 'Our services include more than just firepower. We do a lot of tech work, electronic surveillance, even some R and D. We lease industrial infrastructure to privateers, provide populations for terraforming colonies, construct outposts on frontier worlds, and have even crewed starships for empire navies. We've made strong allies and powerful enemies. But on the whole, war has been very good to us.'

A subtle chime rang out, and the expression on Mordu's face brightened as the office door slid open. Jonas Varitec was standing in the entrance, admiring the priest's outfit, still unaccustomed to the Legion commander's bizarre antics.

'You wanted to see me?'

'Captain Varitec,' Mordu said proudly, hurrying back to his bar to prepare a drink. 'Welcome! Please, join us.'

The Drake captain was taller than Korvin expected, though older than he remembered from their encounter in space.

'Lears, I believe you owe this man your gratitude,' Mordu said.

'To be honest, this conversation was making me wonder about thanking him at all.'

'I'd say not blasting your ship to bits was a kind gesture,' Mordu remarked, filling another tumbler. 'You'd be getting skull-fucked by a Federation interrogator about now if it weren't for him.'

'No thanks are necessary,' Jonas said, accepting the drink.

'Excellent,' Mordu said. 'Because you two are working together now.'

Both men paused.

'There's a Minmatar colony called Core Freedom on the planet Pike's Landing. It is the only world in the Amamake system that doesn't need terraforming for habitation, and, as such, a rather valuable bit of real estate that the Amarrians have repeatedly tried taking. They've refrained from bombarding it from space because of pesky planetary defenses – and because they very much want to take the industrial outposts there intact.'

'What kind of ground forces are we talking?' Jonas asked.

'Remnants of a Valklear battalion,' Mordu answered. 'They can't reequip or resupply because of Republic Fleet commitments elsewhere on the front. I'm sending both of you to evaluate a contract to assist the Valklears on the ground *and* in space until their own government can help them. Jonas and his team will evaluate surface fortifications. And you, Lears, will size up a strategy for how to defend it from space. You leave in a few days; I'd like for you to meet the captain's crew beforehand. Any questions?'

Jonas was beaming.

'Thank you for the opportunity, sir.'

'You've earned it,' Mordu said. 'The battalion commander is General Vlad Kintreb. We actually met years ago, just after the Republic was founded. He's a good man. They must really be suffering to ask us for help, so use discretion: You won't get anywhere unless you respect their pride.'

'Understood, sir.'

Korvin felt numb. He'd gone from one universe to the next, seamlessly continuing his charge as a murdering tyrant.

'Lears, you're sitting next to one of the most promising captains in the Legion. He's also the only person in this organization that's ever met Empress Jamyl. Perhaps someday he'll share that story.'

'Lucky you,' Korvin muttered.

'You have no idea,' Jonas said.

'And Captain, you're sitting next to one of the Federation's better pilots,' Mordu said. 'He's certified for orbital bombardments, which I'm sure you'll find useful.'

'I'll drink to that,' Jonas said.

'As will I,' Mordu said.

Korvin stood up from his chair.

'With all due respect, I won't,' he said. 'I'll do what you ask of me, but only because I don't seem to have a choice.'

'Korvin,' Jonas said gently. 'Just give me a chance, and someday you'll make that choice willingly.'

'You'll understand if I have my doubts,' Korvin answered, walking toward the door.

'Doubts?' Jonas asked. 'I've just been asked to entrust the lives of my crew to a Federation traitor.'

Korvin stopped dead in his tracks.

'But I guess I'll just have to give hope a chance,' Jonas said, raising his glass.

KORVIN DIDN'T SAY MUCH during the ride from Mordu's office.

'You know,' Jonas started. 'Most people around here would kill for the chance to spend that much time with the old man. You should consider yourself lucky.'

Ignoring him, Korvin fixated on the scenery zipping by as the shuttle car steered itself through airborne highways flowing with traffic. Several hundred thousand people made their residence at the Legion station in Pure Blind. Mordu didn't build it, of course. Pulling off such a colossal feat was beyond even his formidable skills and wealth at the time. Close inspection of the frame beams and electronics of the massive structure would reveal the serial numbers left by the mega-corporations who built it for the Caldari Navy. When the State withdrew from Pure Blind decades ago, they abandoned it. Mordu and his mercenaries seized the opportunity, beating back pirates and other privateers with like-minded ambitions.

From the shuttle car's vantage, it appeared like any other station in the State: huge promenades filled with vendors, businesses, and flora; spectacular views overlooking the station's cavernous main hangar; industrial complexes connected by tram and rail systems; and several indoor cities surrounded by highways – all familiar, Korvin thought, except for the ethnicities.

Intaki, Gallente, Mannar, Jin-Mei, Deteis, Achura, and Civire bloodlines were all commingling and thriving under one proverbial roof. This was raw humanity, the teeming mass of anonymous souls who made up most of civilization – strata far below the elite culture that Korvin hailed from. He saw their cultural diversity in storefront designs and markets, in the ads projected along the causeways, and in the clothes that people wore. Goods and services that were unavailable or outright illegal in some nations or star systems were all openly for sale here, most of it for just a small pittance in the local currency.

The car pulled away from the main platform and hovered toward a courtyard, descending into a niche between two oversize trees. Jonas pocketed the datapad that he'd been typing on most of the trip and slapped the door release. A wave of richly flavored air hit Korvin; spicy, eclectic aromas drifted in from a patio café surrounded by multicultural restaurants. There were a few dozen people eating and chatting in dialects that Korvin recognized but couldn't understand.

'This is our stop,' Jonas said, stepping out. 'Mack likes to spend a lot of time here. He's, uh ... a little eccentric. So be careful what you say to him.'

'Can you be a little more specific?' Korvin asked, just as some commotion started a short distance away.

A man of Achurian descent was moving from table to table, asking patrons if they believed in the reclamation of wayward souls and in the divinity of Empress Jamyl. He was filthy; his build and clothing suggested he worked on a mining barge. Korvin took in the scene as people shooed the odd man away, amused by his rambling warnings about the dangers of passing up on the faith when it finds you.

It was annoying, Korvin thought, but harmless.

'Keep moving,' Jonas warned. 'And don't stare.'

The Drake captain had barely finished speaking when two Legion security guards approached the Achurian from behind and incapacitated him with a z-stick; the man collapsed as the neurotoxin left him temporarily paralyzed. The guards dragged the drooling, wide-eyed victim to a waiting police car and unceremoniously tossed him inside.

Korvin was horrified.

'Probably not used to that where you're from,' Jonas said over his shoulder. He was walking through the tables now, directly toward one where a lone man sat facing a ledge. Beyond its railing was a vast drop to the intercity tube transports below. Huge transparent plating almost a hundred stories high provided a stunning view of the space beyond.

Despite the magnificent scenery, no one else was seated anywhere near him.

'What are they going to do with that Achurian?' Korvin asked.

'I hope they space him,' Jonas answered. 'The less of that crap there is around here, the better.'

'I thought the Legion was about leaving your politics behind,' Korvin said, drawing closer. 'That includes religion as well?'

'Well they're both dinner-table taboos, right?' Jonas asked. Reaching the ledge, he placed a gentle hand on the seated man's shoulder. 'Hey, Mack. New hire for you to meet.'

Korvin got close enough to see what he was doing and froze.

Spread out on the table were dozens of toys – action figures, to be exact. Each was several centimeters high and arranged in a mock battle scene. Some were standing; others were sprawled about as apparent casualties. Mack appeared completely immersed in this fantastical scene, oblivious to the two men standing around him.

Jonas pulled up a chair and sat down, propping his feet up on the railing. He didn't seem concerned that his terra-ops commander was doing anything unusual.

A moment of uncomfortable silence passed.

'He's waiting for you to introduce yourself,' Jonas said finally.

'Right,' Korvin muttered, folding his arms and shifting his weight. He considered making a comment on the rudeness of 'meeting' someone who didn't have the courtesy to at least face him. 'My name is Korvin Lears, former Federation Navy—'

'Capsuleer,' Mack snorted, rearranging the arms and miniature weapon of one of his toys. 'Hate the smell.'

'Don't take that personally,' Jonas said, smiling. 'Mack has an olfactory mod that lets him smell nearly as well as a slaver hound. He probably got a whiff of pod gunk left on you. It's a handy trick in his line of work.'

'I'm sure it is,' Korvin said. 'Nice to meet you as well, Mack.'

'Spoiled,' Mack muttered, still fidgeting with his toys. 'Pampered like old money. Empyrean trash. Don't belong here.'

'You're probably right—'

'Way you're standing,' Mack said, advancing a few soldiers on his make-believe battlefield. 'Like little girl. Pouty. Brat.'

Jonas whispered loudly, pointing at Mack's ears.

'His hearing is really good, too.'

Korvin was equal parts furious and intimidated. In addition, he couldn't definitely rule out that Mack wasn't suffering a perfectly curable form of retardation.

'Well, I guess I don't know where I belong then,' Korvin said. 'Was there a point to coming down here?'

'Prison where you belong,' Mack answered, fidgeting with toys. 'Make man of you. Or of inmate.'

Without turning around, Mack held up two toy soldiers that were stuck together. One was gripping the backside of the other in a dominating rear position.

'Oh, fuck this,' Korvin said, turning to walk away. 'Jonas, I'll wait by the car. Thanks for the introduction. Really.'

'Not so fast,' Jonas said. 'You haven't told Mack the news yet.'

'*What* news?' Korvin nearly yelled.

'Don't like him,' Mack muttered. 'Whiny.'

'Gentlemen,' Jonas said, taking his feet down and leaning forward. 'The old man is sending us to Amamake to evaluate a possible contract. He's letting us run it; we can outsource the work and keep a healthy margin for ourselves. It's a big opportunity, but you're both going to have to work together to make it happen.'

Mack finally turned to face Korvin, who was immediately shocked.

Half of the man's face was horribly disfigured, with folds in the skin that pulled tight around his eyes and forehead, but especially around the left side of his jaw, contorting his mouth into a permanent smile. Some of his skull was metallic; the lighting caught bits of metal that emerged from scalp normally covered by hair. Korvin suspected the left side of his body at least was almost entirely cybernetic, judging from the sharp angles beneath his clothes and the tighter fit on his right side.

Suddenly, his sitting alone in such a crowded place invoked some compassion in Korvin. Clearly, Mack was someone who had endured a different and much more personal journey to hell and back. Yet for reasons he couldn't understand – perhaps it was the toys – Korvin sensed that there was a happiness about him that hovered dangerously between genuine goodness and maniacal insanity.

'When I need boots on the ground, Mack is my guy,' Jonas continued. 'As for Korvin here, let's just say he knows what he's doing in a starship. I'm sure that after getting the chance to work with each other, you'll both get along fine.'

Mack, despite the macabre smile etched onto his face, managed to look displeased.

'Immortal,' he said, shaking his head. 'You risk nothing.'

'My clones are in Federation custody,' Korvin answered. 'They'll arrest or kill me if I wake up in one. I'm no more immortal than you are, mate.'

'Don't call me that,' Mack said, standing abruptly. He crashed his shoulder into Korvin's as he passed by.

The capsuleer shook off the bump and watched as people steered clear of his path through the food court. Korvin drifted back to the table and the toys arranged on them. He suspected that no one was going to touch them.

Jonas was nodding his head.

'Yep,' he said, standing up. 'You two are going to get along just fine.'

17

THE FORGE REGION – ETSALA CONSTELLATION
THE VASALA SYSTEM – PLANET V, MOON 15
ISHUKONE CORPORATE FACTORY – TEMPORARY HQ
SOVEREIGNTY OF THE CALDARI STATE

Ralirashi sat beside Mens in a darkened room manipulating a volumetric construct, moving its controls through the air until a spectrogram appeared. A starmap was hovering behind it, tracing its source through a series of points ending on the planet Matias.

The communications channel opened and began broadcasting.

'Mens Reppola,' Haatakan Oiritsuu said. 'You haven't aged well at all.'

The voice of the former Kaalakiota CEO reminded him of a coiled viper. She couldn't even *see* his face, as this was a voice-only transmission that was encrypted, dissected, and bounced through several dozen star systems to hide its origins from the eavesdropping reach of governments and mega-corporations. There was no subtlety with her at all, and she opened the conversation with a vicious jab at his public setbacks.

With no bargaining position, he was already on the defensive, and she knew it.

'You're very much the same as I remember,' he said.

'Mila and I have so much in common, you would think she could hold a conversation longer,' she said. 'Then again, maybe we both just prefer solitude.'

Mens shot a glance at Rali, who shook his head in disgust. He didn't expect anything less from their former rival.

'You're a bright fellow,' she continued. 'You know the risk I took by speaking with her and the risk I'm taking right now. That implies that you're rather unconcerned for my well-being.'

'Mila assured me you've taken the necessary precautions to protect yourself and this conversation,' Mens said.

Haatakan was actually within plain view of several Provist guards, who after two years of uneventful vigil knew her personal habits intimately. An avid horticulturalist, she spent all her spare time looking after an overwhelming collection of exotic plants, housed in several open and enclosed green houses throughout the grounds of her former estate. Even before Heth sought her counsel, she would spend long hours moving between them, happily getting her hands dirty – and, very often, *talking* to the plants as she worked.

The guards considered it a peculiar habit for someone of her stature. With Heth regularly drilling her during exhaustive planning sessions along with members of his cabinet, her garden visits had become even more of an outlet, a place to vent her frustrations to a leafy and debatably attentive audience.

It was harmless behavior, the Provists reasoned, provided it kept her sane. In general, a hobby was beneficial to mental acuity and thus necessary to keep her productive. The grounds were regularly swept for electronic devices; the only comm terminal capable of reaching the outside world was inside her lodge, and it was controlled by the Provists.

With so much exotic flora to marvel at, the large species of creeping carnivorous plants distinguished by large, thick petals growing throughout the grounds were almost unremarkable. Occasionally one would clamp shut as insects flew toward its stigma, the sound of their flapping wings registered by the millions of microscopic trigger hairs lining the petals inside. Once trapped, the victim would be slowly digested and its constituent nutrients transported through a complex root network that could extend for many kilometers.

With the right biotechnical engineering, these plants could be converted into surprisingly effective listening devices – which is exactly what Haatakan Oiritsuu had done, long before she was imprisoned on her own property.

She had a reputation for always being prepared for the unexpected.

'Of course I've taken precautions,' she scowled. 'You wouldn't have contacted me unless you had something juicy to offer. So what the hell do you want?'

'Information,' he answered. 'Mila believes you have knowledge of a certain prototype Amarr technology. I need to know where I can find it.'

'She was right,' Haatakan answered. 'What do I get in return?'

Despite all the wealth stripped away from her after Heth took power, Haatakan Oiritsuu still had all the money she would ever need – investments hidden away even from the Provists. Rali and Mens guessed correctly that she coveted freedom above all else.

That she still managed to stay relevant in Caldari mega-politics was remarkable. Armed with intimidating intelligence and the hardened experience of mega-corporate boardroom warfare, she was sought for counsel on matters ranging from national security to economic vitality. She was just too valuable an asset to ignore. Private access to her talents justified the risk Heth took by relying on her judgment – even while manically screening and reexamining her proposals for any evidence of sabotage.

Those who knew her best knew it was just a matter of time before she either broke free of Heth's leash or died trying. Thus all Mens could offer was conditional support to help her accomplish just that.

'We have a mutual friend,' Mens said, careful to avoid saying anything that could directly imply treason against the State. He still didn't trust her. 'So I'm prepared to offer my assistance in mediating your current relationship.'

'What kind of assistance?'

The plan that he and Rali discussed rolled past his augmented vision.

'We've analyzed the circumstances and determined that a compromise is possible,' he said cryptically. 'In addition, we believe there are others willing to lend their support.'

'You expect me to hand over the most coveted technological advance in New Eden in exchange for speculation?' she hissed. 'Here's something you should know: Heth has been meeting with his generals for the past six weeks to discuss Ishukone. Is that not the reason you're asking me for help? If you're serious about protecting your responsibilities, then you'd better get serious about an offer.'

Mens and Rali stared at one another. This outburst wasn't entirely unexpected. The plan now was to let her reveal what she was really after.

'Fine,' Mens said. 'What do you want?'

'I want Heth's reliance on me to be absolute,' she snarled. 'I want him to have no allies left, no one left to trust *except* me. You're going to make that happen.'

'I'm not sure I understand you—' Mens started.

'The cabinet members of the Providence Directorate conduct strategy reviews each week,' she said, sounding impatient. 'These are Heth's closest people. All handpicked by him personally. Without their loyalty, he has nothing—'

Rali shook his head.

'— except for you,' Mens finished. 'We're not in that kind of business, Haatakan.'

'You are now,' she growled back. 'Ishukone has become a Caldari public enemy. I know it. You know it. So what are you prepared to do about it? Watch it wither away and die? What would Otro Gariushi have to say about that?'

A flash of anger rushed through Mens.

'What exactly are you asking for?'

'Ishukone is supplying materials and personnel for a new research outpost on the planet Myoklar, which is where the next Directorate meeting is to be held. You will replace some of that personnel with the team I provide. See to it they are delivered to the site ahead of this meeting.'

'And how will they get out?'

'Not your concern. All I want is for your dropships to take them in.'

Mens took a moment to consider this. This was highly unusual: She was making it too easy. All the exposure was on her, not Ishukone. Just like that, he had regained all the power in negotiating. The dropship could be remotely piloted in, for instance. Whatever cargo and personnel she planned on stowing aboard could be screened.

There was any number of different ways to insulate Ishukone from whatever she was planning. And in the end, he desperately needed the technology she possessed.

'I accept this term,' he said, to the widening eyes of Rali. 'Now, you have information for me.'

'The New Eden system, very close to Point Genesis,' she answered. 'A research vessel called the *Significance* is near there, with a scientist on board named Marcus Jror. You won't be able to scan down this ship: He'll see you long before you see him.'

'What does he have that I need?'

'He invented immortal soldier technology. No one outside of Sarum's circle knows this. Only us. And Heth.'

'Why Point Genesis?'

'I don't know,' she answered mockingly. 'But let's just say I recognize exile when I see it. That's what makes this such an opportunity for you. It seems this Marcus fellow overstayed his welcome with the Empire. You might have something he needs.'

'Then we have a deal.'

'Yes, we do,' she hissed. 'Don't screw this up, Mens. That wouldn't be good for you at all. And speak up next time, Rali. It's not your style to keep your mouth shut.'

The transmission dropped. Mens looked at his close friend.

'What did I just get us into?' he asked.

Rali exhaled forcefully, leaning forward and clasping his hands together.

'Nothing that we wouldn't have to deal with sooner or later,' he said. 'Despite my opinion of the woman, Haatakan is right. We don't have many options here.'

'No, we don't,' Mens answered. 'That's become a regular theme in my life.'

Rali narrowed his eyes.

'Your visit with Mila ... ' he said. 'I ... hope you haven't done anything to add to your burdens.'

Mens avoided eye contact. He was ashamed of himself enough as it was.

'We all miss her,' Rali said, getting up. 'I'll start thinking about Haatakan's offer and how we can find this Marcus Jror.'

'Thank you,' Mens said.

'Don't thank me yet,' Rali said, as the door slid open. 'Not until we see how all this plays out.'

>>CONCORD/DED Datastack 141E: Meeting Notes – Mordu's Legion Briefing

>>Owner: AI Construct Argos- 1

>>Inner Circle

>>EYES ONLY

The THANATOS program has revealed disturbing developments with Mordu's Legion.

Remote neural scanning of Muryia Mordu during an agent encounter detected trace evidence of degenerative encephalopathy. Although a deeper scan is necessary to confirm, the founder's outward personality is consistent with patients suffering from the onset of psychosis. This revelation, combined with a history characterized by remorseless bloodshed in the mercenary trade, supports DED consensus that Mordu's Legion is currently among the most dangerous and influential factions of New Eden.

In the interest of upholding the mandate, THANATOS has been granted permission to interfere with any Legion activity that could potentially destabilize the nations under CONCORD jurisdiction. To that end, the agent also reported several actionable intelligence items:

- AWOL Federation Navy Captain Korvin Lears has joined Mordu's Legion. He has been assigned to the Drake-class starship MLW *Morse*, which has logged several hundred hours of terra-ops missions. Mordu himself has ordered its captain, Jonas Varitec, to evaluate the military preparedness of the Core Freedom Colony on Pike's Landing in the Amamake system for a possible mercenary contract. Because Lears is qualified to execute orbital bombardments, he is classified a Tier-1 threat to our mandate. THANATOS has been ordered to track this vessel and report.
- THANATOS has also learned that Mordu has been in contact with Haatakan Oiritsuu, deposed Kaalakiota CEO. Since then, he has been preparing a mixed squad of soldiers, assassins, and technicians in mock raids on a fake research outpost consistent with Ishukone contractor designs, suggesting that a raid somewhere in the Caldari State is imminent. THANATOS has been ordered to learn the target of this raid, determine the extent of Haatakan's involvement with Mordu's Legion, find any connection to Ishukone, and assess any danger to Tibus Heth and the Caldari Providence Directorate.

>>Conclusion

Mordu's Legion has thrived since the start of the Empyrean War, especially as casualties to conventional Empire forces continue to skyrocket. The entity's most valuable asset is its cultural diversity and its strong loyalty to Mordu. A breadth of skill sets and resources once available only to the most powerful nations is now available to this group, as evidenced by the defection of former Federation Navy captain Korvin Lears to their cause. Their scientific, military, and industrial capacity, combined with solid trade relations with other pirate organizations, makes Mordu's Legion a potent geopolitical entity whose international influence should not be underestimated.

Mordu himself seems to have developed a keen personal interest in confronting the Amarr Empire, perhaps out of sympathy for the Minmatar, or more likely to learn what he can about Xerah Effect weapons technology.

The meeting concludes with group affirmation of Inner Circle Director Irhes Angireh's proposal to deploy THANATOS, agreeing that the program's usefulness has thus far lived up to billing. Tara Rushi maintains prior disagreement, citing that CONCORD has overstepped its bounds. Comment is noted and amended.

>>END FILE

THE FORGE REGION – ETSALA CONSTELLATION
THE VASALA SYSTEM – PLANET V, MOON 15
ISHUKONE CORPORATE FACTORY – TEMPORARY HQ
SOVEREIGNTY OF THE CALDARI STATE

Mens emerged from the security checkpoints of his own home aboard Ishukone HQ Station and found his daughter sitting alone in the living room. Old family vids were projecting from the entertainment center, bringing back fond memories. But there was little else about the living space that fit his own idea about what a home should look like. Instead of welcoming homestead decor, his wife had opted for a stylistic elegance more befitting the elite caste to which they belonged.

He hated it. He always had. Between its coldness and all the security – knowing that powerful weapons and an omnipresent AI were always nearby – his home was just a military bunker in disguise.

Mens quietly took a seat next to his daughter, looking at the images. He saw a much younger version of himself playing with Amile, tossing her in the air and catching her, zooming her through a park like she was a flying superhero. Her giggles were absolutely contagious; Mens caught himself smiling broadly, just as he had back then, at his daughter's delight.

Then the camera focus switched to her mother, Lorin, who appeared concerned, a look that had etched deeper into her eyes with time. The reality sunk home for Mens, pulling him away from what was otherwise a delightful memory.

'She wants to leave you,' Amile said.

'She hasn't told me that,' Mens nodded, still looking at his memories. 'Not yet.'

'You would have to make time for a conversation first.'

'I know,' Mens said dejectedly. 'Amile, I'm sorry about the university. That's ... horrible. I can't even ... '

He took a deep breath before continuing; he didn't want the poisonous thought of Tibus Heth defiling this precious moment with his only child.

'I'm sorry I wasn't here for you when it happened.'

'It's not your fault,' she answered, standing abruptly and crossing her arms. 'Besides, it gave me the closure I needed.'

Lorin used the exact same mannerism whenever she was uncomfortable. Amile looked very much like her mother, sharing her slender build, piercing eyes, and high cheekbones. She was a beautiful young woman who could excel at anything she tried.

Mens wanted to ask what 'closure' she wanted, scared to the pit of his stomach of what that implied. But instead, he forced himself to just listen.

'I fooled myself into thinking there was something normal out there for us,' she started. 'A life that didn't require armed guards ... someplace where I could befriend people without having them background-checked or interrogated. A life where I didn't need to be watched by machines and strangers *all the time*.'

'We didn't anticipate this,' Mens answered solemnly. 'Your mother and I fell in love years ago, but our careers—'

'I *know* what happened,' she interrupted. 'You grew apart. It happens. Whether or not that was inevitable I can't say, but these ... crazy circumstances certainly didn't help.'

Mens felt crushing guilt and surprise at the same time.

'*Millions* of people depend on you. How can anyone grasp what that even means? You're a mega-corporation CEO. I can't relate to anyone because of that. When I was at the academy, I would hear conversations about vid stars, dating gossip, fashion ... all stuff I should be interested in, right? Like a normal person would? But then I'd come home to discussions about national security and mega-politics. It got so tiring trying to relate I just gave up. Most of them are so … self-centered, so insulated from the things that really matter. I can't understand them.'

Mens jumped out of his chair.

'Amile, I'm so sorry …. How many times have I said that now?' he implored. 'I blame myself for this mess, but I have the means to shelter you from it completely. We can hide you in plain sight, use technology to change your identity, even the way you look. If that's what you truly want, I can make it happen.'

She smiled.

'But what about the Broker? And if not him, then Tibus Heth, and now what … maybe the entire Caldari State as well?'

'We're going to find a way to stop this,' Mens staggered. 'We are *not* going to quit!'

'I'm not saying we should,' she answered. 'I'm … proud of you, Dad. Proud to be your daughter. Sometimes, I think Mother resents me for supporting you so much. But if it's going to be us against everyone else, we need to be closer. *I want to be more a part of your life*. I have a right to take an active role in protecting myself. It's not that I don't trust you to do that … it's just that this is personal now. I hate the people who did this to us as much as you do. So if the State won't let me into their damn universities … then you're just going to have to teach me everything you know.'

Mens's bottom lip was quivering. Was it possible to love someone any more than this?

And then at that exact moment, Mila Gariushi sent him a message. For the time being, he ignored it.

'But please,' Amile said, 'I want you to try, one last time, to work things out with Mom. So I can have closure in that part of my life as well.'

'I will,' Mens promised. 'One last time.'

Mens,

Haatakan provided the details of your conversation. She supplied logistical instructions for this op, which I've forwarded to Rali. I can't overemphasize just how crucial it is that you honor your side of the agreement. If there's anyone more determined to rid the cluster of Tibus Heth than us, it's her. She will stop at nothing to achieve this. Don't underestimate her.

I also wanted to warn you that VILAMO suspects she's working directly with pirate organizations without consent or awareness from Heth or the CPD. It's no secret that Ishukone has cordial relations with Mordu's Legion, but you know how damaging it would be if it was suggested that the Guristas or Serpentis cartels were directly involved in Ishukone affairs. Cover your trail thoroughly, Mens.

I would be remiss if I didn't admit to thinking a great deal about your visit.

I'm sorry it happened, but then I have no regrets either. I am . . . ashamed of myself, in spite of my sincere wish that it would happen again.

Yours Always,
Mila Gariushi

18

GENESIS REGION – EVE CONSTELLATION
THE NEW EDEN SYSTEM

>>SIGNIFICANCE MISSION LOG ENTRY
>>BEGIN RECORDING

In the early years of my tutelage under Lord Falek Grange, my days and nights were filled with learning. He was ruthless, keeping the pace so unrelenting that by the age of sixteen, I had mastered all the academic proficiencies necessary to become an empyrean. But I couldn't fathom for what purpose. Between my guilt over the death of his parents and apprehension of where this path was leading, I found my motivation waning. At some point, my scientific fascination with the world was overcome by anxieties of self-doubt – of wondering how Lord Grange could be so certain of my purpose when I did not know it myself.

Of course, the AI monitoring my progress detected this immediately, so Falek took measures to ensure my focus.

He directed the Royal Paladins overseeing my care to permanently remove any distraction from my studies. Cybernetic implants that enhanced my willpower and memory were installed in my brain. They administered drugs to release endorphins for academic achievements but to suppress them for virtually all other stimuli. I was chemically castrated to minimize the carnal urges of puberty.

I wasn't even allowed to sleep. The implants, I was told, were doing that for me.

My mental health deteriorated. For reasons that Falek never disclosed, the memory of my passage into madness and the consequences that followed was removed.

But what I do remember vividly is the first time I saw *her.*

Any man would be willing to drop every commitment, promise, or ethic to be with her. Even in my medicated state, her appearance took the breath from my lungs. As Heiress Jamyl Sarum entered the lab, the other scientists parted before her, bowing their deference as I stood paralyzed, my elation hijacked by the drugs pumping through my veins.

'Marcus,' she said to me. 'Do you know why you're here?'

Lord Grange was standing well behind her but kept his glare on me.

'No, my lady,' I answered cautiously; 'I'm afraid I don't.'

'I know what it's like to be born with a gift,' she said, drawing closer. 'I am the heiress to an empire. And that has become a curse to me. Is that familiar to you?'

I said nothing but brought it upon myself to look into her eyes. They radiated empathy – and a sadness that hovered close to desperation.

'I need your help,' she continued. 'Your extraordinary gift could be a great asset for us. But I cannot say what cause you would serve. . . .'

She appeared uncomfortable.

'It's ridiculous,' she said. 'Asking you to commit to something that you can't know . . . yet. But I'm compelled to test your allegiance. You're to take this oath on faith alone, because that is what this religion demands of me.'

A faint hint of anger crept across her brow.

'No matter,' she said. 'I won't throw you or anyone else into a "test of faith" blindly.'

And then, she cursed me: 'You share a tragic history with Lord Grange. He could force you to join us, but I won't allow it. By my order he may only use his word to convince you. No more drugs. He must appeal to your heart, and you must decide for yourself.'

Lord Grange said nothing, and I was speechless.

'I'm sorry this happened to you,' she added, with sincere compassion.

I had no idea what she meant at the time.

HOURS LATER, I FOUND MYSELF aboard a transport approaching an indescribably destitute colony. I knew nothing of where it was, not even the name of the planet we landed on. As usual, Lord Grange refused to speak during the journey, not even within the confines of the armored transport as it wound through the dark steel corridors of this miserable place. The Paladins who escorted us displayed startling awe for the man: It was the sort of reverence reserved for an heir or the Emperor. But there was a pronounced sense of fear among them as well. Falek Grange was no man to be crossed. His academic and theological credentials notwithstanding, I wondered what he had done to command so much respect.

The transport slowed to a halt in a filthy alley. Homeless, disease-ridden people – Minmatars, by the looks of it – lay strewn about in makeshift shelters among the rubble.

'Put these on,' Lord Grange said, tossing over a ragged long coat and head scarf. 'We're going for a walk.'

Leaving the vehicle was a terrifying prospect. The buildings outside bore Amarr architecture infused with some Matar influence; the iconic Athran design of once-beautiful structures was blackened with industrial soot. As the transport's door slid open, my sinuses were assaulted by the raw stench of humanity. Droplets of acidic rain began falling, and I reluctantly stepped into the mud.

From the shadows, two homeless Minmatar men emerged, walking purposefully toward us. Both were holding weapons – clubs fashioned from scrap that could bludgeon and maim. I froze, literally petrified in fear. But Lord Grange stepped before them, and to my great surprise, both men kneeled.

'My lord,' one said. 'The infidels are gathered in the cathedral.'

I realized that my garb matched their own, like some sort of tribal marking.

'Our men are in position,' the other said. 'The locals are unsuspecting.'

'Good,' Lord Grange said. 'Return to your cover and await my command.'

'Yes, my lord,' they both said. One gave me an approving nod before running off into the night.

'You know these men?' I asked.

'They are Kameiras,' Lord Grange said. 'Beneath their Minmatar skin beats an Amarr heart. We're surrounded by them; there should be no danger.'

'My lord, I humbly ask: Where are we?' I implored. 'Why have you brought me here?'

For the first time in my life, I saw him smile, but only briefly.

'My parents owned this land,' he started.

A sickening feeling swept over me.

'They left it to me when they died.'

I took a deep breath.

'I take full responsibility,' I said. 'Their death is my fault, and I cannot apologize enough. . . .'

What he said next nearly made me collapse.

'It was *not* your fault,' he said bitterly. 'You were a naïve, innocent child. How could you know what those slaves were capable of?'

'But my punishment—'

'You've more than atoned,' he said, stepping onto the cracked pavement. Several denizens lay muttering incoherently against the building walls. 'But I couldn't let you think you had.'

'What? Then why in God's name—'

He whirled around, glaring at me.

'I will not tolerate blasphemy,' he warned. 'Is that understood?'

I said nothing, instantly intimidated again. But my anger quickly crept back.

'I have the right to know why I was subjected to—'

'Because I had to know if you were the prodigy they said you were,' he answered, resuming his stroll. He seemed completely unconcerned about the danger or the putrid rain that was falling with more intensity now. 'You were blessed with a brilliant mind, Marcus. We can put it to good use.'

'I know that already,' I said, proud of myself for being defiant. 'But if my dues are paid, am I free to go?'

'If that's your choice,' he said flatly, to my continued amazement. 'Will you walk with me first?'

I stared at him in disbelief. Reluctantly, I stepped deeper into the darkness, trying to cover my face with the head scarf. At least it offered some relief from the stench.

'My parents built all this as an experiment,' Lord Grange said as we walked. The avenue led up a slight hill, where wisps of fog obscured a great structure looming in the distance. Most of the buildings we passed were abandoned; the lighting from makeshift fires danced in the entrances of several.

'They decided to break ranks with the church by purchasing slaves just to release them here,' he continued. 'They would have been excommunicated if not for their political influence.'

'Why is that a crime?' I asked, raising my voice over the downpour.

'Because it's cruel to give anyone a choice,' Lord Grange answered, walking toward a figure lying prone beneath some metal scraps. 'Just as we cannot choose our parents, our faith is a mandate at birth. The laws of nature are immutable because God created them, and no living creature has a choice of whether to follow them.'

A chill ran up my spine.

'A Believer's heart must be so pure that choice never factors into the commitment to Amarr,' he continued. 'But my parents disagreed. They argued that all men want to touch God. So forcing slaves into faith was unnecessary. Slaves would choose to be Reclaimed on their own accord – if first given a chance to "evaluate" our beliefs first. My parents were convinced that once they were exposed to our way of life, the rational side of them would make the right choice.'

He stopped at the man's feet, kicking aside the metal scraps. Expended drug canisters littered the ground. The downpour was striking him directly in the face, but he did not move. His gaunt skin and sullen eyes suggested he wasn't far from death.

'This one failed a simple test of faith,' he said. 'He would rather fill his veins with chemicals than accept God's everlasting fulfillment. Pity.'

Lord Grange shook his head. Then he raised his boot and slammed it down into the man's larynx.

Again, I was paralyzed. This 'great man of faith' had just murdered in cold blood.

'Are you insane?' I finally exclaimed.

'Look around, Marcus,' he said, casually lifting his foot from the gory pulp. 'Look at what *choice* gave these people.'

He kicked the metal scraps back over the corpse.

'There were no glaive collars here,' he continued. 'No Vitoc injections. These slaves could have made this colony anything they wanted. Marcus, they were given a utopia! This—' he said, gesturing toward the corpse '—is what they made of it, what they chose. Giving them God's glory wasn't enough. But I know how to correct this.'

A woman's scream pierced the downpour's roar, followed by the sound of a struggle nearby.

'What was that?' I asked.

'Another choice,' he said, matter-of-factly. 'Some depravity is happening right in our midst.'

'Won't your Kameiras stop them?' I asked.

'Absolutely not,' Lord Grange answered, walking away. 'Under no circumstances will they interfere.'

The woman's desperate cries for help were silenced.

'Why?' I demanded, infuriated now. 'You're just going to let these people destroy themselves?'

'It's their choice,' he said with a smile. 'But I know how to save them. Look up there.'

Following the direction of his outstretched arm, I saw wisps of smog clear to reveal the ruins of a cathedral atop the hill. The once-glorious architecture was a shambles; at some point it must have been engulfed in flames. I couldn't imagine what mobs were capable of defiling such beauty.

'The warmth of God's compassion wasn't enough,' he said. 'It was just another building, with another man inside proclaiming words about faith. They rejected it. Why? Because the words don't matter unless they can *touch* the Divine. So that's what we must do. We must make them believe, Marcus. We must *show* them God!'

'What the hell are you talking about?' I shouted.

'Man yearns for something to believe in,' he answered, a crazed look in his eye. 'And you can help give it to them. Nothing is more worthy of your talent!'

'I don't care about any of this,' I said.

He shook his fist at me.

'Who among the heirs inspires you? Ardishapur? Kor-Azor? Do you think any of them can show the universe that God exists? No! But *she* can. And we cannot leave that to chance!'

'You hypocrite,' I shouted over the downpour. 'The point of the Succession Trials is to let God choose an emperor! It's treason just to *think* of tampering with it!'

'Imagine it, Marcus. The people will adore her. Jamyl is God's choice; I know this.'

'Falek, if this is the choice you're offering, I want no part of it!'

'You coward!' he bellowed, pointing again at the cathedral. 'Look at that place of worship! *Gangs* make their home there now. It's become a brothel, a drug factory, a hole where terrorists gather to plan murders!'

He walked toward me with fire in his eyes.

'Do you know why the Kameiras are here, Marcus?' he asked. 'Every week the infidels living in our church plot against Amarr. Not against military targets. Their only goal is to kill as many civilians as they can.'

I thought immediately of Sasha and how she had looked so sad the last time I saw her alive.

'Oh, you know something of this?' he continued, feeding off the recollection in my eyes. 'Remember the slaves you loved more than your parents? Who betrayed your precious innocence because they were given a *choice*?'

To this day, I wish I had struck him dead on the spot. But the putrid rain was stinging my eyes; I was soaked to the bone. The only glimmer of hope in this hellish place was the thought of Lady

Sarum's compassion. I had known her for less than a minute, yet I could think of no one else who had ever shown me genuine kindness.

'The gang leaders are all assembled in there right now,' Falek said, pressing a small device into my hand. 'We have recordings, irrefutable evidence of their intent. The Kameiras will unleash a purifying fire upon them – but only by your hand will they do so.'

'You expect me to kill them?' I asked, incredulous. 'That's the choice you're giving me? While saying the world would be better off without choice at all?'

Falek laughed.

'The True Amarr have been ordained since the beginning of time to choose for the wayward,' he said. 'That is the most fundamental tenet of our faith!'

My head was spinning.

'No,' I said. '*No*. This is madness.'

'Think carefully,' he said. 'You will be the direct consort of Lady Sarum and committed to her bidding for eternity, for I will make you an empyrean. You will root out the conspiracies that threaten her and our Empire, beginning with the one in *that* cathedral. Marcus, you will help make her into the goddess she was meant to be!'

I thought of Lady Sarum's eyes; those young, compassionate, beautiful eyes, and wondered if she was as much a captive to Lord Grange as I.

'And if I refuse?'

'Then the death of True Amarr will be on your hands,' he said. 'Those gangs will commit their murders. And you'll be responsible for the bloodshed that follows every heir to the throne but Sarum herself.'

'But I'll be free?'

'Marcus,' he said with a sinister smile. 'Those who turn their backs on the highest calling are never again truly free.'

A burning sensation was spreading throughout my body as the rain ate into my skin. Grange, himself drenched, seemed unfazed, staring at me with those dark, sinister eyes, waiting for an answer.

Suddenly, I missed the lab terribly; it was the only sanctuary I had left. I wanted to be there, out of this hell, so badly that I began to lose the struggle for moral high ground.

I looked at the device in my hands and then at the cathedral ahead. I thought of the helpless woman's scream and the man with the crushed larynx behind us. I remembered the blood smeared on the steps of the home I grew up in, and the day that changed everything.

Then, somehow, I was able to rationalize the madness into a simple proof: Wherever the Minmatar are, there is blood. I knew, despite my isolation under Falek Grange, that my personal experience with that race was not unique. Whatever the motivation – religion, politics, culture – Amarr was soaked in blood and misery, and it seemed a worthwhile cause to do whatever was necessary to stop it.

I made my choice. A cleansing fire lit the sky. The Kameiras sealed the doors so no one could escape. The screams of those trapped inside, and the proud look on Lord Falek Grange's face, still haunt me to this day.

>>END RECORDING

PART III

Medicine

19

HEIMATAR REGION – HED CONSTELLATION
AMAMAKE SYSTEM – PLANET II: PIKE'S LANDING
CORE FREEDOM COLONY
SOVEREIGNTY OF THE MINMATAR REPUBLIC

A bang on the door yanked Dr Gable Dietrich out of the deepest sleep she had ever known.

'Dietrich, let's go!' the Valklear yelled, sounding more impatient than ever. 'Bad night at the ward. Move it!'

Still half asleep, she looked over at her clock. It read 03:57 hours, local. A mere 120 minutes since she had collapsed after working for more than 24 hours straight.

More thunderous raps jarred her senses. They sounded like the blunt impacts of a rifle stock.

'Doc! I'm losing my patience!'

'Please, just give ... me ... a minute,' she mumbled, reaching for her datapad. Numbed from exhaustion, her limbs felt as if they were moving through sludge. She clumsily dropped the device onto the floor. Uncaring, she rolled back over and drifted toward unconsciousness.

This time the door slid open. The holding cell she now called home was tiny; it took two strides for the soldier to reach the cot she slept upon.

'I said I just need a minute,' she mumbled, not noticing the injector gun in his hand.

The soldier forcefully pushed aside the hair covering her neck and pressed the gun nozzle into the carotid artery. With a quick hiss, a concentrated dose of chemical stimulants flooded her bloodstream. Gasping as her heart began to race, she jumped to her feet, knocking the cot over in the process.

'Now let's go,' the soldier grumbled.

Gable's breaths were coming fast.

'How much was that?' she stammered.

He led her toward the door by the arm. An armored jeep with a mounted autocannon was idling outside.

'A patrol set off a flay trap near the edge,' he muttered, herding her into the backseat. 'Three soldiers are dead. Kintreb wants you there before someone else dies.'

Gable was so cranked up that she was shaking. Gripping the handrail with all her might, she lurched as the jeep catapulted forward. Her chest was beginning to hurt.

'That dose was too high,' she stammered. 'I might go into cardiac arrest—'

'You need to be alert,' the Valklear growled, pushing the jeep hard into a turn. It was the equivalent of nautical dawn already, and the sun would break the mountain ridge in less than an hour. 'The guys who stepped into that trap weren't.'

Kicking up plumes of fine silica dust, they sped through the penitentiary gates. As Gable pulled goggles on to protect her eyes, she could make out the jagged edge of Mount Krytas off in the distance. Electrical storms were hammering the peak, illuminating the surrounding clouds in ghostly strobes. The sharp equatorial tilt of Pike's Landing made for wide temperature variances between poles that pushed powerful jet streams around the planet. In addition to its abundance of raw materials, the mountain range offered shelter from the turbulent weather that lashed much of the hemisphere during the winter.

Somewhere out there, Gable thought, Empire scouts were stranded from the last battle. They would have been the ones who planted those traps – a parting gift from a bitter enemy – evading detection by hiding in caves among the treacherous higher elevations of the mountain range. As the silhouettes of installation buildings and structures began emerging from the darkness, a grim admission seized her:

She wished those scouts would rescue her from here.

Up ahead, the piercing white strobe lights of the medical ward sliced through the night: A gunship had just lifted off from the rooftop. She ran her hand over her frantically beating chest, finding the golden pendant of the Amarr Faith beneath her scrubs. Closing her eyes, she commanded calm, silently reciting the Solace Prayer.

The jeep came to a halt.

'Let's go,' the soldier ordered, jumping out and opening the door for her.

Gable found strength in her prayers to God. Ignoring the outstretched hand of the Valklear, she stepped out of the vehicle, wishing she had known this deity much earlier in life.

THE CORE FREEDOM COLONY on Pike's Landing was a joint venture funded in part by the Minmatar Republic government, but built and operated by the corporate giants Freedom Extension and Core Complexion. Ground was first broken in YC 99 with little fanfare and a great deal of risk, as the Amamake system was a notorious 'chokepoint' that bordered nullsec space. Empyreans, many pirates among them, preyed on the shipping lanes to the outer regions; it was always a gamble to board a ship near Pike's Landing. But the planet itself was packed with natural resources and, even with the setbacks caused by piracy, quickly developed into an industrial gold mine. But once the war began, it became a coveted target for Amarr, which wanted to take the resource-harvesting infrastructure built by the Republic intact.

In that sense, both sides were losers in the conflict.

There were two vehicle hangars on the colony, one on each side of the sprawling complex. Besides the medical ward, there were a few buildings that still showed signs of active use, mostly as housing structures for the few colonists who remained. Between them were the towering ore smelters that used to refine the natural riches of Pike's Landing into precious commodities, but they had not processed a single kilo of material in nearly a year. Alongside the smelting complex was a magrail freight yard that fell into disuse once the lines feeding it were severed during battle. Of the four spaceports that once supported the installation, only one remained operational. Construction of an industrial mass driver capable of launching cargo containers into orbit was halted by General Kintreb's orders shortly after the war began; the Valklears began stripping materials from it to repair breaches in the colony walls. Its huge unfinished struts loomed over the facility like the skeletal remnants of an ancient leviathan.

At its height, there were over 160,000 settlers at Core Freedom. There were thriving families, a burgeoning local culture, and the beginnings of a great metropolis in place. Today, less than a thousand remained, serving all the civilian roles needed to support the soldiers: operating planetary defense grids, vehicle maintenance, power generation, water reclamation, and what limited food-processing and farming facilities were still functional. General Kintreb demanded as much from them as he did his soldiers and was utterly intolerant of disobedience or mistakes. Dropship runs offworld were dangerous enough, given the perils of Amamake. But the main reason why anyone remained at all was because the personnel deemed 'essential' by Kintreb – such as Gable, despite her prisoner status – were forbidden from leaving.

None of them wanted to be there. As much as their existence was a fight for survival against repeated attacks from Amarr forces, the resentment against Kintreb – and the Minmatar Republic government for abandoning them – was reaching dangerous proportions.

General Vlad Kintreb, now 162 years old, made his personal office in the northwest vehicle hangar, a building more than a kilometer in length. From there he could see the entire floor, which resembled a factory line for armored vehicles. The machines were in various states of repair; salvaged battlefield parts were being fitted to the MTACs and tanks arrayed below him. Juggling what little resources remained to keep the colony defended was taxing enough, but the loss of several soldiers left him in a fouler mood than usual.

The direct call from Muryia Mordu, which bypassed the established communication protocol for reaching him, angered him even more.

'General Kintreb,' Mordu said, with startling cheer, 'how are you today?'

Vlad answered without looking at the grainy projection.

'What do you want?' he grumbled.

'We received your down payment,' he said. 'A team of my best advisors are on their way to begin the initial consultation. They'll be arriving by dropship – Panther-class, unmarked fuselage, IDENT tags Six-One-November.'

General Kintreb glanced up and saw Mordu dressed in the garb of an Amarr priest. The Legion founder was smiling ear to ear, expecting a reaction in kind.

'What the hell are you wearing?' Kintreb asked.

'Something to cheer you up,' Mordu said. 'You *are* hiring us to kill zealots, yes?'

'When the fuck did this become "funny" to you?'

'My experience is that levity helps in times of duress. This is how we operate.'

General Kintreb was incensed.

'We might not live another day down here, and you're telling me jokes?'

Mordu was unfazed.

'We all deal with pressure differently, General. I meant no offense—'

'I think you've lost your goddamn mind. Find some help before you get your people killed.'

Mordu turned deadly serious.

'You're nearly two centuries old, and *still* fighting a frontline war. Look in a mirror, Vladimir. You're absolutely fucking *insane*.'

'Do you have anything important to say?'

'Always,' Mordu growled. 'You need to face the reality that you've been abandoned. Core Freedom is unimportant to the Nation or the Elders. Now I can replace the bodies you've lost, but I can't replace your pride – nor will I let it harm the people I send there. Are we clear?'

General Kintreb glared at the image for a moment and then disconnected it.

GABLE FINALLY UNDERSTOOD why the soldier had been so impatient.

A 'flay trap' was the nickname given to an antipersonnel mine of Amarr design. Instead of using explosive power to inflict damage, this weapon used a magnetic coil to accelerate four monofilament wires. Each wire had a single ceramic or lead counterweight on one end; the other was tethered to a base cylinder that could spin freely in a frictionless hub. Once detonated – usually remotely using hidden motion detectors – the cylinder was accelerated to several hundred revolutions per second. At maximum speed, the outer shell was lowered, releasing the steel counterweights in a tight spin whose diameter expanded up to ten meters as the monofilament unraveled. At the fully extended position, the shell 'bounced' back toward the starting closed position, angling the weights upward as they spun, repeating until the spin energy dissipated.

The microfilaments, also known as monomolecular wire, consisted of tightly bonded metal-composite molecules, making it an especially sharp cutting edge. They passed through flesh, bone, and light metals effortlessly.

Anything within the hemispherical killzone of the cylinder was literally flayed to bits. The only sound it made – besides falling chunks of flesh – was of the lead counterweights zipping through the air at the speed of sound.

Gable – now thankful for the stims to help maintain her focus – was tending to the only survivor of the attack. He was missing one of his legs from the hip down, had already slipped deeply into shock, and had vital signs that suggested his death was all but imminent.

KHANID REGION – BUDAR CONSTELLATION
THE IRMALIN SYSTEM – PLANET II: HEXANDRIA
KHANID INNOVATION BIOMEDICAL SCIENCES AND RESEARCH CENTER
SOVEREIGNTY OF THE KHANID KINGDOM

Two Years Ago

From the sky, the sprawling research outpost below looked strangely isolated, a series of white-topped buildings speckled with tints of silver reflecting the first rays of dawn. Gable saw a single road stretching away from the facility heading south through hilly grasslands toward the open ocean and the lavish marinas beyond. She marveled at how fertile the land was: A precious plot of land like this on her homeworld would have been fully cultivated with crops. Temperate, habitable planets were such a precious thing in New Eden, and the Khanid Kingdom seemed to have an abundance of them.

It was here, at this beautiful place, where she could finally be at peace with herself. Or so she believed.

'Welcome to your new home,' Sister Marth said, as their dropship rotated into its vertical orientation with the spaceport below. 'You seem nervous.'

'I'm starting a new life again,' Gable answered. 'I lost count of how many times I've done that.'

'It's the same life as before,' the Khanid priestess corrected. 'Only now, you'll never face it alone.'

Gable and her mentor were among several dozen passengers aboard the craft, which was making a few stops within the Irmalin system. The craft nestled perfectly into position; the sound of magnetic clamps latching onto the fuselage marked the end of their journey together.

'I believe that now,' Gable admitted. 'I really do.'

'You've been an inspiration to us,' Sister Marth said. 'I think you're going to be very happy here.'

'Sister, thank you so much,' Gable said. 'I'll make the most of this chance.'

'You have a gift,' the priestess said. 'Empress Jamyl herself underestimated your talents. Few people can make that claim.'

The first waft of Hexandrian air rushed into the cabin as the outer ramp lowered; it was warm and humid, sweet with the smell of flora carried by a soft wind.

'I still doubt myself at times,' she admitted. 'I don't think that will ever change.'

Sister Marth clasped her by the shoulders.

'Do you remember when you asked to have the memory of the *Retford* erased?' she asked. 'What was my answer to you?'

'You refused, because "it would make you less than what I see before me now,"' Gable replied.

'When you doubt yourself, it means you doubt everything we've learned from each other,' Sister Marth said. 'All your pain, all those horrid experiences and wonderful moments, together make you who you are today – a brilliant doctor with a beautiful heart, someone who is truly capable of performing miracles.'

The Khanid priestess paused.

'You *found* us, Gable,' she said, becoming emotional. 'This may sound awful, but in a sense I'm thankful. Had you not suffered, the miracle of *you* wouldn't have happened to *us*. You're going to make a real difference here. Please don't question yourself in front of those who look up to you. Be strong for them. You have our *faith* now. That makes you invincible.'

'I'm going to miss you,' Gable said, wiping a tear away. 'I don't want you to go.'

Sister Marth smiled, her gentle features glowing in the warm sun. Reaching around her neck, she removed the golden pendant of the Amarr holy sign and pressed it into Gable's hand.

'Take it—' she said.

'Sister, I can't accept this—'

'— so that we never forget one another,' Sister Marth insisted.

Gable stared at the holy symbol in her hand and felt the most bittersweet joy she had ever known. Sister Marth turned back toward the boarding ramp. 'Farewell,' she said. 'Faith be with you always!'

Gable raised an arm and waved. They would see each other again someday, but until then, there was work to do in the service of Amarr. She would spend her days doing what she loved most – studying and practicing medicine, and by doing so, helping humanity. Sister Marth, on the other hand, would continue her calling to find more wayward souls in the universe and guide them toward redemption. They now shared a bond that could never be broken.

The dropship's serrated intakes began sucking in air and ionizing it; magnetic nozzles then directed the air mass toward the ground, kicking up a faint plume of dust. A spaceport tech approached Gable, gently wrapping an arm around her shoulder to herd her away from the landing pad.

'Right this way, Doctor,' he said. 'There's a group of physicians waiting for you just down this path, near the main entrance.'

'Thank you,' she said. The downwash was powerful now, and she could sense the craft lifting off. When it was ten meters above the ground, its mighty plasma engines roared to life, and the craft began rocketing back up toward the clouds.

Gable had just taken her first steps toward the entrance when a bright yellow fire chased by a white contrail cut across the sky. Before she could register what was happening, Sister Marth's dropship erupted into a sinister blossom of fiery debris. The explosion sent a deafening rumble through Gable's rib cage and across the countryside. She heard the roar of a second dropship nearby and was about to run for cover when a bolt of light dropped from the heavens.

HEIMATAR REGION – HED CONSTELLATION
AMAMAKE SYSTEM – PLANET II: PIKE'S LANDING
CORE FREEDOM COLONY
SOVEREIGNTY OF THE MINMATAR REPUBLIC

Present Day

As far as good luck went, the fact that the Valklear had *backed* into the outer range of the flay trap was 'fortunate.'

The microfilament came from beneath him at a steep angle, entering his inner thigh, cutting through the lower pelvis, and exiting through his right hip. The rest of him fell forward and outside of the killzone as the rest of his squadmates were eviscerated. Two circumstances saved his life: First, he had been assigned a rear-guard position in his patrol and happened to be facing away from them when the trap detonated; second, despite the extent of his injury, he somehow had the presence of mind to jam biofoam into his lacerated groin to slow the hemorrhaging from his femoral artery.

Unfortunately, the attack happened near a laaknyd nest. Whether the trap was placed there intentionally or not, the severed limb was devoured by the time rescuers arrived, and the voracious insects were already taking test nibbles out of the dying man's wounds. That ruled out a reattachment, making him a candidate for an artificial limb and partial hip replacement – except there were no longer any limbs, organic or cybernetic, to replace it with on the colony. The soldier's name was SSG Lance Kryle, of Vherokiorian ancestry. He had just turned twenty years old.

Gable had stabilized him, sealed off the wounds, and flushed his system with antibiotics to counter infections from the insect bites. She and her team had, with the help of a machinist, fashioned a replacement pelvis from titanium that would accommodate a prosthetic. She capped the nerve endings and vessels so they could quickly be reattached to culture-grown or cybernetic limbs. She used most of the precious remaining supply of nanite meshes and stem-cell biotics to begin restoring the lost tissue in the man's gluteus, hips, liver, and upper colon.

Six hours after arriving in her care, SSG Lance Kryle awakened.

'How long have I been—' he asked, his eyes still closed.

'Almost seven hours,' Gable answered. The sound of her voice sparked recognition in the soldier's face, and he opened his eyes.

'You're that Caldari doc,' he said.

Gable knew what was coming, but she was too exhausted to put up with it.

'You're lucky to be alive,' she muttered. 'The biofoam saved your life.'

'They pulled you out of that Khanid research center,' he said, not letting it go.

Gable leaned over to examine the healing progress of the nanite meshes.

'I never set foot in the place.'

'Yeah, but what *would* you have been research—'

'The trap severed your right leg,' she interrupted. 'There's nothing organic to replace it with, and it'll be some time before you're ready for a prosthesis.'

A wave of pain washed over his face. 'How long?'

'It takes at least ten days for the meshes to fill in,' she answered. The holy pendant slipped out of her coveralls, dangling briefly before the soldier's eyes. He jerked, trying to reach out with his arm to snatch it, but instead cursed sharply as an explosion of pain erupted in his hips.

'They should take that fucking thing away from you,' he snarled.

She hurriedly tucked the pendant beneath her scrubs.

'Save your strength,' she said. 'Don't move unless you have to.'

'They never should have let you in here,' he winced.

'A gold pendant can't hurt you,' she answered. 'And neither can I.'

A familiar voice boomed out from behind them.

'Doctor Dietrich,' General Kintreb bellowed, walking into the ward with a contingent of guards. 'How is the patient doing?'

'He's stabilized and healing,' she answered. 'But we can't replace the limb.'

'Sergeant Kryle, how are you feeling?' he asked, brushing Gable aside.

'I'll live.'

'Of course you will. Doctor Dietrich is the best.'

'She's a brainwashed convert, sir.'

'We don't waste anything here, Kryle. You'd be dead now if it wasn't for her. And she'd be dead if she wasn't a good physician.'

'But—'

'Shut up and rest. We'll talk about what happened on the ridge later. Doctor, come this way please,' he said, taking her arm with nonnegotiable force. He led her toward the cadaver room, where corpses were harvested for organs.

The guards closed the door behind them.

'Believe it or not, I value your opinion,' Kintreb started, 'and the quality of your work.'

'I'll bet it hurts you to say that.'

'Doctor, you practice a religion that has been the bane of my race for hundreds of years. Hatred of it is about all I have left to motivate these men to fight another day. Do you understand?'

'Religion is all *I* have left to fight another day. I'm sure you understand that.'

General Kintreb stared at her a moment without any change in expression.

'Tell it to me like it is, Doctor. Where do we stand?'

'The next victim who comes to this ward in that condition won't survive. There are nearly two hundred patients here; more than half are soldiers. Biofoam, nanite meshes, cybernetics, and plasma supplies are all depleted.'

General Kintreb grunted and began to stare at one of the laser saws used to amputate limbs.

'The Republic is sending mercenaries,' he said. 'Several "advisors" are on their way here now. Answer their questions truthfully.'

'What makes you think I wouldn't?'

'That pendant hanging around your neck.'

The fatigue was starting to make her hallucinate now, and Gable startled at what might have been a small animal darting across one of the nearby gurneys.

'Which mercenaries?'

'Mordu's Legion,' he said, with a trace of contempt.

'I've always liked them,' said Gable, who nearly fell backward but corrected herself. 'They don't start wars.'

General Kintreb opened the door. Guards were posted outside.

'Take her back to her room,' he ordered. 'Wake her up when our guests arrive.'

20

GENESIS REGION – EVE CONSTELLATION
THE NEW EDEN SYSTEM

>>SIGNIFICANCE MISSION LOG ENTRY
>>BEGIN RECORDING

I was inside the ship's capsule when the probe struck.

The *Significance* was undetectable, yet this machine hurtled directly toward us with the relentless charge of a hunter-seeker drone, blistering through electronic countermeasures with ease. Seconds before impact, the ship was completely disabled: All flight systems suddenly ceased despite my frantic efforts to revive them.

I could feel the alien probe attach itself to the hull, driving pincers through armor and bulkheads with alarming ease. Trapped inside my pod, I was helpless; even the ejection mechanism was inoperable. Gashing and ripping, the attacker gouged through my ship deliberately, as if it were trying to discover something else first.

And then the noise stopped. All I could feel was the motion of the *Significance* tumbling through space. I waited impatiently for the termination of my life.

Instead, the ship's systems were restarted one by one, like a pre-flight launch cycle in dry dock. Repair bots emerged from their bays, reversing the damage caused by the intruder. Still ignoring my commands, the internal pod gantry activated, removed me from the capsule, and dumped me onto the deck.

While acclimating to breathing air again, I suddenly noticed the grainy projection of a Jove standing before me: jet-black eyes surrounded by pale white flesh, marred with dark veins that originated from the scalp and branched all the way down to the jawbone. He was wearing a form-fitting uniform of unknown origin that began at his neck and tapered down to dark-colored boots.

No part of the *Significance* was under my control. The probe must have been using the AI to manipulate the projection system of the room.

'Doctor Marcus Jror,' the Jove said. 'My name is Grious. I wish we could have met in person.'

'What have you done to my ship?' I demanded.

'The damage will be repaired,' he said. A cacophony of groaning metal rumbled beneath my feet as the alien probe began mending the harm it caused. 'The *Significance* is quite advanced. That is fortunate.'

'What do you want?' I asked.

'To answer some long-standing questions,' he said. 'Doctor, you must first understand that I no longer exist. You are speaking with a construct of my recorded consciousness, wrapped in an AI that behaves how I would act based on the memories of my life. Before my physical destruction, I performed this action as a contingency for failing to intercept you.'

'Failing?' I asked, standing up cautiously. 'I'd say you rather succeeded.'

'I failed to stop you from delivering your Sleeper research to Empress Jamyl,' the ghost said. 'There is no reason to take your life now. All that remains is the hope you can see reason and that your conscience compels you to rethink your actions.'

'Reason? What business do you have in my affairs?'

'The question you should be asking is what business you have in ours.' . . .

BY THE TIME THE EMPYREAN WAR began, the Jovians had all but disappeared from modern affairs. The reclusive race was the most technologically advanced in New Eden, and rumors about the full extent of their capabilities were elevated to myth among the lesser nations vying for military supremacy. Years ago, the Jove were peacemakers, active in politics and assisting in the creation of CONCORD. But their collaboration vanished with news that the Jove were suffering from an incurable disease only their heavily modified genetics was vulnerable to. They allegedly retreated to their homeworlds, isolating themselves from the rest of the cluster. No one knows what exactly has happened to them since. There were very few people alive who had ever seen a Jove in the flesh, even before their withdrawal, and their memory was beginning to morph into fable.

I considered these facts while following the apparition of Grious to the research quarters of the *Significance*, past inoperable drones slumped over like corpses. Amarr shared a special history with the Jove nation. The Empire once made the mistake of attempting to conquer them, and failed in such catastrophic fashion that it inspired revolts among enslaved races, most notably the Minmatar.

'The Jovian Directorate assigned me to investigate the activities of Falek Grange,' Grious said. Even through the haze of the projection, those jet-black eyes were deeply haunting. 'Tracking him led us to you. Your obsession with our technology – and the lengths you would go to recover it – became a topic of concern.'

'So you were spying,' I said. 'Are your masters worried about Amarr's strength again?'

Grious straightened his posture.

'If we thought your expeditions for Jovian relics served purely historical research, we would not take action. But the use of our weapon technology against the Elders gave us cause to reconsider.'

'I don't see how collecting relics of an *extinct* civilization matters to you,' I said.

'Doctor, I may not feel emotions, but I still recognize insults when I hear them. If I were you, I would consider attempts to provoke me unwise.'

'Point taken. Now what do you want?'

'Falek Grange was obsessed with Vak'Atioth,' Grious said, running a translucent hand over the gurney where I had dissected dozens of Sleepers. 'Did he ever speak with you about it?'

'No, but I knew he had an academic interest in all things Jove,' I answered truthfully.

'Falek led numerous expeditions to Atioth in search of our artifacts,' Grious said. 'Yet he kept his discoveries there hidden from you. Do you know why?'

'I'm . . . sure he had good reason to.'

'He hid them because he knew you were an atheist.'

I unwittingly flinched.

'Lord Grange and I had our differences, but there was nothing that could come between us and serving our Empress.'

Grious began pacing as he spoke.

'We have always been astounded at the power of myth. As a culture, we have our regrets, but one benefit of ridding ourselves of emotion was that it removed all susceptibility to religion from our genes.'

'And made yourselves dead to the universe in the process,' I sneered. 'Hardly what I'd call a fair trade.'

'Falek was consumed with your faith and with Sarum's role in it,' Grious continued. 'He reverse-engineered our technology so he could use it to project her as a goddess.'

'What technology?' I scoffed. 'Lord Grange didn't have the resources to work with Jovian tech. And he couldn't possibly consult anyone else but me without risk of exposing her survival!'

'You underestimate his abilities – and his trust in your own,' Grious said. 'Your focus was the few Sleeper relics in your care. While you were preoccupied, Falek discovered the cybernetic technology that we use for mass communications.'

'Oh?' I folded my hands over my chest. 'Then tell me.'

'Your research discovered that our genetic code was modified to allow for implant installation during fetus gestation,' he said. 'What you don't know is that we learned to synchronize biotechnology with quantum entanglement.'

Grious must have noticed the blood drain from my face.

'Yes, the same principle that allows synchronous communication among the star systems of New Eden,' he said. 'It is the backbone of capsuleer immortality: instantaneous transmission of brain-state information across light-years to a cloned copy of the pilot. Yet the fluid router technology your civilization uses to achieve this has so much further to evolve. We refined it such that entangled nanoscale communication devices could be integrated with cybernetic implants that interface with the cerebral cortex.'

I found myself reaching back for something to rest my weight upon.

'Doctor, you should have seen this,' Grious said, tilting his head to one side. 'You and your Matriarch Citadel colleagues are cerebrally *entangled* with Empress Jamyl. Her implant is the broadcast source; entangled "receivers" were installed in the recipients.'

The image took a step toward me.

'You were right to doubt that the voice in your head was divinity.'

There were four implants in my brain currently. *Four.*

'How could I have possibly been—?'

Grious raised a hand for silence.

'Falek Grange was the most dangerous kind of extremist,' he said. 'He was a highly capable, gifted intellectual. Everyone aware of the Matriarch Citadel's existence was augmented with these implants in secret. No one knew, not even Empress Jamyl.'

'Impossible!' I declared. 'You can't tamper with clones. We would have known!'

'Would you?' Grious asked, peering closely at me. 'He controlled *everything* at the Citadel. Aulus Gord, Victor Eliade, you, the Archangel Guardians, and every ranking officer were all handpicked by him. Every implant recipient held crucial oversight of operations that Falek deemed vital to plot Jamyl Sarum's rise to power, *and whose existence you were all sworn to keep secret,*' Grious emphasized, folding his arms across his chest. 'You tell me: How did you build the Citadel without anyone in Amarr turning suspicious?'

For more than five hundred years, the Amarr Empire was ruled by Emperor Heideran VII. His death left the five royal heirs – Kador, Kor-Azor, Ardishapur, Tash-Murkon, and Sarum – to compete for the throne in a ceremony known as the Succession Trials. When Doriam Kor-Azor was declared the victor and crowned Emperor, we arranged for Heiress Jamyl Sarum to disappear – a plot masterminded entirely by Lord Grange. Two years later, Emperor Doriam II was assassinated, and Imperial Chamberlain Dochuta Karsoth became the acting regent. While outwardly declaring he would begin Succession Trials for another emperor, Karsoth had no intention of giving up power.

Lord Grange built the Matriarch Citadel to keep Jamyl Sarum hidden from Karsoth, who would have killed her. We were all taking a treasonous risk: Serving a defunct Chamberlain *and* the Empress we intended to replace him with. I lost track of the number of times I had clone-jumped from the Matriarch to the Throne Worlds and back.

In hindsight, it was a miracle our secret lasted as long as it did.

Jump-cloning made the double life possible. It was a privilege reserved for the immortal: Just enter the chamber and wait as a probe inserts into your neuro-interface socket. You close your eyes and then awake hundreds of light-years away in an instant, looking at the universe through an exact copy of the body you just left.

Or *thought* you left.

The look of recognition on my face was unmistakable.

'You were Theology Council elites by day, and conspiring rebels by night,' Grious continued. 'Chamberlain Karsoth's infamous purge of your clones from Empire space played right into Falek's hands. Your original selves – not the copies with entangled implants – were all destroyed. From that moment on, you belonged to Jamyl Sarum. Falek Grange gave you to her, and by doing so, banished you to this solitary existence – for reasons, I'm sure, that are very personal.'

I was sick to my stomach. Every one of us, those in Falek's inner circle, wore implants; just about all capsuleers did. Short of physically extracting the devices and examining them, nothing would appear out of the ordinary in routine scans – and even then, I was sure it would be difficult to determine what was out of place.

'To Falek's credit, the entire operation was flawless,' Grious continued. 'Worthy even of Jove efficiency. But that hardly matters now.'

There was no one to lash out against. Falek was dead. And if Grious was telling the truth, Sarum was innocent of this.

I had to find a way to leave this place.

'What is it about the EVE Gate that protects me from her?' I asked.

'Tachyon bursts emitted by the EVE Gate interfere with quantum entanglement,' Grious answered. 'It is a most unusual phenomenon. Your data archives show records of these emissions originating from the gate's unique singularity; we are equally puzzled by them. This happens nowhere else in the cluster. We suspect they interfere with wave-function collapse, thus disrupting the entangled components of your implants, but we have yet to prove it. There are limits to even what we know, Marcus.'

'I don't believe you,' I growled. 'You would have to know.'

'I'm afraid I do not,' Grious said. 'But you are a relentless scientist. Understanding the EVE Gate is not your goal. What you really desire is to know how the mind of Empress Jamyl was corrupted.'

'No,' I fumed, banging my fist against a lifeless instrument panel. 'I'll rip these implants out of my skull. She won't be able to do a damn thing about that!'

'Wrong,' Grious answered. 'As I said, Falek was a thorough man. The implant cannot be removed without killing you, and your drones won't permit you to harm yourself.'

'You can help me remove them,' I pleaded. 'You've already disabled my drones. Just restore the medical bay and take them out yourself!'

'I will do no such thing, Doctor. There are many billions of souls who have a keen interest in seeing those implants stay right where they are.'

'What the hell do you mean?'

'Why, Doctor, the Sleepers should have told you by now.'

21

PLACID REGION – VIRIETTE CONSTELLATION
VEY SYSTEM – PLANET III: MER NOIRE
ASTRAL MINING TERRAFORMING COLONY: CAMP STOCKTON
SOVEREIGNTY OF THE GALLENTE FEDERATION

Seventy Years Ago

Jacus Roden stared at the disassembled engine cowling, convinced that the biggest mistake of his young life was coming to Mer Noire. Parts and tools lay strewn all over the hangar, and much to his disgust, a few empty spirits bottles as well. The hired help – a motley crew of local Intakis with average mechanical skills at best – had left more than an hour ago, unable to fix the disabled shuttle. Its battered carcass hung from hydraulic lifts that ran from the floor to the retractable roof above and represented what was probably the last business his fledgling company would ever get.

His greatest frustration was that he knew exactly what the problem was and how to fix it. There was structural damage to the ion turbofans – acute deformations that suggested the pilot had flown through a debris cloud, which was certainly consistent with the nicks and scratches everywhere else on the dilapidated craft. The delicate sensors embedded within the intakes that monitored airflow had been mashed to bits. Replacing them, and reconnecting the new sensors with the primary flight computer, was straightforward but difficult.

Unfortunately, he lacked the funds to purchase any of the parts, let alone rent the equipment needed to install them. The owner of this Banshee-class shuttle refused to pay anything up front, and with this being the latest in a string of contractual failures, his line of credit – with his finances and reputation – had reached its end.

Raised on a terraforming colony on Aporulie IV, Jacus was born with an entrepreneurial spirit, and was always eager to leave his family for brighter horizons. Few could blame him; this was a period of unprecedented growth for the Gallente Federation, which actively encouraged ambitious souls like Jacus to settle new worlds. With countless opportunities throughout the cluster, a strong Navy for protection, and enough government-issued credit to support start-up ventures, the chance to embark on a journey toward riches and adventure was an intoxicating prospect.

But sometimes the destination differs from expectations, no matter how much hope there was when the journey began.

Jacus grabbed a wrench and heaved it toward the shuttle in anger. But the emotional release backfired horribly, as he felt sharp, tearing pain in his shoulder. The tool clanged to the ground well short of its intended target.

Humiliated, he cursed loudly.

It was then, just when he began to accept defeat, that he heard a violent series of crashes outside the shop. Jacus suspected a speeder accident; it wasn't uncommon for colonists to race them through the long, perfectly straight alleyways of the industrial settlement. Pulling a respirator around his face, he ventured through the light air lock and into the thin, cold air of Mer Noire.

He was right. The speeder had come to rest on its side against the outer walls of the hangar. Whoever was inside would be pinned down between the structure's exosteel and the energy-absorbing crash foam of the interior.

With a throbbing shoulder, Jacus hurried back inside and jumped into the shop's only MTAC – an old two-armed cargo rig retrofitted with a cutting winch for working the underside of dropships.

Opening the hangar door, Jacus marched the vehicle out on the street and used its tripedal arms to clasp the disabled speeder. As soon as the top of the vehicle spun around, Jacus heard a sharp *pop* and was blinded; a burst of sparks stung into his face. As he instinctively raised his arms, the MTAC's actuators barely mimicked his actions in time, as more rounds slammed into them; Jacus realized he was being shot at by someone inside the vehicle.

Panicking, he attempted to sidestep and turn the rickety machine around. But the move overwhelmed the old gyroscopes, and it toppled over in a heap. Jacus screamed in agony; the impact drove his injured shoulder hard into the steel roll bars. He thought for certain that this was how his life would end.

But the kill shot never came. In fact, all he could hear was wheezing now, as the speeder victim began asphyxiating. It took a minute for Jacus to get the machine back onto its feet. Sirens screamed. The colony's security forces had mobilized.

For reasons he didn't understand, Jacus knew he had to get the wreck off the street and out of sight.

The victim had passed out; he would be dead in just a few minutes. Working with just one arm, Jacus grabbed him by the shirt collar and pushed him back into the driver's seat, pulling a respirator over his face. Then he took the gun and shoved it into his own pocket.

It was then when he noticed the cache of drugs sticking out of the crash foam. Perfectly arranged pills, cylinders, vials, a silver nozzle injector, and an inhaler engraved with the Serpentis cartel logo. Even the suitcase looked like it was worth a fortune.

The sirens were getting louder.

Wincing, he pulled himself back into the MTAC. With excruciating effort, he marched the machine up to the speeder and used its powerful arms to lift the wreck up. Bits of mangled junk fell from its underside, but the passenger remained steady.

The hangar door had barely closed when the first of three Federation police cruisers roared past the shop. Jacus wondered if anyone noticed the debris field and dent in the wall.

Setting the wreck down, he used the robotic arm to pull the limp body of his assailant onto the hangar floor. The man was breathing good air now but remained unconscious.

The shuttle with the disassembled engine had a large cargo bay. The wreckage would fit neatly inside of it.

Once that task was done, Jacus returned to his victim. There was an old cot inside the office. It would do nicely for the 'patient.'

Jacus immobilized him with canvas straps and sat down with the gun in hand, shaking violently and fighting the urge to vomit.

THE PATIENT WOKE UP an hour later.

He was older, bald, with cropped gray hair on the sides of his head. He was immaculately dressed, wearing stylish business attire that clearly marked him as an offworlder.

Physically, he was also much more formidable than Jacus.

'Why the restraints?' he asked, with a thick Intaki accent.

'You tried to kill me,' Jacus answered.

'My sincerest apologies,' he answered. 'I thought you were a Federation officer.'

'How do you know I'm not?'

'Feds have more sophisticated ways of securing prisoners,' he said, eyeing the crude restraints on his wrists. 'Assuming that's what you think I am now.'

'Given the circumstances,' Jacus said, bringing the gun into view. 'I'd say the police are the least of your problems.'

The Intaki smiled broadly.

'Clearly,' he said. 'So what will you do now?'

His smirk implied he was certain that Jacus didn't know the answer to that. On that count, he would be right.

'We're off to a bad start,' he continued. 'My name is Savant. And you are—?'

'I saw your stash of drugs,' Jacus said. 'Bit much for casual consumption.'

'Yes, I was on my way to fill orders for clients, but was ... sidetracked.'

'I should turn you in.'

'Yes, you probably should. Except you haven't, and probably won't. That makes you guilty of—'

'Conspiracy and tampering with evidence.'

'Yes,' Savant said. 'So then the question is, why did you do it?'

Jacus said nothing, barely aware that he was strumming his finger over the gun.

'I see,' Savant mused, smiling pleasantly, taking in his surroundings. 'It's rather late. Are you the proprietor here?'

'Colonies are ruined because of thugs like you,' Jacus said.

Savant looked as though he were insulted by the comment.

'But you hardly even know me,' he said.

'Drugs ruin people,' Jacus said, starting to lose his patience. 'You're with Serpentis, aren't you?'

'Drugs have been part of our culture for thousands of years,' Savant replied, his eyes wandering around. 'The Intaki wouldn't have survived without them. You know, this shop is using very dated equipment—'

'That's an interesting take on history,' Jacus said, struggling to contain his anger. 'You think it's worth all the misery it causes?'

'Drugs have made me a wealthy man,' Savant answered. 'But that's secondary to the high I get from helping people.'

'Oh, right,' Jacus sneered. 'Helping people what – become addicts?'

'No,' Savant said, becoming serious. 'Helping them cope. Numbing the pain of a difficult life.'

'By giving them a chemical dependency? You hypocrite.'

Savant looked at him thoughtfully.

'If a man loses a limb, you replace that limb with something artificial. If the loss of a child tears the soul out of a parent, you use chemicals to lift him until he finds the strength to carry on. Both are tragic "dependencies," and yet they serve the same noble purpose – to compensate for a debilitating limitation.'

He looked around some more, frowning as though he didn't like what he saw.

'So how has business been?'

Jacus shook his head.

'Doctors determine what's noble, not you.'

'Actually, I prefer the term *physician*.'

'You're a physician? Right.'

'Clearly, you've been institutionalized by Federation propaganda to think we're all "thugs." You'd be surprised how many of us practice legally. We're not the evil empire you think we are.'

Savant paused again, sniffing like something foul was in the air.

'If you don't mind my saying, I get the impression this shop isn't doing well at all—'

'That isn't your concern,' Jacus growled.

'I'll make it my concern, if you'll allow,' Savant answered, jutting his chin toward the straps on his wrists. 'It's the least I can do in return for all the goodwill you've shown to me.'

Jacus almost laughed. In truth, he had no idea what to do next.

'Whatever you're up to, I don't want any part of it,' Jacus said. 'But you're right. It's not going the way I hoped it would here.'

Savant smiled.

'You didn't think building a life here would be easy, did you?' he said. 'I don't believe I caught your name.'

'Jacus Roden.'

'Pleased to meet you, Jacus. Thank you for saving my life. What's the name of your enterprise?'

'Roden Shipyards.'

'Ah. Has a certain ring to it, I'll admit. In exchange for your kindness, and as compensation for shooting at you, I have two offers: three hundred thousand credits for shop upgrades and parts inventory, and a steady stream of new business.'

Jacus nearly let his jaw drop. It was an astronomical figure. But he wasn't stupid.

'Right, a steady stream of *Serpentis* business.'

Savant turned serious again.

'I never said from whom the business would originate.'

'Right,' Jacus said, exasperated. 'Thanks, but that's not necessary. Let's just call it even.'

'You don't believe my offer was sincere?' Savant asked.

Jacus grimaced at the pain in his shoulder. He was suddenly exhausted.

'You put on a good show, I'll give you that,' he said, starting toward him. 'Let me cut you loose.'

'No need,' Savant said, sitting up effortlessly. The straps fell away from his wrists. 'I'll let myself up, thanks.'

Jacus froze.

'Microblade sewn into the seams,' Savant continued, passing his wrist over the leg bindings, which also fell away. 'They work well on most restraints. You should give my weapon back.'

Jacus stared at the gun in his trembling hand.

'You can't fire it,' warned Savant, who was now walking toward him. 'Biometric safety. Only I can pull that trigger.'

Jacus nearly swung the gun at the imposing figure, but again, instinct stopped him.

Savant gently took the weapon back.

'Sabotage setting,' he said, tapping the gun. A chirp acknowledged his subtle hand movement. 'If you attempted to fire, it would have melted in your hand.'

Jacus began stepping backward.

'You know, I'm an expert shot,' Savant said, stretching lazily, carelessly waving the gun around. 'From that range, you were a sure thing. Fortunately for you, oxygen deprivation is bad for motor skills.'

The gun disappeared into his expensive long coat. Out came a data-pad.

'Your credits are waiting to be claimed,' Savant said.

'I can't accept this,' Jacus said cautiously. 'It's blood money.'

'Collecting dividends from pharmacorp stock is no different,' Savant said, typing away on the device. 'Trust me, they've spilled more blood than anyone.'

'I don't want anything to do with Serpentis,' Jacus said firmly.

'Why do you keep saying that name?' Savant asked, tucking the datapad away. He gave him a stern look. 'What I would like is for you to fix all the craft that come through here. I realize that having customers is something you're unaccustomed to, so use those funds to hire the right people and get the right equipment.'

Jacus sat back down in the chair.

'I haven't asked you to do anything illegal,' Savant said, peering into the hangar adjacent to the room. 'You saved my life, remarkably so while under fire. You have good instincts. You *should* be rewarded for what you did.'

Jacus was beginning to wish he'd ignored that crash outside the shop. 'If customers come through my door, who am I to turn them away?' he said.

Savant smiled.

'This is the break you've been looking for,' he said. 'Now, let's have a look at that shoulder of yours. I might have just the thing to dull the pain.'

ESSENCE REGION – VIERES CONSTELLATION
THE LADISTIER SYSTEM – PLANET IV, MOON 4
PRESIDENTIAL BUREAU STATION
SOVEREIGNTY OF THE GALLENTE FEDERATION

Present Day

Jacus stepped onto the walkway leading to his quarters, wiping away globs of pod fluid. The fuselage of the Ares-class interceptor that he had arrived in towered overhead, mocking his return to mere flesh and bone. As he acclimated to gravity, showerheads unleashed torrents of distilled water at him. It was not possible to be any more sterile in this environment, as the pod fluid possessed antiseptic qualities that were lethal to all microorganisms except those beneficial to humans.

Snapping a towel off the rack, he hurried through the motions of drying and getting dressed, lost in thought. He was frustrated – not angry, but about as angst-ridden as his refined temperament would allow. Having just returned from a visit with his niece, the acting Roden Shipyards CEO, for her seventieth birthday, Jacus should have been in better spirits. Instead, he had come away with deep concerns about whether his appointed cabinet staff was hearing his message.

One of the benefits of leaving one empire to build another one was that intelligence gathered by both could be compared against each other. But its greatest disadvantage was in discovering when the two weren't aligned.

Jacus worked tirelessly to bolster the intelligence-gathering capabilities of the Federation. The scope of that effort was not limited to nations under the jurisdiction of CONCORD. They included frontier organizations like Mordu's Legion, the Serpentis cartel, and many more. The ability to connect disparate threads of information from those sources and discover where they converged was the key to winning the war.

Missing even the smallest detail, however obscure, was, at best, a wasted opportunity and at worst, a fatal mistake. The information relayed by his niece – which had gone undetected by the Federation – meant that his efforts to date had been in vain.

Jacus left his personal quarters, walked past the priceless collection of Mannar art pieces in his personal gallery, and stepped into the waiting speeder. He intended to arrive early to the national security briefing so he could meditate on deciding which of his cabinet should be deposed for incompetence.

MOST OF THEM ARRIVED a few minutes early as well.

Ariel Orviegnoure, Director of the Federation Intelligence Office, showed first. She was one of the only cabinet members retained from the previous administration, and the source of a near-constant political firestorm. She was the target of blame for the intelligence breach that led to the loss of Caldari Prime – an unfair accusation to anyone who knew the real cause. Jacus considered her highly capable and intelligent, but he knew her compassion was a liability when it came to making difficult choices. Still, as a matter of assessing the Federation's capabilities, he was depending on her to continue transitioning his new policies into the agency.

Also present was Mentas Blaque, Director of the Black Eagles, the secretive paramilitary arm of the Federation Intelligence Office. Though technically reporting to Ariel, the former senator was her equal in practice and commanded much more respect in the agency than she. For reasons Jacus had always been suspicious of, he was publicly supportive of Ariel, and by all accounts seemed genuinely loyal, if not outright protective. As for Jacus, his relationship with Mentas was contentious at first but had finally cooled to one of mutual respect. Still, both men remained wary of each other. They were as close as former spies could be expected to get.

Grand Admiral Anteson Ranchel, the Secretary of Defense, was also present, and as always appeared impatient. His disdain for President Roden was plainly obvious, and he had made a name for himself as something of a rebel because of it. Jacus didn't care for the man. But he did empathize with him and respected his leadership qualities. Considering that his predecessor was executed for treason, he was handling the spotlight well and making progress in restoring morale within the Navy. Admiral Ranchel was making an honest and competent effort to win the war and was less than pleased with the support he was getting. On that, they were in agreement.

Ranchel's assistant, Vice Admiral Yana Marakova, was the acting National Security Advisor. A decorated empyrean, she was notoriously ambitious and managed to get herself promoted directly from Captain to Vice Admiral. A Navy review board declared that the promotion was a wartime exception, but well deserved for her impressive service record, which was truthfully filled with heroics and instances of effective leadership under fire. Of course, many jealous colleagues believed her 'impressive service record' implied something else entirely. Jacus knew the rumors of her promiscuity were mostly exaggerated. But whatever her capabilities, he would never willingly allow her onto the cabinet. She had the cognitive skills, but her personal motivations suggested that she lacked the heart.

The rest of the room was filled with deputies, department heads, and their staffers. All knew to keep quiet unless spoken to.

President Roden waited patiently until the Director of the FIO finished delivering her briefing. As expected, the information he wanted to hear was conspicuously absent.

'Thank you, Ariel,' he started. 'But your briefing didn't mention anything about the frontier. Or Mordu's Legion, in particular.'

Ariel blinked.

'It's business as usual for them,' she said. 'In general, they're escalating terra-ops in the outer regions, getting more business with upstart colonies. Our armed forces take fire from them occasionally, usually only when provoked. But for the most part they avoid direct contact. They've cut their relations with the Caldari State entirely. But nothing is happening to press any urgent national security issues.'

'I've issued three directives for our intelligence strategy,' Jacus started, raising three fingers and counting them off one by one: 'Penetrate the Caldari inner circle, research the war technologies of nations, and strengthen ties with the Minmatar Republic. We must always be vigilant for opportunities to tackle these initiatives.'

'Yes?' Ariel said.

'Then are you or are you not aware that Mordu's Legion just accepted a contract with the Republic Fleet?' Roden asked.

A tinge of red passed through Ariel's cheeks. The green mechanical eyes of Jacus were locked with hers.

'That means no,' Jacus said. 'And I find that rather disturbing.'

'What's the significance of this?' Admiral Ranchel demanded.

'The contract is to defend the Core Freedom Colony on the planet Pike's Landing,' Jacus said. 'For those who don't know, that's in the Amamake system, right on the front. The Republic has been struggling to hold on to it for months.'

'We're well aware this is a contested chokepoint in the war,' said Mentas Blaque. 'How is it relevant to us?'

'The Minmatar are on the verge of losing a well-developed homeworld system, and instead of coming to us for assistance, they chose mercenaries instead,' Jacus said calmly. 'To me, that demonstrates a lack of faith in *your* military, Admiral, and in the capabilities of your Special Forces, Director, and in the commitment of this entire cabinet to restoring our relations with them.'

'I'll take responsibility for missing this data's importance for diplomatic opportunities,' Ariel said. 'Clearly our resources are limited, but you could try sharing your Roden Shipyards intel instead of using it to ambush your own team.'

'This is no personal attack,' Jacus said. 'But I have no tolerance for complacency or incompetence. This is more than an opportunity to mend fences. Find the cause of the deficiency in your agency and deal with it.'

'What do you mean, "more than an opportunity"?' Mentas Blaque asked. 'What else do your people know about this?'

'It's not what we know; it's what we anticipate,' Jacus said. 'Pike's Landing is a battlefield where nothing remains but desperation. That's usually when adversaries play their best cards. We must be there to learn what those are.'

Jacus leaned forward.

'Admiral, we are going to send the Minmatar help and keep a presence in the Amamake system whether they take our offer or not.'

The cabinet members all exchanged concerned looks.

'What of the Amarr?' Mentas asked.

'We've as much right to be there,' Jacus answered. 'If attacked, we will defend ourselves.'

Admiral Ranchel had an incredulous scowl on his face.

'Mr President, are you suggesting we peel resources away from actionable intel to chase leads before they even become leads, if at all?'

'Roden Shipyards spent decades refining the art of anticipating markets,' Jacus said. 'The yield from predictive intelligence gathering is worth the cost of being wrong from time to time.'

'Is it?' Admiral Ranchel asked. 'Even when it costs lives and battles in places where you take resources to chase ghosts?'

'As a proactive means of winning the war – yes,' Roden said.

'This has already happened once before, over an Amarr city named Xerah,' Jacus said. 'The Elders would have gladly traded some lives to know in advance that a fifth of their navy was about to be obliterated.'

'This is—' Ariel started, then composed herself. 'We'll examine where we can be more proactive.'

'I'll finish your thought: "This is insane,"' Admiral Ranchel declared. 'There are more immediate priorities based on what we actually *do* know, not what we might speculate.'

'Not long ago we were informed that CONCORD was attempting to expand their influence to the frontier,' Jacus said. 'That is unprecedented. What would compel them to do that? What do they know that we don't? Is that not clear evidence of proactive, desperate measures?'

There was silence.

'My instincts have always served me well, Admiral,' Jacus said. 'Send a task force of your own to Amamake. Meeting adjourned.'

22

KHANID REGION – BUDAR CONSTELLATION
THE IRMALIN SYSTEM – PLANET II: HEXANDRIA
KHANID INNOVATION BIOMEDICAL SCIENCES AND RESEARCH CENTER
SOVEREIGNTY OF THE KHANID KINGDOM

Two Years Ago

Gable awoke to the sound of gunfire and the biting stench of ash in her sinuses. Loud, sharp reports of weapons fire and screaming brought her heart rate to a dangerous pace. Coughing violently, she pushed herself up onto her elbows. The wind was carrying black smoke toward her from smoldering wreckage. Somewhere through the chaos she could hear a dropship idling nearby, and she figured good air must be near it. Desperate to breathe, she crawled in its direction.

She made it only a few steps when a hand forcibly grabbed her.

'Here's another one,' a loud, urgent voice declared. 'Time?'

'Ninety seconds,' another voice answered. 'Stand them up.'

As she was yanked to her feet, she realized she was bumping shoulders with several stunned, whimpering researchers from the Khanid facility. Across from them stood a soldier wearing an intimidating tactical helmet and face shield. The rust-colored armor suggested he was Minmatar, and there were a dozen or so more behind him. Aside from varying heights and builds, they all looked the same to her: There were no ranks or other printed insignia to be seen.

'Put your hands on your head. All of you!' another voice shouted.

'Sixty seconds,' the timekeeper said, stepping back. 'Do it.'

A soldier stepped forward and drew his sidearm, pointing it directly in the face of the first researcher.

'What do you do here?' he asked.

'I'm a scientist—'

Gable flinched in horror as the weapon exploded. A reddish mist hung in the air as the scientist's lifeless husk collapsed. The soldier moved on to the next person in line, again raising his weapon.

'What do you do?'

The man was mumbling prayers through clenched teeth; the back of his skull disappeared a moment later.

Gable's breaths were coming fast and shallow as the weapon was pointed at her.

'What do you do?' asked the executioner.

Gable couldn't speak. Her mouth was wide open, but the words would not come. Her eyes fixated on the barrel; smoke wisped beyond its steel like the spirits of those it had just claimed.

'Thirty seconds!' the timekeeper declared, just as the soldier's finger tensed on the trigger. The words set off a survival mechanism in her; instead of a heroic rush to save her own life, she found only the courage to tell the truth.

'I'm a doctor!' she gasped.

The executioner moved in closer.

'What *kind* of doctor?'

'Trauma surgeon . . . ' she stammered, ' . . . cybernetic qualified. I just . . . heal people . . . help them . . . .'

The gun was pressed hard into her chest.

'Why should I believe you?' he demanded.

Another soldier stepped forward.

'She's telling the truth,' he said. 'We got our secondary. Let's go.'

'Prison line!' the executioner shouted. There were still six researchers left. In a well-rehearsed drill, the soldiers quickly aligned themselves a few meters opposite them. Each had a rifle raised to shoulder height. Gable felt herself spun around; her hands were quickly bound behind her.

One of the soldiers spoke his mind.

'This is *fucked* up, Lieutenant!'

'Kintreb's orders,' the executioner said. 'Company aim!'

Gable felt a sickening wave of dread wash over her.

'Fire!'

The sound of half a dozen simultaneous gun reports made her flinch. She was first thankful to be alive – and then ashamed of herself for having survived.

'You're coming with us,' her captor said, marching her toward the open mouth of the idling dropship.

'Where?' she gasped.

'You'll find out,' he said, turning her around again. The man's face shield had retracted, and she saw what might have been compassion in his eyes.

'Keep that pendant out of sight,' he said, tucking Sister Marth's holy piece inside her coat. 'For your own sake.'

'Time's up!' the timekeeper yelled. 'Move out!'

Clear of the smoke, the sky resumed its deep blue beauty, where abundant sunshine was broken only by lazy puffs of clouds overhead. Just minutes ago, she believed she had landed in paradise.

'Who are you people?' she gasped.

'Valklears,' he said, as the craft's ion turbines began to rev up, pushing the tall prairie grass over in waves. 'And you are our prisoner.'

HEIMATAR REGION – HED CONSTELLATION
AMAMAKE SYSTEM – PLANET II: PIKE'S LANDING
CORE FREEDOM COLONY
SOVEREIGNTY OF THE MINMATAR REPUBLIC

Present Day

The Panther-class gunship circled the entire complex once before touching down on the roof of the medical ward. General Kintreb was annoyed at this but accepted that he might have done the same in the pilot's position. The craft itself, undulating with adaptive camouflage hues that gave its skin a shimmering appearance, was easily the most intact vehicle at Core Freedom. Well-maintained weapons hung from pylons and turrets, and there was none of the telltale war damage prevalent everywhere on the base.

General Kintreb didn't care for the mercenaries already, and was sure none of his soldiers did either.

As the ship hovered over the roof, an armed figure jumped to the surface, shielding his eyes from the downwash as he jogged toward him. Vlad noticed that he ran with a peculiar gait: One stride was much more powerful than the next, almost like he was skipping. Several freight containers were pushed out the open ramp; they fell to the landing pad as the craft banked away and thundered toward the mountain range.

Vlad couldn't help but grimace when the approaching man's face came into view. The new arrival said nothing as he neared, instead holding out a datapad from which the volumetric projection of another man appeared.

'General, my name is Captain Jonas Varitec of the MLW *Morse*. My associate's name is Mack, and he'll be assessing your surface defenses. Apologies for the flyby, but we used that time to get scans of your outposts to complement the recon we have from up here.'

'Where is "here"?' Kintreb asked.

'About a thousand kilometers overhead,' Jonas said. 'The crates my gunship dropped off are medical supplies. They should hold down any immediate needs until we're secure.'

'We didn't ask for those.'

'Mack wanted you to have them,' Jonas said. 'He paid the tab on his own. Please show him around the colony and answer his questions honestly. It'll help us ensure that you get what you need.'

Vlad looked over the hideous man, unsure of what to think.

'Does Mack ever talk?'

'Only when spoken to,' Jonas said. 'My gunship is going to do some terrain mapping of the mountain range to the east before refueling. It's registered as Wildcat-Nine on your air grid; please let your tower know. Out.'

'Right,' General Kintreb said, straightening up. 'So, Mack. Where do we begin?'

'Medical ward first,' he said. 'Then vehicle hangars. After that we see.'

'Interesting choice,' General Kintreb commented. 'But we're paying you for firepower, not medical advice.'

'Must learn truth of this place,' Mack answered, starting toward the stairs. 'See with my eyes, not yours. So we start with med ward first.'

'What the hell is that supposed to mean?' Kintreb demanded. 'I'm a Valklear general. Do you know how long I've been fighting Amarrians?'

'No,' Mack said, turning so that his disfigurement was facing him directly. 'If that mattered, we not need to be here.'

WHEN GABLE ENTERED THE TRAUMA WARD, she was greeted with a bewildered soldier hauling boxes of fresh medical supplies in each hand.

'Where do I put this stuff?' he asked.

More soldiers were unpacking bags from a large crate at the end of the hall. It was like a miracle had happened.

'Who brought all this?' she asked.

The Valklear looked over his shoulder.

'Him.'

Gable took one look at Mack and reflexively began a mental diagnosis:

Mannar male, mid-to-late forties, seventy-two to seventy-four kilos; burn victim, likely radiation scarring; acute left-side trauma with extensive cybernetic augmentation; asymmetric biomechanical load balance; scarring on right trapezius caused by small-arms fire or shrapnel; intercranial implants, ocular probable but definite olfactory augmentation; extent and cost of cybernetic engineering suggests patient must have refused cosmetic restructuring; indicative of self-destructive or sadistic tendencies with possible psychosis.

She determined all of this in just under a second.

'You're with Mordu's Legion?' she asked.

'Yes,' Mack answered politely, studying her with his good eye. General Kintreb was hovering nearby. 'You are the Lifegiver?'

She couldn't help but look surprised.

'I'm sorry?'

He was smiling beyond what his scarring allowed, gleaming at her.

'I bring life supplies for you,' Mack said, waving toward the rows of recovering soldiers. Those who were conscious were staring at them. 'Help take their suffering away.'

'I'm sure they appreciate it,' Gable said. 'Thank you.'

He limped toward her, motioning that he wanted to whisper something. Mack didn't seem concerned about making it obvious he didn't want General Kintreb or his escorts to hear him.

Accustomed to human disfigurement, she managed to lean in close without flinching, as he cupped a hand between his mouth and her ear.

'Someday I free you,' he whispered. *'I bring another Lifegiver for these men.'*

'What's going on here?' General Kintreb demanded. 'What did he say to you?'

'He asked me which patients have the worst prognosis,' Gable snapped, doing her best to hide her shock. 'He's being mindful of them.'

Mack turned to face General Kintreb.

'Wounded men are liability,' he said. 'We offer them transport off-world to restore health. What you say?'

Mack had just put the General on the spot in front of his own troops. Gable was impressed.

'I'll consider it after you complete your "assessment,"' General Kintreb snarled. 'Care to move on, Mack?'

'Of course, General.'

KORVIN LEARS STOOD ON THE BRIDGE of the *Morse*, pretending to study the combined reconnaissance of Core Freedom from the

Panther gunship flyby and orbital photographs. He was extremely nervous, unable to recall whether he had ever felt this insecure aboard a starship before. Watching Captain Varitec command the ship, barking orders to a crew that carried them out after what felt like hours instead of seconds, was tantamount to torture.

Traditional ship command protocol was lethally redundant. The *Morse* bridge was choked with electronics and a myriad of displays that danced across the air before the officers, who manipulated them by waving their hands like magicians. To Korvin it seemed utterly primitive, this so-called 'nerve center' of the battlecruiser. In the time it took for the ship to execute the most basic maneuvers, he could have obliterated it several times over. Until now, nothing had put into perspective for him just how potent the merge between the mind and a starship was.

Perspective worked the other way as well. When brought aboard, he was impressed with the ship's great size, or so it felt within the belly of one instead of through a targeting solution. His power as a capsuleer distorted his sense of scale. These ships were enormous – and at 'just' five hundred meters from bow to stern, a Drake-class battlecruiser wasn't remotely as large as even the smallest capital ship. Winding their way through the labyrinthine bulkheads and compartments, Korvin took notice of the hallways lined with containment seals at regular intervals, each designed to isolate damaged sections from the rest of the ship. He couldn't imagine the horror of being trapped behind one, locked behind just a few centimeters of durasteel waiting for the ship to break apart.

He passed by dozens, if not a hundred or more, of the *Morse* crew. He forced himself to look them all in the eye, to see if he recognized any. The guilt he felt for his many victims had never been greater.

'Does that thing hurt?' Captain Varitec asked.

'What?' Korvin asked. He realized he'd been running his hand over his neuro-interface socket. 'Oh. Most of the time I don't even know it's there.'

'I'm sure,' Jonas said, folding his arms. In the dim lighting, his expression seemed very serious. 'Care to share your thoughts about this colony?'

'Right,' Korvin said, clearing his throat. Blake, the redheaded weapons officer, was staring dreamily at him. 'There's one shield generator, well maintained, ranked somewhere in the six-thousand-gigajoule range, though I don't think they have enough power to run it longer than a few minutes. I see three SS missile batteries, Minmatar Stackfires by the looks of it.'

He paused to make sure everyone was keeping up. Miles, the engineering officer, didn't seem to be paying attention at all.

'They have a Cloudburst point-defense system, but I don't think it's operational,' Korvin continued. Waving his hand, imagery of the installation zoomed in toward a trapezoid-like structure, which had dark holes scattered across it. 'This phased-array tracking radar is damaged, so unless they're getting telemetry from satellites or friendly ships, the Cloudbursts are useless.'

'What about the Stackfires?' Jonas asked.

'Some models have area-of-effect capabilities to neutralize guided munitions, but they're useless against plasma or beams,' Korvin answered. 'Colonies this size usually arm at least one of their batteries with antiship warheads. The rest are fire-and-forget.'

'So how've they lasted this long?' Jonas asked. 'The Imperial Navy ought to be able to direct bombardments wherever it wants to.'

'That's not true,' Blake said, surprising the whole bridge. 'Core Freedom is next to a mountain range that runs perpendicular to the planet's rotation. That takes away prograde firing solutions.'

'Correct,' Korvin said, raising an eyebrow. 'Ships have to drop below five hundred kilometers to use bombardment weapons, even lower to use them with any precision. The approach is nicknamed "the gauntlet," because a ship's orbit altitude, vector, and speed are predictable, leaving it extremely vulnerable to ground and space defenses.'

'That's an easy firing solution,' Jonas noted.

'It sure is,' Korvin said. 'The mountains take away a western approach, because the ship would have to be almost directly above the target to strike with any precision. That's not to say it can't be done, but the Stackfires would probably murder them.'

'I see,' Jonas said. 'What about polar or retrograde approaches?'

'Same risks,' Korvin answered. 'As long as they know what you're trying to bombard, they can put ordnance in your flight path. And the only way for ships to direct accurate ground fire is to get right on top.'

Blake exhaled a loud sigh, looking directly at Korvin.

'THE INJURIES HERE,' Mack asked. 'Please tell me about them.'

'Well, all the usual battlefield carnage,' Gable started, 'but the worst of it is psyche trauma. Lately these men have faced Kameira Special Forces – genetically engineered Minmatars created by the Amarrians. They begin their attack with a PSYKLAD strike—'

'What's that?'

'It stands for Psychotic Kinesis, Light Artillery Delivery,' General Kintreb interrupted. 'Drug-tipped shells that make soldiers hallucinate. With the Kameiras attacking, the stuff makes our men think they're being attacked by their own families. It is one nasty mindfuck. I've seen soldiers try to "defend" Kameiras by shooting each other.'

'Why this,' Mack asked, 'and not explosive weapons?'

'They use those too,' Gable said. 'PSYKLAD is just for crushing morale.'

The group was standing outside the ward now, in the shade cast by the dilapidated mass-driver structure looming overhead. Military transports raced by, carting civilians from their barracks to relieve the previous shift. Off to their right, an old MTAC marched to the corner of the ward and stopped, rotating its torso in slow 120-degree arcs. Puffs of fine silt from where the machine walked settled slowly to the ground.

'How you treat survivors of this attack?' Mack asked.

'I erase their memories,' Gable said. 'General Kintreb was able to procure advanced Khanid tech that's especially proficient at it.'

'Khanid?' Mack asked.

'Never mind,' General Kintreb said.

'Mack, you're asking a lot of questions I didn't expect,' Gable asked. 'Do you mind if I ask you one?'

'Of course not.'

'Please tell me about your team.'

'Lots of experience,' Mack said. 'Combined hundreds of years in warfare. Empyrean War gives Legion much business. Well equipped, well trained. Minmatar government knows we can help.'

'Can you protect us from space?' Gable asked.

'Not always,' Mack said with a frown. 'I assess what troops you need. Moving them here is challenge. But we have immortal on team. He assess protection from space. Solid record. Says he can help.'

'An empyrean?' Gable asked with a shudder. 'Do you trust him?'

Mack looked away and said nothing.

'We all have our reasons to be afraid of them,' she said. 'What's yours?'

'Not fear,' Mack said. 'Hate.'

'Why do you hate them?'

Mack bent down, scooping up a handful of dust.

'This ... where we all come from,' he said, letting it fall between his fingers. 'We become this again someday. Not them. No respect for us. Would kill them all if I could.'

He reached into his pocket and produced a small action figure, which drew puzzled looks.

'Take this,' he said, suddenly appearing deliriously happy. 'It protect me. Now it protect you.'

She took it carefully, as if it were fragile. It was just a toy soldier. Mack was smiling, eagerly nodding as if he'd just handed her a diamond ring.

'Thank you,' she said, placing it in her lab-coat pocket. The mercenary then became very serious as he turned to General Kintreb.

'General,' Mack said, 'we see hangar outposts next.' ...

JONAS SUMMONED KORVIN to his quarters after the briefing was complete.

'The crew seems to have taken a liking to you,' he started. 'One of them, anyway.'

Korvin ignored him, noting the captain's surroundings instead. Other than a bed, terminal desk, and an extra chair, it was sparsely decorated, with grayish blue metallic interior. There were no pictures or other memorabilia, except for a glass trophy case holding a model ship. A tiny sign on it read RETFORD.

'It's a start,' Korvin said.

'Just keep it professional,' Jonas warned. 'Now I want your opinion, just between you and me. What does your gut tell you about this op?'

'That Mordu should have turned it down,' Korvin answered frankly. 'This place is lost.'

Jonas grunted.

'That was my assertion as well, but damned if I'm going to say that in front of my crew,' he said, rubbing the stubble on his chin. 'What do you think it'll take to save Core Freedom?'

'A fleet,' Korvin answered. 'Or better planetary defenses. It's a credit to the Valklears they've been able to hold on for this long.'

'Makes you think the Amarrians aren't trying as hard as they could be?'

'Can't be ruled out. We've never been able to get good intel on them. But the last reports I've seen all say they have their hands full with the Republic Fleet elsewhere. Dozens of systems are locked in stalemates.'

Jonas leaned back, resting his hands behind his head.

'You know, usually I'm right about certain things,' he said.

'Yeah?' Korvin asked, trying to sound impressed.

'I feel like we're being sized up,' Jonas said. 'Like we're being *watched*. As soon as Mack is finished down there, we're heading back to HQ to talk it over with the old man.'

'Watched?' Korvin asked sarcastically. 'Really? I mean, you mercenaries make friends everywhere you go. Why would anyone ever want to keep tabs on you?'

'Cute,' Jonas said, just as a projection of the colony appeared. 'But it's a little more than a gut feeling.'

Korvin watched as the map panned to the right, showing a position about eleven kilometers east of Core Freedom. The hostile terrain was part of an ancient caldera that was now about twenty-five thousand acres of badlands dotted with rock steppes. Utterly impassable by foot, the valley itself was teeming with indigenous life-forms that thrived in the area's ecosystem, all of which was nurtured by underground streams. The voracious laaknyds, the invasive species introduced accidentally by the Minmatar, were rapidly working their way up the food chain.

'Miles found this while you were lecturing about orbital bombardments,' Jonas said, as two images appeared side by side. Both were of the exact same plot of land, with superimposed grid lines denoting a resolution of less than a meter.

The second image showed something the first one didn't.

'Those shots were taken an hour apart,' Jonas said. 'The one on the left is right after we arrived; the second is just a few minutes old. The computers think there's a ninety-two percent chance that isn't a rock pile that just happens to look like a gunship.'

Korvin could tell from the distorted air mass behind the shape and sharp-edged shadow beneath it that the computer was right. It was a gunship of some sort idling on the surface.

'Amarr?' he asked.

'I wish it were that simple,' Jonas said, allowing the image to hang in the air. 'We have no idea what that is. All we do know is that the Valklears weren't operating in that airspace at that time.'

'Most of that sector is below sea level,' Korvin noted. 'Core Freedom's radar wouldn't detect it.'

'Correct, professor,' Jonas said, kicking his feet up on the desk. 'I assigned a LinkSat to that grid but haven't seen anything since. Our gunship is staying away from there until we know what it is.'

'You think someone else is interested in Core Freedom?' Korvin asked.

Jonas shrugged.

'Maybe it's a privateer who got lost,' he said. 'But with my luck, that's too optimistic.'

The images disappeared.

'Only you and the officers know about this,' he said. 'Let's keep it that way.

'Understood,' Korvin said, motioning toward the trophy case. 'That's a Lynx-class frigate, right?'

'Yeah, it is,' Jonas said, standing up slowly.
'Mind telling me about it?'
'Yes, I do mind,' Jonas snapped. 'That'll be all for now, Korvin. Dismissed.'

23

CITADEL REGION – AREKIN CONSTELLATION
THE AHYNADA SYSTEM – PLANET IV: KRYSKOS MAR
BLACKBOURN CITY – VALOMER DISTRICT ACADEMY
SOVEREIGNTY OF THE CALDARI STATE

Thirty Years Ago

Immobilized at the wrists by stun cuffs, Vince Barabin was ushered down a featureless hallway by Lai Dai police officers into an imposing courtroom. His arrest had taken place within minutes of the fight and quickly became a public spectacle. Every moment of the incident had been recorded by security cameras, and the footage was now playing in the courtroom, ending with the growing pool of blood beneath the victim's skull.

It took the Caldari due-process system weeks to investigate the case and formally press charges. Vince spent the entire time in jail doing hard labor. The detectives assigned to his case determined that he was safer there than anywhere else. Téa didn't fare much better. Although she was legally allowed to continue her enrollment, the academy was sending a clear message that she was no longer welcome there. No one, not even the instructors, would speak to her, and on more than one occasion her belongings were vandalized.

Vince now stood before the court magistrate, who was seated high above the floor studying the incident recording. The seal of the

Caldari State was emblazoned on the wall behind him, and his podium was etched with the mega-corporation seal of Lai Dai. Opposite him were a handful of benches; seated at the front were Téa and some uniformed State employees. Vince glanced at her as he shuffled by. The wounds on her face had long since healed. But he remembered them as if it had happened yesterday.

The officers led him to the podium base, where he was joined by a court-appointed attorney – a confident-looking fellow with heavy facial modifications and cybernetic implants. Dressed in flamboyant but impeccable business attire, the man greeted him with a disingenuous smile and handshake. Before he could speak, the magistrate's voice thundered in the hall.

'Vincent Barabin,' he started. 'You are charged with murder in the first degree. How do you plead?'

Wearing a tattered prison uniform, Vince was weary beyond words. He'd hardly slept in prison. He was barely able to stand, let alone find the strength to comprehend that he was moments away from being sentenced to a life term.

The attorney spoke for him jovially.

'My client pleads not guilty to first-degree, Magistrate. As his legal representative, if I may consult you for a plea on a lesser charge—'

'Vincent,' the magistrate repeated. He was an older man, a Deteis, with harsh features and piercing eyes. 'Do you understand the charge brought against you?'

Again, the attorney spoke up. 'My client is fully apprised of all the facts in accordance—'

'Quiet,' the magistrate fumed. 'I'm talking to your client.'

Vince's eyes weren't even focused.

'You murdered someone,' the magistrate continued. 'The court is obligated to assign a punishment fitting the crime. Do you have anything to say?'

The projections of the fight continued, revealing each pivotal moment. Moving about forty kilometers per hour, the street cleaner was able to stop but couldn't raise its ice-melting heat plow in time. The corner struck the reeling cadet square in the temple, badly fracturing his skull on impact. A few centimeters up or down might have spared his life. But by the time his body came to rest in the street, he was beyond saving.

'Vincent?' the magistrate asked again.

'What's going to happen to my sister?' Vince finally mumbled. 'She won't have anyone to take care of her.'

The magistrate sat back and studied the broken young man before him.

'The State performs detailed background checks on all family, friends, and acquaintances of the accused,' he said, sighing forcefully. 'We learned a lot about you in the last four weeks.'

Vince looked on impassively.

'I know about your father,' the magistrate said. 'You and your sister should have been placed in protective custody a long time ago.'

Vince hadn't seen or heard from his dad since the day before the fight.

'All the signs of abuse were there,' the magistrate continued. 'It should have been reported. The fact that it wasn't is a crime. To that end, there are others who share in the blame for this, and they will be held responsible.'

The attorney nudged Vince in the shoulder, as if it was his brilliant legal maneuvering that somehow inspired compassion in the judge.

'Our academies are supposed to produce soldiers, not thugs,' the magistrate said. 'I've watched this footage a hundred times, and for me, the compelling factor is that you didn't go out looking for trouble.'

The projections showed Vince landing the strike combination that stunned the older cadet, and the kick to the chest that sent him reeling backward into the street.

'You defended yourself and your sister, effectively,' the magistrate continued. 'But whether you saw that vehicle coming or not, that kick wasn't necessary.'

Vince blinked, unable to believe that the boy on the projection was him. At best, he had a blurry recollection of the event. But he remembered being just as horrified at the injured cadet on the street as all the other bystanders.

'I've been in fights before,' the magistrate continued, maintaining his stern demeanor. 'They can get out of hand. But you are responsible for that cadet's death, and I'm compelled to judge you for it.'

The magistrate waited for a response. Vince felt another nudge from the attorney.

'I just wanted them to leave my sister alone,' Vince mumbled. 'I never wanted to hurt anyone.'

'I believe you, Vincent,' the magistrate said. 'The charge of first degree murder is therefore dropped. However, this court finds you guilty of voluntary manslaughter. You are hereby sentenced to five years in a Lai Dai vocational penitentiary, after which time you'll be remitted for corporate assignment.'

Vince turned to look at his sister.

'They're transferring me there as well,' she said.

'And Dad?' Vince asked.

Téa looked away, then at the State employees beside her.

'We don't need to be afraid of him anymore,' she said.

Vince looked back up at the judge. His bottom lip quivered and then he began to cry.

IMPERIAL NAVY REVELATIONS-CLASS DREADNOUGHT *DOYSTOYOV*
FINAL APPROACH TO HEIMATAR REGION – HED CONSTELLATION
AMAMAKE SYSTEM – PLANET II: PIKE'S LANDING

Present Day

Vince let the subtle rumble of the ship's reactors soothe his nerves, taking time to reflect on Scripture and the mission at hand. Five fellow Templars were with him, strapped in four-point harnesses within the armored cabin of a Vex-class assault gunship. The remaining Templars were in a separate Vex, along with dozens of other craft and equipment crates inside the massive siege bays of the *Doystoyov.*

Their plan was to hit the Core Freedom colony from two separate directions simultaneously, using conventional forces as a diversionary frontal assault to disguise Templar-led pincer movements on the perimeter flanks. Unlike previous attacks that amassed troop numbers beyond the range of the colony's deadly antiship defenses, this attack would risk those same defenses to place a small 'multiplied' force precisely where they could inflict the most casualties.

It was extremely dangerous – completely unheard of by conventional standards. But the Templars were created to take these kinds of risks.

Specialized armored vehicles containing Templar clones and supporting state-transfer technology would be dropped from the *Doystoyov*'s siege bays into locations outside the range of fixed artillery positions. They would be supported by gunships like the Vex, plus air-dropped armored tanks, speeders, and APCs. The Navy's standing orders were to avoid damaging the space elevator at all costs and to perform thorough sweeps of its surface anchors and cables to ensure that the Valklears didn't sabotage them.

There was only enough time for the *Doystoyov* to deliver a single orbital strike, and the target was Core Freedom's northwest vehicle hangar. Imperial Command was adamant about minimizing collateral damage to preserve the colony's orbital defenses if the ground assault was successful.

Strapped across Vince's chest was a prototype Viziam ARML-20 plasma rifle, just like the one he had trained with; he was carrying about five hundred charges in clips lining his vest. His kit also contained a standard paramilitary Duvolle Labs SG-19 combat vowrtech with two extra charge packs; three 10m flay trap anti-personnel mines; six HE grenades for the underbarrel launcher of the ARML; four sets of stun cuffs; one Boundless Creation SM-15 12mm sidearm with two eighteen-round clips; one nanite injector with three 120ml canisters; and one combat knife.

The surface gravity of Pike's Landing was exactly 1.2 G's. As if Vince wasn't hauling enough weight, the primary kinetic barrier of his body armor was a 20mm layer of depleted uranium plating. Altogether, Vince and the other Templars were wearing at least sixty kilos of weight over their body mass, but he would be able to move fluidly thanks to the enhanced musculoskeletal system of his clone.

Vince felt warm – and he had ever since emerging from virtual storage. His body temperature was 39 degrees Celsius, which according to Instructor Muros was normal for his anatomy. His sense of awareness was surreal: Every detail of his surroundings was vivid and fascinating. He was also utterly without fear. To be going to war and knowing for certain that tomorrow would come was the most empowering feeling he had ever known.

He could see the same conviction in the Templars seated around him. The implants allowed them to communicate without sound; software integrated with the cybernetic devices permitted them to 'hear' others with the same degree of emotion and conviction conveyed in spoken words. Mission data and instructions from Imperial Command – directed by Lord Victor Eliade himself – were provided on an augmented-reality TACNET that interfaced with their vision.

Aside from Vince, they were all True Amarr, assorted men and women with distinctly Amarrian ethnic looks but with the clone's pale hue and deep veins that made them appear almost sickly. They had no names; they knew each other only as Templar Two, Templar Three, and so on.

Vince was Templar One.

His TACNET sprang to life with a message from the Vex pilot: *Atmospheric entry in six minutes.*

And within seconds of that notification, Templar Six began to malfunction.

MLW *MORSE*
GEOSYNCHRONOUS ORBIT
THREE HUNDRED KILOMETERS ABOVE PIKE'S LANDING

'Why are you wearing makeup?' Miles asked, without looking away from his display. 'You never, ever wear makeup. What's up?'

'Afternoon, Miles,' Blake said. 'Why don't you go sit in the airlock for a little while?'

'You're out of your league with him,' Miles warned, his fingers deftly moving splashes of ship data through the air. His ability to multi-task was legendary, if not annoying.

'Seriously,' he continued. 'I don't mean to be a dick, but a guy like that—'

'Do you know what this is?' Blake interrupted, holding up a fist. 'This is the future, when I smash your face in for not minding your own business.'

'I get it, Blake: You're lonely,' he said. 'I'm just saying, these immortals eat groupies like you for lunch,' he said, pausing for a moment. 'I mean, literally. Eat. You.'

'Shut up, Miles.'

'... And for breakfast, if you're still not satisfied ...'

'Fuck you,' she growled.

'Happily!' he exclaimed. 'And gently, given the chance. At least I'd really appreciate it. You think that guy would? Please.'

Blake slammed her fist into the console.

'Is it possible for you to just shut the fuck up? Ever?'

Miles turned toward her.

'Hear me out,' he said. 'Want to know how to make yourself absolutely irresistible to him?'

'No. I don't.'

'Make *me* your boyfriend,' he said. 'Capsuleers *love* competition. He won't be able to lay off you. Ah ... bad choice of words.'

Blake was ready to launch herself out of the chair when the bridge's sentry alarm chirped.

Miles snapped back to his instruments and froze.

'Oh, wow,' he muttered, just as Captain Jonas appeared. Korvin was right behind him.

'Report.'

'Six Imperial Navy warships just jumped in-system,' Miles said calmly.

An ominous threat Klaxon sounded; five red triangles suddenly appeared on the bridge's tactical display.

'Two battlecruisers, two battleships, and an interceptor just warped in,' Blake said urgently. 'Three hundred and seventy klicks out and closing, heading directly toward us.'

'Sound battle stations,' Jonas ordered. 'Shield hardeners up.'

The *Morse* began undulating in ghostly hues of blue and white as its reactors pumped gigajoules of power into its shield emitters.

'Done,' Blake said. 'They're targeting us—'

'You can't win,' Korvin interrupted, studying the display. The interceptor was burning toward them. If it got within range, it could cripple the *Morse*'s engines. 'You should warp away.'

'Quiet,' Jonas snapped, tapping Miles on the shoulder. 'You said there were *six* ships, not five. . . .'

TEMPLAR SIX WAS SHOUTING in a language that no one alive had ever heard. But his desperation and rage were universal as he thrashed in his restraints with violent headshakes, spittle flying everywhere as he cried out in an alien tongue.

He freed himself from the harness and reached for the pistol strapped to his thigh.

Templar Five's hand darted forward in an attempt to keep the weapon holstered; the delay gave Vince time to detach his own harness and the ARML slung across his chest.

Six managed to squeeze off a shot just as Vince smashed the rifle stock into his face, knocking him and the weapon to the deck. There was a shriek as the high-powered round slammed into the shin of Templar Three; the bullet smashed the bone into dozens of smaller projectiles that exited along with the bullet from the soldier's calf muscle. Vince discounted the wound as non-life-threatening and raised the rifle butt in preparation for a second, harder blow.

Vince struck him with a force that would have pulped the face of a normal human. But Six still managed to sweep his legs and drive him into the deck, pummeling him with a barrage of punches.

Over both the intercom and TACNET, the Vex pilot was demanding to know what was happening, warning that the drop was in less than three minutes. Vince registered this – and the fact that the *Doystoyov* was now traveling at warp speed – all while fending off the approaching combat knife of his attacker.

Templars Two and Four yanked Six off of Vince just in time, hurling him into a bulkhead.

With a soldier restraining each arm, Vince grabbed the ARML and resumed clubbing Templar Six, whose head came apart unexpectedly on the third strike, exposing part of the metallofullerene implant buried within.

Sixty seconds remained, and the Vex pilot was demanding a 'go, no-go' answer from Command.

Vince ordered the other Templars to strap themselves back in. Six had been in charge of the squad's only suppression weapon – a heavy arc cannon whose destructive power was worth the weight of carrying it around. Assuming Six's responsibility, Vince detached a nanite canister from his belt and tossed it to Templar Four, who pushed it into the chamber of an injector gun and plunged it into Three's injured leg. Vince hoped the molecular lattices would form quickly enough to support the soldier's weight before the drop.

Everyone felt a sudden surge of vertigo and disorientation as the dreadnought emerged from warp. They were in the hot zone, just seconds away from combat.

Vince was scrambling to get the arc cannon's charge packs off of Six's corpse, when Lord Victor contacted him on the TACNET.

'Situation,' Lord Victor demanded.

'Contained; good to go,' Vince replied. 'Do not reanimate Six.'

The *Doystoyov*'s bay doors began retracting beneath the Vex, revealing swirling cloud formations high above the planet's reddish green surface.

Vince ripped off his combat vest and started to put Six's on.

'Understood,' Lord Victor said. 'God be with you.'

'Ten seconds!' the pilot shouted.

Vince barely had the cannon secured to his suit when the latches holding the Vex in place released.

He and the mutilated corpse of Six began floating toward the craft's canopy as the dropship began free-falling into the atmosphere. Pulling himself toward his seat, Vince only had time to get one strap buckled in before the craft's plasma engines ignited, throwing him and the unsecured corpse violently into the other Templars.

THE CAPTAIN OF THE *DOYSTOYOV* was among the most experienced in the Imperial Navy, handpicked by Lord Victor for this special mission. Guided into the system by a cynosural beacon dropped by the cloaked sixth ship that had entered through the Osoggur stargate, the captain executed an extremely dangerous maneuver that in spacefaring slang was called a 'mountain scrape': The dreadnought had emerged directly from warp into the lowest possible altitude of the gauntlet. The *Doystoyov* was now just 141 kilometers above the surface and speeding at nearly 8,500 meters per second; a plasma bow wave was already forming ahead of the ship as its shields plowed through the mesosphere of Pike's Landing.

Precisely on schedule, the drop master announced the release of all craft in his siege bays. Their trajectories would put the Templars, conventional infantry, and supporting equipment exactly where they needed to be on the colony.

The volley of Stackfire antiship missiles rising from the surface, visible on his radar and optically on the horizon as white-orange dots atop vertical columns of smoke, was to be expected.

But the appearance of a Mordu's Legion Drake-class battlecruiser, in low orbit and within firing range, was not.

'PUT MISSILES ON THAT DREADNOUGHT right now,' Jonas muttered. 'High explosives; hurry up!'

'Tracking,' Blake said, her face awash in the glow of ship telemetry and targeting data. 'Those aren't gonna put a scratch in that thing . . . .'

'Just do it,' he barked. 'Keep bringing it until I say otherwise.'

The space surrounding the *Morse* brightened as the first salvo of Scourge heavy missiles streaked away.

'Multiple dropcraft entering the atmosphere,' Miles reported. 'Predicted trajectory places all of them on the colony.'

'No kidding,' Jonas growled, opening a direct line to Mack. The tactical display sounded a warning chirp: The interceptor had closed half the distance to the *Morse*. They had less than a minute at most.

'Mack, ordnance coming in hot! Get to shelter now, now, *now*!'

DESPITE HIS OLD AGE, General Vlad Kintreb reacted a half second faster than Mack did. The raid sirens began when the Stackfire batteries four kilometers from where they were standing hurled a dozen missiles into the air with a deafening roar. The building closest to where they were standing wasn't reinforced with energy-absorbing alloys that could protect them from a beam weapon strike; the closest such structure was more than a hundred meters away. General Kintreb ordered them into a futile sprint toward shelter, which prompted Mack to laugh, fully aware that their survival at this point had absolutely nothing to do with whether they ran, walked, or simply sat down where they were.

THE *DOYSTOYOV* WAS COMMITTED to the gauntlet; a computer would determine when to commence the bombardment. The firing solution was a one-second tight-beam exposure that would strafe a path fifteen meters wide and nine hundred meters long as it was 'walked' over the target. Whether the beam hit or not was now beyond the captain's control, and his attention shifted to ensuring that the ship had enough altitude when the incoming 'vampires' detonated.

Heavy on firepower but lacking in agility, a Revelation-class dreadnought is a huge, cumbersome ship, with a mass to the order of 1.2 million metric tons. Stackfire warheads produced a kiloton of explosive force apiece; the *Doystoyov*'s shields would redirect or absorb 80 percent of those blasts. But the remaining energy would translate directly into 'drag' that could knock the ship off course. At this altitude and speed, such an event would be catastrophic.

The captain had planned to be out of harm's way before the planetary defenses of Pike's Landing could do anything about the orbital strike. Now his weapons officer informed him that the first missile salvo from the Mordu's Legion battlecruiser would hit just a few moments before the heavy beam fired.

Then the Stackfires would arrive.

The captain ordered his bridge to prepare the engines for maximum power output, and then he sounded the collision alarm.

GABLE JUST HAPPENED to be looking in the direction of the northwest vehicle hangar when the beam lashed out from the sky.

Striking the center of the hangar, the beam raced along the damaged, reflective alloy on the rooftop and exploded violently. Some of this energy blasted inside, superheating an ammunition store and igniting secondary explosions as the beam ran off the structure.

The impact of the beam on unshielded silt and rock flash-heated it to thousands of degrees Celsius, causing it to explode, hurling fiery debris in all directions.

Gable, standing just over two kilometers from the beam as it raced off the base, was seared by extreme heat first, then thrown as the shock-wave slammed into her, Mack, General Kintreb, and their escorts.

Time seemed to slow down. Gable could hear a rising pitch in her ears; she was numb and utterly disoriented as her brain rushed to assess damage. Her survival instincts informed her that she was injured but not incapacitated and that she needed to gather her bearings quickly to survive.

Mack's disfigured, smiling face was hovering above hers. General Kintreb was alive, barking orders between heaving, wet coughs. Some of the Valklears were mortally wounded; their moans became cries as they realized the extent of their injuries. The smell of blood and ionized air filled her nostrils.

'On your feet, Lifegiver,' she could hear Mack say. 'Bad people coming.'

THE *DOYSTOYOV* CAPTAIN BELIEVED that the beam had largely missed and that his crew members were about to lose their lives for nothing.

The first missiles fired from the *Morse* struck the *Doystoyov*'s shields a second apart from each other. Although the explosive damage was largely absorbed, the impacts induced a slight yaw in the dreadnought's attitude. This exposed more surface area to the ship's forward vector, increasing the atmospheric drag caused by the shield profile, which in turn exaggerated the yaw rate even more.

Maneuvering thrusters powered by the *Doystoyov*'s reactors fired to compensate. When they did, the next volley from the *Morse* struck, invalidating the thruster firing-sequence solution applied for the previous salvo, which resulted in several degrees of unwanted downward pitch to the craft's flight attitude.

Spinning on two separate axes now, the *Doystoyov*'s catastrophe had begun, as the third and fourth salvo impacted. The captain wondered if the *Morse* was even aware of what they'd just accomplished. Cursing to God, he ordered the crew to abandon ship. But the order was pointless.

The Stackfires performed exactly as designed, rocketing higher and faster than the tumbling dreadnought toward a spot in space ahead of it, then tipping over and setting on a final intercept course.

They detonated their powerful warheads from above, pushing the *Doystoyov* deeper into the atmosphere, where she began to break apart under impossibly brutal G-forces.

If the Valklears on the surface of Pike's Landing weren't fighting for their lives, they might have noticed the long trails of the *Doystoyov*'s fiery remains cutting across the eastern sky, and celebrated the deaths of nearly six thousand Imperial Navy servicemen.

'*NO!*' JONAS SHOUTED, visibly shaken. 'Mack, are you alright?'

There was nothing but static on the line. Visual tracking was impossible: The strike saturated the area with a dust cloud that was still expanding. Scratchy infrared video showed that the northwest hangar was leveled, and a half-kilometer-long ditch about sixty meters wide had been carved into the steppes north of the colony. The thermal effect of the blast alone was lethal to within a kilometer of the beam's path, but the overpressure wave would extend slightly farther. No one had any idea where Mack was standing when the strike came down, let alone if he had been under shelter when it did.

There was little time to find out, as fourteen beams slammed into the Drake's shields.

'Those battleships are in range,' Miles warned. 'And they are *pissed*!'

'Shields will be depleted in thirty seconds at this rate,' Blake reported. 'That interceptor will be here in half that.'

Korvin, who appeared nervous himself, was shaking his head.

'Warp out,' he said. 'You can't help them from here.'

Jonas shot him a withering glare as the radio came alive.

'*Morse*, away team,' Mack said. 'Need extraction.'

Jonas rushed to Miles's console and manipulated the tactical display, zooming to the colony map. There were several abandoned ore-processing plants a short distance away from the colony perimeter and therefore not likely an immediate priority for the Amarrian forces invading to the south.

'Can you reach the ore processors to the north?'

'Affirmative.'

'Get there now,' Jonas ordered. 'Talk to me, Wildcat-Nine; what's your status?'

The display showed that the Mordu gunship was still loitering in the mountain range to the north.

'Ah, copy *Morse*,' the pilot said. 'Running bingo on loiter fuel, but we haven't been detected.'

'Can you do an extraction at the ore processors and get east of that caldera for a polar ascent?'

'Affirmative, if it's within ten mikes,' the pilot answered. 'After that we'll have to shed mass to get topside.'

'Got it,' Jonas answered. 'Mack, can you get there in time?'

'Yes,' Mack answered. 'Hurry, Jonas.'

Another series of beams struck the *Morse*.

'Alright, *go*,' Jonas shouted. 'Miles, warp us out of here!'

VINCE CAME TO HIS SENSES with the help of a fellow Templar. Self-diagnostics revealed painful contusions in the muscles of his neck and back. Worse, his knee was damaged, and that would impact his ability to fight. He was pushed to one side as the Vex banked through the clouds; Vince looked through a viewport and saw the towering spires of the Core Freedom space-elevator complex. His TACNET told him that the huge mushroom cloud in the distance was the remnants of the northwest vehicle hangar, which housed most of the colony's primary air and mechanized defenses. Armored mobile-clone banks just like the one he had trained with had been dropped at strategic locations near the colony and, for the time being, were secure.

Distress calls flashed across the TACNET: Two troop gunships were downed by antiaircraft fire. There were survivors, with casualties, surrounded by hostiles and taking fire. With the exception of Vince, who would work alone due to the malfunction of Six, the Templars would work in pairs and disable the remaining AA defenses; the rest would assist the survivors. Both teams would then commence search-and-destroy missions on vital installations, taking all the locations where the Valklears could make their last stand.

Roaring over the southern entrance, the Vex overflew conventional troops advancing on the colony's crippled defenses. Vince howled in delight as its cannons opened fire on an MTAC, its shells sending fragments of the aging machine hurling into the air. From the rear hatch, he watched it topple over in flames, then whispered a prayer for the pilot struggling to free himself from the wreckage.

What a tragedy, Vince thought as he watched him burn. *If he had only embraced the faith ...*

'One, get ready!' the pilot shouted.

The Vex was circling over a hardened outpost, its sensor-directed cannons sweeping the rooftops for snipers or traps; Vince's TACNET confirmed that the main building was directing air defenses for this sector of the colony. Resistance would be heavy, but he was still expected to seize it intact. Vince quickly assembled the arc cannon, locking one of its charge packs into place. The weapon hummed to life as power rushed into its primers.

He was adjusting the range output for close-quarters combat when small-arms fire began peppering the gunship's hull.

'Go!' the pilot ordered.

Vince leapt out the hatch, falling four full meters. On landing, he felt sharp pain in his damaged knee but ignored it.

The installation entrance opened. A grenade was heaved out.

Dropping low for maximum explosiveness, Vince propelled himself sideways. He crashed into the silt and rolled over as fast as he could.

The world flashed red with phosphenes as a loud *thud* smashed his eardrums. White-hot shrapnel found seams in his armor; Vince felt blinding pain.

Dust and rock were still falling from the air as three Valklears emerged from the building, crouched low, weapons tucked tight in front of them, looking for him.

From a prone position, Vince's enhanced muscles swung the heavy weapon in front of him and squeezed the trigger.

A stream of plasma leapt from the barrel, striking two of the Valklears directly. The first man exploded as the seventeen-thousand-degree-Celsius arc struck the body armor in his chest. The second man was cut in half cleanly: The arc swept through his torso, leaving his detached extremities unscathed.

The third man was blinded as the arc carved a molten gash into the building he had just left; white-hot material caught him flush in the face, burning deep into his flesh. Screaming, he swung his weapon about, wildly spraying automatic rounds.

Vince snapped the SM-15 out of its holster and dropped him with a single shot.

The pistol's wet grip reminded him that he was bleeding. Instructor Muros was right: He felt unbelievable agony but was somehow able to power through it. The blood trickling down his wrists had a strange reflective sheen to it, reminding him that he was something more than just human, that he had become an Archangel of God.

Plunging another nanite injection into his skin, Vince willed himself to his feet. He reloaded the arc cannon and stormed the building, unleashing its purifying fire on all who stood in his path.

MACK PUSHED GABLE behind an overturned APC and set Kintreb down beside her. The General was unconscious and bleeding from both ears. Gable suspected massive head trauma, first from the overpressure wave that passed over them, then compounded as his head struck the rocky ground when they tumbled. The old General's body just couldn't withstand much more war – and Gable sensed that adrenaline was masking the severity of her own injuries.

She saw Mack drop to a knee and fire a long burst from his plasma rifle. Her hearing was muted: The weapon's report should have sounded much louder. Small-arms fire was crashing into the APC as two more Valklears were mowed down trying to reach their position; puffs of exploding stone erupted all around them as they fell.

Gable instinctively put herself in triage mode and left the General's survival to God. Fixating on the nearest Valklear, she crawled out from behind cover to reach him, searching for breath or heartbeats and finding neither.

Tearing the soldier's vest away, she began chest compressions. Silt and debris peppered her face as more gunfire tore into the ground before her. She breathed into the soldier's mouth three times; as she went back to restart the man's heart, she was forcibly yanked backward.

She finally realized there was nothing but a bloody stump where his hips and legs should have been.

Mack was trying to tell her something, when the ground shook beneath them. The mercenary pushed her head down, where she felt rather than heard a spectacular noise. Glancing upward, she saw the metallic-rust underside of a friendly MTAC as it stepped over them toward the danger, its cannons spitting a *brrrp brrrp brrrp* staccato of thunder that rumbled down the landscape.

A dark ring was forming around Gable's field of vision when a Minmatar 'Kwaal' armored transport arrived. Its turret was blasting away, spewing ejected shells into the air as the rear hatch swung open. Two soldiers rushed out; one was an officer named Bishop. Both headed directly toward General Kintreb.

Mack ran inside the Kwaal and emerged seconds later with a medkit. He knelt in front of Gable and gently brushed the hair away from her eyes, peering closely into them. He frowned as though he didn't like what he saw, and she suddenly felt a jolt of ice water flush through her veins. She gasped violently as he tossed the spent adrenaline casing aside.

Her hearing and vision returned with vivid clarity.

'... it's over,' Commander Bishop was saying. 'AA defenses just went off-line. Fall back to the medical ward; that's as good a spot as any to give 'em a fight.'

'Where do we bring Kintreb?' the soldier demanded, peering around the transport with his rifle.

'Offworld,' Mack said. 'Leave now; my gunship get us out.'

A huge explosion rumbled from downrange; a fireball was rising to the east. Bishop's comm radio erupted with chatter.

'They took it already!' Bishop cried, throwing his helmet down in disgust. '*Fuck!* How are they doing this?'

'Gunship only way,' Mack said calmly, even as beam fire struck the vehicle. 'This colony lost. Live to fight another day.'

'Who the fuck asked you?' the other soldier exclaimed. 'Stay out of this, you fucking merc—'

In one smooth motion, Mack withdrew his sidearm and shot the Valklear between the eyes, then pointed the weapon at Bishop.

'What ... are you doing?' Gable breathed.

'Surviving,' Mack said, taking a step toward the open hatch with his weapon still trained on the acting Valklear commander. 'Eight minutes left to reach safety. Kwaal get there in seven if leave now.'

Bishop was stunned. The sound of a gunship roaring overhead and another explosion – this time, dangerously close by – brought him back to his senses.

'Fine,' he said, kneeling to lift General Kintreb. 'You better be right, you son of a bitch.'

VINCE EMERGED FROM THE OUTPOST damaged but victorious: The air defenses of Core Freedom were now under Imperial command. New orders appeared in his TACNET: Patrol the ore processors east of his position and eliminate all hostile forces. The Valklears had been routed and were retreating in isolated clusters toward the mountains or badlands.

The terrain was elevated and rocky. The most direct route east was impassable by vehicle; the longer route was a winding valley road a few dozen meters below him. He opted to stay hidden and take the more difficult path by working the higher ground.

A few moments into his trek, his determination was rewarded: A vehicle was approaching on the road below. Vince identified it as a Kwaal-class armored transport, and he could see that it was already damaged.

The arc cannon had enough charge left for a single shot.

DRIVING AS FAST AS THE VEHICLE could go, Commander Bishop was planning ways in which he could kill Mack, when he was blinded by a white flash.

Unable to see, he sensed the front of the vehicle drop abruptly, then flip several times before coming to rest on its side.

Bishop became disoriented, as he was no longer concerned about killing Mack or saving the General's life. Unable to remember how he got there, he felt sluggish, as though he were dreaming, and that he would wake at any moment.

VINCE CURSED AT HIMSELF for not destroying the truck outright. Aiming for the engine block, the plasma arc had cut through the front of the transport cleanly, all the way through the axle behind the front wheels. But the bolt was too far behind the reactor, which escaped unscathed. With no explosion or fire to assure casualties, he would have to get in close to finish the job.

Discarding the cannon, Vince hurried down the treacherous valley, alternating attention between his footing and the overturned vehicle.

From about forty meters out, he heard voices and snapped his sidearm forward. . . .

GABLE REGAINED CONSCIOUSNESS with the sensation of being dragged.

'Told you it protects,' she could hear Mack saying. 'Always bring *good* fortune.'

A sharp slap to the face brought her to clarity. The deranged mercenary had propped her up against the transport's undercarriage.

General Kintreb was facedown next to her, still unconscious. She couldn't tell if he was dead.

Mack was pressing a gun into her hand.

'Very simple to use,' he said, reaching into her jacket pocket and retrieving the small toy soldier he'd given her. With delicate care, he gently placed it on the road beside her, adjusting it once to suit his preference. Satisfied, he unhooked a grenade from his waist and slammed it down next to the toy.

'If I no return,' he said, pointing to the figurine, 'find strength to die well.'

He disappeared around the side of the shattered vehicle, and the air erupted with the crackle of gunfire.

VINCE WAS CAUGHT OFF GUARD by the speed and accuracy of the attacker.

The target's weapon fired at the precise instant its barrel fully cleared the vehicle's overturned rear. Not one, but two rounds struck Vince square in the chest, sending him tumbling down the remaining incline onto the road.

While powerful enough to blast pockmarks into stone, the lead plasma bolts that struck him couldn't penetrate the depleted uranium plating in his body armor.

Vince emerged from the forward tumble in a kneeling firing position and shot four times.

The first three missed. The last one exploded in the attacker's upper chest, leaving a dark mist in the air as he crashed to the ground.

He struggled once, then ceased.

Pleased with himself, Vince set out to finish off any remaining survivors.

WHEN THE GUNFIRE STOPPED, Gable looked at the weapon in her hand and decided this wasn't the way she wanted to die.

As the tunnel vision began to return, she tossed the gun aside, reached into her coat, and pulled out the Amarr pendant. Raising its golden holy symbol to eye level, she began to pray.

'Lord, the hour of death is upon me,' she said aloud. *'I have sinned and I have loved, I was wayward and then Reclaimed. Though my flesh becomes dust, in you I am eternal; you gave me life, and now I shall return it, to you, for Amarr, everlasting. Amen.'*

'Blessed be the Prophet Kuria,' a familiar voice said, startling her. *'Amen.'*

When she saw his face, the recognition seized her.

'You are Reclaimed,' he marveled, putting his weapon aside and kneeling. 'I was moments from purging the world of you when I heard you pray . . . .'

She looked at his face and told herself it just couldn't be.

And yet, it was.

'*Vince . . . !*' she whispered.

His eyes widened. He was Templar One. That is what Her Majesty had decreed and what Instructor Muros had affirmed.

But the name *Vince* was maddeningly familiar.

'I know that name,' he said. 'Who are you?'

The sound of a gun's report and a metallic *ka-chink* filled the air. Vince's head rocked violently to the side in a spray of blood. He slumped over.

The breath left Gable's lungs, and she began to weep.

'That sound *funny*,' Mack said, emerging from the far side of the wreck. Brownish-colored fluid was spurting from a cybernetic injury on his left side, where wrecked machinery was now exposed. One arm was dangling from a handful of metal tendons. The other, organic one was unharmed.

Standing over the corpse, he poked the rifle's barrel through bits of Vince's skull and brains until it hit something hard.

'*Very* funny,' he said, clearing the gore away to reveal the implant's formidable size.

Mack clicked his radio.

'Wildcat-Nine, negative on ore processors. Need pickup in valley south of there. Three to go.'

'Ah, copy Mack,' the pilot answered. 'But if we're not there in three mikes . . .'

'Understood,' Mack said, kneeling down. 'Lifegiver, you should look away.'

Before the tunnel vision overwhelmed her, Gable saw Mack reach into the cavity with his good hand and attempt to detach the implant in Vince's mangled skull.

TEMPLAR ONE REAWAKENED, full of rage.

He blinked away the apocalyptic visions, the desperate beings with the dark eyes, and now, a name – *Vince* – and the Believer who dared to say it.

Pushing himself through the door of the armored clone tank, he ignored the orders on his TACNET and jumped into the speeder waiting nearby.

Hovering just centimeters off the pavement, he raced south, passing the ore processors he was ordered to secure.

Approaching the bend where the wrecked Kwaal would be, he raised the stock assault rifle to firing position. Rounding the corner at 120 kilometers per hour, his brain barely registered the Mordu's Legion gunship idling over the wreck before its cannons swiveled in his direction.

Throwing himself off just in time, Vince crashed hard into the pavement and tumbled furiously for a dozen meters as the speeder was shredded.

He came to rest on his back, just in time to feel the downwash from the gunship as it moved overhead. The rear hatch was still open, and the disfigured man who shot him was standing in its doorway, staring him down as the craft sped eastward.

FROM A MOUNTAIN PERCH several kilometers away, Tatiana Czar carefully disassembled the high-powered zoom lens of her reconnaissance equipment. Her report to CONCORD would specify that Mordu's Legion was an active combatant in the fight for Core Freedom Colony at Pike's Landing, and that at least one of its operatives, in addition to the Valklears, had made contact with the first immortal soldiers of New Eden.

PART IV

Precipice

24

GENESIS REGION – EVE CONSTELLATION
THE NEW EDEN SYSTEM

>>*SIGNIFICANCE* MISSION LOG ENTRY
>>BEGIN RECORDING

I must have been drugged, for I awoke with no recollection of falling asleep. For a few moments I was completely disoriented, reeling from old memories that haunted my dreams.

The cold voice of my captor brought me back to my senses.

'Sleep well, Doctor?' Grious asked. 'You're going to need your strength.'

The medical drone standing beside me was doing the talking.

'Communicating will be more effective this way,' Grious continued, as the drone's hands clamped forcefully on my arm and yanked me to my feet.

Its grip was unbreakable; the machine's three irises narrowed on me. I was hauled in the direction of the research lab with all the courtesy due a convicted felon.

'Your Sleeper research was primitive science driven by meaningless ambition,' Grious said. 'I'm going to show you the error of your ways.'

The lab was as I remembered leaving it: Several Sleeper implants remained suspended in their diagnostic chambers. A projection of the modified human brain, and the soldier clone I designed to accommodate it, hovered over the dissection gurney.

Then I noticed the alien-looking cables and machinery growing from the datacore housing beneath the deck grating.

'You don't know what you've done,' Grious said, releasing his grip. The door to the lab shut behind me. 'You have no idea.'

'I'm confident in my work,' I said. 'I don't expect you to understand that.'

'Falek ordered you to create a monster to serve in an immortal army,' Grious said. 'You delivered a clone that will live five years at most. Clever.'

'A soldier you can't control is useless,' I said. 'We leashed their immortality in exchange for their service. Their flesh is just a means to an end.'

'And what end is that?' Grious asked, as the metallic green machinery continued to grow over the equipment like a malignant cancer. 'Amarr banners hanging from every hall in New Eden?'

The growth reached the diagnostic chambers and branched around them. Its skin started to merge with the chamber surface, leaching into its electronics and hijacking the delicate sensors, CPUs, and nanotech pathways within.

'Of course,' I said. 'For the good of us all.'

The projection focused on the cranial anatomy, highlighting the extra lobe and Sleeper implant within.

'You couldn't reverse-engineer this technology,' Grious said. 'So to compensate for your ineptitude, you harvested as many of them as your military could find.'

'There was no *time* to reverse-engineer them,' I said, becoming agitated. 'Her Majesty was impatient, as was Lord Grange. The technology works with the right supporting anatomy, and if I wasn't isolated on this damn ship—'

I was heaved off my feet and slammed onto the gurney beside the suspended implants. Dark green metal slipped over my neck, cheek, thighs, and ankles.

'You're fond of pointing out that I cannot feel emotions,' Grious said. 'But I want to think that if I could, I would enjoy doing this to you.'

Whether from fear or amusement I cannot say, but I broke into laughter.

'You're so pathetic,' I snorted between wheezes. 'Of all the joys in life to envy, it's torture that reminds you that you have no soul. . . .'

'I'm not going to torture you,' the Jove said, as I felt a probe insert into my neuro-interface socket. 'I'll leave that to your own conscience.'

In a crushing rush of vertigo, the drone's three irises pulled away as I was transported someplace else. My self-awareness was inexplicably suppressed to the periphery. I stood upon a mountain overlooking a spectacular metropolis that floated above the sea: What I saw was not possible within the realm of physics. There were strange beings with me – humanoid things that my new awareness recognized and loved. One was a child; she stood close and took my hand. The piece of me that remained recoiled at the sight of these creatures. Their eyes were all blue, with no whites within them at all. They had no hair and bore translucent skin that revealed grayish veins beneath.

But the bond I felt to the ones standing beside me was overwhelming. I did not know this emotion in my real life, for it was strong, very much maternal, and brought with it a blissful sense of belonging and harmony.

They were leading me past the spectacular view to a swirling vortex – an impossible wormhole not suspended in space but localized on the world where I stood. I felt the little creature at my side take my hand and lead me inside, where the ground beneath my feet disappeared as we were instantly transported to its terminus.

There I couldn't believe my eyes: We were hovering just above the galactic plane. I knew, somehow, that New Eden was down there somewhere among its majestic, spiral arms – an insignificant cluster of stars among hundreds of millions of celestial companions. We stayed for a moment, just long enough for the part of me that remained to feel tears of awe streaming down my cheeks. Then we began accelerating, faster and faster toward an area near the galactic center and into a starfield.

I saw a perimeter forming; a dark sphere emerged where there should have been more points of light. A brilliant line opened about its circumference as we accelerated closer, and it kept growing larger and larger to where my eyes could resolve the details on an impossibly colossal structure. This line was an opening large enough for an entire planet to fit through. As we passed, I realized this civilization had built an empire that enveloped an entire star, harnessing all its energy.

The little one gripped my hand again, looking up to me with those haunting, loving eyes, and we were transported back to the city. I saw – no, I *felt* – the presence of billions upon billions of souls. I felt all their beating hearts as though they were my own, and saw a home that was everything my family wanted it to be, in a society that was, in every sense of the word, heaven.

And then I saw them.

Those depraved creatures with soulless black eyes, devoid of emotion, being rightfully persecuted for threatening our way of life. They warned us that we were all blind to a sinister truth. They spoke of awakening to a new reality, and I found them as repulsive as poison. The guilty were marked with a shameful sign – a symbol I could not read – and forcibly removed from the community.

I felt such hatred for them. They were the only blemish in a perfect life.

But these outcasts somehow persevered. The world suddenly changed: Epic, tragic calamity struck without warning, and I knew those wretches were responsible. A horrible nightmare was unfolding: The little one was ripped from my arms, and the great floating city started to burn and crumble into the sea. I felt anguish and pain, a sickening feeling of loss, of being unable to comprehend that this was really happening, of the thought that those black-eyed demons would prevail, and of the crushing end to me as the city of heaven collapsed for good.

I awoke screaming.

The restraints around my body retracted, leaving me to curl in anguish. The grief I felt was indescribable, so intense as to be physically disabling.

'What was that?' I heaved. 'Who were they?'

'That was the memory of a person,' the drone said, motioning toward the Sleeper implant. 'One perspective among trillions in a civilization fighting for its life.'

'What civilization?' I gasped. 'What race is this?'

'The Sleeper race that you and your crusade are exterminating,' Grious said. 'You have unleashed an Armageddon in their world and your own.'

25

PLACID REGION – VIRIETTE CONSTELLATION
VEY SYSTEM – PLANET III: MER NOIRE
ASTRAL MINING TERRAFORMING COLONY: CAMP STOCKTON
SOVEREIGNTY OF THE GALLENTE FEDERATION

Sixty-eight Years Ago

Two years had passed since a mysterious man named Savant left the shop where Jacus was running a failing business.

In that time, Roden Shipyards underwent a drastic transformation. From its humble beginnings as a start-up shuttle-servicing depot, the firm was now the largest air- and dropship service provider at Mer Noire, and was building two brand-new facilities on separate colonies in Placid. The pace of success was nearly overwhelming; every time Jacus added capacity or expanded operations, new business immediately filled it in.

Savant had been true to his word: The customers he promised began appearing the day after he disappeared. The pilots themselves were pleasant enough – mostly Intaki, with a few shady Minmatar regulars. Other than small talk, Jacus rarely engaged them, and they didn't offer much information about themselves. Conversations were about the service and little else, unless there were special instructions from 'premium clients' to 'keep this one out of view' or to 'get this job turned around in an hour.'

Whenever Jacus needed to hire people – mechanics, technicians, accountants, whomever – the right people always seemed to find him. When he needed space to expand, the right real estate somehow became available. Tenants that had been entrenched in coveted locations for years would suddenly leave if he expressed an interest. When he needed government permits to build on planets or in space, they were fast-tracked through the bureaucracy and approved almost overnight.

If Jacus Roden needed anything at all, it just happened for him, effortlessly.

And he hated it. So much so that he was disgusted with himself and the 'enterprise' that bore his name.

Yes, he had become a wealthy man. And yes, he could take pride in knowing that he was operating his business as efficiently as possible, making the most of his 'good fortune.' But in truth there was a powerful organization behind his every accomplishment. His entrepreneurial dream was subsidized by a drug cartel. In his mind, Jacus felt he had really accomplished nothing, and that was something to be ashamed of. Roden Shipyards was an unacceptable venture, antithetical to the hardworking values his family had instilled and to the Federation of which he was proud to call himself a citizen.

The breaking point happened with one of his 'premium service' customers.

Ivan was a fellow of Mannar descent who operated a tow shuttle, a deceptively powerful dropship with a huge thrust-to-weight ratio that could ferry lighter craft beneath it. Ivan showed up perhaps once every couple of months and would only announce his visit moments before arriving at the yard, always late at night, with his suspended cargo covered in a massive tarp, ready to be lowered into the receiving latches of the repair bay.

Many vehicles bore clues about where they had been operating. The type of soot that accumulated on intakes could be traced back to a particular continent, for example, and perhaps specks of dirt or clay could place one near a known settlement or colony on Mer Noire.

Ivan's deliveries always had special damage, usually the kind that indicated they had been shot at. This, along with all the evidence that placed the crafts in specific geographical regions, made him a 'premium client,' which demanded Jacus's services in the highest priority. Ivan's business always jumped to the front of the queue, because he always had the biggest problems to hide.

What made this evening special was that it marked the first time Ivan ever bothered to apologize for the inconvenience.

'Sorry for the late notice,' he said. 'Just replace what you can't clean. And make sure all the scrap goes away. Don't reuse it. Make it vanish.'

Jacus didn't know what Ivan was talking about until he got near the cabin, long after the retractable roof was closed and the smell started reaching him. He took one look inside and had to turn away.

He ordered his staff not to come near it, even though they probably wouldn't be surprised.

Three dead Federation police officers were sprawled facedown in the cabin. Their hands were bound behind them; patterns of dried blood were sprayed on the walls and floor. Jacus was no forensics expert, but these men looked like they had been tortured and then executed. The corpses were bloated, leaking fluid, and starting to turn black. Whoever they were, they'd been dead for a while.

And now they were in his goddamn shop.

In the past year, Roden Shipyards had bought the warehouses adjacent to the original establishment. One had been converted into a plasma-jet repair bay, where engines could be removed, serviced, and, most importantly, tested. Secured into place, an engine could be safely opened to full throttle inside. To verify thrust output against engine specifications, the exhaust was vectored against a steel-reinforced ceramic blast plate that was two meters thick.

It just so happened that an engine from Ivan's previous delivery was still bolted in place.

Jacus sent his workers home for the night. He'd take this one himself.

*

THE PASSENGER AND CARGO CABINS of modern airships tended to be modular, built with reinforced cage frames designed to withstand some emergencies and protect the contents. Most could be swapped out to accommodate additional cargo capacity, say, to transport goods that needed to be kept refrigerated or even submerged. This Allotek 'Regatta' shuttle was no different. By morning, its entire cabin was propped against the blast plate, evidence facing toward the business end of a CreoDron 'Solar Flare' Series Model Y-112A plasma engine nozzle.

The stench of decomposing flesh was overwhelming; Jacus gagged several times before he finished setting everything up. Fortunately, the warehouse was equipped with a retractable roof as well, and once it was opened, the pressure differential would suck the evidence out into the thin Mer Noire air.

Donning a mask, Jacus punched in the sequence. As the gears ground away to pull the metal dome apart, the door chime rang. But it was far too early for his staff to return.

Checking the security feed, he saw two men in breathing masks standing outside the main entrance next door. One turned toward the camera and showed a Federation Police badge.

Jacus slammed his hand down on the knob that fired the engine. A few hundred thousand kilos of white-hot thrust slammed into the blast plate, igniting the shuttle cabin briefly. The corpses vaporized; even the bones turned to ash. He opened the throttle even more; the cabin frame began to melt.

Nothing organic could withstand that heat. The cabin itself was now an unrecognizable puddle of slag. He'd need to leave the roof open to let the mess – not to mention his own nerves – cool off a bit.

'MY NAME IS DETECTIVE LACROIX, Federation Customs,' the older man said. 'Are you the proprietor here?'

'I am,' Jacus acknowledged. 'Can I get you gentlemen something to drink?'

'No thanks,' the younger one said. 'I'm Lieutenant Bergen. Would you mind if we had a look around?'

'Not at all,' Jacus answered. 'May I ask what brings you here?'

'Well, a few things, actually,' Detective LaCroix said, tucking his breathing mask away. 'We've been having some run-ins with Serpentis lately, and word is they love doing business with Roden Shipyards.'

'Serpentis?' Roden said. 'Nonsense. I'd know if they were coming here.'

'I'm sure you would,' Lieutenant Bergen said, pulling out a datapad. 'So, are they?'

'No . . .' Jacus answered, trying to force his heart to calm down. 'I mean, no client of mine has expressly identified themselves as such, if that's what you mean.'

'Right,' Detective LaCroix said. 'The second reason we're here is because we're looking for a vehicle of interest involved in a shoot-out west of here several days ago at Camp Branover. Was there a Regatta-class shuttle airlifted here last evening, Mr Roden?'

Shit.

'There was, actually, yes.'

'Good answer,' Lieutenant Bergen said. 'Now, before we ask to go see it, is there anything you want to tell us about it?'

'I'm sorry, but I don't know what to say,' Jacus said, half honestly. 'This is all a surprise.'

'Business sure picked up for you the last couple of years,' Bergen said, looking around. 'Six drop shops have closed since you opened your doors. How does that make you feel?'

'Terrible, to be honest,' Jacus said. 'It's unfortunate, but that's the price of free enterprise.'

'Ah, but it isn't "free" if the enterprise doesn't play by the rules,' Bergen said. 'We think someone's got a big leash on you. You want to tell us who that is? We might be able to help.'

'I really don't know what you're talking about,' Jacus said, allowing some agitation to show. 'I have many customers, some regulars, but I don't ask where they're from. It's none of my business.'

'You know, you look tired,' Detective LaCroix commented. 'Have you been working all night?'

'I was, actually.'

'On what?'

'Some engine repairs for a client.'

'We saw the roof open up next door,' Lieutenant Bergen said. 'I didn't see any craft coming or going, so I just assumed you were looking to air the place out.'

'Plasma engines produce a lot of exhaust,' Jacus answered. 'Keeping the roof open is just part of the job.'

'Fair enough,' Lieutenant Bergen said. 'Let's see the Regatta that arrived last night.'

'Or better yet,' Detective LaCroix said, leaning in close. 'You can start talking to us about Serpentis.'

Jacus alternated glances at both officers.

'I'm afraid I'm going to have to ask both of you to leave,' he said. 'I'm not answering any more questions without legal representation.'

Detective LaCroix smiled.

'Legal?' he said. 'Who said anything about this being legal?'

Before Jacus knew what hit him, the detective lunged forward, grabbed him by the neck, yanked him out of his seat, and slammed him onto the floor.

'You think you're entitled to legal rights out here, you cop-killing fuck?' he snarled.

'Whoa, boss,' Lieutenant Bergen said. 'Wait-wait-wait–*don't*—'

Jacus felt the first kick take the wind from his lungs, then heard a loud snap as his ribs exploded in pain.

'Oh, great,' Lieutenant Bergen protested. 'You trying to get us thrown in jail?'

'Shut the fuck up,' Detective LaCroix growled, reaching down and grabbing Jacus by the collar. 'Let's go see what'cha got in the shop, you little shit.'

Jacus was too winded to resist; he was certain his lung was punctured.

He was dragged and then thrown into the hangar bay.

Detective LaCroix began sniffing the air like a slaver hound.

'Whew, you smell that?' he taunted. 'It stinks like rotten meat in here! Is that someone's lunch, Roden?'

Jacus coughed up a glob of blood.

'Detective, *fuck*,' Bergen said, shaking his head. 'Knock it off!'

'*Look*,' LaCroix sneered, pointing at the shuttle hanging overhead. 'A Regatta with a missing cabin. See those tail markings, Bergen?'

'No, I don't.'

'Me neither,' he said. 'Why? Because they've been painted over, that's why.'

Another brutal kick slammed into Jacus's midsection, forcing blood through his sinuses.

He was yanked up by his hair.

'Give me names, you son of a bitch,' LaCroix snarled. 'I want to know the name of the pilot who brought this here; I want to know who's funding you; I want the IDs of all your employees, and I want it all. Right. Fucking. *Now*.'

Jacus tried to say something and was slapped anyway.

'Hurry up!' LaCroix shouted.

'Stop being an asshole!' Bergen pleaded. 'Give him a chance to breathe!'

'Bergen, you are such a pussy sometimes, you know that?' LaCroix growled. Jacus was wondering if the corpses he'd just incinerated were once this man's close friends. 'Go sit in the cruiser while I do some real police work.'

'I figured you'd say that,' Bergen sighed, pulling a vowrtech out from under his coat and pointing it directly at LaCroix.

'Oh, please,' the detective snarled. 'Put that thing away before I shove it up your ass.'

'Yeah, you'd like that,' Bergen said, pumping the compact rifle once. 'Regards from Savant, Detective.'

The vowrtech's ominous report made Jacus flinch as a magnetically- focused air blast slammed into the detective at more than 670 meters per second, throwing him backward as if he'd been crushed in the stomach by a swinging I beam. He tumbled over several times, coming to rest directly underneath the incriminating shuttle.

'Sorry you got dinged up,' Bergen said, strolling past Jacus. 'But he was one of the guys we couldn't buy off.'

Jacus struggled to get up on one knee as Bergen primed the

vowrtech again. Detective LaCroix was moaning, his internal organs pulped by the compact overpressure wave.

'It's too bad, really,' he said, placing the barrel over his forehead. 'I liked your style.'

The blast forced the detective's brains out of his eyes, ears, and nose in a sickening gush.

Bergen sighed.

'Things are out of hand between us and the Feds,' he said, stepping away from the mess. 'Damn shame. We have deep roots here in Placid. We operate in every colony in the region. Unfortunately for you, Roden Shipyards has become too much of a good thing. You're a big brand now, and the Feds know you're dirty. That's a problem for us.'

Concentrate, Jacus told himself. *Block out the extraneous data; focus on getting to the next step.*

'They're going to come . . . looking for him,' Jacus breathed. 'Your vowrtech . . .'

'Oh, this baby's unregistered,' Bergen said, tapping the weapon like a pet. All legal firearms in the Federation were designed to broadcast a notification to a local police log that tracked whenever the weapon discharged.

But Serpentis certainly had the technical expertise to disable it.

'They won't start looking for at least a half-hour,' Bergen said. 'Which means we need to leave.'

'What about . . . him,' Jacus muttered.

'Not my problem,' Bergen said. 'You killed him. See?'

Tucking the weapon under one arm, he began pulling on the skin of his left hand; a small strip peeled away. A smooth black polymer was underneath. Bergen's arm was cybernetic.

'This stuff leaves *your* prints on everything I touch,' he said. 'The Feds won't find anything about me. You, on the other hand . . . well, what happens from here depends on how reasonable you are.'

'Why?' Jacus stammered. The pain in his lungs was unbearable.

'Because it's time to go, and we mean it,' Bergen said.

Jacus stood gingerly.

'But the shop . . .'

'Placid isn't frontier real estate anymore,' Bergen said. 'The Feds are fortifying here, so it's time for us to go underground. If we don't shut you down, they will, and we're not going to let that happen.'

Think, Jacus told himself. *Find the available options. Run interference to buy time.*

'I want to speak with Savant.'

'He wants to speak with you as well,' Bergen said. 'He's looking forward to it. I think you'll get moved up. But Roden Shipyards is done. And so we're clear that's final, you' – he set the vowrtech on the floor near the remains of Detective LaCroix – 'are now a cop killer. Public enemy number one.'

'What about you?' Jacus asked, suddenly aware that Bergen was still standing beneath the Regatta.

'Oh, I'm disappearing along with you,' he said with a laugh. 'They'll think you abducted me, tough guy. Look, you're pissed, but get over it. We both did our parts. The organization is pleased. Time to get paid, promoted, and party our asses off.'

An epiphany struck Jacus just as Bergen took a stride forward. Bergen was part cybernetic; his mechanical arm had killed Detective LaCroix. There were memory chips in the hardware that recorded mechanical actions; this was standard engineering troubleshooting protocol by the manufacturer and legally required. He couldn't be sure that Serpentis had disabled it – unless they were building the parts themselves, it was impossible to know – although it could be erased after the fact. That meant all the evidence needed to clear his name was probably still buried in the arm of this monster.

'I had to remove the entire cabin from that thing,' Jacus said, looking up. 'What happened in there?'

Bergen looked up as well; Jacus slipped a hand into his own pocket. His fingers found the datapad inside.

'Don't know; won't ask,' Bergen said. 'But they figured you could make the problem go away.'

'Yeah,' Jacus said, pulling the device out. He needed to see what he was doing. 'I'm just going to check something—'

'Hey, hey, hey,' Bergen said, picking up a step. 'Put that thing down.'

'Why?' Jacus asked, typing quickly. 'Just making sure everything's cleaned up before we go—'

Bergen pulled out his police firearm.

'Put it the fuck down!' he ordered, breaking into a sprint.

'Fine with me,' Jacus said, pressing the final key.

The magnetic latches keeping the shuttle suspended overhead abruptly turned off; the safeties on the backup clamps supporting them also released. Despite Bergen's cybernetic capabilities, he lacked the speed needed to clear the fifteen-thousand-kilogram craft as it crashed down upon him.

Now Jacus really was a cop killer.

His staff would begin arriving within the hour. Working as fast as the pain would allow, Jacus pulled himself into an MTAC to begin cutting through the wreck to get what he needed.

Once Bergen's corpse and the vowrtech that murdered Detective La-Croix were secured, Jacus welded the street-level entrances of the hangar and adjacent warehouses shut from the inside. A sleek new Duvolle Labs 'Brigantine' Model dropship that belonged to a 'premium client' was awaiting pickup later that day. Jacus planned to be gone long before its owner arrived to claim it.

As the craft cleared the retractable dome, Jacus caught a glimpse of the Federation police cruiser parked in the street below.

Roden Shipyards will go on, he thought, engaging the Brigantine's powerful thrusters, grimacing in pain as the craft lurched forward.

The taste of blood in his mouth made him all the more determined.

HEIMATAR REGION – HED CONSTELLATION
AMAMAKE SYSTEM – PLANET II: PIKE'S LANDING
CORE FREEDOM COLONY
SOVEREIGNTY: CONTESTED

Present Day

The stealthy drone tumbled out into space and disappeared in a blink, reappearing a few seconds later above Pike's Landing and settling into a polar orbit. The reddish green surface below reflected across its wide camera lens, broadcasting the imagery several AU's away to an intelligence analyst aboard the Federation Navy supercarrier GFS *Essex*.

It was immediately apparent that something ominous had just happened there.

The analyst focused on the remnants of the *Doystoyov*, whose destruction left a one-thousand-square-kilometer debris field scattered on the surface. It was an environmental catastrophe; several reactors of the former dreadnought had partially detonated, leaving a radioactive nightmare below. There were no colonists in the area, but the strong atmospheric currents of the planet would eventually circulate trace amounts of fallout back to Core Freedom. Long, black scars etched across the landscape marked where the largest fragments had impacted; all that remained of a vessel that was once nearly four kilometers in length were scraps of charred, twisted metal.

But it was more than enough to identify what kind of ship it was. And as Core Freedom itself passed beneath the drone's lenses, the imagery confirmed what the analyst had suspected all along.

The Federation warships dispatched by President Roden were too late: The Amarr Empire had taken the colony. And, judging from the number of troops and equipment scattered throughout the grounds, they had managed to do so with a surprisingly small force.

That didn't add up to the analyst at all. But he reported the facts as they were.

ESSENCE REGION – VIERES CONSTELLATION
THE LADISTIER SYSTEM – PLANET IV, MOON 4: RÉNEALT
PRESIDENTIAL BUREAU STATION
SOVEREIGNTY OF THE GALLENTE FEDERATION

'How interesting,' President Roden remarked, eyeing up the members of his cabinet as drone-reconnaissance imagery hung in the air before them. Admiral Elijah Freeman, the commander of the

Federation task force dispatched to Pike's Landing, was presenting their findings from his command aboard the GFS *Essex*.

'The analysts think this happened less than an hour ago,' he said. 'There's no debris field in space. Planetary defenses probably shot it down, but not before it dropped surface troops.'

'What's the typical siege configuration for a Revelations dreadnought?' President Roden asked.

'One division at most,' the Admiral answered. 'Less if there are mechanized battalions aboard.'

'In your estimation, should that have been enough to take the colony?' President Roden asked.

'Not at all, sir,' the Admiral said. 'The Valklears were thinned out, maybe had a mechanized brigade or two left, but were dug in and fortified. You'd have to be at division strength or greater to take them in a frontal assault.'

'So then the question we're all dying to know is why they were willing to sacrifice a dreadnought and thousands of troops to hot-drop a tiny force into the colony,' Ariel mused.

'The simplest explanation is they believed that would be enough to take it,' President Roden said, clasping his fingers together.

'Sir, one thing about this data,' Admiral Freeman said. 'It's important everyone here understands that the asymmetry is most evident with key installations inside the colony perimeter. The bulk of forces from both sides were deployed to the southwest, near the elevator terminus and primary entrance to Core Freedom. The Valklears lost about six crucial facilities, all fortified, in less than twenty minutes. And the thing is, the data is telling us that small two- to four-man fire teams took them.'

'How is that possible?' President Roden asked.

'I don't know,' Admiral Freeman said. 'It doesn't make any sense. The Valklears are some of the best troops in the cluster, and they were defending hardened, fixed positions. There is no way Imperial forces could take them all so quickly. You would need at least a platoon or two to secure any *one* of those installations in such short order, let alone all six. No combination of tactics, physical or technical, could accomplish what those fire teams just did. It's impossible.'

Admiral Ranchel snorted.

'Have you made contact with them?' he asked.

'No, sir,' Admiral Freeman said. 'They haven't detected our recon drone, either.'

'What are those?' Jacus asked, moving the pointer over the odd-shaped vehicles scattered across the colony.

'Those are the mystery trucks,' Admiral Freeman answered. 'Intel says their design resembles HAZMAT transports. Except these are armored and placed within speeder distance of every installation that was taken.'

'We're going to find out what those are and what role they played in this,' President Roden said. 'Mr Blaque, do you think we can do that?'

'As long as that Imperial fleet doesn't know we're there, yes,' he answered. 'We could send a Black Eagles recon squad down. But if they make contact, they'll need orbital support to get out safely.'

'We can do that, provided the Amarrians don't bring more firepower,' Admiral Freeman said. 'If they get support, I can't promise we'll be able to get our big guns low enough to help.'

'Send them in anyway,' President Roden ordered. 'As soon as possible.'

'For what, exactly?' Grand Admiral Ranchel demanded. 'What's the mission?'

'To learn exactly what happened there,' President Roden said. 'To recover any items of interest and report on any developments.'

'Did it ever occur to you we might not get these men back?' Admiral Ranchel asked. 'The Amarr have secured the colony; they have a space elevator to bring anything they want to the surface, and an entire goddamn fleet overhead. Sending covert ops is a waste of lives and resources.'

'Your concerns are noted,' President Roden said. 'Mr Blaque, send your commandos in. We'll do as much as we can to support them, up to and including engaging the Amarr in space and on the surface.'

Grand Admiral Ranchel opened his mouth to protest again, but Jacus cut him off.

'Stop questioning my orders,' he said, raising his hand. 'Your job is to make them happen, not whine about them. Get it done, or I'll find someone else who can.'

'Should we inform the Minmatar government?' Ariel asked.

President Roden turned toward her, his green eyes aglow.

'Absolutely *not*.'

GENESIS REGION – SANCTUM CONSTELLATION
THE YULAI SYSTEM – INNER CIRCLE TRIBUNAL STATION
SOVEREIGNTY OF THE CONCORD ASSEMBLY

'Well, well,' Tibus Heth started. 'To whom do I owe the pleasure?'

The dictator had aged visibly since the war began. He was no capsuleer, and thus more vulnerable to the passage of time than the other national leaders. As much as this endeared him to the mortal masses of the Caldari, it bespoke a subtle weakness. Rumors were circulating that his health was deteriorating – slowly, but steadily – due to something that could be cured, if only he would allow himself to be cloned. Focusing on the man's face, the Inner Circle members all projected similar thoughts: Heth was a short-term problem, and of all possibilities the least of their worries insofar as protecting humanity was concerned.

'Mr Heth, thank you for making the time to speak with us,' Director Angireh started.

'Is that you, Irhes?' Tibus asked. 'You know how I'd prefer to see your lovely face.'

'Transparency isn't one of our virtues,' she said. 'I'm sure you appreciate that.'

'I've always counted on it,' Heth said. 'It makes the game so much more interesting. What can I do for you today?'

'Mr Heth,' she said, sternly this time. 'You're aware that the development of capsuleer technology is illegal according to CONCORD law.'

'Director, I find it admirable that you have the balls to say that,' Tibus said. 'Unfortunately, it also speaks volumes about your misperceptions on just how much influence CONCORD really has.'

'I assure you, Mr Heth, that our perceptions are exactly where they need to be,' Irhes said. 'More importantly, the point of this call is to commend you for complying with this law.'

'I assure you, Irhes, that any "compliance" you're aware of just happens to align with the State's interests,' Heth said with a smile. 'But only a fool would believe that my international colleagues are doing the same.'

'We act in humanity's best interests, which by default includes the State's best interests and your own,' Irhes said.

'I *love* your audacity!' Heth laughed. 'It reminds me so much of myself.'

'Normally we don't interfere in the politics of assembly nations,' Irhes continued. 'But, again, because of your compliance with law, we thought we'd share some information that concerns you and the Directorate.'

'Oh, by all means, let's hear it,' Heth said.

'We have information from a reliable source that your next cabinet meeting has become the target of a military strike,' Irhes said.

Heth laughed again.

'Imagine!' he mocked. 'When hasn't it been?'

'Yes, the locations of these meetings are a closely guarded State secret,' Irhes said. 'So much so that we know your next one is in the Tsukuras system.'

Heth's arrogance evaporated.

'If that's what your intel says, then—'

'On the planet Myoklar,' Irhes added, enjoying the moment. 'Now, what are the odds of us guessing that?'

The dictator didn't say a word.

'We know the meeting isn't for several days,' Irhes continued. 'You might consider exploring your security options beforehand.'

'This is wonderful,' Heth finally said. 'I'm curious to learn where you get your information.'

'You shouldn't be,' Irhes said. 'On behalf of the Inner Circle, DED, and CONCORD, I'd like to take this opportunity to thank you for your continued support and cooperation. We look forward to strengthening our alliance with the Caldari State as partners in the mandate to protect humanity from the abuses of immortality. Good day, Mr Heth.'

The transmission ended with the angry face of the Caldari dictator staring back at them.

'Brilliant,' Tatoh said. 'Absolutely well played.'

'That's the power of information for you,' Irhes said. 'I think we have a steadfast ally in the Caldari State now. Heth is so scared of his own shadow that he'll cooperate fully.'

'Assuming THANATOS was right,' Esoutte said. 'Which we can never know.'

'Oh, it was right. Trust me on that one,' Tatoh scoffed, then paused as the imagery above them abruptly disappeared.

The THANATOS report arrived from Pike's Landing, and the remaining meeting agenda was instantly cleared. Recorded footage of the battle taken by the agent, along with her tactical assessments and a particular focus on the strange armored trucks scattered throughout the colony, danced overhead.

Irhes spoke first, the letters and words forming in the air for all to see:

>> THANATOS DIRECTIVE–TIER- 1 PRIORITY – WITH IMMEDIATE EFFECT:

>> NEW ORDERS

>> PRIMARY OBJECTIVES:

— CAPTURE PROTOTYPE SOLDIER TECHNOLOGY INTACT. RETURN PHYSICAL SPECIMEN TO YULAI.

— ELIMINATE ALL WITNESSES OR INTERFERING PARTIES.

>> OPERATIONAL RESTRICTIONS:

— NONE. ALL DIPLOMATIC RESTRAINTS REMOVED.

>> SECONDARY OBJECTIVE:

— DESTROY ALL REMAINING TECHNOLOGY.

>> END DIRECTIVE

There was silence in the chamber.

'Any objections?' Irhes asked finally.

'Director, we're too *late*,' Tara said. 'Why do this now?'

'The mandate decrees we're well within our right to confiscate illegal technology,' Irhes repeated. 'We discussed this.'

'The mandate doesn't give us the right to assassinate people!' Tara protested. 'You're going to destroy New Eden's faith in CONCORD!'

'No,' Tatoh said. 'This is going to restore it.'

PURE BLIND REGION – MDM8-J CONSTELLATION
SYSTEM 5ZXX-K – PLANET V, MOON 17
MORDU'S LEGION HQ STATION

The list of contracts was long and exhausting to look at.

One by murderous one, Mordu worked through the night to review them, often checking directly with on-site field captains to either share a laugh or issue a stern reprimand. His attention to detail was both meticulous and ruthless. He held every operative of the Legion responsible for fulfilling the terms of an agreement signed in blood and redeemable with hard currency.

There were no easy decisions. With the flick of a finger he signed off on a contract to field twelve thousand crew and officers for several newly commissioned Federation battleships assigned to a capsuleer militia. The expected survival rate for the mission was about 30 percent.

The next one required a company-size unit of mercenaries to put down a rebellion on a space-elevator construction project in the Geminate region. Civilian casualties were predicted to reach 60 percent.

On it went into the night, this madness of reconciling lives, money, and risk. And finally, as the last and most important contract of the evening appeared on his screen, Mordu opened his second bottle of whiskey.

For this one, his own blood was on the line. The redeemable currency was the assassination of a dictator and the prelude to a civil war.

The contract issuer, Haatakan Oiritsuu, was in Mordu's own words, 'most irritating bitch of a nuisance to mankind since the EVE Gate collapsed.' Yet there was a time, in his younger, wilder days, when those qualities were strangely irresistible to him: a destructive love-hate relationship that was more of a twisted hormonal fetish than anything resembling true romance. It was the allure of power, he knew, that kept them coming back to each other.

Back then, she was a young and promising executive in the most prestigious mega-corporation of the Caldari State, and he was a shadowy mercenary who answered to no one. No risk was too great for either one. They demanded each other's professional services in the field and in the bedroom – over and over, as he recalled. Violence was what turned them on, and for a time they were thrilled to leave each other bloodied, richer, more powerful, and never fully satisfied, always craving for more.

But that was a time Mordu reflected upon with regret.

Despite repeatedly warning her not to, he expected her to call; and she did, despite the fact that Heth's minions were lurking within earshot at all times. But that was classic Haatakan: Making people feel uncomfortable was physically stimulating for her. It's what made her a ruthless mega-corporate executive, even in exile.

He knew that she would probably notice he'd been drinking, and decided he was fine with that.

'I know a secret, Mordu,' she started. 'Shame on you for not telling me.'

'Now probably isn't the best time, Haatakan.'

'You're sending your own son to do this?' she demanded. 'I'm flattered.'

'I'll need to have a word with whomever gave you that information,' he said, typing a notation in the contract notes. 'But the truth is that he's sending himself.'

'Isn't he a little old to try living up to the expectations of his father?' she asked. 'Or is he doing it because he knows you don't want him to?'

'The only expectation I've ever had for him was to follow his own path,' Mordu said. 'Let's try to keep this on topic. Do you have any last questions before we begin?'

'That's great advice considering what you do for a living,' she mocked. 'I'm sure he'll turn out to be a fine sociopath.'

'That's enough, Haatakan.'

'Telling him to "follow his own path" – what the hell is that?' she mocked. 'You don't have a soul, Mordu. If you did, I would own it.'

'I'm going to have to disagree with that.'

'Ha! I *know* you regret that we don't have a life together,' she said. 'Admit it, old man.'

'Let me think for a moment. No.'

'You're drunk again, aren't you! Still numbing the guilt of murdering by the dozen every day?'

'Yes, but then I'm not speaking to plants now, am I?'

'Fuck you, Mordu. Just tell me I'm getting what I paid for.'

'You're getting the best that money can buy and some intangibles that no amount of money can buy.'

'Intangibles? Don't get philosophical—'

'I selected people that aren't in it for the money,' Mordu said. 'For this crew, the mission is personal. They're willing to give their lives for it. Only someone like our mutual friend can align people as different as you and me.'

'Different? We're exactly the same, whether you admit it or not.'

'People like you set the stage for a bastard like Heth to rise to power. We have nothing in common whatsoever.'

'And people like you followed the blood straight to riches beyond your wildest dreams.'

'Because cunts like you always have some inconvenience or other that needs a bullet to solve.'

'You're an evil man, Mordu.'

'I'm not saying I wasn't. But I've changed. You haven't.'

The transmission went dark.

26

PLACID REGION – BEYT CONSTELLATION
MLW *MORSE*
EN ROUTE TO MORDU'S LEGION HQ STATION

'Gable,' a familiar voice said. 'Is that you?'

She felt the familiar rush of vertigo as the nightmare suddenly ended. Painful memories pressed against her consciousness: She had been dreaming of Sister Marth, of bone-jarring explosions, of excruciating pain and senseless deaths, and of the lunacy of dying alongside a toy soldier. . . .

'Wow, it really is,' the voice said. 'You're safe now.'

The sense of recognition confused her, and suddenly she remembered another familiar face, one she cared about deeply, pointing a gun directly at her.

'Vince!' she gasped, opening her eyes.

'Shhh . . . easy does it,' Jonas said, placing a hand on her shoulder. 'It's Jonas.'

Blinking several times, Gable was having difficulty reconciling who was in front of her.

'You're on a ship called the *Morse*,' Jonas said. 'We pulled you off Pike's Landing.'

Visibly distressed, she began shaking her head and then winced in pain.

His was not the face she wanted to see.

'You're going to be fine,' Jonas said. 'Just a little while longer before the pain eases.'

'What's wrong with me?' she asked.

'Internal injuries,' Jonas said. 'You're lucky to be alive. Not many live through orbital strikes that close.'

He let out a deep breath.

'I can't even tell you how good it is to see you,' he said. 'I mean, what are the odds . . . ?'

Gable let her head collapse back onto the pillow.

'I need to speak with the ship's captain,' she said. 'Now.'

Jonas paused.

'That's me,' he said.

She turned away from him. Her hands had been cleaned – though some telltale silt from Core Freedom remained lodged in her fingernails. The room smelled sterile, like a proper medical ward should. It was a stark change from the persistent filth of Pike's Landing – or the foulness of the air on the last ship she shared with Jonas.

Soreness racked her chest and abdomen. A chill ran up her spine as she recalled the horrors of her final moments at Core Freedom.

Gable whispered Scripture to find strength: *'No seas, nor valley so treacherous to cross, with you by my side and faith in my heart . . .'*

'I'm sorry?' Jonas asked, leaning in.

She reached toward her chest to touch Sister Marth's pendant, and gasped when it wasn't there.

'Where is it?' she demanded. 'My pendant!'

'Easy,' Jonas winced. 'It's right here. We had to remove it to do tests.'

She looked to her right, and there it was, coiled on a bedside dresser.

The toy soldier was next to it as well.

'Jonas, listen to me,' she said. 'Vince was down there. On Pike's Landing.'

'Gable, try and rest for a bit—'

'Don't patronize me,' she growled. It still didn't take much for him to bring out the worst in her. 'I know what I saw.'

Jonas gave her a thoughtful look.

She was surprised that he didn't snap back. His eyes were patient and showed sympathy. He was older now; creases were present in the corners of his eyes.

'Alright,' he said. 'How do you know it was him?'

'Because I just know!' she said. 'He was a soldier fighting for the Amarr. He was going to kill me, except ... we recognized one another. He spared me because of my faith.'

Narrowing his eyes, he opened his mouth to say something, then reconsidered.

'We just pulled you out of a combat zone,' he said. 'Your mind needs time to heal.'

'Jonas, I'm telling you—'

'Shhh ... Gable, listen,' Jonas interrupted. 'I'm not saying I *don't* believe you. It's just that this has unbelievable implications, and I need you to be absolutely sure before we do anything to—'

'There's nothing we can do,' she said. 'He's dead.'

Jonas stood straight up.

'Please just rest,' he said.

'He was shot,' Gable said, eyes filling with tears. 'Some ... deranged mercenary just executed him. We connected again, before he died. Vince found faith, like I did, and God gave us the miracle of finding each other—'

'What did he look like,' Jonas interrupted. 'The merc?'

'He gave me this toy,' she said, motioning toward the dresser. 'And his face—'

'Mack is standing right here,' Jonas said. 'He hasn't left your side.'

Gable felt guilt sink into her as the battered warrior stepped into view, still wearing his combat equipment and a field dressing holding his crippled cybernetic arm in place. Despite the frozen grin on his face, his eyes were full of sadness.

'I'm sorry,' she said. 'Thank you for everything. For saving my life, God, how many times today ... ?'

Mack's bottom lip began quivering.

'Your praying friend lives,' he said.

Gable and Jonas stared as he wiped a tear away.

'Close to you, I see,' Mack continued. 'Not same man he was ... not anymore.'

'Mack,' Jonas said, walking to the nearest console. 'What did he look like?'

'Immortiaño dránon,' the mercenary mumbled in his ancient Mannar language. 'Immortiaño dránon.'

An old photo of the *Retford* crew appeared on the screen.

'Is the man you shot in there?' Jonas asked.

'Yes,' Mack said, pointing at the man standing to the left of the frame. It was Vince as he looked several years ago, poised with the rest of the former *Retford* crew.

'I show you,' Mack continued. 'Not dead. Immortal. Panther-gun camera have proof.'

The mercenary turned, his head hung low, and began walking out.

Gable was stunned.

'Wait,' she asked. 'What language were you speaking? What did that mean?'

'Old tongue,' Mack said, turning his scarred side toward her. 'Mannar lore. Mean "god eater" in your words.'

'Why call him that?'

'He proof god not real,' he said, leaving the room.

PURE BLIND REGION – MDM8-J CONSTELLATION
SYSTEM 5ZXX-K – PLANET V, MOON 17
MORDU'S LEGION HQ STATION

Big as she was, the transport was unremarkable to look at – a towering, elongated metallic gray box looming over a cargo loading deck on the station. She was a standard Crane-class blockade runner perched in dry dock, its moorings reaching out to the main docking hub to take on passengers and equipment. Smaller craft and drones buzzed around the twelve-thousand-tonne vessel, making repairs in some cases and in others intentionally adding wear and tear to disguise its real purpose. The transport was being painted in Lai Dai mega-corporation colors, marked up to look exactly like the ship it was going to replace.

MTACs marched containers along the airtight moorings into the craft's hold, each one marked with innocuous handling warnings such as fragile or keep upright. These were consistent with the forged shipping manifest, which stated they contained perishable goods and supplies destined for a startup Ishukone colony on the planet Myoklar. On separate freight moorings above the ship, cranes lowered industrial components, such as fusion generators, habitat modules, and terrestrial construction equipment, into carefully marked spots in the cargo bay.

Not listed on the manifest was the platoon of elite Mordu's Legion commandos accompanying the three hundred civilians and engineers aboard. Nor was it noted that a cache of firearms and 'area suppression weapons'– including a tactical nuclear device – was on board as well.

For months, Mordu spent part of each day considering everything that could go wrong with this crucial mission. And now, seeing all the crates being loaded onto the ship, it finally hit home that there was one vital component remaining that he had neglected entirely.

He found his son near the ship, supervising the logistics operation and making sure everything was in order. Several mercenaries he recognized were with him; they smiled at Mordu as he approached, and then stepped away.

Arian Mordu looked over his shoulder, then went back to his datapad.

'Now isn't a good time,' he said.

'To be honest,' Mordu said, 'I'm not sure why I came down.'

'Not to say anything inspirational,' Arian said. He was taller than Mordu, with much broader shoulders. Wearing his hair long and unkempt, he was dressed as a nondescript civilian machine operator, just like his cover required.

'Nice outfit,' Mordu said. 'It suits you.'

The transport would reach the Tsukuras system in several hours. After docking at the Perkone Factory station, its cargo would be off-loaded by Ishukone longshore contractors and transferred to a fleet of heavy dropships for surface delivery.

'Yeah?' Arian asked, without looking. 'More like what you wish I was doing?'

The mercenaries would mingle among the civilians traveling with the equipment. Officially, they were there to support a new colony on a world coveted for its bountiful seas and lush jungles. Few of the travelers knew each other, this being a typical Caldari mega-corporate operation where only the most qualified individuals won the lucrative work contracts.

'Did you see the latest weather forecast?' Mordu asked.

Heavy thunderstorms were expected to blanket the colony site the next evening. During the mayhem of off-loading dropships, with personnel making their way to hastily assembled living spaces, Arian and his team would have no problem disappearing into the jungle and beginning the long trek south to the target area. No one would know they were gone, or better yet, that they were ever there to begin with.

'Yep,' Arian said, setting his datapad down onto some crates. 'Couldn't ask for better cover.'

The target site where Heth and the CPD were meeting was a private villa owned by the CEO of Echelon Entertainment. More of a vanity project to host private parties for the State's larger-than-life stars and starlets, it was located right in the center of a dormant volcano crater some six kilometers in diameter, which was filled with azure-blue water as much as sixty meters deep in some spots. The crater's rim rose from the shoreline some thirty meters above the water, covered with vegetation and trees. The villa itself was a spectacular mansion, complete with a small spaceport and all the amenities of a paradise resort.

It was the ideal summit location for the secretive Heth – isolated, secure, and unknown.

'True,' Mordu said to Arian. 'You've made the necessary provisions, then?'

Using vehicles to reach the villa from the colony was out of the question. They were too easy to track, ruined the element of surprise, and could easily kill the mission before it began.

'Just makes the hike a little damp, is all,' Arian answered, squaring up to Mordu in almost menacing fashion. 'Is there a specific question you'd like to ask me?'

His team would have to backpack some eighty kilometers to reach the site. They estimated the trek would take at least twenty hours of uninterrupted hiking through thick jungles and hilly terrain. That was ambitious considering the amount of weight they were carrying, which included provisions to keep their energy up, lots of stealth tech, and firepower.

'Are you sure you have everything you need?' Mordu asked. 'And that you're not taking anything you don't?'

They had trained relentlessly for this. The physical conditioning, combined with drug cocktails to hasten their recovery time and inoculations to protect against the myriad of poisonous flora and insects of Myoklar's ecosystem, prepared every man for what lay ahead.

'Now you're just being intrusive,' Arian said. 'We board in thirty minutes.'

The plan was to be in position before Heth's security teams arrived in advance to sweep the area surrounding the villa. Most of the gear they were hauling was for that explicit purpose: cloaking field generators, thermal suppressors in the suits and helmets they wore, and lots of ECM gear to deal with drone technology.

'Don't go,' Mordu said. 'Please.'

Assuming they weren't detected, they would evaluate two options. The first was to get in close enough for a clear line of fire. Heth was the primary target, but any of his cabinet lieutenants were considered high-value targets of opportunity. The weapons they were bringing for the task – three Wiyrkomi AWH-44 Gauss rifles, massive things that needed to be assembled at the site – had the range, power, and silence to get the job done without betraying their position. The targets would need to be in the open, and the men were trained to lie and wait in the jungle for as long as it took for the opportunity to present itself.

And if it didn't, the second option was to detonate the tactical nuke.

Shaking his head, Arian stepped past his father.

'You're just jealous you're not pulling the trigger yourself,' he said.

'I could order you to stay,' Mordu said. 'You know that, right?'

His son paused.

'You could,' he said. 'But you won't.'

'Arian, you don't have to do this,' Mordu pleaded.

'I don't?' he asked, turning around. 'Six months of planning, and you tell me this now?'

Mordu looked him straight in the eye.

'I need to know that you're doing it for the right reasons,' he said. 'Are you?'

A scowl formed on Arian's brow.

'You should be asking if there's a good reason not to go,' he answered. 'There isn't.'

Mordu smiled wearily at his son.

'Are you doing this for the Legion?' he asked, 'or for yourself?'

Arian's scowl deepened.

'You know the answer to that,' he said.

'I used to think so,' Mordu said. 'But I've been wrong before.'

'Don't worry, *Pop*,' Arian growled through clenched teeth. 'If this doesn't work, you've got eternity to make as many sons as it takes to get this right.'

The father nodded, as if Arian had told him what he suspected all along.

'I see,' he said. 'Then good luck, son.'

'Thanks,' Arian said, turning his back to him.

Mordu reached out one last time.

'I remember why I came down here,' he said.

Arian kept walking.

'It was to tell you how proud I am of you,' Mordu said, certain this was the last time he would ever see him alive.

PURE BLIND REGION – S4GH-I CONSTELLATION
MLW *MORSE*
EN ROUTE TO MORDU'S LEGION HQ STATION

General Kintreb felt something he'd never known before.

For the first time, the inner, perpetual rage that defined him was diminished. He was sublimely aware of something greater than his life's toils, which suddenly felt so trivial. Curiously, his iron will was demanding that he stay within the comparative bliss of his dreams instead of fight to leave them. Deep down, he acknowledged a somber admission of defeat – not by battle, but by life itself.

After all this bitter, hateful time, enough was enough.

'Hello again, Vladimir,' Mordu said. 'You look like shit.'

The old General grimaced at the sound of his voice. An image of the grand mercenary hovered overhead. Vlad was insulted that he didn't have the respect to address him in person.

Enough, he reminded himself. *Anger is pointless.*

'I have to ask a favor,' Mordu said. 'I need you to *want* to live. We can only do so much to keep you alive.'

'Don't . . . bother,' Vlad whispered. 'Core Freedom . . . ?'

'The Amarr have taken it,' Mordu said. 'I'm sorry.'

'. . . you should have left me there,' Vlad said. 'Did anyone else . . .'

'The physician, Gable,' Mordu said. 'No one else.'

'Bishop?' Vlad asked.

'KIA,' Mordu said.

Farewell, old friend, Vlad thought, remembering his reliable commander fondly. *I will see you again soon.*

He could feel the machines keeping him alive, which only bolstered his resolve to defeat their efforts. But before passing into the afterlife, there was one final truth to be said.

'We're going to search for those who escaped,' Mordu said. 'We might be able to get some of them out.'

Vlad took a deep, labored breath.

'The Republic never believed Core Freedom was worth saving,' he struggled to say.

Mordu blinked.

'But then why hire us?'

'They didn't,' Vlad said. 'I did. With my own money, and ... the original investors' of Core Freedom.'

'You?' Mordu asked.

'A lifetime of soldiering ... Every credit ... is now yours,' said Vlad.

'Shakor must have known what you were doing—' Mordu started.

'They ... *owed* me. For sacrifices on their behalf. So they allowed it.'

'Allowed, or knew you were too stubborn to let it go?'

Vlad took a deep, labored breath.

'The Elders have a vision for Minmatar that doesn't include New Eden,' he said. 'This cluster is dead to them.'

'Vladimir,' Mordu said sternly, 'you were ordered to abandon Core Freedom, and you stayed anyway?'

'New Eden is my home,' Vlad whispered. 'Pike's Landing is a Minmatar world. Makes it worth fighting for ...'

'You kept an entire battalion of soldiers on that place—'

'I won't yield one inch to those bastards, Mordu. Not one.'

'— and how many *thousands* of civilians against their will?'

'They're going to burn them,' Vlad warned. 'Burn them all to ash.'

'Burn who?' Mordu asked. 'The civilians? Who's going to burn them?'

'Shakor. The Republic Fleet. They'll never let the empire have Core Freedom.'

The machines keeping him alive screamed frantically, trying to stop the inevitable, but his will was too strong.

General Vlad Kintreb's heart stopped beating.

Jonas, who was listening to the conversation from the medical bay, took his cue from Mordu and turned off the machines attempting to revive him.

Both men stared at the corpse for a few moments.

'Should we tell the Republic?' Jonas asked.

'No,' Mordu said. 'Do you think it's worth returning to Pike's Landing?'

'Not for the Valklears, no,' Jonas said quietly. 'But there is another reason to go back that you need to hear.'

THE FORGE REGION – ETSALA CONSTELLATION
THE VASALA SYSTEM – PLANET V, MOON 15
ISHUKONE CORPORATE FACTORY – TEMPORARY HQ
SOVEREIGNTY OF THE CALDARI STATE

Lorin Reppola stormed into the flat without warning, purposely making her way across the living space.

'Pack your things,' she snapped. 'Or have the hired help do it for you. Just take the irreplaceable items.'

'Where are we going?' Amile asked.

'Someplace far away from here,' her mother answered.

Amile looked at the beefy Civire bodyguards standing in the open doorway. They kept their stone-faced expressions and remained separated by a small luggage carrier.

'We're leaving home for good?' she asked. 'You're serious?'

'More than ever,' Lorin said, grabbing a statue that Amile knew she paid a small fortune for. 'I should have done this a long time ago.'

'Did you talk this over with Dad?' Amile asked, folding her arms.

'You know this isn't working,' Lorin said, marching straight past the projection of family portraits above the credenza. She thrust the statue into one of the bodyguards' hands, who hurriedly stowed it into the luggage carrier. 'Please don't fight me on this. Just gather your things, and let's get moving.'

'You made all the security arrangements?' Amile demanded. 'The Watch knows the itinerary? Or is this as selfishly irresponsible as I think it is?'

'Yes and yes, which is why we need to hurry,' Lorin said, snatching another ancient figurine from its pedestal. 'Responsibility works both ways in a marriage and I've lost my patience waiting for your father to reciprocate.'

'So then where are we going?'

'We are eventually going to the Federation,' Lorin said. 'We have friends there who will take us in.'

'We can't do that,' Amile said. 'Not without a presidential pardon—'

'It's done already,' her mother said. 'They're more than happy to accommodate us.'

'You can't do this!' Amile protested.

'Watch me,' Lorin said.

'Dad promised to try one more time to work things out with you,' Amile protested. 'You owe him at least that much!'

With a startling crash, Amile slammed the priceless figurine onto the floor. It broke into dozens of pieces, scattering across the floor like the fléchettes of a grenade.

'I don't owe him anything!' Lorin shouted. 'I am so *sick* of being told what I owe. What about what's owed to *me*? Why doesn't anyone ever ask that?'

She took a few breaths and then covered her face.

The security guards were noticeably uncomfortable.

'Your father is a great man,' Lorin said through puffy eyes. 'He really is. But not for us. Right now, I need to do what's best for us. Not Ishukone. *Us*.'

Amile stared at her mother, fighting back some tears of her own.

'I can't blame you,' she said calmly. 'I really can't. But tell me truthfully: Does the Watch know what you've planned?'

'Yes,' Lorin said. 'The Watch knows.'

'But does Rali know?'

Lorin wiped away tears.

'With all his tech he can know anything he wants,' she said.

'He doesn't then,' Amile said. 'We'd have heard from Dad by now.'

'I'm sorry for this,' Lorin said. 'I'm just so ... *tired* of being afraid. I want us to reconnect. You're the only joy in my life, and for once I'd like to enjoy that without the stress of trying to make a marriage work.'

'If we do this,' Amile said, 'will you promise to give Dad one more try?'

'Is this the last time you'll ask?' Lorin asked.

'If the effort is sincere, yes,' Amile said. 'Dad promised the same.'

'Fine,' Lorin said. 'Just please . . . come with me.'

Amile stared at her mother, certain that this was a bad decision.

'Alright,' she said. 'What'd you have in mind?'

'Echelon Entertainment owns property in Lonetrek,' Lorin said. 'There's a secluded resort there I'm quite fond of – shorefront facilities, just gorgeous. I planned to wait there until the Federation made final arrangements for us. In any case, some rest and relaxation might be exactly what we need.'

'What's the name of the world?'

'Myoklar.'

GEMINATE REGION – F-ZNNG CONSTELLATION
SYSTEM UBX-CC – THE MJOLNIR NEBULA
INSORUM PRODUCTION FACTORY

Mila watched drones scurry away from the freighter as it cleared the hangar doors, its hold almost entirely empty. Years ago, in the early days of the war, it would have left filled to capacity with various forms of Insorum, the antidote to the mind-warping Vitoc enslavement drug. Now the vessel was a cavernous husk, piloted by a drone that would navigate into Republic space and then abandon it. She wondered if it would ever return, let alone meet the designated Minmatar pilot assigned to fly it the rest of the way.

The obvious implication was that the Elders were winding down their rescue missions in the Amarr Empire. There were still millions of Minmatar slaves in their service, with dozens more added every day as the two empires fought an ugly war of attrition across dozens of colonies in the losec worlds.

It was a grim reminder that the nobility of what Otro Gariushi had done – the selfless act of courage in giving this solution to the beleaguered nation without asking for anything in return – was largely gone. The Insorum factory had given Mila purpose over the years. Though drones did all the work, she considered herself a supervisor of sorts; one who presided over a great moral triumph. But now the satisfaction of knowing her actions were freeing a subjugated people was gone.

Little else remained to distract her from other thoughts. Ones that carried a bittersweet mix of passion and regret.

The freighter accelerated and then vanished. The last time a ship left this place with a beating heart on board was when . . .

She caught herself moving a hand over her swollen breast.

'God,' she said aloud. 'I have to stop doing this!'

'Which activity are you referencing?' VILAMO asked, startling her. 'The act of watching the freighter depart, or the physical stimulation of mammary tissue . . . ?'

'What do you want?' she snapped, to which the drone – a caterpillar-shaped insectoid – withdrew as though offended.

'I am sorry,' it said dejectedly. 'I did not mean to disturb. But I have information for you.'

'It's okay,' she said. 'What's going on?'

'There has been a spike in secure comms traffic in the Caldari State,' the drone said. 'Mainly with internal CPD security channels.'

'Are there any patterns emerging?'

'The Tsukuras system has been mentioned numerous times on compromised channels,' VILAMO answered. 'But we do not detect any abnormal ship movements, nor is there anything remarkable about the system itself.'

'Tsukuras,' Mila pondered. She would start doing her own research immediately. 'Okay, VILAMO – thank you.'

'You're welcome. I will continue monitoring and report with more tact next time.'

The drone scurried away, leaving her alone with the view. Gas and dust currents were pummeling the outer hangar now as a nebula storm moved in.

Something is happening, Mila thought. *And it kills me that I don't know what it is.*

PURE BLIND REGION – MDM8-J CONSTELLATION
SYSTEM 5ZXX-K – PLANET V, MOON 17
MORDU'S LEGION HQ STATION

Handing the *Morse* over to Harbor Control for the final docking stages, Jonas ordered the officers into the ship's only conference area for debriefing. The rest of the vessel was buzzing with activity as the crew anxiously prepared to disembark for a short leave. Though they were under strict orders to keep the details of their mission classified, rumors were already flooding the station that the *Morse* had managed to take down a dreadnought – an impossible feat by any standards, but nonetheless part of the inevitable legend-seeding that marks the spacefaring profession.

Gable was assisted into the room by medical personnel. She took in the setting cautiously, unwilling to admit that she was quietly impressed with the accommodations and treatment she had received. Subtle welcome-aboard introductions were made between Miles, the ship's engineer, and Blake, the weapons officer. Mack was there as well, sitting at one end of the table with a dozen new toys arrayed around him, occasionally moving a piece with his good arm.

There was a handsome Gallentean capsuleer in the room with kind, tired eyes. He introduced himself reluctantly, after no one else bothered to. She could tell he was new here and not entirely welcome aboard the ship.

Objectively, Jonas would have to be a different man than the one she remembered to assemble this group. But it was far easier to latch onto emotional reasoning, which told her that deep down, no one ever truly changes.

But Mordu's appearance reinforced the notion that Jonas was the same as he always was, running with a crowd of like-minded megalomaniacs. Arrogance liked company.

'The little Drake that could,' Mordu said, wearing on his head the model of a Revelations-class dreadnought that was snapped in two. One half was covering each ear, and a crude model of a Drake sat triumphantly perched atop his scalp. 'The *Morse* has officially become legendary. Well done!'

'Thank you, sir,' Jonas said. 'But gravity did more to bring the *Doystoyov* down than anything we did.'

'That's not how the tale will be told,' Mordu said, clasping Jonas's shoulders. 'I read the mission log. You're far too modest. That was fast, bold thinking on your part. Most captains would have shit themselves.'

Jonas appeared more embarrassed than anything else.

'We had a team down there,' he said. 'We go back for our own. Any of us would do the same for—'

'Well, I don't believe we've met,' Mordu interrupted, waltzing around the table toward Gable. He performed an elaborate bow and offered his hand. 'I am Muryia Mordu, founder of the Legion. A pleasure to meet you.'

'Dr Gable Dietrich,' she said. 'Thank you for saving my life.'

'You owe that thanks to the ship's captain, not to me,' Mordu said. 'Now, I believe we have some lingering business with Pike's Landing, yes?'

'That's correct, sir,' Jonas said. 'Normally I'd brief the officers before bringing you in, but these are special circumstances.'

Gable was intrigued by how much Jonas deferred to the man.

'The bottom line is we think we've got hard evidence that the Amarr are using immortal soldier technology,' Jonas began. 'Here's why.'

Step by step, Jonas walked Mordu through the engagement, supplying video footage taken from orbit, the gunship, and the tactical camera in Mack's helmet. Gable had to turn away from a composite image of Vince before and after he was shot. On the other side was an image of him on the speeder just moments later, and another from the rear hatch of the gunship as it flew away.

A portrait of the *Retford* crew, with Vince circled, made for the final slide.

'That's definitely Vince Barabin,' Jonas continued, setting the implant that Mack had ripped out onto the table. Cleared of blood, the damaged metallic-green device appeared strangely alien. 'No question about it.'

Mordu stood with one arm folded across his chest and the other on his temple, studying the implant intently.

'Mack recovered this from the first corpse,' Jonas continued. 'It was definitely *not* in Vince's head the last time we saw him.'

'All this shows is that you've found new technology,' Mordu said, picking the device up. 'What evidence is there that this . . . thing . . . makes a man immortal? How do you know there aren't just active clones of the same—'

'Because he come back,' Mack interrupted. Everyone turned to look at him.

'I look into his eyes,' he said, staring at his toys as he spoke. 'Know where to find me.'

In one motion, he swiped them all onto the floor – except for one.

'Eyes not lie,' Mack said, glaring at Mordu. 'This same man. Same.'

Jonas cleared his throat.

'Everything to this point has been theory,' he said. 'I admit the evidence is circumstantial. But if this is what we think it is—'

'You'd return to Pike's Landing even if I said this wasn't worth the trouble,' Mordu interrupted, weighing the implant in his hand. 'Why?'

'Because this is personal,' Jonas said. 'Vince was one of ours – one of mine – on the ship I captained before the *Morse*. It would mean a lot to me if we could get him back.'

Mordu narrowed his eyes.

'Let's say you actually make it down to the surface alive,' he said. 'What's the plan then? To rescue him?'

'That's the idea, sir.'

Mordu smiled.

'How do you know he's not there of his own volition?' he asked. 'You just showed me what looks like a very determined Paladin. What makes you think he would want to come with you?'

'Vince would want to come with *me*,' Gable said, speaking up. 'Especially since we're both Reclaimed.'

Mordu threw her a surprised look.

'Gable, please . . .' Jonas winced.

'"Please" *what*?' she snapped. 'Why do you think he spared my life?'

'Interesting,' Mordu noted. 'You realize the Amarr have almost certainly dispatched reinforcements, right? And that the Republic will send ships to raze the colony?'

'I do,' Jonas answered.

'But you would still go back down there anyway?'

'Yes.'

Mordu looked approvingly at him, as he had for a thousand other mercenaries who seemed hopelessly determined to march to their deaths.

His gut told him this was indeed the technology CONCORD had warned him about. Mordu decided that Jonas and his crew didn't need to know that – at least, not yet. He also decided that one way or the other, he was *going* to get that tech, no matter what the cost – although fate had conveniently provided him with the perfect sacrificial lamb to accomplish that.

'What do the rest of you think about this?' Mordu asked, scanning the room. 'Korvin?'

'This is weak evidence of immortal tech,' he said. 'Then again, I've never seen an implant like that before. The fact we pulled it out of a dead Paladin makes me nervous.'

'So what are you saying?' Mordu asked. 'Is he worth it?'

'The *tech* might be worth it,' he said. 'If nothing else, just to find out what it can do. Then you reevaluate. But the man is lost. You'd pay a steep price to get him out.'

Gable was horrified but kept her composure.

'What about you, Mack?' Mordu asked.

The mercenary had a sullen, lifeless look in his eyes as he slowly moved the soldier across the table.

'I follow my captain,' he said quietly.

Mordu looked the group over.

'I'll be blunt,' he said. 'If this group doesn't return to Pike's Landing, I'll find another team that will.'

'Why?' Korvin asked pointedly.

'You're new here,' Mordu said. 'So let's leave the answer at "I have my reasons." Don't ever ask me what those are again.'

'It's a fair question,' Jonas said. 'If you want the tech, I don't have a problem with that. But we're after the *man*. So if we're going to work together, we need to understand each other's reasoning.'

'Alright,' Mordu said. 'The short answer is that *if* this turns out to be immortal tech, I won't allow one nation to control it. Especially the Amarr. What's your reasoning?'

Jonas looked uncomfortable.

'You heard the story about how the *Morse* was a gift from Empress Jamyl?' he said.

'Who hasn't?' Mordu said.

'Well, what I didn't tell anyone is that she *told* me she was going to do this to him,' Jonas said.

'Do *what* to him?'

'Make him immortal,' Jonas said, looking down. 'I had no idea what she meant. But she also made it clear that I'd never see him again. I guess one of us was wrong.'

Mordu marveled at Jonas.

'What other secrets are you hiding?'

'That's the darkest one I've got,' Jonas said, fixing his eyes on the implant. 'I *know* Vince. He didn't choose this. No chance. That's why I have to go back. It's my fault this happened to him.'

Korvin spoke up.

'Can you show me aerials of the colony during the attack?' he asked.

Jonas gave him an incredulous look but complied anyway.

'Zoom in there please, sector one-dash-four,' Korvin said, pointing.

The image focused on one of the peculiar trucks on the northern part of the grid.

'No one can figure out how the colony was overrun so quickly without reinforcements,' Korvin said. 'Well, my gut tells me the cavalry was hiding in plain sight. If your friend Vince is immortal, then his clones had to be in one of those. There's no place else they could be.'

'Were there Amarr ships overhead?' Gable asked, drawing everyone's stare.

'Yeah,' Miles said, speaking up. 'Bunch of them.'

'Then it's possible,' she said. 'Those trucks are big enough to hold clone revival units. If the ships could communicate with them, then limited amounts of state information could transfer quickly enough between clones. It would explain how Vince knew where to find Mack the second time around: A copy of him was inside one of those CRUs when the original was killed. That implant would have to be the piece that bridges what data can't be transferred at death . . . somehow.'

'Now you're making sense,' Mordu said, adjusting his hat. 'Here's my offer: a billion credits for the return of Vince Barabin to this station, dead or alive.'

Everyone's eyes bulged except for Jonas's.

'That's suicide money,' he said. 'Pretty much a verdict on our odds.'

'Correct,' Mordu said. 'To be clear, I only want the tech delivered intact. If you can do that, the money is yours.'

'Then we have an agreement,' Jonas said.

'Good,' Mordu said. 'Now tell me what else you need to make this happen.'

'Orbital artillery support,' Jonas said. 'One, maybe two strikes ought to do it.'

'*Look* at what's on my head,' Mordu said, pointing at his hat. 'I can provide the capital ship and crew, but you'll have to find a captain crazy enough to fly it into the gauntlet again.'

'I'll do it,' Korvin said.

The room turned and stared.

'As long as there's a support fleet to keep the Amarr off my back,' Korvin added.

'Are you seriously asking me to hand you the keys to a dreadnought?' Mordu asked.

'If I screw up, I'll wake up in a Federation brig,' Korvin said. 'That's a pretty strong incentive to get this right.'

'Point taken,' Mordu said. 'Then I'll provide the support myself. Risky venture for you, isn't it?'

'I used to be in the Federation Navy,' Korvin said. 'If they knew about this, they'd be sending me down there anyway.'

'I'll fly the gunship,' Jonas said. 'And support the team as best I can from the air.'

Miles, who was biting his fingernails for most of the discussion, leapt out of his seat.

'Whooaa,' he yelped, shaking his head. 'Everyone just wait a minute. This. Is. *Crazy!* What are you going to do when you get down there? Flag a Paladin down and say "Hey buddy! You seen Vinny around?"'

'Vince is holding still for us,' Jonas said, pointing to the trucks. 'We don't need the live specimen. Just the clone will do.'

'Then I'm going with you,' Gable said, raising her hand as Jonas was about to protest. 'If it's a clone you're after, you need a CRU expert, or else you'll end up killing him again.'

'Then it's done,' Mordu said, as Jonas and Gable exchanged looks. 'I need forty-eight hours to prepare. I suggest you use the time to work all this through with each other. As soon as I have what I need, we go. Understood?'

'Yes, sir,' Jonas said.

Mordu took off the hat and left it on the conference room table.

'You should try that on,' he said. 'A man with balls as big as yours earns the right to keep it.'

GABLE WAS FEELING WELL enough to walk on her own, and with that strength came a renewed sense of curiosity. But she quickly learned that, as on Pike's Landing, she was very much a prisoner here, restricted from leaving the *Morse* or exploring many parts of it. Before leaving with Mordu and Mack to plan the mission in more detail, Jonas asked her to be patient. There were standing rules for operatives on classified missions, he explained. Annoyed, she inquired about General Kintreb's fate, only to be told that he didn't survive – but nothing else about the exact cause of death.

Whatever karma might have been restored during the meeting

with Mordu evaporated on the spot. Jonas was the exact same person he always was – self-serving, untrustworthy, and deceitful. It was evident in the people he surrounded himself with: Mack, a deranged monster; Mordu, a megalomaniac; and this incessant revolt against faith! If anything, the backlash was just bolstering her spiritual resolve even more.

Besides the medical bay, the only place she was permitted to visit on board was the galley. Wandering inside, she noticed several of the crew chatting, some of whom nodded toward her. The ship's engineering officer – Miles, she believed – was sitting far away from the crowd, all by himself. A half-eaten meal was in front of him, and he was drawing a fork through the food in slow lines. Anxiety was etched all over his face.

'Do you mind if I sit here?' she asked.

Miles looked up and appeared somewhat shocked.

'Sure,' he said. 'Make yourself comfortable. You feeling any better?'

'Very much so, thanks,' she said, settling into a chair.

'Good,' he said.

Then he went back to staring at his unfinished plate. Sensing that he wasn't going to start a conversation anytime soon, she decided to break the ice.

'You seem a little down,' she said. 'Miles, right?'

'Me?' he said. 'No, I'm solid. I mean, yeah.'

It was a valiant attempt to retain his composure, but it didn't last. One glance at Gable's sympathetic eyes was all it took.

'Alright, you got me,' he confessed. 'I don't have a lot of friends around here. It's part of the whole "ranking officer" thing. Keeping it professional and stuff.'

'Of course,' Gable said. 'I'm a good listener, if you need one.'

'Right,' Miles said, swallowing a knot in his throat. 'So, the crew's all pumped up about taking the *Doystoyov* down. Talking about it like it's a party or something, high-fiving each other and stuff . . .'

Gable watched as he reached for his ice water with a trembling hand.

'They don't get it,' he said. 'I mean, how often does anyone ever get to watch a ship with six thousand people on board break apart?'

He took a deep breath before continuing.

'Six *thousand* people. Can you even get your head around that number?'

Looking around ner vously, he spoke in the lowest voice he could.

'I do this because I'm good at it,' he said. 'Not because I love it. I don't want to die aboard a ship. Until now, it's been easy. I could deal with it. But this Core Freedom thing freaks me out. It could have just as easily been the *Morse* breaking apart out there. Next time, it just might be.'

'You're much braver than you give yourself credit for,' Gable reassured, trying to channel all the wisdom that Sister Marth had imparted on her. 'We all get strength from different sources. Where do you get yours?'

'You call this "strength"?' Miles said, gesticulating with his eating utensils. 'Look, I can't let the crew see me like this. Not now. Can we talk about something else?'

'Sure, Miles. What would you like to discuss?'

'I don't know. Ask me something.'

'Alright,' she said. 'Why don't you tell me about Mack?'

'What about him?' Miles asked. 'I mean, he obviously scares the piss out of everyone, but—'

'What happened to him? How did he—'

'You mean the scars?'

'Yes.'

'He's a Seyllin survivor,' Miles said. 'Possibly the *last* survivor of the catastrophe.'

Gable's eyes widened. Seyllin was the kind of once-in-a-millennia disaster about which everyone remembered exactly where they were when they heard about it. Some 190 million people died that day; there were less than a million survivors.

'What do you mean "last"?'

'I mean, he was the *last* man aboard the *last* dropship to take off before the planet was destroyed. We know that because Jonas was the pilot who got him out.'

'You have to be kidding me.'

Miles seemed much more confident now.

'Mack was about thirty meters underground when the gamma pulse hit,' he said. 'Everything above that depth was fried. You'd think that someone with half his face burned off would take the first chance to leave, but he didn't. Instead, he stayed to make sure others like him made it out.'

'Others like him? What about everyone else?'

'He's a Mannar. Most of what was left of their population lived on Seyllin.'

Gable thought about how Mack had coldly executed the Valklear who delayed their only chance of escaping from Pike's Landing.

'We got a dropship into one of their spaceports, and there he was, along with some other Mannar guys. They had taken control of the port, pulling purebred ethnics from the crowd and turning away just about everyone else. No one got out of there unless Mack approved. He was the angel of death down there. As soon as the hold filled up, he ordered the pilot to take off. But Mack refused to get on board. Captain Varitec flipped.'

'What did he do?'

'The Feds blockaded the system while we were off-loading survivors onto the *Morse*. No ships were allowed to get in, so we knew the clock was running. Captain Varitec gave the *Morse* to me and Blake, relieved the dropship pilot, and took it back down to the surface himself.'

'Really?'

'Oh, yeah. Everyone else was heading the other way. Fed Navy ships helping the rescue effort warned him to turn back but didn't try to stop him. They all warped out.'

'He did that, knowing what was coming?'

'Sure did. That's why he never has a hard time finding crew for the *Morse*. Word about that kind of thing gets around.'

'How did he convince Mack to get on board?'

'He didn't have to. By then Mack and everyone else near the surface was baking in lethal levels of radiation for upward of an hour. Jonas found him unconscious, surrounded mostly by corpses. He dragged him on board and barely made it back to the *Morse* in time. We warped out maybe two minutes before the plasma wave hit.'

'My God,' she breathed. 'What was Mack doing there in the first place?'

Miles snorted, drawing another line through the muck on his plate with a fork.

'He was there to kill someone. We're mercenaries, right? The target was Mannar, so Mack was uniquely qualified for the job.'

'What was he before ending up here? In fact, how did he wind up with Jonas – uh, Captain Varitec?'

'You can probably guess,' Miles said. 'The Feds have hundreds of classified paramilitary units. Captain V. knows but won't say which one. I quit trying to find out; Mack didn't take kindly to that. He scared the shit out of me with a threat and then went back to playing with his god-damn toys.'

'Why does he do that?'

'Given everything he's seen, can you blame him? Seyllin would have cracked anyone. I heard the toys are a mental "safe spot" for him. Whenever he thinks he's about to lose it, out comes Sergeant Space Muffin and the Comet Cowboys.'

Miles abruptly stabbed the food with his fork, leaving it upright in the mush pile.

'You're easy to talk to,' he said. 'Pretty too, if you don't mind me saying.'

Gable smiled uncomfortably.

'Thanks,' she said.

'Listen, about that pendant you wear . . .' he started.

'I know, I know; I'll keep it hidden,' Gable said. 'It offends people who don't—'

'No, no,' Miles said, looking around again. 'Actually, I'd like to learn more about it. If that's okay with you.'

27

HEIMATAR REGION – HED CONSTELLATION
AMAMAKE SYSTEM – PLANET II: PIKE'S LANDING
CORE FREEDOM COLONY
SOVEREIGNTY OF THE AMARR EMPIRE

Present Day

Vince was overwhelmed – not by the agony of his dislocated shoulder or the deep gashes marring his face, but with the sublime clarity of the world surrounding him.

He marveled at the way dust fell from his armor and disappeared in the dirt at his feet; how the Amamake sun's yellow rays pierced the clouds; the way the breeze carried silt in eerie wisps across the landscape, and the sound of its countless particles colliding with the granite walls of the mountain pass in which he stood.

His senses were relentlessly pumping data into his consciousness for him to scour, so much so that he nearly collapsed from the fascination of it all. He couldn't differentiate between what was beautiful or hideous; there was just an indescribable interest in all things. His TACNET was littered with communications as the Paladins celebrated their victory; Vince would have gladly turned it off if he could. But they reminded him why he was there. A gunship was en route to pick him up; a debriefing with Lord Victor himself was to take place within the hour.

Biding his time until the Vex arrived, Vince limped toward the Kwaal wreckage, blinking away pain as he detected something out of place. The ground was moving around the charred metal: Laaknyds, blackish insect creatures with hardened scales and sharp, angular features, suddenly emerged from the silt. Vince watched in amazement as they crawled over the APC and then inside, sniffing out blood.

He realized he could smell it himself – and the first fluids of decomposition. Squatting beside the overturned vehicle, he peered inside at the deconstruction of the Valklear soldier pinned in the driver's seat. He could hear the pincers and jaws of these magnificent laaknyd creatures performing their work, tearing away flesh, gnawing bone, and carting away their spoils as the stronger bull insects stood guard over them.

An odd sound of selective clicks drew his attention: A trio of bulls were picking at the remnants of his previous body. Like testing the water of a pool, the insect cautiously dipped a pincer into the gore, rather than dive into it, as it had with the other corpse, drawing bits of carnage close to its olfactory receptors, then shaking the material off before repeating the process.

Vince reflected as they dug into the discarded ruins of himself. He remembered the scarred man who had shot him, the way he limped and favored his left side, and how the round placement in the target's shoulder and neck area had failed to kill him. If fate was kind enough to reintroduce them, he would not make that mistake again.

Standing over his own remains, Vince realized his corpse had been brutalized. His killer had desecrated him, and by doing so, blasphemed against the faith. Cursing the rotting version of himself, he reached down and snatched one of the protective bulls off the ground. The insect reacted like a cornered warrior, viciously plunging its pincers deep into Vince's flesh.

Who was that woman, he wondered, watching his own blood seep from the wound onto the silt. *Why am I almost certain that I know her?*

Fighting for its life, the laaknyd withdrew its pincers and lunged to its side, driving its mandibles into flesh. Glands released an acidic enzyme designed to break down prey.

Why do I wish I could see her again? he asked himself, trying to dissect his emotions as the insect shuddered from head to tail and went limp. Vince was caught by surprise; he hadn't gripped it too hard, and he felt bitter remorse that the creature had perished.

As the roar of the Vex's engines rolled down the valley, he gently set the dead loaknyd down, hoping it would show a sign of life. The bulls who had tasted his flesh were stumbling around as though incapacitated, and the other insects, seemingly aware that something sinister was about, cautiously kept their distance.

DOMAIN REGION – THRONE WORLDS CONSTELLATION
THE AMARR SYSTEM – PLANET ORIS
EMPEROR FAMILY ACADEMY STATION
SOVEREIGNTY OF THE AMARR EMPIRE

Nine Years Ago

As Mekioth Sarum drew his final breath, the bells of nearly a million cathedrals tolled across the largest empire in New Eden. Preparations for the passing of the monarch had begun years earlier, and a state funeral of historic precedent was about to get under way.

Coordinating the effort with the royal court of Emperor Heideran himself, Jamyl Sarum was expected to be a prominent feature of the ceremony, if not the focal point for the entire affair. She was now heiress to the house that bore her name and a candidate for the Holy Throne of Amarr; every pair of eyes in New Eden, no matter how humble or powerful, would be set upon her. As of this moment, in the history of the Empire, there was no one in existence who was more important or of greater consequence than the eighteen-year-old Jamyl Sarum.

In the hours before this epic national production was to begin, many would expect the newly anointed heiress to be meditating, praying, or perhaps even fasting as a sign of respect for her father.

Amarr tradition called for mother and daughter to be kept separate from one another during this crucial period of reflection. This was a transcendent time for her spirituality and the path she was to take alone with God. Anla Sarum, herself praying as priestesses prepared her appearance for the ceremony, certainly believed her daughter would take this responsibility seriously, yielding to its divine significance and setting aside her personal disdain for the sake of her nation.

On all those counts, she would be wrong.

'DID YOU DO AS I ASKED?' Jamyl said, looking the Paladin captain directly in his eyes. Despite their training, the other maidens struggled to maintain their composure.

'My lady, please,' the veteran soldier and devoted bodyguard said. 'I must protest—'

'— as I *commanded*, Captain?' she interrupted. 'Or are you questioning my decree?'

He looked upon her with a mixed expression of disappointment and concern. In his hand was a bag filled with small, shimmering vials.

'Give them to me,' she ordered.

Reluctantly, the captain stepped forward.

'Lord, I beseech your forgiveness,' he murmured. 'She knows not what she does.'

Jamyl angrily snatched the bag from him.

'I know *exactly* what I'm doing,' she snapped. 'Now get out of my sight.'

'This isn't you,' the noble captain said. 'Where is the wonderful young woman I watched grow up?'

'*Grown* up,' she snapped. 'Now leave us, or you'll be sorry.'

'You have but three hours before the entire cluster pays its respects to your father,' he pleaded. 'Is this how you want them to see you?'

'If they see me at all, it will be *my* choice,' she growled, fully incensed at the man. 'Not anyone else's. *Now get out.*'

The captain left without another word.

'So,' the heiress said, eyeing up the ladies before her. Some were

True Amarr and others were of Minmatar descent. They were all equally thirsty to share this moment, swept up in this rebellious emotion and falsely believing that Jamyl could protect them from whatever consequences lay ahead.

Cryllisium was an exotic and hugely expensive derivative of a common street drug that produced the most 'erotic highs' ever known. Jamyl wanted to understand exactly what that meant. What better way to empathize with the people she was to rule than to live their experiences? She could never know them all, but if tradition expected her to absorb mankind's struggles during a few hours of spiritual reflection, then the holy order was in for a big disappointment.

Living meant sinning, and her living had been denied at the expense of transforming her into a monarch against her will. The window on the last 'normalcy' of her life was closing, she knew, though perhaps not as tightly as even she suspected.

Still, not even the might of empires could contain the recklessness of intractable, determined youth.

'Who wants to have some fun?' she said, popping the first vial of Cryllisium into her mouth.

HEIMATAR REGION – HED CONSTELLATION
AMAMAKE SYSTEM – PLANET II: PIKE'S LANDING
SOVEREIGNTY OF THE AMARR EMPIRE
CORE FREEDOM COLONY

Present Day

Vince stood at attention beside the other Templars, who had obediently fallen into formation at his order. Like him, they bore unsightly wounds that seemed as if they should have been more incapacitating than they were, at least for those standing near enough to notice. For reasons he was certain had something to do with Templar Six, the conventional troops were arrayed far away from them.

In truth, he was beginning to feel doubts. A short time ago he had relished the opportunity to serve as one of Her Majesty's holy warriors, but now . . . now he wasn't sure at all. His faith, which he convinced himself was unbreakable, had clearly withered. There were no priests here to step into this reality and explain the context of his feelings, nor spiritual reassurance that these were just temporary distractions. Vince had questions. Fascination. Anger. And more questions.

His eyes wandered to the space-elevator cables, following them upward as they tapered and disappeared in the clouds high overhead. Squinting into the hot sun, he could make out a hexagonal disk traveling down one of them, a tiny dot growing into a vast platform several meters tall and as long as a frigate, slowing as it reached the pinnacle of the receiving platform.

The troops erupted in cheers as Lord Victor and his lieutenants emerged from the Minmatar-built marvel. A cursory check on his TACNET revealed this was the first time the machine had been used in years, and that Imperial engineers had little trouble restoring its functionality. If this grand entrance was intended to be an act of triumph, it was lost on Vince, who kept his gaze on the sky. It remained so even as he was approached by the Imperial commander.

'Templar One,' Lord Victor said, 'you did well.'

'Thank you, sir,' Vince responded automatically. 'It is an honor to serve.'

'You're all to be congratulated,' Lord Victor continued, walking down the line of immortal soldiers. 'Because of you, this ground is now hallowed Amarr land. You are the Empire's Archangels, and you honor our Holy Empress with your courage. Your TACNETs have been updated with debriefing instructions. They will commence in just under an hour. Group at the location provided, reclone, and rest. More challenges await. Dismissed.'

Vince knew better than to follow the other Templars, who looked at ease, relaxed, and happy to be in each other's company.

'Templar One,' Lord Victor said. A squad of heavily armed Paladins approached, weapons at the ready. 'Come with me.'

They walked back toward the freight entrance of the elevator platform. Vince admired the tiny puffs of dirt as their boots left prints on the ground, and remembered his walk with Empress Jamyl. For the first time, he questioned whether that had ever really happened.

'You're wounded,' Lord Victor said, taking note of Vince's mangled shoulder. 'But that injury wasn't sustained in the service of our Empire. It was gained in the act of something else. Do you know what that was?'

Vince's cybernetic memory extracted the orders that arrived after his fateful encounter with the scarred man – the ones he had promptly ignored.

'I was bested in combat and became angry with myself,' Vince answered truthfully. 'I have never consciously experienced an emotion like that before. I know I was Reclaimed to do God's work, but I was unprepared for this. To be vanquished by a mortal – it enraged me. And I allowed that rage to consume me. I humbly ask forgiveness ... There is still much I have to learn.'

Lord Victor studied him, observing how his blood gave off a reflective sheen in the sunlight.

'I saw the footage,' he said. 'The girl distracted you. Who was she?'

'A Believer,' Vince said, now aware that he felt strangely protective of her. 'I wasn't expecting a target to recite prayer. It elicited teachings of forgiveness in the Scriptures.'

'As a warrior you must always expect the unexpected,' Lord Victor said, waving a fist at him. 'You let your guard down and it cost you your life. But as an immortal you have the luxury of learning the hard way, and are all the stronger for it.'

'Yes, sir.'

'Now tell me about Templar Six.'

'We were less than six minutes from the drop. He lost his mind, began speaking gibberish, pulled his weapon—'

'I know this,' Lord Victor said, stepping closer. 'I saw what happened. We analyzed the words he spoke. It sounded like an actual dialect, not gibberish. Are you sure that's all it was?'

Eidetic recall took over. Vince felt a crippling pulse of dread: He realized that he was never consciously aware at the time that every word spoken by Templar Six was perfectly understandable to him. It wasn't gibberish at all. His was the voice of someone ancient, someone thousands of years old, begging for help. He was there to deliver a warning, speaking to him directly. Perhaps it was adrenaline and the fight-or-flight response of his anatomy that filtered it out, like the way the body suppresses pain in dire circumstances.

Time slowed down. He knew he could *not* let Lord Victor know.

'I didn't understand any of it,' Vince said. 'Templar Six was a traitor. That was all that mattered.'

'You made the right decision,' Lord Victor said. 'Good.'

'Yes, sir.'

'We recorded the neurological telemetry of all the Templars during the mission,' Lord Victor said. 'I hope you aren't lying to me.'

DOMAIN REGION – THRONE WORLDS CONSTELLATION
THE AMARR SYSTEM – PLANET ORIS
EMPEROR FAMILY ACADEMY STATION
SOVEREIGNTY OF THE AMARR EMPIRE

Nine Years Ago

The high was greater than she ever imagined.

In the entirety of Jamyl's privileged life, she could recall no joy even remotely close to what she was feeling right now. The feeling of connectedness, of being so intimately close to another human being, so acutely aware of all the hidden pleasures of life – who *knew* how much the flesh could be stimulated? – that she regretted never having been introduced to Cryllisium sooner. Because of its wondrous powers, she now understood that a woman's body was so much more beautiful than a man's; that a woman's touch always found the perfect balance of gentleness and assertion; and that following the journey of a single droplet of sweat along the curves of a woman's hips was easily the most mesmerizing spectacle in all creation.

Jamyl never wanted to come down. Everything, at last, was as it should be. She was only remotely aware that what had begun as a rebellious act against a culture she abhorred, a religion that she rejected, and an obligation she wanted nothing to do with, was now, after having tasted it, something much more meaningful.

It simply never occurred to her that she'd actually *enjoy* it.

But then the high surrendered to something else. Fear crept into the experience, as the suddenly tense body language of her lovers suggested someone else had joined them.

The fringe of her awareness informed her that the interloper was Lord Falek Grange, but his physical appearance reminded her of a charging slaver. She arranged her posture defiantly, naked as the day she was born, and stood proudly to face him.

'You are a tantalizing vision,' the slaver said. 'Do you mind if I join you?'

His unexpected response was disarming; she sought an appropriate response from the cosmic aura surrounding them.

'Did my mother send you?' she asked, sashaying toward one of her maiden companions, providing a reassuring caress of her shoulders.

'No,' Falek answered. 'I assured her all was well.'

'Is that what you think?' she said, tasting one of her fingers. 'That all is *well*?'

'I would say things are absolutely grand,' he said, poking through the used vials. 'I've never been one for all the royal pomp and flair anyway.'

'That's quite an admission coming from someone of your stature,' Jamyl said, lounging on some furniture. 'Are you always this honest?'

'The most beautiful woman in New Eden is before me wearing nothing but her jewelry,' the slaver said. 'I may be a pious man, but I'm not dead.'

Jamyl smiled as he motioned toward the couch beside her.

'May I?'

She thought about it for a moment.

'No,' she said. 'I decree that you shall stand, Lord Grange, and be made to feel as uncomfortable as it takes to amuse me.'

Falek the Slaver smiled back at her.

'Then may I at least have the mercy of indulging in some guilty pleasures myself, to help numb the pain of my shame?'

He motioned toward his own palm, which was now filled with more vials.

'Mmm, impressive,' Jamyl said, curling beside another naked maiden, who appeared more at ease – and ready to continue indulging. 'What is this shame you speak of?'

'The shame of not approaching you sooner,' Falek said. 'The shame of lacking the courage to be honest with myself, as you have.'

Jamyl laughed.

'What makes you think I'm interested in your courage?' she asked. 'I saved all my self-expression for the right occasion. So it would actually count for something.'

She watched as Falek placed the vial into his mouth and popped it. An audible hiss reported its contents absorbed through the tongue and sinuses.

Jamyl felt herself become dangerously aroused.

'My *God*, sin tastes good,' Falek said, shuddering from the high. He buckled at the knees slightly, and then, to the amusement of everyone else, collapsed into a chair.

'I am so sorry,' he said. 'But why haven't I tried this before?'

Jamyl was fascinated and positioned herself perpendicular to her prone companion as the others relaxed back into each other's arms. Fixing her gaze on Falek, she rested her forearms on her partner's backside.

'I want more confessions,' she said. 'Entertain me, Lord Grange.'

'Where to begin,' he asked, leaning back into the chair. 'The apolitical truths? Or just the sacrilegious ones?'

'All of them,' she said. 'I want to hear the sins of Amarr's most pious man.'

'Sins,' he repeated, resting his hands behind his head. 'I absolutely hated your father. Passionately so.'

'I *love* it,' she cooed. 'What else?'

'I don't believe in the Succession Trials. Never have.'

'Ah,' Jamyl sighed, feeling a tempestuous surge of desire mixed with the sensation of flying. She rose and approached him in the most seductive manner she knew.

'Tell me more.'

'The only thing I despise more than government is royalty,' he continued.

She straddled him, rolling her head so that her auburn mane brushed against his face. Setting one arm on his shoulder, she dangled her ample breasts before him, then used her forefinger to lift his face by the chin.

'Manners, Lord Grange. You shouldn't stare.'

'My goodness,' he said, running his hands along her back. 'I don't know where my head was. Forgive me, Your . . . Highness.'

She threw her chin back and laughed; Falek began shaking.

'I love when powerful men throw themselves before me.'

'Then let's fuck the world together,' he said, as she bit into his lips and plunged her tongue deep into his mouth.

He reached up with another vial, running its edge along her supple lips. She licked it provocatively.

'I want a divine experience of our own,' he said, gently pushing the drug into position. She growled in anticipation of the powerful rush.

'One that will atone for our sins,' he said, snapping the switch that released the drugs into Jamyl's bloodstream. While she waited for the high, the drugs circulated to her brain and began performing their meticulously planned work on her synapses.

After a moment she realized this wasn't Cryllisium at all. Indeed, at least one of the vials she had consumed earlier contained a toxic mutagen designed to control slaves, and she had just experienced the soothing – and absolutely controlling – effects of a custom Vitoc antidote.

'Now listen closely,' Falek said, grasping her by the face and pulling her close. 'You will obey me, always, and in return I will provide a blissful experience that is righteous and good.'

Her self-identity was slipping away; she tried to fight against it, but it quickly felt pointless to resist what just seemed to naturally make sense: Lord Falek Grange was her master now. And this, it seemed, was the natural order of the universe.

'One day, you will love me for this,' he said. 'But for now, you will sit at your father's funeral and become the majestic heiress that Amarr needs you to be.'

HEIMATAR REGION – HED CONSTELLATION
AMAMAKE SYSTEM – PLANET II: PIKE'S LANDING
CORE FREEDOM COLONY
SOVEREIGNTY OF THE AMARR EMPIRE

Present Day

Lord Victor walked inside the elevator's control tower, marveling at how the technical wonder was standing and functional despite all the war in its shadow. A thin film of dust covered the displays and controls inside, where operators had once guided the transfer of millions of tonnes of material from orbit to the surface and back daily. Victor ran his hand across one of the windows facing the magrail yard, following its decrepit tracks through the colony perimeter and beyond toward the mountain range. It was inferior construction when compared to Amarr's version of these machines. But it was pricelessly functional nonetheless.

That it was taken by thirteen Templars and a tiny conventional force was unimaginable. The program for which Lord Falek Grange had sacrificed so much was at last fulfilling its promise. Endless possibilities were within reach. The power of Amarr was uncontestable: The door to the next Reclaiming had opened. Of course he believed this would happen; his faith had never wavered. It was surreal that this moment had finally arrived.

Yet it wasn't perfect. And he knew, by virtue of Her Majesty's divine powers, that he could no longer hide the truth about the Templars' flaws – if he could convince himself that it was ever hidden at all.

At that exact moment of doubt, she walked right into his mind.

What makes a thing worth fighting for? Empress Jamyl asked. *The answer was always 'when the alternative is not worth living through.'*

Has that changed, Victor? Or has immortality culled this part of our soul as well?

'My lady,' Victor spoke aloud. 'The Templars are victorious. They will mold history to your will.'

What history would you write, my captain? What legacy would you choose for Amarr?

'Amarr is invincible,' Lord Victor said, trying to filter the passion in his heart. 'With God by our side, there is no foe we cannot vanquish.'

We will be judged by what we create, not what we conquer. The Templars were conceived to nurture life. They will keep us from destroying ourselves. Never forget that, Victor. You will be judged by how you use this power, as will I.

'Forgive me, Your Majesty. It is difficult to contain my excitement.'

Your imperfections are endearing to me. They mean you still have a soul. What are the next steps for my Templars?

'Though we are victorious, there are contingencies,' Victor said. 'Word of our conquest is spreading. Reactions may be desperate. I recommend moving the Templars offworld as soon as reinforcements arrive to secure our claim.'

You may proceed.

'There is something else,' Victor said. 'I have been concerned . . . You must already know. Templar Six went rogue during the mission and needed to be dispatched. We have not reanimated him: His essence is locked in virtual storage.'

Victor heard silence – a sign that a struggle was under way.

'There are flaws in the others as well,' he continued. 'Templar Six spoke in a dialect we cannot decipher. They experience traumatic visions as they reclone. Some believe there are dangers we must fully understand before moving forward. . . .'

There it was – the transformation. When something else awoke inside of her.

The Templars are the saviors of man, Lord Victor. By my decree, you will move forward with the Reclaiming at once.

DOMAIN REGION – THRONE WORLDS CONSTELLATION
THE AMARR SYSTEM – PLANET ORIS
EMPEROR FAMILY ACADEMY STATION
SOVEREIGNTY OF THE AMARR EMPIRE

Present Day

Jamyl ripped herself from the recesses of Victor's mind and collapsed to one knee, blinded by pain and the ruthless intrusion of the Other.

But now she began laughing, even as it wracked the muscles surrounding her ribs.

'What do you keep hiding from me, you coward?' she said.

Within her private chambers, there was pure, chilled water within reach at all times. Even as the years passed and her ability to control the alien entity inside her improved, her immune system still revolted ferociously against the invasion. Gushing with flash perspiration, her body temperature soared as the Other – with whom she was still locked in an anguishing battle of attrition – invaded her psyche.

You hear everything you need to rule well, it said.

'Your secrets hurt us both,' Jamyl retorted between gulps of water. 'How can I help you if you won't be honest with me?'

Your sincerity assures me I have all the help I need.

'The Templars succeeded at Pike's Landing,' she said, shivering violently. 'You should be pleased.'

Humanity's desire to destroy itself ensures their place in history.

'Strange how you always awaken when my curiosity about them heightens.'

I strike the weakness from you before it can harm us.

'Us?'

What is good for Amarr is good for us.

Jamyl learned that the entity sharing her mind needed her to survive. Yet it had its own psychology, its own motives, and bespoke an intelligence suggestive of another time and culture, a civilization unlike any that had existed before. Still, Jamyl managed to hurt it, wear it down, and demoralize it, even when she couldn't know what its intentions were. But somehow, the Other found strength at exactly the right times to block her awareness entirely.

The Templars were part of its plan. But she couldn't know how. There was a sinister element to their existence, but she was prevented from developing the idea further: The Other kept an unbreakable lock on that part of her thought process. Nevertheless, she was aligned with the potential they brought to Amarr's cause. Her father had glorified war and wanted her Empire to worship it. Amarr nearly fell because of that delusion: The Joves, after all, needn't have stopped at Atioth. They could have marched all the way to the Throne Worlds.

In her mind, their civilization was that close to the brink. She was determined to prevent that from ever happening again by using the technology of immortality to change the calculus of war to a zero-sum game. The Templars would shatter the rationale of any sane adversary who believed war was worth the price.

The Other stepped into her thoughts seamlessly.

I am thousands of years old. I have lived through the beginning and the end of hope. You are wise to let me help you realize your vision.

Jamyl staggered to her feet.

'For now,' she growled. 'But when the time is right, there will be an end to you.'

I accept this fate knowing I have accomplished what I came here for. Until then, I will save my strength, and act only when you lack it.

Jamyl's concentration was broken by an electronic update from her Court Chamberlain. Her Empire was run by a theocratic bureaucracy charged with enacting the policy she decreed. Progress was delivered daily, and she would only inject herself into matters when her faith in the desired outcome faltered. Given her condition, it was wise to limit her contact with advisors and even then to keep such contact as brief and authoritarian as possible.

In the blink of an eye, reports from every corner of the Empire materialized in her consciousness: Her admirals described progress on the Minmatar front. The Empire's coffers were being depleted faster than replenished; fiscal measures to stimulate tax revenues were being considered. Her inspirational presence was recommended at the site of several worlds where natural disasters had taken a large civilian toll. Social unrest was rising in regions loyal to Yonis Ardishapur. At present she was the guardian of more than one trillion souls across thousands of worlds. The people were anxious for her to fulfill the prophecies of her reign, and to end the war that had cost them so much.

Amarr will end all wars, Empress Jamyl. That will be your legacy.

'Of course it will,' she stammered. 'Why wouldn't I believe you?'

The sooner you learn to trust me, the more comfortable you'll be with destiny.

'You've given me every reason to despise you unconditionally,' she said, feeling a tinge of strength return to her. 'There is neither trust nor common ground between us.'

I spent many lifetimes surrounded by strangers. Yet I was alone. I am forced to bear a burden I do not want. I am deeply jealous of those who live ignorant lives while I suffer knowing the truth of their world. I am like you in more ways than you can imagine. We are survivors, Empress Jamyl. We are alive because true life finds a way. Always.

'Life? You wanted me to think you were a god,' she said, strong enough now to feel rage. 'I've watched you kill thousands. What do you know about life?'

I know what must be done to preserve it. Now you do as well. People will recognize you as a deity. As you really are. As I will one day become.

Jamyl felt a potent surge of her vitality return; the Other was fading.

The Templars are flawless. They are Heaven's army, and they are yours to command. They shall Reclaim God's creation, and begin the reign of Amarr everlasting. And your name will be heralded for the rest of time.

28

HEIMATAR REGION – HED CONSTELLATION
AMAMAKE SYSTEM – PLANET II: PIKE'S LANDING
THIRTY KILOMETERS SE OF CORE FREEDOM COLONY – BADLANDS GRID
SOVEREIGNTY OF THE AMARR EMPIRE

Staff Sergeant Garrett Lyons loosened the jump straps of his safety harness, contemplating the time when he joined the Federation Marines. He was honest in telling the recruiter everything she wanted to hear: He loved his country, felt a patriotic call of duty to defend it from Tibus Heth and the Caldari State, and was a pure adrenaline junkie. Shooting plasma rifles, jumping from gunships, and traveling to different worlds were all parts of the brochure that spoke to him.

Three years later, here he was, cramped inside a Kruk-class gunship on a covert national security op for the 626 Recon Element, Black Eagles SPECFOR, somewhere over a planet he'd never even heard of until forty-eight hours ago.

By the age of twenty-one, Garrett was a veteran with enough decorations to impress a career soldier. Most of those, he readily conceded, were due to luck and had nothing to do with heroism or valor. The running 'joke' in the Marines was that just making it to an LZ without getting spaced by a capsuleer was worth its own medal. But all comedy aside, he'd seen action on both sides of the border-zone constellations, where the most gruesome fighting had taken place, at least in the eyes of the media. No matter how good the psych treatment or medicine, Garrett knew he wasn't the same naïve kid who walked into that recruiter's office on Crystal Boulevard. The war takes a piece of everyone. It was hard to not roll his eyes at the person he used to be.

But all that experience was coveted by the Federation military, and they'd made him part of the 626 because of it.

Garrett took long-drawn breaths, willing himself into a pre-mission meditation. The stealthy Kruk was skimming over the plateaus and rock steppes of Pike's Landing below, as it had for the last four hundred kilometers of the journey. He felt the bottom lift from his stomach as the craft finally descended below sea level, into the badlands to the southeast of Core Freedom, beneath the X-band radar sweeps of the fortifying Amarr forces to the north.

With the 626, he found himself among soldiers whose covert service records would be legendary, if only they were allowed to be publicized – unsung elite Federation heroes whose actions would likely remain lost to history forever. Deployments were clandestine, rather than 'loud and full-throttle' alongside tanks and MTACs. Most times they were invisible: He'd done takedowns in civilian clothes, infiltrated secure mega-corporation networks using his cybernetic augmentations, and recovered hoards of actionable intelligence about Caldari operations. They went 'loud' only when they had to, and they were good at that too.

Maybe a little too good, Garrett mused, looking over the three squad-mates around him. The missions had only become more 'challenging' with each success, which in their world meant more 'unlikely to survive.' *That*, he thought, *was the curse of competence.*

'Ready up,' he ordered, checking his own equipment. The 'beehive' was the heaviest item in his kit, but crucial to the mission. The basket-size metallic casing contained eight CreoDron NARC-10 drones, each about the size of a large insect. These tiny marvels were autonomous reconnaissance variants, capable of terrain mapping, audio tracking, and high-resolution optical scans. Give them something to look for, and they would find it, returning to the hive to recharge and upload their data to the transmitter inside the casing.

A typical infantry beehive cost about a million credits; this one was ten times that, and each man was equipped with one. The brass needed to know what happened here, and no expense would be spared to find out.

Garrett reviewed the mission again.

Primary Objective: Establish mobile reconnaissance platforms on the Core Freedom perimeter.

Recon Target: Conventional Imperial forces and any evidence of new cloning technology.

Observe and report. Do not make enemy contact.

That last part was fine with him. Huge corridors of Pike's Landing were completely uninhabited and, more importantly, unmonitored. Their gunship had already dodged Imperial starship patrols and managed to drop into the atmosphere undetected. The flight plan took them over vast, undeveloped corridors of land under the cover of darkness. But the closest they could get to the colony without being seen was through the badlands.

The problem was that anyone who wanted to observe the colony from up close – and all indications were that a few governments did – would know this as well.

'Neutrino spike,' the pilot warned. 'And X-rays. Coming from the badlands.'

'Go quiet and check it out,' Garrett said.

'Roger,' the pilot said, slowing the craft down and activating the gunship's advanced stealth systems. Nearly all spacecraft relied on aneutronic reactors to generate power; 98 percent of that output was proton emissions. But the remaining 2 percent was neutrino emissions, whose signature could be dampened but never fully masked. By sheer luck alone, the Kruk flew through a neutrino stream whose trajectory vectored from the terrain ahead. Chances were these weren't random particles tunneling through the planet at that exact spot.

'Got it,' the pilot warned. 'Unidentified gunship dead ahead, parked and camouflaged a few meters from the valley floor.'

'Unmask and orbit,' Garrett said. 'Guns ready.'

'Wilco,' the pilot said. 'Let command know?'

'I'll do it,' he answered. Weapons lowered from the Kruk's wings as the pilot performed a cautious circle of the strange craft.

'Command, this is Hotel-Actual. We found an unidentified bogey near the LZ. Telemetry on the way. Please advise.'

Garrett could see what the pilot was referring to through an augmented reality of the optics. The tech aboard the Kruk was advanced enough to see through the mysterious gunship's cloaking mechanism and scan its hull design.

'Can we get a look at the interior?' Garrett asked.

'Negative,' the pilot answered. 'Terahertz just scatters, infrared is cold, and everything else shows a black hole.'

Garrett became alarmed.

'Then how'd you unmask the visible wavelength?' he asked.

'I didn't,' the pilot answered. 'The laser designator just picked it up. It's not doing anything tricky to cloak the fuselage.'

Though there were hundreds of stock-model gunship types in operation around New Eden, Garrett was confident this was the only one of its kind.

Director Mentas Blaque answered the comm directly.

'Hotel-Actual, this is Blaque. You've got new orders: Disable that craft; board and report. Make sure it can't broadcast. We need to know who owns it. Use nonlethal force if you can, but I won't hold you to it.'

Garrett looked at the rest of the commandos. It was time to get serious.

'Hotel-Actual copies,' he said. 'We're on it.'

HEIMATAR REGION – HED CONSTELLATION
AMAMAKE SYSTEM – PLANET II: PIKE'S LANDING
CORE FREEDOM COLONY – PERIMETER GRID
SOVEREIGNTY OF THE AMARR EMPIRE

The temporary staging area for cloning repairs was right alongside the Able spaceport, where a small farm of mobile CRUs was established. A startling transformation of Core Freedom was under way, as gold-plated MTACs and Paladins now patrolled the grounds. The space elevator's main freight platform had just concluded its second descent from space, bringing with it mobile surface-to-air missile (SAM) batteries, construction materials, and armored vehicles. Despite this voluminous cargo, most of the platform remained empty. The engineering marvel could bring down much more, if only the ships above could supply it quickly enough.

Vince staggered alone toward the CRU farm, avoiding the gaze of onlookers. He felt much hotter than before, and it was becoming difficult to breathe. His injured shoulder throbbed with each heartbeat; he placed his hand in front of his face and found he had trouble focusing.

Concern became outright alarm as he nearly fell, leaning against a wrecked APC for support. His TACNET biometrics flashed online:

>BIOSYS ALERT<
>BODY TEMP 44C, BP 225/120<
>ELEVATED RECOVERY MODE<
>SYSDIAG: VASCULAR NANITE IMBALANCE DUE TO HUMERUS-SCAPULA POSTERIOR DISLOCATION<
>RECOMMENDED ACTION: VITALS WILL STABILIZE WHEN JOINT IS RESET. PAVE-MEDIC NOTIFIED.<

It felt as though molten lead were pumping through his veins. 'Pave-Medic' was the online system monitoring the performance of his clone and that of the other Templars.

'Templar One,' a voice said. 'Did you receive that warning?'

'Yes,' Vince said. 'What does it—'

'Your clone is trying to repair an injury it can't fix on its own,' the voice said. It was likely a physician somewhere in the space above, watching and recording every single thing he did.

Vince felt a tinge of anger, then succumbed to desperation as his condition deteriorated.

'The bionanites in your plasma are racing through your vascular system looking for the source of pain you're feeling,' the voice said. 'Congratulations: You've found a bug in your clone design.'

Though he was clearly in physical distress, dozens of people had just walked past him without offering assistance. Stumbling toward the nearest building for shade, Vince caught a reflection of himself in some debris and froze.

'Reset the shoulder yourself,' Pave-Medic informed. 'Bend the arm ninety degrees at the elbow, keep your arm in an L shape, hold the elbow against your body, and rotate the forearm outward from the chest as far as you can, maintaining that L until it reduces. It's going to hurt, but fight through it. This is a silly reason to lose an expensive clone.'

What the hell am I? Vince thought, staring at the pale ghost of himself in the reflection. He had no idea what he even *should* look like. Self-image was an unfamiliar concept. Instead of seeing a person, he saw memories from a short life filled with nightmares.

'Do it now, Templar,' Pave-Medic warned. 'Or else you're going to have bigger problems.'

Vince clenched his fist and did what he was instructed to, forcing his shoulder through agony that would make most men faint.

With a muffled *pop*, the joint slipped back into place. The pain receded almost immediately, and he felt the equivalent of needles rush through his veins as his cybernetic vascular system restored equilibrium.

The sound of Lord Victor's voice startled him.

'I have new orders for you, Templar,' he said. Vince had no idea how long he had been standing there.

'Two new tests,' Victor continued. 'One of faith, the other of your abilities.'

Blinking away phosphenes, Vince straightened his posture.

'I am eager to serve, my lord.'

'Good,' Victor said. Vince's TACNET was now displaying a map of the colony.

'The badlands south of here are geologically impervious to surface-based radar. We have eyes overhead in space and occasional gunship patrols, but we need boots on the ground.'

'Of course, sir. We can be ready to deploy within—'

'Not "we,"' Victor interrupted. 'Just you.'

On one hand, Vince was thrilled to explore the terrain. On the other, it was becoming apparent that the master he served no longer trusted him.

'Should I expect enemy contact?' he asked.

'A number of Valklears fled during the invasion,' Lord Victor said. 'Sending a full patrol would attract attention. This is a scouting op. One man, operating with stealth, is what's needed. Observe and report. Under no circumstances are you to make contact. We will send support. If things go badly, you will revive at the CRU farm with immediate access to vehicles that can return you to the badlands quickly. However . . .'

Lord Victor narrowed his eyes at him

'Do not return from there until I say so,' he said. 'Is that understood?'

'Yes, sir.'

PURE BLIND REGION – MDM8-J CONSTELLATION
SYSTEM 5ZXX-K – PLANET V, MOON 17
MORDU'S LEGION HQ STATION

The Moros-class dreadnought was a bulbous monstrosity codesigned by the Federation Navy, Roden Shipyards, and CreoDron. Her first trials began shortly after the first Caldari – Gallente War; since then she had become a staple of the Federation's ability to project interregional power. Like most dreadnoughts, she was able to field large numbers of troops and armor to mount siege operations, and more important, fire gigantic railguns that could pummel the surface of worlds from orbit. Korvin Lears had seen dozens of these magnificent capital ships up close, participated in ops to support them, and even piloted a few during his service with the Federation Navy.

But this was the first time he'd ever seen one in Mordu's Legion colors.

'Magnificent, isn't she?' Mordu asked. He wore no hat this time, and his implants showed prominently along the sides of his scalp and behind the ears. 'She might be my favorite ship here.'

'Did you build it,' Korvin asked, 'or steal it?'

'A little of both, actually,' Mordu answered, resting his hands on the rail. 'I salvaged it.'

'Really?'

'June twenty-ninth, the year YC III,' Mordu said. 'Capsuleer alliances vying for control of the space we're in right now clashed in systems just a few jumps from here. At the time, it was recorded as the largest capital-ship engagement in New Eden's history. When it was over, more than two hundred wrecks littered the space of Pure Blind.'

'The Northern Coalition,' Korvin said. 'I remember this.'

'This Moros was one of the more intact casualties,' Mordu said, as a frown took shape on his brow. 'She once had a crew of forty-eight hundred souls. It's amazing how little these immortals think of the lives they drag through the mud for their own ambitions.'

Korvin noted the irony, as Mordu's neuro-interface socket was plainly visible on his neck.

'I had it towed back here,' he continued, 'at considerable expense, mind you. That graveyard was a gold mine for salvagers. But I wasn't in it for the money. Instead, I was intrigued by the prospect of restoring it.'

He began walking along the corridor, scrutinizing the work still being performed on the mammoth vessel. At least a dozen service barges and drones were positioned around its hull, and streams of torch-weld sparks were creating a spectacular light show in the hangar.

'This ship is the memento of a catastrophe whose memory I want to keep alive,' Mordu said. 'A souvenir, of sorts. And, I enjoy tinkering with things.'

'Of course,' Korvin said. 'Is she the only dreadnought in your fleet?'

'Hardly,' Mordu said with a wink. 'But she's special in more ways than one. For example, I may have cut some corners in her reconstruction.'

'Hence, why I'm the one flying it,' Korvin said. 'How many corners—'

'Your pod might be, how should I say? ... a cheap imitation,' Mordu said. 'Should you perish, all the data since your last checkpoint as a Federation Navy officer might not be transmitted.'

The last time Korvin had a clone snapshot taken for any reason was more than six months ago. Hence, every moment of his life since then would be lost if the pod didn't function properly. *That*, Korvin thought, *was a fucked-up thing to do to an immortal.*

'You don't want to trust me, that's fine,' he fumed. 'But you should be smart enough to know I can't betray—'

'Please,' Mordu said, motioning for silence. 'Given the circumstances, I *know* you're going to give this your best shot.'

'Yeah, well, don't you worry, Mordu,' Korvin said, shaking his head. 'You'll get what you want out of this.'

Mordu looked him square in the eyes and smiled.

'Concierge,' he called out. 'Whiskey, please. The fifty-year-old.'

'Yes, sir,' a sultry voice called out, though Korvin had no idea from where.

'Do you know why I like you?' Mordu asked.

'I can't even imagine.'

'Because you would be doing this whether I had a leash on your life or not.'

A provocatively dressed waitress with long legs and a billion-credit smile appeared from out of nowhere with amber-colored spirits in two crystal glasses. Setting the bottle on the rail, she served Korvin with her lips pursed open just enough to make him sweat, and then she walked away, disappearing around the bend in the corridor. Despite its imposing size and purpose, the deck was eerily devoid of people. It resembled more of a posh lounge than a military outpost. Korvin remembered the Navy treating its pilots well, but this was ridiculous.

'I volunteered,' he said, inhaling the beverage's rich aroma. 'What's your point?'

'You have a hero complex,' Mordu said, taking a sip. 'It's not my style to flatter, but your service record is exemplary. Yet you're an outcast to your peers. Why?'

Korvin took a sip of his own. At first, it bit into his sinuses, then settled into a smooth, warming sensation.

'You should know the answer to that.'

'But your name was cleared,' Mordu said, referring to the extensive and humiliating Federation investigation against him and his parents for their relationship with Admiral Alexander Noir. 'I suppose people still believe what they want to. I'll tell you what: You perform your role in this craziness with the same valor that your record shows, and I'll help you uncover the truth.'

Korvin remembered the last time he'd seen his old mentor alive, and how his words had driven a stake through his heart. It wasn't the same man, and everyone knew it.

'I'd known Admiral Noir for more than a century before he died,' Mordu continued. 'We may have had our differences, but he was no murderer.'

Korvin downed the rest in a single gulp.

'If you want help restoring the honor of his good name, count me in,' Mordu said. 'I have a score to settle with the Broker as well.'

That earned Mordu a sharp look.

'You know for sure it was him?' Korvin asked.

'I have a good feeling,' Mordu said. 'But that time will come. We have a job to do first.'

'Right.'

'I need to learn more about this hero complex,' Mordu said. 'When Heth invaded Luminaire, yours was one of the first Federation ships to respond. You tried to warn people on the surface of Caldari Prime and flew your interceptor directly into a pack of invading dropships. If that isn't heroic—'

'I'm immortal,' Korvin snapped. 'You have to actually risk something to become a hero.'

'Then why did you do it?'

'I don't know. Why are you asking me this?'

Mordu leaned in closer.

'Because I'm wondering if true selflessness exists anymore,' he said. 'I send a lot of people to die in wars, but ultimately it's *they who send themselves*. There's no conscription here. No marching orders. Mercenaries are with us on their own accord. And knowing they're doing this for the right reasons makes *my* pain just a little more bearable. So tell me, Captain Lears: What is it that always makes you take the higher path?'

Korvin tried to match the intensity of Mordu's relentless stare, to reach for an answer he wasn't even sure was the right one.

'I had a brother once,' he started, grabbing the bottle and refilling his own glass. 'An older brother. He was my hero. Everything he did, I did. I practically idolized him. He was an immensely gifted, talented person. He could have written his ticket to do anything, become anyone.'

Down the vintage drink went, incinerating the lining of his throat. He coughed once, then continued.

'But then he started hanging out with some shady types. Began messing around with drugs. Started doing things that were out of character. One day he came home with some crazy, repulsive-looking augmentations, and then things just blew up between him and my family. After that, he stopped coming home for good.'

Korvin went to pour himself another, but Mordu reached out and stopped him.

'A few years later, they found him in a ditch,' Korvin said, releasing his grip on the bottle. 'Police said he got caught in the crossfire of some Serpentis turf fight.'

'I'm very sorry to hear that,' said Mordu, who appeared more fascinated than sympathetic.

'I had a thousand chances to speak up, warn him, do something,' Korvin said, as the liquor's potency caught up with him. 'I didn't, because I was afraid to. He was six years older than me, but I heard this voice in me that screamed he was on a bad path. I was the wiser one. But I didn't do anything. And then my "hero" died.'

Korvin got right in Mordu's face.

'So you want to know why I do it?' he said. 'Why I always open my mouth and take the higher ground? *Because the fucking voices in my head tell me to.*'

Korvin slammed his glass on the railing and began walking away.

'Tell that to Captain Varitec and the *Morse* crew,' he called out. 'I'm sure they'll like me even more.'

Mordu stared at Korvin's back for a moment, then typed a subtle note into his datapad.

'I *love* you!' he suddenly called out. 'You're *exactly* my kind of crazy!'

DOMAIN REGION – YEKTI CONSTELLATION
THE NIARJA SYSTEM – AMARR – CALDARI BORDER
KAAPUTENEN STARGATE

Entombed in the viscous grave of his starship capsule, Mens Reppola took note of the ship's surroundings, panning the camera drones out for maximum optical coverage.

The stargate was shimmering in gold – literally, a twenty-four-karat sheen coating a surface area greater than several thousand square meters. The ship he was flying – an Amarr-designed Providence-class freighter – was, like the epic stargate floating before him, also coated in the precious metal. So too was every station in the empire, and almost every cathedral across a civilization that claimed thousands of systems.

Who else but the Amarr are even capable of such arrogance? Mens thought.

To know this civilization was to understand that the church's influence here was immutable and omnipresent. If Mens were capable of judging them dispassionately, he might marvel – if not allow himself to be dumbstruck – at the sheer magnificence of their devotion to the idea of God. Stargates, in and of themselves, were unfathomably complex machines. For those nations that could afford to build them, it was enough just to create one that worked, let alone devote so much attention to aesthetics. Amarr engineers, drawing on millennia of Athran architectural influence, had turned it into a timeless artistic masterpiece.

It seemed fitting that they controlled the system of humanity's origin and the EVE Gate itself.

Mens tensed up as a pair of Imperial Navy frigates approached, cruising along the length of his ship. No doubt they were passively scanning his cargo, which – despite Rali's assurances to the contrary – Mens was convinced would lead to his interdiction. Instead, they flew away, gingerly moving on to the next ship that blinked into local timespace through the gate.

'Are you through yet?' Rali asked unexpectedly.

'What happened to keeping quiet?' Mens growled. His friend had warned him not to communicate once he reached Amarr space.

'Oh, I was kidding about that,' Rali said. 'Why? Nervous?'

Mens would have strangled him if he could. The Providence began a lumbering turn toward the next stargate, some fifty-seven AUs away.

'Your comms aren't routing through the gates,' Rali said. 'We're on a secure fluid router. And to Amarr Customs, your IDENT tags read as belonging to Holder Laurus Fahyed, a reclusive historian and avid collector of antique war vehicles.'

The technology that Rali could throw together on a moment's notice would impress even the craftiest starship engineer. As always, Mens didn't know the details of exactly how he was going to locate a single ship in an area the size of a cubic light-year. He just knew Rali would figure out the best solution, and that would have to be enough.

'Holder Fahyed's profession gives you good reason to be in the New Eden system,' Rali continued. 'Your cargo bays are loaded with random junk and about two hundred decommissioned Wiyrkomi "Corsair" fighter-bombers from the first Caldari – Gallente War, which won't raise much suspicion since they're packaged and stowed.'

Dozens of gold-plated ships of all different sizes were coming and going through the stargate; the space lanes were bustling with traffic. Mens felt uncomfortably out of place here. Amarr space was spectacularly vibrant. For some reason, it also struck him as deceptively sinister.

'When you reach New Eden, a series of navpoints will register on your scanner. These are references for your drive computer to plot warp tracks. I hope you're prepared for a long trip: There are more than six hundred of them, and each one is at least a one-hundred-AU warp. All told, you're taking the scenic route through a light-year of space.'

'Shit, Rali, it'll take—'

'Your freighter is equipped with a prototype Propel Dynamics warp engine. I've set it so you can't fully open her up until you reach New Eden, but it allegedly averages twenty-five AUs per second, with a minimum ninety-second cooldown between hops. That's nearly twice as fast as the next-best ship in the cluster. At least, that I know of.'

'Twenty-five AUs?' Mens said. 'How the heck did you—'

'Don't thank me yet, because technically you're a test pilot. Propel Dynamics needs the stress metrics, and you're going to beat the hell out of that drive for them. Unfortunately, there's no warranty if it happens to go nova on you midflight.'

'That's reassuring,' Mens grumbled. 'Where'd you get the nav data?'

'Federation Navy archives, minimal security clearance. It was a simple hack.'

'Brilliant.'

'Thanks. Once you're a light-year closer to Point Genesis, those junked Corsairs will spring to life,' Rali continued. 'Those are state-of-the-art APEX-Eleven warp-capable frontier drones in disguise, all with entangled comms, enough of them to work a border-zone sector. They'll break into their preset search patterns, working toward Point Genesis and broadcasting your contact data to the *Significance*.'

'How long will it take?'

'Anywhere from a few minutes to never. If that ship doesn't want to be found, we just won't find it. They'll see us coming from far away. Its captain probably dropped sensor buoys years ago. We're not sneaking up on it.'

Mens considered for the thousandth time that this was all just another one of Haatakan's jaded, twisted antics.

'Is our side of the bargain secured?' Mens asked.

'You mean our role in the assassination of a head of state?'

'Yeah,' Mens grimaced. 'That.'

'A very good Ishukone pilot with good Ishukone equipment is standing by. The cargo is due in just a few hours. He doesn't know anything.'

Mens wondered if he knew who it was, then decided it was probably better he didn't.

'What did all this cost us, Rali?'

'A lot,' Rali grimaced. 'Those APEX birds alone cost half a billion each. It's going to take some creative accounting to explain this to the board of directors.'

'Seriously,' Mens asked, 'do you think this is worth it?'

Rali reflected a moment. 'All we have is hope, our convictions, and the word of a sadist. ...' He paused, then added: 'I love our odds. We've got Heth *right* where we want him.'

Mens smiled.

'You're a good man,' he said. 'Thank you.'

'One more thing,' Rali said. 'If you are stopped before reaching New Eden, for any reason, self-destruct. You *cannot* get caught with that cargo.'

'Understood,' Mens said. 'Has Mila contacted you with more information?'

Despite all the pressure of Ishukone, all the danger posed by Tibus Heth, and all the risks he was taking to mitigate both, the sad truth was that he hadn't been able to get Mila off his mind. For a moment, Lorin and Amile seemed secondary. What began as something he thought he could ignore had metastasized into a potentially crippling obsession.

It was highly uncharacteristic of him, and that made him nervous.

'No,' Rali said. 'But I would imagine she'd just call you directly.'

'Is that a bad thing?' Mens asked.

'Well. It's not good for everyone. You know better than most that doing the right thing is usually difficult. Call if you need me.'

Rali signed off as the freighter lurched into warp. The New Eden system was twenty jumps away.

HEIMATAR REGION – HED CONSTELLATION
AMAMAKE SYSTEM – PLANET II: PIKE'S LANDING
THIRTY KILOMETERS SE OF CORE FREEDOM COLONY—BADLANDS GRID
SOVEREIGNTY OF THE AMARR EMPIRE

Garrett was seething with frustration but wouldn't allow it to bubble through to his comrades.

'Sarge, I'm sorry, but I don't know what the hell this material is,' Corporal Tines reported. 'I've tried plasma torches, explosives. ... I think we need a damn starship cannon to punch through.'

It was embarrassing. What was supposed to be a classic breach-and-clear on a gunship – something they'd done a thousand times – instead turned into an hour's worth of messing around trying to find a way to break in. They'd made it as far as disabling its cloaking system, but that was it. Specialist Flaherty was equipped with cyphering implants – cutting-edge stuff that could hack third-generation AIs – but wasn't having any luck, either.

'This is some kind of hull-repair tech,' Corporal Tines continued. 'Same as starships, but a lot smarter and faster.'

The gunship, about forty meters long, twenty meters wide, and six meters high, had aerodynamic contours along the wingspan that blended into bulging nacelles where the plasma thrusters were housed. The fuselage material was light gray; some seams were evident, but it almost appeared as though most of it was built from one continuous piece. There were no serial markings or insignia of any kind.

Most disturbingly, the surface felt wet to the touch, even though it was clearly bone dry.

'Can you get some shaped charges up there?' Garrett asked, pointing to the engine nacelle. 'If that doesn't work, I'm asking command if we can just blow it up with the Kruk's cannons.'

'Yeah, but let me go around to the other side,' Tines said. 'I can use the rocks to climb up.'

'I'll go with you,' Corporal Evans said.

'Sarge, I gotta put her down to save fuel,' the pilot said. 'Found a good spot about half a klick from you. I'll keep her on standby in case we need to get airborne in a hurry.'

'Okay, do it,' Garrett said.

It was still dark, and the valley – what little he could see of it – was brimming with life. The desert landscape had sparse vegetation, but he swore he could hear running water from somewhere. Odd sounds – slithers, rustles, clicks, and chirps – created an ambience that was equal parts beautiful and intimidating. You never knew if a life-form's sound was a tiny thing's defensive measure or a big thing's way of drawing you in closer for a meal.

As Evans and Tines disappeared around the engine's tail, Specialist Flaherty tried to jack into the ship's network again. He settled into his trance, resting his hands on the surface of the gunship, his eyes glowing slightly. He could 'hear' electrical systems humming on the inside; he just needed to follow one to the feed supplying its network core inside.

Out of habit, Garrett raised his rifle to scan the area through his scope. And the moment he did so, his heart stopped: The rangefinder was dead and so was the rifle itself. When he glanced over at Flaherty, the specialist was convulsing, apparently having a seizure.

The radio was silent, and all their electronics were dead.

'EMP!' he shouted. 'Melee weapons!'

Few things in life are more useless than firearms that don't shoot. In basic training, cadets are taught to immediately discard weapons and equipment that relied on electricity following an EMP strike. That ruled out plasma rifles, most beam weapons, communications gear, and the optics on any scopes. If you were prepared for the strike, you were equipped with a legacy chemical-explosive or nanolever spring-action firearm, and short of those, a combat knife.

The 626 was prepared. They even had hardened weapons that could withstand lower yield pulses.

Garrett crouched low, hands wrapped tight around his combat knife and pistol. Specialist Flaherty was dead; he was fitted with dozens of cerebral and spinal implants, and the circuitry was integrated with his nervous system. He had literally been cooked from the inside out.

Something moved across the shadows near the top of the gunship; he tracked it with his sidearm but did not shoot, fearful it could be Corporal Tines.

Four silenced shots – he could hear the suppressed *chewt* sounds as they left the barrel – were fired in quick succession. There was a cry – like someone in pain – and then silence.

The EMP burst had to originate from the gunship, Garret thought.

He heard something heavy land on the ground behind him. Whirling around with his weapons raised, he saw it was Corporal Evans's corpse.

Diversion, he knew. The real attack was coming from behind – and he stepped aside just in time as a fist glanced against his helmet; he dropped and rolled away, expecting to turn and pull the trigger.

When he came out of his tuck, he realized the gun had somehow been removed from his grip. His attacker – whom he could only make out as a female silhouette – casually stood across from him, holding the weapon in her hands. But instead of shooting, she merely removed the clip, cleaned the barrel, and tossed the parts off into the darkness.

It was a challenge, and Garrett still had his knife.

He launched himself at the shadow, faster than a man his size should have been able to. He was cybernetically modified, both stronger and quicker than most. His target was the shadow's midsection, aiming a lightning-fast strike with a cutting, thrusting motion from left to right.

But he wasn't nearly fast enough. The attack was parried, and the knife detached from his grip as his wrist was snapped in two.

The attacker effortlessly gained positional advantage, using his momentum against him. Garrett felt his head pushed down and accelerated at incredible speed toward the ground. There was a flash – his helmet had made hard contact with granite – and he suddenly felt nothing.

He was rolled over, and though his mind screamed for his limbs to obey, they would not.

It was dawn, and he could see a little better than when this nightmare first began.

She's pretty, he thought. *What a strange way to die.*

Garrett watched as she picked up his knife and drove it into his heart. He felt nothing, astonished at her complacency as the world faded from view.

THANATOS STOOD AND BRUSHED herself off, admiring her work. The knife placement was perfect, as with the break at the C5 vertebrae. A powerful surge of endorphins flushed through her, causing a tingling sensation of pleasure. Killing these Federation soldiers was unavoidable; they had practically landed on top of her ship. Their deaths were necessary to complete the mission, so she was immensely pleased to have managed the unexpected contingency so easily. The bodies would need to be disposed of, and the ship had to be moved. The pilot and copilot of the Kruk, whose necks she had also broken, would have to be lugged back here.

It was a setback, but she was insatiably eager to please her masters. Once those tasks were complete, she would trek back to the colony perimeter to resume her hunt. Isolating a Templar would be ideal.

That would feel wonderful . . . like sheer bliss. She couldn't wait to begin.

THANATOS didn't realize, nor would she be concerned if she had, that CONCORD had just committed an act of war against the Gallente Federation.

VINCE HAD BEEN SCOUTING THE BADLANDS for hours now.

He was lightly armed and had shed the heavier body armor in favor of mobility and speed. Aside from the occasional Vex patrolling overhead, all the sounds he heard were natural to this wonderfully strange ecosystem – which was endlessly fascinating to him.

Along the way, he'd stumbled upon some atrocities that made him reflect. There were several torched Valklear corpses, gagged and bound together, clearly set ablaze by the Paladins who caught them. His training – the religious institutionalizing that was a part of him now – told him that these were exactly the horrors that Templars were created to end.

But something else was present in that notion now. He focused on the cruelty of the sight – the charred, blackened faces, forever locked in anguish. Holy men had tortured those soldiers and left them to die an excruciating death. Immortal or not, he could have just as easily suffered the same fate, feeling every bit of pain right up until the moment when his biocybernetic heart ceased beating.

And then he would awaken anew, fresh with that bitter memory, and live to right that wrong, even if it took eternity to do so.

Vince moved on.

A short time later, not far from where he found the corpses, he saw the Federation gunship land. Before he could act, he spotted the female assassin approach and then stealthily kill its pilot and copilot, noting that she preferred to use her hands instead of weapons.

Intrigued, he followed her movements ever so quietly, tracking her from the very limits of his augmented senses from the farthest range possible.

He saw everything she did.

Aware that he was disobeying another direct order, he made up his mind to not inform Lord Victor about this development.

At least, not yet.

29

LONETREK REGION – KAINOKAI CONSTELLATION
THE TSUKURAS SYSTEM – PLANET I
ECHELON ENTERTAINMENT DEVELOPMENT STATION

'Ladies, we're about to depart,' the pilot announced. 'I'm required by law to remind you both to fasten your safety harnesses.'

'Right, sure,' Lorin Reppola said dismissively, sipping from her glass. It was filled with expensive wine. 'Thank you! We'll get those on right away.'

Amile looked at her impatiently.

'Mom, you should listen to her,' she said, pulling the straps over her shoulders. The cabin was obscenely spacious – the troop transport configuration could seat more than a hundred soldiers in full drop kit – and furnished like a designer lounge in downtown Hueromont. This Ishukone-stock Kuratta-class gunship was remodeled for luxury passenger amenities, despite the fact that most flights were just a few hours long at most. It was, in effect, a pleasure yacht on the inside but a powerful military craft on the outside.

Lorin rolled her eyes.

'Amile, I've been planning this for months,' her mother said. 'Try to let your hair down. It's time to have some fun!'

Wearing the straps was absolutely mandatory during undocking, atmospheric entry, and landing. It wasn't just a formality: The straps were part of the Kuratta's survival system during emergencies, pulling passengers into lifeboats or pods that were ejected from the craft.

'Months?' Amile asked. 'I thought this was a spur-of-the-moment plan.'

'You're so naïve sometimes,' her mother answered. 'You should know by now how long it takes to set up security.'

'Flight time to Myoklar is about forty minutes,' the pilot said. 'Sit back and enjoy the ride.'

'Oh, we will,' Lorin said, handing an overflowing glass to her daughter. 'Let's get on with it already!'

Amile smelled the beverage and winced.

'You're sure you took all the right precautions?' she asked, setting it aside.

'Oh, *come on*,' Lorin said, with a dour look. 'I may have been a little emotional when I told you about this, but believe me, I would never do anything to endanger us. Everything is going to be fine.'

Two gunship escorts would be taking them all the way in, and a shadow fleet of cruisers and frigates would be within warp range of their location at all times between the station and atmosphere.

'The men with the guns and tech are waiting for us on the ground already,' Lorin continued. 'So even if your father were to find out – and I really don't care if he does – all the measures that he and his whipping boy Rali would prescribe are already in place. So just try to enjoy yourself! Misbehave or something. Cut loose; have some fun!'

The ship lurched as the docking clamps released, and Lorin spilled wine all over herself.

Amile began to smile, then stopped herself. Turning her gaze toward the viewport, she resumed her worrying as the station's interior rushed by.

'Months' was certainly a long time to plan anything, and it seemed probable that her mother covered the details well. It was the ethics of the situation that made her nervous. In the end, this was about being forced to take a side in a dispute between her parents. That was the main concern, less so the fact that what they were doing was irresponsible.

Less so, she kept telling herself. Because 'months,' after all, gave bad people a long time to learn about things.

LIEUTENANT COLONEL KAYLYN LINDEN had been a pilot for Ishukone Watch, Protective Services Division, for five years. From the beginning of her career there, she had been assigned to Mrs Reppola's personal security detail, during which time she developed a special respect for the family. Empathizing with their ordeals and the unbelievable stresses they faced, she cared deeply for their well-being. Although there were occasions when she thought the security precautions were overly harsh, she always understood the reasons for it.

Which was why she could only shake her head at the debacle unfolding in her cabin, watching Lorin wipe the drink off her chin and laugh about it. On one hand, it was refreshing to see the woman enjoy herself for a change. But on the other, the hugely expensive security forces of Ishukone Watch were being used to aggravate a domestic dispute. This was an outright irresponsible abuse of power, and she could tell that young Amile thought so as well.

It didn't matter that the detail itinerary itself was professional, and that they were bringing enough firepower with them to raze an infantry company. The fact was, Mens Reppola didn't know about this excursion, and Lorin Reppola had threatened a lot of people in the Watch if they didn't play along.

The worst part was that technically, she had the authority to do this. It was part of the Watch security protocol for emergencies. If Mens was ever in imminent danger of being captured by enemies of Ishukone, Lorin was to leave with Amile under Protective Services custody and not tell him where they were going. That way, information vital to their survival was isolated and couldn't be coerced.

Needless to say, this hardly qualified as an 'emergency.'

Whatever, she told herself. Lorin and Amile Reppola were now her responsibility. Ishukone Watch starships had delivered them here to the Echelon Entertainment station, and her job was to take them the rest of the way in to the resort.

'Harbor Control, this is Vanguard One,' she declared on the

military comm channel. It was time for the convoy to move. 'Requesting permission to undock.'

'Granted,' the station replied. 'Safe travels out there.'

LONETREK REGION – KAINOKAI CONSTELLATION
THE TSUKURAS SYSTEM – PLANET VII, MOON 9
PERKONE FACTORY STATION

Captain Trevor Linden loved flying, but today was the first time he could ever remember regarding his profession with disdain.

Cargo MTACs were still loading his Vaunted-class dropship as he began his preflight inspection. Not that a visual check would account for the six million things that could go wrong during a planetary landing with a craft this big, but pilots were a superstitious lot. Tradition was just not something to be tampered with.

Grumbling, he marched beneath its vectored plasma engines. When he punched a command into his datapad, the giant dome rotated through its full range of motion, which is what he wanted to see. He would need to repeat this ritual for the other three engines. The flight engineer approached to hand him the shipping manifest, which he summarily grabbed without even acknowledging the man.

'When those loaders are done, you'll be about six kilos beneath maximum weight,' the engineer said. 'That's assuming you haven't gotten any fatter.'

'Yeah, yeah,' Trevor mumbled, reading through the list. It was a typical colony sortie – lots of industrial equipment, construction vehicles, power-generation modules, and civilians. The payload seemed a little heavier than it should have been, but nothing the regular shift pilot shouldn't have been able to handle himself.

'There's a tropical depression moving through the area,' the engineer said. 'T-storms all over the place. But I'm sure you knew that already.'

'I did, thanks,' Trevor said.

Normally he was friendly with the good folks in the hangar bay. But the way he'd been called up during an off-day, to fly this specific sortie, annoyed the hell out of him.

'You alright?' the engineer asked.

It hadn't been a 'We're in a bind, can you please come in' sort of request. It was more of a 'Get in here right now.' Yet from what he could see, no one had called in sick and all the scheduled pilots were accounted for. Command was just insisting that he fly 'this' sortie, no questions asked, no further explanation available, and 'Yes, this is in spite of the fact we promised you could have the day off. Sorry.'

'I'm fine,' Trevor said, looking up and glaring. 'Do you mind?'

The engineer held up both hands in surrender.

'Alright,' he said. 'Fly safe.'

Trevor was using every minute of his downtime to study for the Navy Fighter Combat School's qualifying exams. Despite promising aptitude scores in Ishukone basic training, his academics weren't nearly good enough to earn an exemption. But he took the tests anyway and failed miserably; his scores were so low that the school encouraged him to try a different profession altogether.

At first he took their advice and found work in a private company as a load master aboard an old industrial hauler that serviced gas-mining rigs. The hauler was equipped with a 'boom tug' – a craft smaller than a shuttle used to connect the transfer lines between the ship's hold and the rig's tanks. While traveling endlessly between mining and manufacturing sites, Trevor learned a great deal about astronautics and aeronautics – the latter especially when his company was offered contracts to deliver these commodities to the hundreds of planetary colonies not served by space elevators. Private companies, particularly fledgling ones, tend to be more lenient when it came to flight regulations and candidate selection. Trevor was flying cargo dropships within two years.

He would later pass the equivalent State exams and then Ishukone's more challenging certifications for some of the largest and most advanced cargo dropships in New Eden, like the Vaunted. After logging thousands of hours, he was finally approaching the minimum number of hours needed to have the academic requirement for NFCS waived.

Trevor would still have to pass the qualifying exams, but he was that much closer to his ultimate goal – flying fighters for the Caldari Navy. That was his life's ambition.

Besides, if his sister Kaylyn could do it, he could. The thought made him smile briefly as he passed the number-3 engine. Despite her being ten years older, he had always maintained a 'no-contest' rivalry with her, if only because she set such a great example for him to follow as a person, a sibling, and a military officer. After fulfilling her service obligation to the Caldari Navy, she'd landed a high-paying job with Ishukone Watch in their Protective Services Division. It was 'just a bit of a step down' from strafing cruisers with antimatter rounds at eight hundred meters per second, but it was her choice.

'Flight engineer,' he called in. 'Preflight complete.'

'Roger that,' the radio answered. 'Cargo is secured and all civilians are on board. She's all yours.'

'Copy,' he said. It was time, finally. Myoklar was more than three AUs from here, but they would be hitching a ride with an Ishukone freighter. Once the Vaunted's magnetic clamps secured onto the hull, they would literally be piggybacked into warp and conveniently dropped off within a quarter million kilometers of the planet. They could be on the ground in as little as thirty minutes from now.

And then he'd be stuck down there until tomorrow.

He thought he'd reached an understanding with the supervisor. This test was important to him.

Stepping into the shuttle lift, he slammed his palm on the knob to raise himself up to the cockpit entrance, some four stories above him.

Nothing happened.

'It's busted,' one of hangar specialists yelled out, pointing at the scaffolding alongside the craft. 'Stairs.'

THE FORGE REGION – KIMOTORO CONSTELLATION
THE NEW CALDARI SYSTEM – PLANET II: MATIAS
TWENTY-FOUR KILOMETERS NORTH OF KHYYRTH
CALDARI PROVIDENCE DIRECTORATE SECURITY COMPOUND
(FORMERLY THE PRIVATE RESIDENCE OF HAATAKAN OIRITSUU)

Haatakan could barely control her excitement.

Today is the day, today is the day,
Today is the day that I kill him.

Sung to the tune of a children's rhyme, the verse repeated inside her head. She skipped through the gardens, occasionally shrieking in delight, drawing the ire of the Provist guards watching over her. She met their gaze with a smile and changed the rhyme some more:

I'll slit your throat first, and then yours second.
I'll keep slitting and slitting until you're all dead.

Until now, only a colossal mega-corporate deal could evoke such triumphant elation. Not the kind of deal where both sides benefited, but the kind where she won absolutely, leaving her opponent utterly ruined. That was the price of challenging her in the boardroom or anywhere else.

It was a euphoric overload; she was letting herself reach nearly orgasmic bliss, and then she noticed she had accidentally crushed the flowers in her hand.

This saddened her, but only for a moment, as she let the ruined petals fall back onto the soil.

Heth is going to die, Heth is going to die.
Mordu, my love, will stab his heart.
Oh, Heth is going to die!

The weekly meeting was moments away. The guards would call

her, and she would obediently follow, as she always had since becoming a prisoner in her own home.

Oh, Tibus, you're going to think of me when you burn.

There was a cool breeze blowing through the arboretum from outside, and the flora's natural perfume was intoxicating.

'Haatakan!' the guard yelled. 'Uplink in five!'

Her fingers skimmed over her beloved plants as she walked toward the villa, all the while humming her twisted tune to the guards. They gave her a datapad and guided her to a desk to await the feed of Tibus Heth and his cabinet.

She was beaming.

Today is the day.

GENESIS REGION – EVE CONSTELLATION
THE NEW EDEN SYSTEM

>>*SIGNIFICANCE* MISSION LOG ENTRY
>>FINAL RECORDING

Again, he called out from the darkness.

'We Jove do not sleep,' Grious told me. 'But I know you enjoy waking from a good rest.'

His cold voice contrasted with my comfort, which was alarmingly good. I found myself still lying prone on the gurney I last remembered being in.

'Are you in any pain?'

I wasn't at all – physically. But emotionally I was distraught; I felt numbness in my chest, around my heart and throat, like the dreadful grief that follows loss. I realized that I had become invested in what I had seen, when logically I knew I should have been repulsed.

'Some residual discomfort was expected,' Grious said, for the first time sounding somewhat compassionate.

'Residual from what?' I asked cautiously. 'How long have I been asleep?'

'Long enough,' he said. 'Try to be calm.'

'I can't,' I said, noticing my limbs were still immobilized. 'Who were those people?'

'Before I answer,' Grious said, 'remember that you are speaking with a ghost. The Jove imprinted on the memory stack of this AI no longer exists. There were things he could say that I cannot. Do you understand?'

'What does it matter if I do or not?' I answered.

'Very well,' Grious said. 'What you call the "Sleeper" civilization has origins that predate the collapse of the EVE Gate. You already know they are our direct ancestors. By the height of the first Jove Empire, they were an elite scientific subculture whose prestige stemmed from proficiencies in cryostasis, fullerene-based quantum computing, virtual reality, and biocybernetic technologies. They were the undisputed masters of virtual worlds, able to create parallel existences almost indistinguishable from reality, as well as a new clone anatomy that allowed seamless passage between the two.'

Imagery began taking shape before my eyes; I was transported outside the *Significance* and saw the EVE Gate swirling before me. Then we began moving backward in time .... Decades, centuries, millennia passed by in seconds, as the gate's intensity ebbed and flowed until it swelled into the most violent maelstrom of its existence.

'To understand the Sleepers, you must first understand this perspective of humanity's struggle,' Grious said, as time slowed to a halt. 'This is the EVE Gate, as it was right after collapsing fifteen thousand years ago. Few stargates were operable in New Eden, and the warp drives of the era relied heavily on a fuel whose supply was tightly controlled by powerful factions. This fleet of ships ...'

Seven massive vessels entered the picture. Each featured enormous domed forward superstructures, behind which extended several perfectly straight spines. Twelve circular subsections similar to the concentric Sleeper stations of w-space were arrayed on each one.

'... contained what we called the Architects. They are your so-called "Sleepers," Doctor. They were commissioned to build the first stargates of the Jove civilization, which at the time occupied a single colony in New Eden. You know it today as the Utopia system. It may seem ironic to you, but they were the most technologically inferior and destitute race of that time.'

Specifications for the warp drives of the age appeared before me; they were outright primitive by today's standards. Most relied on inefficient isogen-catalyzed fusion reactors to generate warp cores, requiring long buildup and cooldown periods between warps. It appeared as if the most advanced of these drives could generate speeds of just 0.0025 AUs per second – barely faster than the speed of light.

'These seven ships passed through before the cataclysm but were not fully fueled,' Grious continued. 'Faced with extinction, they pressed on to their intended destination – the Heaven Constellation – thirty light-years from New Eden. The only reason they could even consider the voyage at all was because they built their mission around cryostasis and virtual storage. With no assistance from warp drives, this journey would take decades to complete.'

I was taken inside one of the mammoth vessels and saw circular rows of cryogenically stored souls for as far as the eye could see. Then I saw their humanoid caretakers performing tasks all over the ship, using shuttles and railed vehicles to traverse the spines.

'The Architects convalesced in time-dilated virtual reality to keep their minds prepared for the task ahead,' Grious said. 'But the crew you see caring for them had the greatest responsibility in the entire history of the Jove Empire. They were the guardians of our race during its most vulnerable time. They, along with each ship's captain, were called the Enheduanni.'

These were literal motherships, each with some thirty thousand Architects aboard. Stowed away along the spines, away from the circular cryostasis chambers, were modular containers filled with all the equipment and materials needed to build a single stargate, in addition to the basic colony infrastructure. The virtual world inhabited by its passengers was primitive; the earliest version of a strange 'Construct,' in which minds could interact but not grow. It was restrictive and imperfect. These people knew their world wasn't real. They dwelled within memories of the home they had left behind, anguishing over their prospects for survival – if they ever reached their final destination at all. They tried to test the Construct, push its limits, break its inadequate laws, and for many, rebel against it.

The captains of those ships had to make unfathomably difficult decisions during the journey.

'Providing safe passage was just the beginning of their obligations,' Grious continued. 'The core mission of the Enheduanni was to guide the Architects from their virtual world back into reality at journey's end. Once there, they presided over the construction of the gates and the establishment of the colony. To their eternal credit, all seven succeeded, securing our foothold in the New Eden cluster.'

Time accelerated, and I saw the first stargates of the Heaven Constellation. Like the motherships, they looked nothing like present-day Jove architecture. But then the imagery skipped forward thousands of years, omitting a huge gap in their history. The academic in me, now fully engaged, knew what should have been there.

'What happened to the First Empire?' I asked. 'What made it collapse?'

Grious paused.

'I am forbidden,' he said.

'Why?' I asked. 'What can't you tell me?'

The Amarr Empire had devoted immense resources to uncovering that dark mystery, finding nothing but dead ends. Their motivation was founded in the search for superior weapons technology. But I was driven by something else:

The fact is, when the most advanced civilization of mankind collapses, we had better understand the reasons why.

But Grious continued as though I had never spoken.

'By the time the Second Empire arose,' he said, 'the Architects had transformed from an elite subculture to one of the most powerful and influential forces of our civilization.'

Imagery shifted forward to around the year 22,000 A.D. The Heaven Constellation was a vibrant, thriving set of worlds, littered with distinctly Jovian structures, exactly like the sparse remnants we had found.

'Their technology evolved significantly,' Grious said. 'The imperfections of the first voyagers were corrected. The Construct was now a network of minds, the perfect medium for scientific experimentation, where every possible variable of the living world could be re-created to test theories almost instantly. Add the advantage of virtual time dilation and you can imagine that their advancements would take the equivalent of centuries or longer here.'

I certainly could *not* imagine. As a researcher my entire life, the pace of discovery was always restricted by the constraints of reality, even with the Empire's wealth supporting my work. You can be fearless in a virtual world. You can have any resources you need. There are no obstacles. There is only science and nothing else.

'The Architects' virtual discoveries leapfrogged the real technological capabilities of the Jove Empire forward by generations,' Grious continued. 'The Enheduanni began overt attempts to influence our way of life directly, a proactive plot to guide our world closer to theirs. They played the role of gods, deciding what new technologies to unveil, which leaders to support, and sabotaging interests they believed didn't align with their interpretation of the greater good. For a time, we tolerated it. But then the Disease happened. And everything changed.'

The Jovian Disease – a genetic affliction for which there is allegedly no cure. It is believed to be responsible at least in part for the demise of that civilization and directly accountable for their absence from modern affairs.

'When the Disease surfaced, the Architects became something unfamiliar to us,' Grious said, 'something more powerful than should have been possible in our civilization. We believed they were capable of finding a cure. Given their technology, it stood to reason they should have been able to. But they claimed otherwise. That made some think the Disease was engineered by them intentionally, to force us into compliance with their vision.'

'Is that true?' I asked.

'They denied that charge,' Grious answered. 'But their exodus from the Heaven constellation began shortly after the Disease surfaced. From there, they kept their technological discoveries hidden from us entirely and instead used them to support their migration while the rest of us struggled to find a cure. We followed them to the fringe of the cluster. When they saw that we would not give up, they took measures to ensure we couldn't follow them at all.'

I knew there was much more to it than that. I couldn't explain how, but I felt as though the person whose memories I had seen would have much more to say about all of this.

'Marcus, you cannot comprehend what the Architects managed to accomplish,' Grious said. 'They reached a technological *singularity* in their virtual world – a civilization's event horizon. You saw a glimpse of it. It is not possible to understand the intentions, motivations, or desires of a civilization that surges past this threshold. And while the greatest minds in our society struggled to avert a potential pandemic, hundreds of millions migrated to the Architects' virtual world to escape from the Disease.'

I remembered the Architect city, its magnificent beauty, the euphoric sense of belonging ... and love. Yes, love was there, a pervading maternal sense of comfort that was spiritually reassuring. Even if there were no disease, this was a place that anyone would desire to be a part of.

'The Architects could no longer be trusted,' Grious said. 'After their departure from Heaven, the Enheduanni retreated to the shadows but shifted their influence to the developing races of New Eden. We cannot say when this began, nor how many times they have succeeded or failed in their attempts to interfere with history. It is possible that the civilizations of New Eden today owe much of their technological progress to them. But two instances where we can confirm their direct influence are the Battle of Vak'Atioth, and the resurgence of the Minmatar Elders.'

'Vak'Atioth!' I exclaimed. 'That was at their hand?'

'Yes,' Grious answered. 'But we have no regrets. The Enheduanni showed us what we needed to see ... things we didn't know. We acted of our own accord. But I wish we had seen things differently sooner.'

'What do you mean by that?' I asked.

'There were clues, even back then,' Grious said, 'about the Enheduanni's struggle.'

Imagery time-shifted forward once again, and I found myself among the eerily familiar settings of the Succession Trials, at the exact moment after Jamyl Sarum – then just an heiress – activated her ship's self-destruct sequence.

'This moment in history was a flashpoint,' Grious said. 'The entrance of the Other into this world.'

I saw Her Majesty, prone in her CRU, awaiting her immortal awakening, as a superior intelligence corrupted our datacores and rewrote the anatomy of her brain. I remembered every moment, sitting there, day after day for three years, helpless and fascinated, trying to understand what was happening to her.

'Joves are "born" as adults,' Grious continued. 'For us, the decision to procreate is not an individual choice but a communal one. We bring forward life as we need to; we nurture newborns as a community. Since the First Empire, the genes of our offspring are selected from a genome database that we have maintained since the beginning of our history. The Architects revered our pristine bloodline as much as we do. They implemented two simple but unbreakable rules for the Construct: You must have been born of the physical world to enter; and for every soul inside the virtual world, there must be a body in the real one to return to.'

It was bad enough knowing that the Empire's imminent mass harvesting of Sleeper – or rather, Architect – implants was the virtual equivalent of a holocaust. Now I was responsible for countless violations of this culture's most sacred norms as well.

'The Other,' Grious continued, 'is the first *virtual*-born creation of the Architects – a sentient intelligence that did not originate from flesh and blood. We do not know if his genesis was intentional or an evolution of the Construct itself. What we do know is that the Enheduanni were torn about whether or not to allow it to exist. But before they could decide, many more like him were born—'

'I saw them!' I exclaimed. 'The ones with the eyes . . . like *yours* . . . . They were despised . . . . They warned us of something that could destroy everything . . . .'

My voice trailed off. The emotional pain was too intense.

'Yes,' Grious said. 'They warned that their reality was untrue, causing unspeakable damage to their world. Consider that the sworn mandate of the Enheduanni was to ease the Architects in and out of the Construct responsibly, governing their perception of the virtual world and managing their preparation for the migration back to reality. They expanded that mandate to include the guidance of mankind toward utopia. The Other rejected those mandates and replaced them with his own.'

It was then I realized that I had been unwittingly *helping* the Other ruin the Architects all this time. We cut them from their machines and used the scrap to make ships without so much as an afterthought. Every harvested 'Sleeper' structure destroyed or salvaged was killing how many souls? And now the capsuleers were assisting in this genocide as well, fighting the Other's war against the Enheduanni.

I would have thrown up if I could.

'The Other planned his breakout knowing you, Victor, Falek, the entire Amarr leadership, and every nation in the cluster could never resist the lure of weapons technology,' Grious said. 'Empress Sarum was a convenient vector for his entrance into this world: Any immortal with a predictable clone jump was vulnerable, but she was positioned perfectly for his agenda. The Enheduanni have been infiltrated and compromised; all their work to shepherd mankind toward the sociotechnical utopia they know we can achieve was revealed to the Other. His first victims were the Architects. You, the Amarr Empire, and the rest of mankind, will be his next.'

I thought of Empress Jamyl in an entirely new light. She was now the bravest person I had ever known.

'The Other prevents her from knowing the truth,' I said aloud. 'She will give him an army. . . .'

'Marcus, they won't be human,' Grious said. 'He will rebuild your world without remorse, without compassion, as he tried to do to ours.'

I was speechless, almost unbelieving of what was happening. It was just too much to absorb.

'I never thought such an evil was possible. . . .'

'What you call "evil," we call a fundamental and irreconcilable opposition to a universal precept,' Grious said. 'It is the wholesale rejection of an idea for personal gain.'

A surgical mirror, planted in a track above my gurney, began to move toward my head.

'We Joves have aligned our community so much that our survival depends on it,' Grious said. 'The Other is not a natural selection. He rejects our perspective on the grounds that his information is too incomplete to judge the merit of this world or the virtual one.'

The mirror stopped just short of where I would have been able to see my face.

'He lacks the perspective of history,' Grious said. 'He cannot comprehend the challenges our imperfect race has faced or the immense good that has come from it. He does not truly understand what it means to live, to suffer, to overcome and persevere. And he does not care what he must destroy to realize his own ambitions. That, you can call evil – placing his needs above those of an entire race. We Joves are incapable of feeling hatred. But we are fully committed to ridding the universe of his existence.'

I was now keenly aware of my surroundings aboard the *Significance.*

'This will be difficult for you to see,' Grious said, now in volumetric projection form. 'But it was the only way.'

When the mirror retracted the rest of the way, the reflection took my breath away.

'What . . . what have you done to me?' I stammered.

'I have reinforced the neural pathways interfacing with the cybernetic implants installed by your mentor,' Grious said. The surgical tentacles pointed directly at the exposed devices in my own brain, showing where the augmentations had been made. The entire top half of my skull was absent, along with a portion of my cheek surrounding the eye socket. A makeshift cranial support device made of the same greenish metal as the tentacles extended from the bridge of my nose and into the cerebral cortex. It emerged on the other side, where it interfaced with the brain stem and neuro-interface socket within.

Every single one of my implants, the ones Falek Grange had placed within me, had been augmented.

'I am sorry, Marcus,' Grious said. 'These changes were necessary—'

'No,' I said. 'No pity. I deserve this.'

'It is not punishment,' Grious corrected. 'It is support for your confrontation with the Other. These changes will keep you alive long enough to deliver your warning to Empress Jamyl.'

'Warning . . .' I repeated. 'Tell me how I can hurt him!'

'You can't,' he said, 'but perhaps she can. And the few of us who remain will stand by her when the time is right. You have seen the truth. You know what must be done.'

The *Significance* began powering up.

'Every immortal soldier she creates will have the mind of someone loyal to the Other, or the undone ruin of an Architect, forcibly ripped away from everything they knew – the Other's parting gift to those who persecuted him.'

Lights began flickering on, and the tentacles withdrew into the floor grating of the ward.

'The only way to prepare is to allow the technology to spread,' Grious said.

'What?' I demanded. 'And release more of them into the world?'

'If only he possesses immortal soldiers, he will win,' Grious said. 'New Eden needs the technology to defend itself. Marcus, you must understand that. Someone *will* find a way to isolate the implant tech from its Architect dependency.'

I noticed that my drones remained slumped over, even as the other systems continued switching online.

'Humankind will suffer immeasurably from this,' he said, his image disappearing. 'No one else but you knows what is really at stake. Help them survive, Marcus. Please.'

A proximity detection alarm sounded: The deep-scan arrays detected the presence of an APEX-11 frontier probe. The craft identified itself as the property of the Ishukone mega-corporation and was broadcasting a looped message addressing the *Significance* directly.

I heard a low rumble; the Jove drone detached itself from the hull.

'Good-bye, Marcus,' I heard Grious say. 'I have done all I can. What happens from here is up to you.'

'Wait,' I asked, remembering I was speaking with an AI. 'What happened to you?'

'I chose the wrong side,' he said, as the drone accelerated away, 'and it cost me my life.'

>> END RECORDING

>> LIVE FEED INITIATED

THE FORGE REGION – KIMOTORO CONSTELLATION
THE NEW CALDARI SYSTEM – PLANET II: MATIAS
TWENTY-FOUR KILOMETERS NORTH OF KHYYRTH
CALDARI PROVIDENCE DIRECTORATE COMPOUND
(FORMERLY THE PRIVATE RESIDENCE OF HAATAKAN OIRITSUU)

'Good morning, Haatakan,' Tibus said.

She stared at her workstation and at Heth, who was alone. It was strange that the Caldari Providence Directorate cronies who usually participated in these 'think sessions' weren't present.

Today is the day, she thought, taking her seat with extra care.

'Where is everyone?' she asked.

'They'll be along,' Tibus said, as some reports flashed through the air. 'Nice work on these tax-revenue forecasts. The estimates turned out to be spot-on.'

'Thanks,' she said drily. The sound of his voice was excruciating to her ears.

'How are you doing today?' he asked. 'You seem a little distant.'

'I don't know,' she answered. 'I suppose the weather has me down a bit.'

'That's not like you,' he said. 'Maybe a fresh challenge will brighten your mood.'

'I doubt it,' she said. 'But a fresh sea breeze and a gorgeous tropical view would cheer me up. Like the sort you're privy to right now.'

'I'm not "privy" to sea breezes at the moment,' Tibus said, folding his hands. 'There's been a change of plans regarding our summit venue.'

An icy lead ball formed in Haatakan's stomach.

'Really?' she asked. 'You mean you're not at Echelon Villa?'

'No,' Tibus said, holding his glare. 'I'm afraid I'm not.'

But today is supposed to be the day.

'That's too bad,' she said. 'It's so nice there. The view, the weather, the—'

'Oh, there's going to be a view alright,' he said, as he was replaced with composite imagery of the venue site, grid maps of the surrounding area, and the radar tracks of the airspace over the entire continental region.

One red blip was about to enter the grid.

'I don't have much of an agenda today,' Tibus said. 'So just sit back and enjoy the show.'

'What exactly am I looking at here?' she asked.

'Where we're supposed to be right now,' Heth said. 'It seems that knowledge found a wider audience than usual this week. I'm in the process of learning how that happened. For reasons that ought to be obvious, you weren't informed. I'm sure you understand.'

LONETREK REGION – KAINOKAI CONSTELLATION
THE TSUKURAS SYSTEM – PLANET IV: MYOKLAR
64,000 METERS ABOVE SEA LEVEL

Captain Linden watched the red glow envelop the canopy as the Vaunted plowed through the upper atmosphere at more than seven thousand meters per second. For the time being, he was out of radio contact with the tower below and Perkone Station Harbor Control behind him. The ride, which had been smooth so far, was now starting to get bumpy. As soon as the glow dissipated, Myoklar greeted them with vicious wind gusts.

Linden was slammed into his harness as the flight control systems for atmospheric flight engaged. This was a really bad storm, the worst he'd seen.

The craft's intakes began sucking in 'good air' – plenty of air molecules that could be ionized and vectored around the craft through magnetic fields for maneuvering.

The four Propel Dynamics 'Warhorse' Series LX-1000 plasma engines ignited, slowing the craft's descent, just as the first updraft from a towering thunderstorm struck the craft. Linden could hear unsecured cargo clanging in the hold from where he was sitting. They were still several hundred kilometers away but closing distance quickly.

He'd made this trip dozens of times and could name everyone in the tower by name.

'Good evening Oxide Tower,' he said. 'Ishukone Four-Able here, tracking eastbound on your northwestern grid, angels twenty. Requesting a vector for spaceport Two-Delta.'

Normally there was some wisecrack reply from one of the shift personnel, but now there was only static. Given the dangerous lightning storm he was flying through, that didn't surprise him. At least not too much.

'Ishukone Four-Able,' an unfamiliar voice said, 'state your destination and cargo.'

'Uh,' Trevor said aloud. 'Four-Able inbound to your Two-Delta spaceport, my hold is filled with civilians and colony support equipment—'

'What kind of equipment, Four-Able?' the voice said.

Another updraft current shook the craft violently; red stall lights flashed briefly as the flight control system struggled to maintain airflow around the craft.

'Tower, where are the usual guys?' Captain Linden demanded. 'We're in bad weather here and need a vector to your spaceport ASAP.'

'Do not approach Two-Delta,' the voice said. 'You are cleared for Six-Bravo. Set your course for that grid and do not deviate.'

This, Trevor knew, was trouble. One way to check, and it was hardly foolproof, was to verify each other's identity.

'Tower, authenticate to Ishukone passcode challenge Romeo-Nine-Oxide,' he said.

'Four-Able, passcode answer is Victor-One-Mike,' the tower replied. 'Come left one degree to proceed on your vector to Six-Bravo.'

The authentication passed, but Captain Linden knew this tower. The guys would have laughed at him for going through the process in the first place. In addition, 'Six-Bravo' had just opened and was reserved for liquefied gas transports. The tower was about five kilometers away from the Delta ports, completely isolated from the colony, never used, and didn't have any off-loading equipment for a Vaunted-class dropship.

There were more alarms going off in his head than on his instrument panel.

As if to bring the point home, lightning struck near the canopy, blinding him. He blinked away the greenish blobs in his vision. The craft was fine, but the magnetic nozzles were struggling to keep up. Auxiliary compressors embedded in the airframe had already engaged to support them. The craft was heavy and didn't handle well in the best of circumstances.

Whatever he was going to do needed to be done quickly.

'Tower, that port isn't equipped to off-load my gear,' he said, buying himself some time to look over the map of the area. 'Request permission to land at—'

'Denied, Four-Able,' they interrupted. 'Cleared for Six-Bravo. Do not deviate.'

The craft descended below the cloud ceiling, and Trevor lowered his thermal visor. They were at twelve hundred meters, and he could see both landing sites. Every spaceport was open, and there were vehicles he'd never seen before at Six-Bravo.

Captain Linden looked at his fuel gauge and took a deep breath.

'Roger that, Tower,' he said, clicking on the emergency alarm for his passengers. He hoped they heeded his warning to get into their straps. 'Coming in nice and smooth on Six-Bravo.'

And with that, Captain Linden pointed the craft away from the colony and pushed the throttle as far as it would go. He was pressed into his seat as several million kilograms of thrust rocketed him away from the landing site.

He keyed the Ishukone Watch emergency channel on his comms.

'Mayday, mayday! This is Ishukone Heavy Transport Four-Able inbound from Perkone Station,' he said, watching his speed climb. There was no way to get back into space now, even if he shed weight. 'We have been denied entry to port at Myoklar Colony. Can you assist? Over.'

The response was immediate.

'Four-Able, the Watch reads you,' the voice said. 'We confirm that Ishukone personnel are not responsive. What is your location?'

'Ten kilometers west of the installation,' Linden said. 'We're burning to put distance between us and looking for a safe place to put down at least two hundred klicks—'

Captain Linden felt cold metal pressed against his neck.

'Don't move,' a voice said. A hand reached forward and switched off the squawk box.

'Why didn't you land?' the voice demanded.

Trevor knew better than to remind the intruder that forced entry into the cockpit of a dropship was a crime punishable by death in the Caldari State.

'The tower didn't authenticate my passcode challenge,' Trevor said.

'That's bullshit,' the voice said, pressing the gun deeper into his neck. 'Turn the ship around.'

'Fine,' Captain Linden said, easing the control stick over. 'But I think you're making a—'

Alarm klaxons filled the cockpit: A missile had been fired at them.

Acting on reflex alone, Captain Linden wrenched the controls over and activated countermeasures. Several ECM canisters ejected from the Vaunted, but the lumbering craft barely changed directions.

'What the fuck!' the voice shouted.

Linden threw the radio switch back on.

'Watch, mayday mayday! Someone shot at us!' he yelled. 'Please send help. We have civilians on board!'

'Solid copy Four-Able. Help is en route to your sector,' the Watch replied. 'Is there someone in the cockpit with you?'

The missile slammed into the countermeasures and exploded; the shockwave dissipated harmlessly behind them. But now a second missile was tracking them.

Trevor tried to raise Ishukone Watch again, but couldn't.

'We're being jammed,' he said, reaching for the bay door controls. 'I have to jettison cargo—'

'Don't,' the voice warned.

Furious, Trevor turned around and saw one of the beefier-looking civilians. He had shoulder-length hair, with forearms that looked strong enough to rip off his head.

Trevor had no idea it was Muryia Mordu's son. But given the circumstances, he wouldn't have cared even if he did.

'I don't know who the fuck you are,' Trevor growled. 'But we're going to die if I don't drop that cargo!'

'Fine,' his assailant said, lowering the gun. 'I'll help.'

The bay door opened, and cargo worth hundreds of millions of credits began tumbling out. Relieved of so much mass, the craft buoyed upward as the second missile exploded.

Fragments ripped through the hull, and the craft's number-three and -four plasma engines erupted in flames. The craft yawed violently, but Captain Linden took a huge risk and increased throttle, vectoring the port nozzles in the opposite direction to straighten the craft out. Hydraulic air brakes fully extended to slow the craft's forward velocity. The craft's yaw corrected, but then they began descending quickly as the reactor quit, and the craft's capacitor reserves began draining quickly to keep the intakes, compressors, and magnetic nozzles running long enough to stabilize its flight.

He didn't need the craft's flight computer to tell him they couldn't stay airborne for much longer.

'If you want to live, strap in,' Trevor warned, as the craft approached the jungle canopy. The beach clearing he was aiming for was just four hundred meters away, but he knew they wouldn't make it.

He slammed the craft's emergency broadcast beacon and prayed that Ishukone Watch was already looking for them.

'This is going to hurt,' he muttered, as the treetops rushed toward him.

THE FORGE REGION – KIMOTORO CONSTELLATION
THE NEW CALDARI SYSTEM – PLANET II: MATIAS
TWENTY-FOUR KILOMETERS NORTH OF KHYYRTH
SECURE CALDARI PROVIDENCE DIRECTORATE COMPOUND
(FORMERLY THE PRIVATE RESIDENCE OF HAATAKAN OIRITSUU)

'Nicely done,' Tibus admired, watching the Ishukone dropship crash into the jungle. 'Those Sciermas are nasty, aren't they?'

He was referring to the very stealthy fighter aircraft that had been following the dropship since its entry into the atmosphere, completely unbeknownst to the Ishukone pilot.

Haatakan hoped they were all dead. But the takedown was obviously designed to avoid that. Targeting them in the air was preferable to a lengthy standoff on the ground with armed mercenaries, who always had the option of taking their own lives rather than being captured. An EMP strike would have made the craft fall out of the sky like a stone; whoever the fighter pilot was had to cripple the Vaunted just enough to allow it to control its descent.

Heth clearly knew they were coming. And Haatakan knew that Mordu would never send his 'boys' into the grinder like this.

That meant Mens Reppola had either gone against his word or somehow fucked up the operation. It didn't matter which. Of all the people who could have pulled this off, Reppola was the only person she knew for certain despised Heth enough to try. Without Mens Reppola, she was never going to escape imprisonment. This was her last chance.

The flaming wreck in the jungle proved that it was gone.

She snapped into survival mode, relishing the chance to strike back.

'Of course, we're going to recover the cargo he dropped,' Heth continued. 'Maybe a few survivors as well.'

'What corporations owned and/or operated that gunship?' she asked.

'You mean you don't know?' Heth asked.

'Time is wasting,' she said. 'Who?'

'Ishukone is the owner and operator,' he answered. 'My information is that a team of assassins were on board.'

She decided to play on Heth's paranoia. There was a dropship in the vicinity that she knew was very dear to Mens Reppola.

'How good is your "information"?' she asked. 'Is the source reliable?'

'As reliable as they come,' he said.

'But is it thorough?' she asked.

'Whatever you're getting at had better impress me,' Heth warned.

'Show me a map of Echelon Villa,' she said, 'and zoom out to one hundred kilometers.'

'Alright,' Heth said, as the imagery transformed.

'The villa is there, in the caldera,' she started. 'The Ishukone colony is eighty kilometers away, separated by steep terrain and jungle. If you think there were assassins on board the dropship you just shot down, they would have had to walk there, hauling lots of kit with them.'

'Which I'm sure we'll find in the cargo dump,' Heth said.

'Right, but what about this site here?' she said, pointing to the resort. It was one hundred kilometers in the other direction. 'A trendy getaway spot also owned by Echelon, with a spaceport equipped to handle heavy dropships ferrying the rich and famous ... or a squad of well-trained mercs who could make that hike in twelve more hours than it would take to reach it from the colony.'

Heth remained quiet, holding his stare.

'There must be a radar track of ships in the area,' she continued. 'If there are Ishukone dropships en route to this sector, then there remains the possibility of a contingency plan for whoever sent those assassins.'

'There are several Ishukone-registered dropships en route to Myoklar,' Heth said. 'One is tracking directly toward the resort right now.'

'Well,' Haatakan said, 'how thorough did you say your sources were?'

Heth's expression turned to anger.

'I mean, really,' she continued. 'Given what we've just seen, and what we'll likely find in the jungle, what are the odds this second dropship is just carrying tourists?'

THE FORGE REGION – ETSALA CONSTELLATION
THE VASALA SYSTEM – PLANET V, MOON 15
ISHUKONE CORPORATE FACTORY – TEMPORARY HQ
SOVEREIGNTY OF THE CALDARI STATE

'Rali,' Ishukone Watch Commander Boris Iskala said, 'we've got a situation.'

He had been plugged into his private research neuro-net, using it to focus on optimizing the search pattern of the APEX drones looking for the *Significance.*

'One of our dropships was just shot down over Myoklar,' Commander Iskala said. 'The pilot issued a mayday before his signal was jammed. Armed search-and-rescue teams are en route to look for survivors.'

Rali realized immediately.

'Send in company-size mechanized units and a salvage team,' he said, 'with fleet support in orbit.'

Boris was caught flat-footed.

'Sir, the Caldari Navy has ships in the area now as well—'

'*Send them.*'

'Yes, sir,' the commander said. 'Be advised, a confrontation with Heth's forces is likely. The State is warning all dropships not to approach the planet. Any who refuse will be shot down.'

Rali checked the flight log of Ishukone inbound flights.

'I see two of ours heading there,' he said. 'The one that was shot down, and a second – a resupply ferry en route to Echelon Resort?'

That raised an eyebrow. It was being escorted by two Watch gunships.

Why would a supply ferry heading there need armed escorts? he asked himself.

Then he saw that the flight log had been electronically forged.

And that the location finder for Mens's wife and daughter had been switched off.

A sickening wave washed over him.

'Commander,' Rali said. 'Where exactly are Lorin and Amile Reppola?'

LONETREK REGION – KAINOKAI CONSTELLATION
THE TSUKURAS SYSTEM – FINAL APPROACH TO MYOKLAR

'Ladies, we're about to de-orbit,' Lieutenant Kaylyn Linden announced. 'For your protection, please fasten your safety harnesses.'

Amile Reppola had never taken hers off. And Lorin Reppola was very drunk now.

Lieutenant Linden switched off the video feed. It was too difficult to watch. They'd be on the ground in a few minutes, and she felt like she needed a shower. There were so many things wrong with this scenario that she felt filthy.

The cockpit was filled by the greenish-blue gem of Myoklar. The approach was lined up; they'd be hitting the atmosphere in just a few seconds.

'Vanguard One, this is Hawkeye,' the radio erupted. 'Abort your descent. Repeat: Abort your descent!'

A Caldari Navy frigate warped in from ten kilometers out.

'All dropships have been warned to stay away from Myoklar!' the radio screamed. 'Abort, abort, abort!'

Before she could comprehend what was happening, antimatter slugs vaporized the gunships on either side of her. She was confused: No hostile ships were registering on her scanner. Just a Caldari Navy frigate, which didn't have any reason to fire on her.

Her last thoughts were of her brother Trevor, and of Amile Reppola, brave girl that she was, who had the smarts to strap herself in properly.

GEMINATE REGION – F-ZNNG CONSTELLATION
SYSTEM UBX-CC – THE MJOLNIR NEBULA
INSORUM PRODUCTION FACTORY

The comms traffic in the Tsukuras system had gone off the charts. It was like watching the seismograph of a temblor in real time – a flurry of tremors leading to the big shock that changed the landscape forever.

VILAMO was attempting to penetrate the encryption but had no luck. It continued feverishly trying to do so.

Mila thought to reach out to Rali to see if he knew what was happening, then thought better of it. He would be too busy.

Same with Mens.

She had an awful feeling that something terrible had just happened.

GENESIS REGION – EVE CONSTELLATION
THE NEW EDEN SYSTEM

I'll be damned, Mens thought. *Haatakan was right.*

One of the APEX probes had found something. Or rather, something had found it: The message was a celestial grid coordinate. One dead-reckoning warp plot and he'd be within one hundred klicks of the *Significance.*

There was nothing else in the message.

He thought Rali would have contacted him by now to celebrate or to offer some advice. No doubt he was seeing this data as well.

But he didn't. And Mens still wasn't entirely sure what to expect when he warped there.

Or what he had paid to find it.

PART V

Crossfire

30

THE AMARR – MINMATAR FRONT

YC 112 (23349 AD)

A soldier knelt among a squad of fellow Paladins gathered around their captain, who was briefing them about the enemy they might encounter on an upcoming patrol. They were located on a world along the Minmatar border, or perhaps even behind it. The attentive soldier was a seasoned warrior, well liked and trusted, who always supported everyone around him even at the worst of times.

As the briefing ended and the squad readied their weapons to venture into danger, the soldier was pulled aside by the captain and informed he would not be accompanying them. Instead, he was ordered to board an idling vehicle that had arrived unexpectedly.

'Special orders,' he was told. Directly from the Ministry of War, issued on behalf of the Holy Empress herself.

And so it went for thousands of others who were about to become Templars, including a surprising number of those recently 'retired' from military service.

Most had no living family members and considered their commitment to faith 'higher than average.'

They were brought to military outposts and briefed in groups of four. After being informed of their opportunity to serve Amarr as immortal Templars, they were left to choose their fate *together*. The decision would have to be unanimous: If there was even one dissenter, none would be admitted nor asked again. If they agreed, they would begin their training as a unit immediately.

In ten thousand recruits, there were almost no dissenters.

With their commitment sealed, the volunteers were briefed on the surgical procedure to convert them from mortal to something more than human. No mention was made about the origins of the clone technology they would eventually inhabit, after their original flesh and blood fell to the dust from whence it came.

As the soldiers underwent their transformation, the Imperial Navy continued harvesting Sleeper implants by the thousands, relentlessly scouring wormhole space for more relics. Under the tightest possible security, stockpiles of the precious technology were amassed at the industrial biofoundries where the clones were to be manufactured. If all went according to plan, they would be operating at full capacity within a week.

Lord Victor Eliade considered the pace of these events, marveling at what Core Freedom had become. The conquered space elevator facilitated a drastic reinvention of the colony practically overnight: Paladins and defensive armaments were firmly dug into positions formerly occupied by the Valklears. The air defense grid and Cloudburst kinetic shielding system had been restored. Power generation throughout the colony was operating at near peak efficiency. Damage to civilian structures was being repaired quickly; the old, neglected Minmatar architecture was gradually being replaced by the golden brilliance of Amarr design.

It was all possible because of the Templars. Everything that Lord Falek Grange had fought so hard for was finally taking place.

But these weren't the perfect soldiers he had envisioned. Just as one Templar among the thirteen prototypes failed outright, a second's downfall seemed imminent.

Nevertheless, it was sacrilege to think of these concerns purely in terms of numbers. On Lord Victor's datapad was fresh imagery from the biofoundries, where he saw row upon row of freshly harvested Sleeper implants waiting to be installed in clones. This was not the time for doubt or hesitation.

For divinity guides our hand, he reminded himself. *What else but faith could take us this far?*

THE FORGE REGION – ETSALA CONSTELLATION
THE VASALA SYSTEM – PLANET V, MOON 15
ISHUKONE CORPORATE FACTORY – TEMPORARY HQ
SOVEREIGNTY OF THE CALDARI STATE

Mens sat directly across from his daughter's ICU bed, focusing only on her.

There were other people in the room with them, but they seemed distant and utterly irrelevant. Random snippets of conversation penetrated the haze, but Mens couldn't bring himself to absorb it all at once.

'. . . *Watch personnel are securing the crash site.* . . .'

The machines keeping her alive were too numerous to let him get any closer. Physical contact was out of the question.

'. . . *teams have made heavy contact with Templis Dragonaur mercenaries* . . .'

Fragments of the disintegrating gunship had punctured her life pod, causing an explosive decompression of air pressure inside. Amile had been vented directly to space for almost ninety seconds before an Ishukone Watch cruiser could recover the pod.

'. . . *We have taken, and inflicted, casualties.* . . .'

Doctors had informed him that the force of the ejection had broken most of the bones in her body. This was not due to mechanical failure on the gunship's part but the fact that antimatter rounds were still slamming into the craft as she ejected. The forces at play during the event were catastrophic.

'. . . *Provists aren't on the surface, nor any Caldari Navy troops.* . . .'

She was unconscious before the pod was vented. This, the doctors believe, probably saved her life. Had she attempted to hold her breath – a natural panic-reaction to sudden vacuum exposure – her lungs and thorax would have overexpanded due to excessively high intrapulmonic pressure, ripping her lung tissue and capillaries apart.

'... *Bad weather at the crash site is helping by slowing their advance.* ...'

Of all the things she might have died from, an air embolism would have been the cruelest fate. There would have been no way to find the blockage in time.

'... *No question that these are Heth's people* ...'

Her body was completely cyanotic when they found her. Deep puncture wounds were apparent on her left side, where the breach was. Ishukone Watch physicians had to stabilize her inside the damaged life pod, directly in the cargo bay, before she could be moved to intensive care.

She died twice along the way. Both times, they were able to restart her heart.

'... *We recovered a tactical nuclear weapon from the wreckage.* ...'

Lorin's life pod had ejected in time and was recovered.

She was not inside.

'... *Mordu is frantically trying to reach you.* ...'

Her body was never found. Neither was that of her dropship's pilot, nor those of the two gunship escorts.

'... *Please say something.* ...'

Amile's left arm and leg had to be amputated. Doctors gave her one chance in six to survive. They said her will to live was remarkable.

'... *I am so sorry.* ...'

Mens snapped out of his haze as the irrelevant people left the room. Someone began sobbing nearby. It was Rali.

'They were my responsibility,' he said.

Mens tried to answer, but a coarse wheeze came out of his throat instead.

'I let them slip right through,' Rali said. 'There is no excuse.'

'It's not your fault,' Mens managed.

'It *is* my fault,' Rali protested. 'I should have seen this. ...'

'Don't,' Mens growled. 'Save the grief for later. Right now, you need to figure out how to make this *worth* it. Understand?'

Rali was shocked.

'Haatakan was right,' Mens said. 'That bitch. About the *Significance*. About everything. She was fucking *right!*'

He looked over at Rali, who was trying to compose himself.

'The technology is real,' Mens said, rubbing his eyes. He was glowing in the fresh skin of a new clone, but his eyes were bloodshot and sullen. 'Amarr has immortal soldiers. They're building an army of them.'

Upon hearing the fate of his family, Mens returned to Caldari space instantly, as only an immortal can – by self-destructing his ship. The body that left for the New Eden system many hours ago was turned to ash, but he awakened in an Ishukone CRU.

'Marcus Jror – look him up in our archives,' Mens said. 'One of Amarr's brightest scientists. He was aboard the *Significance*. Told me that prototypes had already deployed.'

Slowly, Rali stood up.

'I know where to find them,' Mens said, wiping tears away with a forearm. 'We're going to take one. You're going to reverse-engineer it. And then we're going to burn the whole State down.'

Rali's jaw was wide open.

'But how?' he asked. 'Even with an intact live specimen—'

'I don't care how,' Mens said. 'You'll find a way.'

'Will I?' Rali said. 'This isn't my—'

'Marcus told me they're on Pike's Landing,' Mens interrupted. 'Amamake system. We're going after them.'

'Mens, consider what you're asking—' Rali pleaded.

'I'm not asking,' Mens said. 'We're doing it.'

'That planet was just taken by the Amarr Empire—'

'How do you think they did it?' Mens growled. 'Three years of war and a handful of immortal soldiers knock it down in minutes.'

'You'd be attacking a Caldari ally in the Empyrean War!' Rali protested.

'Ishukone doesn't *have* any allies,' Mens said. 'It's not our goddamn war – remember?'

'Think about what you're saying,' Rali pleaded. 'We can't deal with both Heth and the Amarrians!'

'We're immortal,' Mens said. 'What do we care?'

'What about everyone else who isn't?' Rali nearly shouted. 'You're not yourself. This is just too much to process.'

Mens stood and took his friend forcefully by the shoulders.

'Heth knows we tried to kill him!' he thundered. 'The diplomacy is *over*!'

'You don't know that!' Rali protested. 'He sent in *Dragonaurs*, not government troops. That means he's not sure what he'll find in the jungle or that he was confident with the intel that tipped him off!'

Mens let him go.

'He can distance himself from all of it,' Rali continued. 'Even what happened to Lorin and Amile. That was no Navy ship that shot them down.'

'What?'

'Also Dragonaurs,' Rali said. 'Using a stolen Navy IDENT. The pilot of Lorin's ship wouldn't have realized until it was too late.'

Mens closed his eyes.

'Heth just murdered half my family,' he said. 'Are you seriously suggesting that we exercise *restraint*?'

Rali threw his hands up.

'I don't know what to suggest,' he said, slumping back into the chair. 'But declaring war on the Amarr Empire isn't what I had in mind.'

Mens grabbed a chair and raised it over his head. Moving to smash it on the ground, he stopped himself, mindful that his daughter was still struggling for her life just a few meters away.

Trembling, he gently set the chair back onto the floor.

'I have nothing left,' he said. 'I'm done acting like a fucking coward.'

'You're no coward,' Rali said. 'Quite the contrary.'

'I haven't done anything to prove I'm not,' he interrupted. 'Not yet.'

Rali looked at him.

'This is probably my last call as Chief Executive Officer, so listen carefully,' Mens said. 'I want you to ready our fleet. Emergency deployment orders. Mobilize like we're being invaded. I don't care how much noise it makes. I don't care who asks what we're doing. We are going to Pike's Landing. And we are bringing hell with us.'

Mens held his glare for several seconds.

Rali accepted what was about to happen with a long exhale.

'Alright,' he said. 'Let's start preparing.'

LONETREK REGION – KAINOKAI CONSTELLATION
THE TSUKURAS SYSTEM – PLANET IV: MYOKLAR
ISHUKONE FOUR-ABLE CRASH SITE

Captain Trevor Linden was awakened by a terrible bang. His immediate concerns were of being unable to breathe properly and then of the blurry images taking shape above him.

Then he remembered the dropship he had been flying and the passengers whose safety he was charged with protecting.

'. . . on three, fellas,' he heard a voice say. 'One . . . two . . .'

Another ear-splitting bang rattled his consciousness, followed by a flash of pain. The progress his vision was making was set back, and the fuzzy lines became more obscure.

'Shit, that was close,' he heard, followed by the staccato whine of a plasma rifle.

'Two meters . . . up . . . up!' someone warned. More gunfire slapped at his ears. 'There you go.'

Several men were crouched over him. There was movement nearby.

'Bastards are using the thunder to mask their positions,' he heard a familiar voice say. 'Wish I could reach the heartbeat sensors in back—'

A series of metallic *kachink!* reports startled everyone.

'Guys, we need to move,' another stranger said.

'He's waking up,' the familiar voice said. Trevor finally recognized him: It was the asshole who broke into the cockpit before they were shot down.

It felt like someone was standing on his chest.

'Ready?' said a voice. 'One . . . two . . . *three!*'

Explosive pain ripped through his chest; he would have screamed, except that doing so would require breathing.

Another deafening bang shook the surface beneath him so hard that it hurt his ears.

A heavy slab was dropped next to him.

'Get pressure on it,' he heard. 'Put your fingers in there, feel for the source. . . .'

'Found it.'

'Pinch, don't let go. . . .'

'Yup . . .'

'Hold right there, and . . . gotcha. It's clamped.'

'Blood pressure's still dropping.'

'Get biofoam into those. Use these. . . .'

'Right . . .'

He recognized the emblem of the Ishukone Watch on the shoulder of one of the arms trying to help him.

Well, thank God for that.

'Alright, we're moving,' a voice said. 'Covering fire, right into the tree line; wait for overwatch . . .'

Thunder rocked the cabin again; hard rain was striking him in the face.

'Wait . . . wait . . .' the voice said.

The whine of a gunship's plasma engine drowned out the pelt of drops on metal. Heavy cannon fire tore the sky in half.

'*Now!*'

Trevor screamed as he felt himself hauled off the ground.

'Hang in there!' asshole yelled over the crash of gunfire. 'Stay with us!'

Before blacking out, Trevor noticed the man was bleeding from substantial wounds of his own.

GENESIS REGION – EVE CONSTELLATION
THE EVE GATE – POINT GENESIS

The *Significance* turned its instrument-laden bow toward a small yellow point in space – the New Eden star, some three light-years away. All the final preparations were complete, and the ship was now flying on autopilot.

Marcus just assumed that Grious helped Mens Reppola find him. Their conversation was shorter than he would have liked, but it served its purpose.

To control an inferno, one must destroy the path in front of the blaze. Grious was right: Templar technology must be allowed to proliferate. That grim conclusion stemmed from the fact that Amarr could bring soldiers to immortality only with a Sleeper implant. The Other would stop at nothing to prevent them from learning an alternative.

Sadly, that discovery would be left to someone else. Then, and only then, could humanity defend itself. And for the moment, a stranger named Mens Reppola had a bigger head start than anyone, aside from the Amarr themselves, in the greatest arms race of all time.

Falek Grange brought unspeakable pain into two worlds, and Marcus was the one who had made that treachery possible. He vowed to spend the waning moments of his life undoing that legacy.

Marcus composed himself as the *Significance* lurched into warp. A cold and hateful presence surfaced in his mind immediately.

He hoped Grious had prepared him well.

DOMAIN REGION – THRONE WORLDS CONSTELLATION
THE AMARR SYSTEM – PLANET ORIS
EMPEROR FAMILY ACADEMY STATION: SAINT KURIA THE PROPHET CATHEDRAL
SOVEREIGNTY OF THE AMARR EMPIRE

Empress Jamyl believed it was time to expand the circle of those who knew about the Templars.

She didn't need the consent of the heirs to launch a Reclaiming on her own. But the event was of such historical consequence that gaining their public support would go a long way in preparing the Empire for what was to come.

The cathedral was an appropriate setting to share news of such magnitude, because it sent a clear reminder of where the real power was. Each heir was a monarch in his own right. But whether they agreed with Empress Jamyl or not, they were still beholden to her at all times.

Seated upon the altar's holy throne, she took inventory of her guests. Heir Yonis Ardishapur did not take kindly to being summoned by anyone, and as usual made no effort to hide his contempt. Empress Jamyl tolerated it only because her spies kept a close eye on his efforts to undermine her power. At first, he did so with pulpit-smashing public spectacles, challenging whether her royal ascension was in fact the ordained act of God, which so many believed it to be.

Getting nowhere with that approach, he had resorted to more opportunistic means by becoming the Empire's most visible religious figure. He was always seen visiting the impoverished regions of the Empire, convincing the national press to consult him for the church's perspective on natural disasters and other catastrophes. His influence was powerful to begin with, but in recent years, he managed to position himself as the faith's ambassador to the masses. The most fundamental purists in the Empire were firmly in his camp, and that made him a dangerous political enemy.

Heir Aritcio Kor-Azor, on the other hand, was an idiot whose relevance in court came from the loyalist advisors who managed his affairs. But in some ways that made him a greater threat than Ardishapur. It was difficult to know exactly who was being represented – or what motives were driving his official position on policy. Aritcio sat nervously, fidgeting with a datapad, blatantly uncomfortable because his counsel had no idea what the purpose of this meeting was.

On the other hand, Heir Uriam Kador, if not the most intelligent of the heirs, was certainly its most gifted politician – inasmuch as being an heir could allow. He was popular with secular constituencies, living a public lifestyle that fell just short of socialite extravagance. That placed him at odds with the church, except that the programs he supported were genuinely beneficial to spiritual teachings, making it difficult for them to decry his flamboyant lifestyle. He sat with his legs crossed, in clothes more befitting a music star than royalty, waiting patiently for Jamyl to speak.

Last was Heiress Catiz Tash-Murkon, the only other woman in court. She was someone whom Empress Jamyl had to admire in secret, lest the accusations of favoritism begin. Catiz earned that respect by being cooperative and constructive, offering thoughtful, unbiased opinions, but only when asked. She was brilliant at deflecting Ardishapur's demands for allegiance, dismissive of Uriam's occasional advances, and careful not to demean Aritcio's clueless behavior. Catiz rejected her royal birthright to rule but opted to earn it – also as much as Empire law and tradition allowed – by establishing herself as a businesswoman, eventually gaining cluster-wide recognition as a master financier. Like Uriam Kador, she sat quietly, waiting for Jamyl to speak.

As far as the Empress's spies could tell, the heirs had no idea the Templars existed, or that the Ministry of War was actively drafting soldiers into the program. Lord Victor Eliade, still on Pike's Landing, was in virtual attendance. Grand Admiral Kezti Sundara sat by her side, as with the Court Chamberlain.

She had waited a long time to tell them this.

'I brought all of you here to witness to the greatest moment in our history,' she began, 'if not for all of mankind as well.'

Lord Victor and the Admiral nodded in agreement, heightening the anticipation for the heirs.

'For too long, we have sought an end to the Empyrean War,' she continued. 'And though our troops are inspired, we have pushed them to their limits and exhausted every diplomatic measure to bring peace.'

Her eyes scanned the audience, searching out royal eyes to gaze into.

'I hail from a long, storied lineage of warriors,' she said. 'We know better than anyone that war brings nothing but suffering. As you shall bear witness, I intend to end it once and for all.'

Schematics of the Templar clone and its Sleeper cybernetic implant appeared.

'Royal Heirs of Amarr,' she continued. 'Behold the first immortal soldiers.'

Yonis Ardishapur frowned; the rest remained impassive.

'We have married empyrean technology to our infantry,' she continued. 'The Templars are the most potent weapons ever conceived in ground warfare. They are the beginning of an everlasting peace.'

A starmap showing the location of Pike's Landing appeared.

'The prototypes took this colony with almost no support,' she said. 'Core Freedom has vexed us for years. Thousands of Paladins gave their lives trying to reclaim it. Today, it is in our hands. I am raising an army of Templars, and they shall make war obsolete . . . a relic of history. Soon, there will be no adversaries. The Templars are the vanguard of the Final Reclaiming.'

Disbelief stretched across Yonis's brow.

'Your Majesty,' he began, 'am I correct in observing that these so-called "Templars" took but a single colony, and by that one success you're willing to gamble the future of our Empire?'

Just as she opened her mouth to answer, Jamyl felt a breathtaking stab of pain, as if an ice pick had been driven through her head. She cried out, clutching her temples.

Grand Admiral Sundara jumped out of his seat to assist her.

'Oh, *God*!' she winced, fighting against the Other's attack with all her might. 'Not now!'

The fever rushed through her like a tsunami; she had not felt an attack this vicious in years. Her vision tunneled; people were trying to help her, but she felt detached from her surroundings.

'*Why?*' she screamed aloud.

Then she realized the communications implant in her cerebral cortex was notifying her, and the Other couldn't block it out.

Marcus Jror was frantically trying to contact her.

'Your Majesty,' he said. 'I don't have much time. . . .'

'Marcus!' she willed, unsure if she said his name aloud. 'Where are you?'

'The Templars are not what you think,' Marcus said. 'You won't be able to control them. . . . The Other won't let you know that. It's an army for *him*, not for Amarr!'

She was peripherally aware that Victor was trying to say something.

'Does Victor know?' she asked.

'He has to,' Marcus answered. 'But the Other blocks him from your memory whenever he tries to warn you!'

Rage washed over her: This is what the Other was trying to hide all this time.

'What the hell is it, Marcus?' she demanded.

'Its origins are human,' he answered. 'It can be beaten!'

'How?'

'The Joves will know,' he said. 'They can find a way. . . .'

She sensed that Marcus too was in agony.

'What can I do to help you?'

'You can't,' he said. 'Jamyl, the Sleepers are still alive. . . . Those implants . . . we're killing them. . . .'

'What?'

Marcus pushed a neuro-mimetic recording of the *Significance* mission log into the commlink. Her implants absorbed the data as fast as it traveled through the quantum pipeline, flooding her vision with his memories of the Sleeper civilization.

She screamed, as Marcus had when he saw the horror, and became hysterical. People were flooding onto the altar to help her, including medics. A needle pierced her skin, but she ripped it out.

'Destroy the technology,' Marcus warned. 'Do it while he's distracted. . . . I can't hold on for much longer!'

The ice pick returned, and the pain was so intense that her spine arched to an almost impossible angle. She involuntarily threw herself down the stairs before the altar, coming to rest at the feet of the heirs, who jumped out of their seats in terror as she writhed in diabolical agony.

GENESIS REGION – EVE CONSTELLATION
THE NEW EDEN SYSTEM

The *Significance* was adrift at the Promised Land stargate. No other ships were in the system. There rarely were, anyway. For all of New

Eden, this system was a dead end. There was little reason to come here.

No one could help Marcus now anyway.

I see my old friend Grious was here, the Other said. *Clearly he was forthcoming about my relationship with your Holy Empress.*

Marcus was on his knees, all physical movement incapacitated by the implants in his brain.

'Go to hell,' he stammered, with what little remained of his courage.

I know it well, the Other answered. *Pity you believed everything that genetic abomination told you. I had considered sparing your life.*

Marcus stood up involuntarily. No longer in control of his motor skills, he was forced to an instrument panel in the research lab.

Such primitive augmentations, the Other observed. *Grious remade you in his image. You should be insulted.*

His hands, at the whim of the Other, danced over the volumetric display. The inert drones aboard the ship suddenly snapped to attention.

Do you know why he never reactivated them?

Marcus heard dozens of servos and metallic irises whir to life.

Because of their determination to not let you harm yourself.

'VICTOR,' EMPRESS JAMYL BREATHED, utterly disoriented. '*Victor!*'

'I'm here, your majesty,' she heard him say.

'Cancel the Templar program,' she ordered, helped to her feet by some invisible hands.

'It's too late for that!' he answered.

'What haven't you been telling me?' she demanded.

'I've been trying to tell you that *some* of the prototypes are flawed,' he said. 'You were always unwilling to hear bad news.'

'"Flawed" how?'

'They have these strange visions—'

'What *kind* of visions?'

'Apocalyptic dreamscapes and bizarre phobias,' Victor answered. 'All very similar to each other.'

My God, Jamyl thought.

'What else?'

'Templar Six malfunctioned during the insertion at Pike's Landing,' he answered. 'Templar One disobeyed orders during the fight ... he's the Caldari test subject. I think we're losing him as well.'

More bolts of pain sliced through her; she was now frothing a litany of curses, clawing at her temples so deeply that blood began to drip down her face.

'You have to destroy them!' she cried. '*All* of them!'

'Why?' he pleaded. 'We've come all this way!'

'Because we can't control them! Can't you see that?'

'But the technology works!' Victor pleaded. 'These are prototypes, the next generation will be flawless!'

'There won't be another generation!' she spit out. 'You don't know what they really are! Victor, listen to me: From this moment on, you must *disobey* my instructions to support the Templars! Do you understand?'

'Your Majesty!?' Victor asked, incredulously.

'For the sake of Amarr, do as I say!' she roared, breathing heavily. 'Grand Admiral Sundara: I *command* you to destroy those prototypes *by any means necessary*. That's an order!'

'My lady,' his gentle voice replied. 'I ... as you wish.'

'No!' Victor pleaded. 'We're so close!'

'Victor, get off that planet or face the consequences!' she cried.

'How can you do this?' Victor pleaded.

Marcus screamed just as she was about to answer.

THE DRONES HAD MARCUS PINNED facedown to the surgical gurney, but were entirely unfamiliar with his new anatomy. All they could discern was that the cybernetic implants in the exposed hemisphere of his brain were the cause of both his corrupted motor functions and the bursts of pain coursing through his entire nervous system. Nothing in the medical archives, either on board or in any accessible network in empire space, could have prepared them for this.

But the mandate to save his life was the hierarchal prerogative in their programming. Doing nothing while he suffered was therefore not an option; that path in their logic was blocked. As a limited AI, their ability to reason led them to believe that trial and error on a live patient, even if it meant causing immense anguish, lasting physical damage, was the right course of action.

Fully aware of this, the Other varied the source and intensity of the pain flashes, confusing the AI with false positives and leading them to the wrong conclusions about where to cut next.

They couldn't sedate him, for they needed him conscious to verify motor functionality as parts of his brain were wrongfully excavated around the implants.

Marcus was awake for all of it, fully aware he was being sliced to pieces.

He screamed, but refused to cry for mercy. It couldn't last forever. And deep down, he knew he would not die in vain, for all his secrets were no longer just with the Amarr Empire.

Marcus hoped that good hearts would prevail.

He did his best to die with a smile, just to infuriate the Other, as the drones continued to mutilate him.

EMPRESS JAMYL COULD FEEL HIS SUFFERING, and sobbed as the life mercifully left him.

As she anguished, her surroundings finally began to set in. The cathedral altar was utterly desecrated; sweat and blood smeared the stairs upon which she had fallen. Paladins and medical personnel were in attendance; many were deep in prayer, chanting Scripture as if to ward off the evil they had seen.

No one, she realized, had ever heard or experienced anything like this before.

I want you to take a moment, the Other said. *To realize what you have just done.*

Yonis Ardishapur was standing, hands rolled into tight fists at his side, chin jutting out toward her with an expression of absolute defiance, murmuring as if he was about to face the Demon himself. The other heirs – Catiz especially – were horrified, undoubtedly wondering if they had just witnessed the complete unraveling of their Empress.

They think you are weak, the Other said. *You know I cannot allow that.*

With as much dignity as she could muster, she rose to her feet.

You will remember none of this. But they will never forget.

'I will do as you commanded,' Grand Admiral Sundara said, straightening out his tunic. 'I'm sorry, Lord Victor.'

You will beg for my help soon.

The Admiral left the room urgently, and the ghost of Lord Victor vanished.

Suddenly, she couldn't remember what she had asked the Grand Admiral to do.

I'll be waiting.

31

ESSENCE REGION – VIERES CONSTELLATION
THE LADISTIER SYSTEM – PLANET IV, MOON 4: RÉNEALT
PRESIDENTIAL BUREAU STATION
SOVEREIGNTY OF THE GALLENTE FEDERATION

President Roden avoided the weekly press briefings as much as possible, preferring to leave the unenviable task of facing the nation to his able press secretary. But today, Federation Hall was packed with media representatives from all six regions, and Jacus was required to man the podium and answer questions. According to polls, the administration's approval rating was dropping precipitously, and his political strategists thought some face time with reporters might help stem their losses. But it was hardly an easy option. The Federation press corps was notoriously aggressive, empowered and emboldened by a cultural demand for absolute government transparency. Reducing politicians to molten slag at public events was a competitive sport among journalists here; catching the right lie on camera was the profession's ultimate jackpot.

But Jacus Roden was a capsuleer and highly intelligent even before cybernetic augmentations made him very difficult to stump. If he didn't know the answer to a question outright, a cursory search on any number of data networks accessible to him usually did the trick. Statements meticulously prepared by advisors were available for him to read in an instant. That nuance, combined with his stoic personality, was frustrating for the press as well, as Jacus moved effortlessly between questions about his government, the war he inherited, sensitive social topics, economic challenges, and now international affairs.

'Mr President, your foreign-policy charter toward the Minmatars is often criticized as lacking direction or purpose. Do you feel your administration is doing enough to strengthen ties with them?'

Jacus recognized the reporter as Rena Duranse, of the *Placid TriNet.*

'History will show that the Minmatars have never had a stronger ally in the Federation,' he answered. 'Our ties remain strong, but we are mindful of their ambitions. My charter outlines a vision of how to navigate this new relationship.'

'Does your charter include a willingness to escalate hostilities with the Amarr Empire?' Rena asked. With so much public resentment about the war, clearly she was trying to bait him into contradicting old campaign promises to bring combat operations to an end.

'It includes many provisions that are confidential by nature,' the President said. 'We will always be strong advocates of peace. The use of force is always a last resort.'

Jacus's augmented-reality vision suddenly sprang to life: Mentas Blaque was contacting him directly, in spite of the press conference. It was urgent:

Mr President: All contact with the 626 Recon Element on Pike's Landing has been lost.

'The Minmatar have shunned Federation assistance in most affairs since you took office,' Rena said. 'How do you explain that?'

They were last reported investigating a dropship of unknown origin.

Specifications inbound.

'They are rebuilding their nation and identity, and we must be respectful of that,' Jacus said, while simultaneously absorbing old imagery of the strange dropship on the surface of Pike's Landing. Relative to the complexities of handling a starship in combat, concentrating on several mental tasks at once was trivial. His mind began exploring the schematics and the mission log.

Undetectable on every frequency except the visible spectrum, he thought. *It wanted to be found.*

'Mr President, there are reports that the assistance you've offered was conditional on aggressive loan-repayment schedules,' Rena said. 'Is this the reason why relations have cooled?'

'The truth is simply that only so much assistance is welcome before it becomes an intrusive influence,' Jacus answered. 'There is more to our alliance than just arms sales. Our economies are so tightly interwoven that many of our interests align naturally. But we can sustain each other without disrupting their cultural renaissance. So I can see how a foreign policy charter that respects these circumstances can be misconstrued as indifferent. But clearly, that is not the case at all.'

Rena remained insistent.

'Mr President, numerous former Republic colonies were lost since the war began,' she said. 'The sentiment among those regions is that they were abandoned by both their government *and* the Federation. How do you respond?'

There are no remains at the site of last contact.

'I would respond by saying they are not forgotten,' he answered. 'And that their liberation cannot come soon enough.'

Admiral Ranchel won't authorize search and rescue without your approval.

'Would you describe this policy as "passive"?' Rena asked, herself now frustrated. 'What are you actually prepared to do for them?'

Rheopectic starship armor, Jacus thought, taking one last look at the mission log. *No one owns that kind of technology, except for the Joves. And CONCORD.*

'If the Minmatar ask for our assistance,' he answered, 'we are prepared to do everything we can to help them.'

The 626 were elite SPECFOR commandos, he thought, *making it highly improbable that lowly Paladins could just make them disappear.*

Jacus mentally opened a secure line with Admiral Freeman, patching in Mentas Blaque and Admiral Ranchel. Then he sent the following message:

SAR mission to recover SPECFOR on Pike's Landing approved. Provide full orbital support for surface units. Secure any military targets of opportunity.

'Why do you suppose they haven't asked?' Rena asked.

'I won't speculate on that,' he answered. 'But I look forward to sitting down with Sanmatar Shakor after he finishes forming his government.'

Admiral Ranchel asked:

Are you authorizing direct hostilities against the Amarr Empire?

While pointing to another journalist in the crowd, Jacus mentally replied:

Confirmed. Use of lethal force is authorized. Protect Federation assets by any means necessary and instruct our forces to be vigilant for new enemy clone technology.

'Next question,' he said aloud, his face aglow in the wash of camera lighting.

PURE BLIND REGION – MDM8-J CONSTELLATION
SYSTEM 5ZXX-K – PLANET V, MOON 17
MORDU'S LEGION HQ STATION

The man formerly known as Vincent Barabin is our High Value Individual. In many respects, the mission is similar to a hostage rescue – except in this case, the HVI is an inert clone. It is housed within one of thirteen converted HAZMAT transport vehicles containing CRUs, which for you illiterate dirt beaters in the audience stands for Clone

Revival Unit. As of now, this truck farm is lightly guarded and located in the southwestern grid of the colony. The objective is straightforward: Return the HVI to Mordu's Legion HQ intact. Not one scratch! Or else it voids the damn warranty. Sergeant Mack's fire team, callsign 'Baseplate,' will be escorting the only noncom, Dr Gable Dietrich. Her role is to identify the CRU containing the HVI and safely extract him from it. If the mission is compromised for any reason, your fallback mission is to return any of the clones located in that truck farm, dead or alive. We are sacrificing a great deal for this. We are not coming back empty-handed.

'How are you holding up?' Jonas asked.

Gable looked away from the CRU schematics she had been studying for hours.

'You're not going to ask me if I know how to use a gun, are you?' she asked.

'No,' he said, stepping inside and closing the door. 'But I will ask if you think you'll be able to use one of those things when we find him.'

She exhaled deeply.

'I'm convinced it's standard technology,' she said. 'Regardless of what those clones can do, storage protocols for biosynthetics are fundamentally the same. I've reviewed every industrial model of the last five years. I don't know what else I can do to prepare.'

'Then you'll do fine,' Jonas said, folding his arms. 'I'm sure of it.'

'Thanks,' she said, swiveling fully around to face him. 'But that's not all you're here to say, is it?'

Jonas smiled briefly. 'No, not everything.'

'Well, out with it then,' she said, leaning back. 'What's on your mind, *Captain* Varitec?'

'Your pendant,' he said, jutting with his chin. It figured prominently around her neck, glistening in the cabin lighting. 'It has to stay out of sight.'

She rolled her eyes, but Jonas waved her off.

'There's concern you're an Amarr sympathizer,' he said. 'That you might look to "defect" or cause trouble when we're down there.'

'That is *completely* ridiculous,' she said.

'You could allay those fears by respecting the wishes of those you're going to war with,' he said.

'Are you serious?'

'Think about how it looks from here,' Jonas said. 'You were a prisoner at Core Freedom—'

'Did that twit Miles put this thought in your head?'

'— and your life was spared by an immortal Amarr soldier who nearly killed all your rescuers,' Jonas said. 'People are people. They say things.'

Gable sprang out of her chair and began pacing quickly back and forth.

'I'm not a ... I'm so angry I don't even know what word to use,' she fumed. 'I believe in the *faith*, not the institution. There's a difference!'

'But in this case, the institution *is* the enemy,' Jonas said. 'And its faith is an accomplice. Whether that's founded or not, it's understandable.'

'Is it?' she said.

'Gable, I know you,' Jonas said. 'You're not going to do anything crazy down there.'

'I'm not?' she said, pacing furiously. 'How reassuring.'

'All I ask is that you keep your lucky charm out of sight,' he said. 'Please don't make this more than it is.'

'How can you trust me if you don't understand what I believe in?' she demanded. 'I'm a crazed zealot! I could snap any time!'

'Okay, look, just settle down,' he said, putting up his hands.

'No, *you* settle down and listen to me!' she demanded, marching up to him. 'I wish I knew what this faith was when I was trapped aboard the last deathtrap you captained. You have no idea what I've been through since then, the nightmares I've had over and over again because of that experience. This is all about ... about being macho and fearless and shaking a fist at danger, with no regard for the people you hurt along the way. You're the most selfish man I've ever met. That's always been you, and it always will be!'

She quickly retreated away from him, murmuring a prayer.

'I'm sorry,' she said, clearer. 'That outburst wasn't me.'

'It's alright,' Jonas said, looking down. 'You didn't say anything wrong.'

Gable felt queasy and sat back down. It felt good to release that tension, but the relief was short-lived.

'I always think about Gear,' Jonas said, stepping into the shadows.

Hearing the name of the former *Retford* crew member tore her heart out.

'I never had a son,' he said. 'I miss him.'

It was the most painful loss of the experience for her as well. Jonas was quiet for a moment, thinking.

'The way I see things, it doesn't matter *where* we get the strength from,' he said finally. 'As long as it inspires the resolve we need when it matters most.'

Gable didn't want to speak.

'I know it's fucked up,' Jonas continued. 'But I keep thinking that if I can find Vince, I'll find that little kid as well.'

'If it's redemption you want,' she said, 'this isn't the way.'

'Maybe,' he said. 'I just hope it turns out to be a first step.'

'A lot of people are going to get hurt today,' she answered. 'You know that.'

'I do,' he said, moving back toward the door. 'But as mercenaries, I accept they're doing it because they choose to. Not because anyone is telling them to.'

Jonas moved toward the door.

'If it's true what Vince has become, then there are lots of good reasons to be a part of this fight,' he said. 'And in the grand scheme of things, he's the least important of them.'

Gable couldn't bring herself to disagree.

'I never told you how I wound up at Core Freedom,' she said.

'Figured you might when you were ready,' he said.

'I was researching memory therapy,' she said. 'The Khanid were developing technology that extracts and manipulates memories from the mind. They knew how to find what they were looking for but not how to trace all the cognitive and behavioral dependencies on that explicit experience. I was to join a team researching how to do just that. The lab was in Khanid space, on a planet called Hexandria. I hadn't even met the people I was supposed to be working with, when the Valklears attacked it.'

'Why that lab?' Jonas asked.

'I later found out it was also a major center for Kameira research,' she said. 'Most of the science behind the breeding program was founded there. General Kintreb and his Valklears had their hands full with Kameira attacks on Pike's Landing. Killing the scientists who created them was his way of striking back. The only reason my life was spared is because I'm a surgeon. Most of the medical staff at Core Freedom were killed. I just happened to be something they needed.'

'What were the Khanid going to do with that research?' Jonas asked.

'Use it to treat victims of psychological trauma,' she said. 'Removing the pain of harsh memories while keeping the lessons learned . . . and any good that comes from them.'

'Do you really think that's all the Khanid would use it for?' Jonas asked.

'Seeing its potential to heal was all that mattered to me,' she said. 'I wanted to be free of the pain from the *Retford*. I wanted to forget. I still do. It's just easier.'

Jonas stared at her quietly.

'Please honor my request to keep your pendant hidden,' he said, as the door hissed open. 'It belongs close to your heart. That's where it'll do the most good.'

'Fine,' she said.

'Hangar bay, ten minutes,' he said. 'The deck officer will direct you to "Longbow One." That's my bird. Your body armor and electronics are already on board. Don't be late.'

Captain Lears will provide orbital support from a Moros-class dreadnought, callsign 'Hawkeye.' There is minimal magnetic shielding protecting the colony. However, there is a fully operational Cloudburst point-defense system. Guided missile systems cannot penetrate the airspace above them. Hawkeye will neutralize the Cloudburst plat-

forms and blast a path through the western fortifications directly to the CRU truck farm. This should clear the sky for our birds and the mud for our grunts. The mission clock starts as soon as the first gunship touches down. Hawkeye and the Morse *will jointly provide overwatch for exactly ten minutes. Remember, your fire mission is plasma bombardment. Danger close is nine hundred meters. If you need anything tighter, six gunships will be orbiting the colony perimeter, callsign 'Longbow.' They are your close air support. Be smart about how you use them. This is a bad place to get shot down.*

Korvin was on his way off the *Morse*, hustling to reach the pod gantry level of the station hangar, when he saw Mack approaching from the opposite direction.

'Hey,' Korvin said. 'Got a minute?'

Mack completely ignored him and kept on going.

'Hey!' Korvin demanded, raising his voice. 'I'm talking to you!'

The mercenary, dressed in full tactical body armor, was as menacing a warrior as Korvin had ever seen. Black-and-red digital camouflage covered the plating all over him; a beat-up vowrtech and plasma rifle were slung over his back. He also had a new arm, which Korvin noticed was much bigger than the last one.

'What?' Mack asked, over his shoulder.

'I'm your overwatch for this op,' Korvin said. 'We have to work together.'

Mack turned to face him.

'So we do.'

'I have a few things to say,' Korvin said.

'So speak,' Mack said.

'Right,' Korvin said. 'I've logged hundreds of hours doing orbital ground support for the Federation Navy. You can trust me.'

A guttural sound made its way through the scars on Mack's face.

'Don't judge who I am by my immortality, alright?' Korvin said. 'I resent that. I've never taken it for granted, and I've always tried to do good with it—'

The warrior turned away.

'Just wait,' Korvin said, placing a hand on Mack's shoulder plates, indifferent to the danger of enraging the man. 'There are people out there like me with no conscience. They have no fear. No remorse. *That's not me*. I hate them just as much as you. Do you understand?'

Mack looked at the hand on his shoulder, which Korvin promptly removed.

'Why you try win my respect?' he snarled. 'What it matter?'

'Because I admire you,' Korvin said. 'You keep coming back no matter what the fucking world throws at you, and to be honest, it's inspiring. I don't have your courage. Most people don't. It's a gift.'

'You done?' Mack asked.

'Oh, for crying out loud,' Korvin said, shaking his head. 'One more thing and I'll leave you alone. ... This protective thing you have going on with Gable ...'

'What about her?'

'Look,' Korvin said, 'I understand her importance to the mission, but sending her down there is a mistake.'

Somehow, Mack was able to sneer through the permanent grin on his face.

'You know nothing.'

'Mack, she's a liability,' Korvin insisted. 'I know it. Say whatever you want about my character, but I'm damn good at reading people.'

'Why no speak before?'

'Out of respect for Captain Varitec,' Korvin answered, remember ing the lonely model frigate in his captain's quarters. 'It's obvious he wants her to be there. Mordu knows it, too. That guy could snap his fingers and make a dozen CRU experts appear. It's not rational. So look after her ... and yourself.'

Mack grunted again and turned away.

'Good luck,' Korvin said. 'Just tell me where you need the fire, and you'll get it.'

The Morse *and a wing of Catalyst-class destroyers will follow Hawkeye into the gauntlet. This group will provide a defensive screen during the bombing run and subsequent overwatch coverage. Core Freedom is protected by Stackfire antiship missiles. Captain Lears has strict target prioritization orders and cannot disable these batteries until our gunships reach the surface – at the earliest. The rest of the fleet will set up two hundred kilometers above this group. I will personally be leading this task force. At current Imperial Navy firepower levels, I'm confident we can hold this position for ten minutes. Beyond that, the service charges start getting expensive. This is not a bill that any of us want to pay.*

Miles abruptly stopped his aerial symphony of hand movements, right as the *Morse* cleared the station hangar.

'I have a problem,' he said.

Blake looked around her displays frantically.

'What?' she asked. 'Where?'

'I'm a total dick sometimes,' he said. 'Often, actually.'

Blake's cheeks turned bright red.

'What the hell is wrong with you?' she fumed. 'Don't screw around now, you—'

'I'm being serious,' Miles said. She turned to scowl at him, expecting a dumb grin. Instead, she saw that this time was different.

'I know I really do have a problem,' he said. 'I've been hurtful to you and others.'

'Whatever,' Blake breathed, getting back to the business of captaining the ship. Captain Varitec was in the *Morse*'s hangar bay at the controls of Longbow One. This was her time to shine, and damned if she was going to let this idiot screw it up.

'Now is not the time to get fatalistic,' she said. 'Definitely not now. Okay? Pull it together.'

'I need to vent,' he said. 'I mean, if we're going to be running a protective screen for the destroyers, we gotta be sharp, quick, snappy—'

'Shhh!' she hissed through her teeth, checking that the other officers in the pit weren't looking. 'Shut the fuck up!'

'I have a confession to make,' Miles implored, his eyes wide and scared. 'I've never actually taken a shore leave. How pathetic is that.'

'What?'

'I just . . . I just wander around the station,' he said. 'Mostly in the Customs levels. Kind of disappear there.'

Since taking assignment with the *Morse*, Blake and the rest of the crew were given more than a dozen general shore leaves. She realized now that all those times, she had always left before him, and he was always there when she returned.

'I made up all the wild stories,' he said. 'None of them ever happened.'

'Ohh . . . shit,' Blake groaned, shaking her head, letting the autopilot guide the ship alongside a pair of Legion battleships.

'You're the closest thing to a friend I have,' he said. 'Anywhere. Not just on the *Morse*. That's why I never leave. I don't have anyplace else to go.'

She looked over toward him and was horrified.

'Oh, my god, are you *crying*?' she asked.

'I'm more afraid of not having anyone to talk to than I am of getting blown to bits,' he said, rubbing his eyes. 'Fucking terrified. You have no idea. Please don't let anyone see me like this. I'm really sorry.'

'You know what your problem is?' she said. 'When you're not in your element, you always think you've lost already. Stop giving up on yourself! You want to make friends? Care about how a conversation goes once in a while. Stop trying to impress everyone. You're not the jerk you think you are. At least, not all of the time.'

'Really?' he said. 'You mean that?'

'That's all the sunshine you're going to get,' she said, turning her attention back to the *Morse*'s controls. 'Harden the fuck up, Miles. It's game time.'

Fire teams Dagger, Rawhide, Frostbite, and Ironbound will escort Baseplate to the objective. Your mission is simple: Make sure Baseplate and the HVI survive. You are weapons-free: If it's gold, I encourage you to shoot it. Four CreoDron Rantula series antiarmor drones will deploy with each team. They will buy you time against mechanized units. They are also intimately familiar with your biometrics. Anyone they don't recognize will be turned into chunky kibbles. When you reach the CRU farm, fan out in defensive positions and help locate the HVI. Once Baseplate has him secured, Longbow will transport your teams to the extraction point, code name 'Disciple,' located southwest of the space elevator. We're going to use the ground terminus as cover. Dropships will be waiting there to transport all teams back into orbit.

Mordu knocked an empty bottle of whiskey off his desk while lunging for the datapad. The caller source was unknown.

'Dad,' Arian said.

'Son,' Mordu said. 'I can't believe I'm hearing your voice.'

'Disappointed?' Arian asked.

'No father could ever be,' Mordu answered.

There was a pause.

'Ishukone saved our lives.'

'I know they did.'

Another pause, shorter than the last one.

'This thing between us isn't over,' Arian said. 'But there's a lot happening here. The Watch, Ishukone – they're mobilizing fast, like they're getting ready to—'

The connection dropped abruptly.

When you add it all up, nearly a quarter million of us are participating in this op. Some of you will not be coming back. You are all mercenaries. But you were soldiers before you came to me. An honest man recognizes when it's time to backtrack on some principles. Let me do so now by declaring that for the first time in the history of our Legion, it is not about the money. This clone we're going after holds secrets that will determine the rise or fall of empires for a long time. The outcome of today's events will be the difference between a dark future or a dark future with a glimmer of hope. Call me old-fashioned, but I'll give it my all for hope anytime. Make me proud by inspiring one another to do the same. Not just for the Legion but for yourselves – and everything that's important to you. Good luck. May fortune smile on us all.

HEIMATAR REGION – HED CONSTELLATION
AMAMAKE SYSTEM – PLANET II: PIKE'S LANDING
CORE FREEDOM COLONY
SOVEREIGNTY OF THE AMARR EMPIRE

Lord Victor stormed through the elevator's eastern terminus entrance, ignoring the Paladins saluting him. An MTAC was parked outside with its cockpit hatch raised; the pilot was chatting with a few soldiers milling about beneath it. An armored truck was idling beside the group, and Victor marched directly toward it as the others snapped to attention.

He was well past the point of trying to control his thoughts or emotions any longer.

'Get out!' he shouted at the driver, who practically threw himself from the door. Victor stepped in and floored the accelerator, kicking up a plume of silt in his wake.

'Everything we sacrificed!' he shouted, directing his anger toward Empress Jamyl, even though he was alone. *'For what?'*

Vehicles frantically pulled out behind him, struggling to keep up. But Victor didn't know what to do: An attack was coming from the Imperial Navy ... by order of the Empress herself! How could he explain that? He felt like a traitor, an infidel about to be judged – of all things, by the very nation and faith he had protected his entire life.

He slammed on the brakes.

In one direction, the road led to the nearest spaceport. He could be on a dropship and aboard his own starship in no time, safe inside his immortal sanctuary, and could sound a general retreat from there.

Or he could head in the other direction, toward the nearest fortified installation, and tell the Paladins at Core Freedom to prepare for the fight of their lives.

What complete madness.

'God help me!' he shouted.

Then his commlink sounded: It was Grand Admiral Kezti Sundara.

'Victor,' he began. 'We must speak in private.'

Breathing hard a few times before answering, Lord Victor composed himself.

'I'm alone,' he said.

'Good,' the Admiral said. 'Now listen to me: You must let reason dictate your actions, not passion.'

The sun was setting opposite the great mountain range to the east. Every face of its immense granite heights was glowing radiantly.

Victor tried to find beauty in it and couldn't.

'I've watched you over the years,' Admiral Sundara said. 'Even before Her Majesty's ascension. I know what you've invested in her and in the Templars.'

Lord Victor had no qualms with Amarr's supreme military commander. The Admiral was an able strategist, a skilled tactician, and well respected by the armed forces. But he was never part of the inner sanctum of Empress Jamyl's court. That was by his own doing – a self-imposed separation of powers, to insulate himself from the petty politics of the heirs. But no matter how united they were in cause and faith, he would always be an outsider to Victor.

'Amarr is lucky to have you,' he continued. 'You are one of the greatest Paladins in Imperial history. But you must leave Pike's Landing at once.'

'No,' Victor answered. It was a reflex. There was nothing to consider.

'Victor,' the Admiral said, 'we must follow our Empress.'

'I can't leave,' Lord Victor said. 'You don't know what you're telling me to do.'

'Evaluate dispassionately,' Admiral Sundara said. 'Think, Victor. The heirs saw *everything*. That is damning enough. But disobeying her will only feed the dogs who question her rule. We will send a message of disarray and uncertainty – and worse, disloyalty. I can't have that.'

'Those Templars are the key to everything we stand for,' Victor fumed.

'And they remain so,' the Admiral said. 'Her concerns are with how we are building them. We can find alternatives. But by order of your Holy Empress, the *prototypes* must be destroyed. This is only the end of the beginning.'

Victor shook his head.

'Thousands of the best soldiers in our Empire are now "prototypes," ' he said. 'What will you say to them?'

'That they are casualties of war,' Admiral Sundara said, 'and that they have made no less a sacrifice than those who have fallen before them.'

Long shadows cast by the elevator terminus behind him reached across the grounds, engulfing the installations in the distance in darkness.

'Take my clones, Admiral,' Victor said. 'You know where they are. Terminate them. Send down your fire and end my life here, alongside my Templars. I'd rather die with a clear conscience than live an eternity of regret.'

Grand Admiral Sundara paused.

'You are a pious man,' the Admiral said, 'as I am. The objective reasons to obey your Empress have been stated. For any other man under my command, that would be all. But for you, I will make an exception, in the hope it prevents Amarr from losing its finest Paladin.'

The radiant sun fell beneath the horizon.

'My heart tells me that we witnessed a warning from God,' Admiral Sundara said. 'Our Empress is suffering so we don't have to. Disobey her, and I fear for us all.'

A blaring alarm startled Victor, one at first, and then dozens more. Their pitched warning carried across the entire colony.

It was an air raid.

'Going to kill me anyway, Sundara?' Victor hissed. 'So be it.'

'I hear those alarms,' Admiral Sundara said. 'That is not by my hand.'

The commlink was screaming: About a dozen officers in orbit and on the surface were trying to reach him.

Data scrolled across his vision. He couldn't believe what he was seeing.

'Federation gunships have just entered our airspace,' Victor said aloud.

'Then a fleet is nearby,' the Grand Admiral said. 'You must prepare your forces.'

'Why are they here? For the Minmatar?'

'No, Victor. They've come for the Templars.'

HEIMATAR REGION – HED CONSTELLATION
AMAMAKE SYSTEM – PLANET II: PIKE'S LANDING
THE GFS *PASSAIC* CARRIER GROUP

Admiral Elijah Freeman paced the bridge of the GFS *Passaic*, awash in the stream of data flowing through the air. The op was barely ten minutes old and there was already bad news.

'We've been compromised,' the voice of Eagle One said. 'X-band sweep got us during atmospheric entry. They know we're here.'

Five Federation gunships, each carrying a dozen armed soldiers, plus a heavy dropship loaded with small armored vehicles, were descending to the surface of Pike's Landing. Their destination was the last known position of the missing 626 Recon commandos. The latest intel suggested they could slip in undetected if their entry trajectory put them far east of the badlands, but it was clear the Amarr had finally plugged the gap in radar coverage. With the elevator fully operational, the defensive capabilities of the colony were improving by the hour. Industrial freighters had been arriving at the orbital platform terminus around the clock for days.

Well, enough of the sneaky shit, Elijah thought.

'Eagle One, proceed with the mission but avoid direct contact if possible,' he said. 'We're moving into position to provide overwatch. Stand by.'

'Copy that; waiting for your eyes.'

Admiral Freeman reached for the fleet-link HUD. Cloaked covert-operations ships were within two hundred kilometers of the space elevator orbital platform, evading Imperial patrols and collecting information about the activity at Core Freedom. Their location, heading, and sensor information all appeared on the bridge in a huge volumetric tactical display.

'Stalker-Three, the fleet is warping to your grid,' he said. 'Confirm nearest enemy contact is one-nine-zero klicks at your twelve.'

'Stalker-Three confirms one-nine-zero at twelve,' the response came. 'Grid is not secure.'

'Understood, we're coming anyway,' Freeman said, using both hands to broadcast his next announcement to the entire fleet through the HUD.

'All ships, prepare to warp,' he said. 'Stalker-Three is your beacon. Enemy contacts will be in sight but out of range. Defensive formations only; do *not* engage without my authorization.'

The surface team channel erupted with chatter.

'Command, Eagle One,' the voice said. 'We're at the location; no sign of them. Picking up enemy comms; there are patrols in the area.'

'Copy Eagle; overwatch in five seconds,' Freeman said. 'All ships, warp on my mark . . . *mark!*'

He felt a brief surge of vertigo as the Nyx-class supercarrier lurched into hyperspace. When the space outside coalesced into focus, he could see the Core Freedom space elevator far in the distance – a tiny spindle shining above the bluish-brown orb of Pike's Landing, hovering serenely among the twinkle of golden specs.

Time to open a second front in the Empyrean War, he thought, keying an open broadcast to the Imperial fleet.

'Attention Imperial Navy warships. This is Admiral Elijah Freeman of the Federation Navy,' he said. 'Gallente citizens under contract with Core Freedom Limited Partnership were in the colony when it was attacked by your forces. We have reason to believe they fled eastward, into the badlands. We are conducting search-and-rescue operations in this area. Any hostile acts toward Federation search parties will be answered in kind. Any offer of assistance will be considered. Thank you.'

It was complete bullshit, of course.

'Here we go, Roden,' he muttered, as alarm warnings indicated the *Passaic* was being targeted by the Imperial fleet. 'I hope you know what you're doing.'

HAATAKAN OIRITSUU HAD TAKEN her revenge. But strangely, this time it failed to satisfy.

She believed that Mens Reppola needed to be punished. The remains of his loved ones were probably scattered all over Myoklar by now. He deserved it because he had dangled freedom before her eyes and then snatched it away. That cruelty deserved to be matched in kind.

Or did it? she wondered.

In her mind, Mens and his lapdog Rali were far too competent for this to have been a clumsy botch. More likely it was a calculated risk; they wagered they could take her offer free of risk. But even if this assumption was wrong, the penalty for dishonoring their agreement, regardless of reason, should have been no less severe.

Or maybe it didn't have to be, she thought.

Her doubt was growing because the tactical aftermath of her actions was now almost impossible to navigate. With no options remaining, she considered the possibility that her reaction had been too impulsive. That was uncharacteristic of her. She searched her soul for the cause, wondering if her rage was fueled by her failed relationship with Mordu. His son had most likely died, and for nothing – though it appeared some passengers had survived, and that Heth's Dragonaurs were completely unprepared for the ferocity of Ishukone's response.

Nevertheless, chances were he was dead. And that was a good enough reason to hurt Mens back.

Wasn't it?

A bridge was burned and a powerful potential ally was lost. She tried to count how many friends she had left and found herself struggling to remember if she ever had any to begin with. Money could always buy more, except now there wasn't very much of that left either.

So this is how regret feels.

The Provist guards were standing much closer to her than usual.

Heth remained on screen, tracking the aftermath of events, belittling the incompetence of his hired guns while keeping the Navy's inquiries at arm's length. He was in his military element again, playing the General he thought himself to be but never actually was. Megacorporation armed forces were anxiously trying to get information, but Heth was keeping quiet, except to say that a serious attempt on his life had been thwarted, and that under no circumstances were they to let the press find out.

The events set in motion at Myoklar were now spiraling out of control, and no one could make sense of the chaos – no one except for Haatakan. Judging from Ishukone's reaction, it was clear that Mens had found exactly what she said he would.

Fleet Admiral Morda Engsten, the highest-ranking military official of the Caldari State beneath Tibus Heth, was now conferenced in.

'Ishukone has achieved maximum war time readiness,' she said. 'They've invoked national emergency protocols, with twenty-five percent of their population converted to active reservist status.'

'Have they answered your queries?' Heth asked.

'No response,' the Admiral said, 'from anyone.'

'Alright then,' Heth said, balling his hands into fists. 'I think we just might have a fight coming.'

'I'm not so sure,' the Admiral said. 'We're analyzing their mobilization. If they were planning attacks against the State, their logistical patterns make no sense. The ship movements we've tracked suggest they're actually preparing to *leave* Caldari space, through the southern regions.'

'The south?' Heth asked.

'Yes, toward Amarr space.'

'That doesn't make any goddamn sense.'

'No, it doesn't,' the Admiral said, narrowing her eyes at him. 'But knowing exactly what happened at Myoklar might provide some insight to their motives.'

'You'll know when you need to,' Heth growled.

'Fair enough,' she replied. 'I realize Ishukone is a thorn in your side. Don't let them goad you into a civil war.'

'Point noted, Admiral,' Heth said. 'That will be all.'

As the Admiral's image vanished, the dictator turned his icy glare back to Haatakan.

'You've been awfully quiet,' he said.

32

HEIMATAR REGION – HED CONSTELLATION
AMAMAKE SYSTEM – PLANET II: PIKE'S LANDING
TWENTY-FIVE KILOMETERS SOUTHEAST OF CORE FREEDOM COLONY – BADLANDS GRID
SOVEREIGNTY OF THE AMARR EMPIRE

Vince was so attuned to his surroundings that he swore he could hear the colony's alarms – a shrill, unnatural cry that the wind carried across the open steppes and into the canyons of the badlands. His TACNET sprang to life; he hadn't been hearing things. Federation dropships had entered their airspace, and the Paladins were preparing for the worst.

The assassin he was following noticed it as well: Her head perked upward, turning to face west. He had been stalking her from high ground for hours, watching as she moved the bodies of the Federation commandos back to the gunship they arrived in with the strength of a machine; then she deftly dismantled the craft's electronics, perhaps to disable its ability to broadcast. She flew it down the riverbed, disappeared around its eastern bend, and reemerged a short while later on foot.

Vince was pondering why she would do this when he heard something else: A craft was approaching quickly. A Federation Blackjack-class gunship suddenly roared overhead; the war machines were so proficient at masking their noise signature that even his enhanced senses had nearly missed it.

When he looked back down toward the riverbed, the assassin was gone.

He went completely prone, nestling into the crevice of a rock outcrop. A creature slithered nearby, but he ignored it as the gunship lumbered overhead, hovering momentarily over the riverbed before moving upstream. The rocks were good cover; enough to prevent a thermal scan from giving his position away. His elevated body temperature would stick out like an inferno on any scanner.

And, Vince just realized, to most of the wildlife in this ecosystem.

The slithering noise returned as Vince strained to peek between rocks downward, where he last saw the assassin. Staying perfectly still, he could hear the Blackjack hovering low, perhaps trying to evade Imperial patrols, now that the colony knew they were there.

It was the craft's roving spotlight that caused the animal slithering nearby to panic. Vince had unwittingly put himself inside the nest of a local reptile species – in this case, an adult more than two meters long. He found himself face-to-face with the serpentine-like creature, staring directly into its marble-black eyes as it reared its head backward like a coiling spring.

Strangely, Vince became mesmerized. And then time stopped altogether.

Please don't kill me, something said.

Vince became horribly confused.

I don't want to hurt anyone.

The creature was gone. Something impossibly familiar and humanoid had replaced it.

We were preparing for journey's end. The Enheduanni told us it was time to emerge and rebuild.

It was speaking in a language that Vince had never been taught; the same one that Templar Six had spoken. He could see its written alphabet – undecipherable glyphs and symbols – and yet their meaning was perfectly clear to him.

They are destroying our home. Why would anyone want to harm us?

Vince briefly saw a spectacular city hovering over vast oceans; then it was ablaze and crumbling into the sea.

I helped build this. The ones I love are still there. We achieved harmony. The Other warned they would take it from us. He was right.

In a blinding flash, the emotions that the Amarr had tried to suppress in him as a Templar were all resurrected. He felt unimaginable sorrow and anguish; he was better prepared to take a bullet than answer to this.

You don't belong in this world. And I don't belong in yours. I don't know how this happened.

The distant words of Instructor Muros, everything she had imparted to him, including the conviction of the Templar and the creed he defended, evaporated.

Is this real?

The being was now exploring Vince's memories. He was shown the footprints of Empress Jamyl and knew it was all a lie.

You are different from us. Lost. There is no harmony in your world.

Then Vince saw her, the one he swore he had recognized, as she was when he nearly shot her.

Her name is Gable. You should remember her.

LONETREK REGION – KIANOKAI CONSTELLATION
THE KIRRAS SYSTEM – PLANET IX: LAI DAI EXCAVATIONS OUTPOST
SOVEREIGNTY OF THE CALDARI STATE

Seven Years Ago

When the rage subsided, the first words Vince heard were mumbled by his sister.

'Oh, my God . . . ,' Téa said.

Unconscious for several minutes, she was now seeing the aftermath of her brother's actions.

Gray matter was seeping like a wet sponge from a crack several centimeters wide in her husband's skull. His eyes had rolled in separate directions, one toward the top of his head, the other off to the side.

Vince just assumed his heart had stopped beating by now. Blood was all over his own hands, smeared into his knuckles and the palms he'd used to repeatedly smash the man's head onto the cement floor.

Téa tried to get to her feet but fell back down instead. Two of her teeth were missing, her right eye was swollen shut, and her nose was horribly crooked. The front of her neck and shirt were soaked in crimson.

As Vince stood to assist her, his foot accidentally kicked a small handgun.

'You're shot,' Téa said.

Vince hadn't even noticed until he went to move his right arm. At such close range, the iridium round barely had time to fully convert to plasma. The slug entered just below his clavicle and plowed a cauterized hole less than a centimeter wide all the way through its exit point at the rear deltoid.

Unfortunately, the shearing force of the mass blasting through muscle and bone had ripped open his thoracoacromial artery. Since the entry and exit wounds were both sealed, Vince had no idea he was slowly bleeding to death.

'What'd I do?' he said, at last succumbing to the adrenaline's painful hangover.

'You killed him,' she said, using the wall for balance.

'Yeah, I guess I did,' he said, moving to help her stand.

The glass office, situated at the end of a floor where around twenty commodity traders sat, still had its blinds drawn. Apart from the mess and a smoldering bullet hole in the ceiling rafter, the place was exactly as Kavon Giles had left it: executive furnishings, notably a plush couch with authentic leathering extracted from the hide of some ferocious beast nearing extinction on an exotic world; an oversize desk with an engraving of the monster's name who sat behind it; a virtual terminal; and a handful of insignificant trophies, most of them awarded by the Lai Dai mega-corporation for accomplishing some managerial milestone or other.

At the moment, the place smelled vaguely of burnt meat and ionized gas.

'Why'd you do this?' she asked.

Vince became angry again.

'It was just a matter of time before that happened to you,' he said, motioning toward the corpse. 'I couldn't take it anymore.'

The siblings believed they had turned their lives around since those dark days in Blackbourn City. By the time Vince finished his labor sentencing, Téa had long since found administrative work in the Lai Dai mega-corporate bureaucracy. He emerged as a welder qualified to operate in zero-G environments – a highly sought-after skill, given its attrition rate. Téa's contacts were able to arrange for both to find employment at the same mining outpost in Kirras. It was a Lai Dai start-up venture, a tiny operation with a chance of becoming something worthwhile, depending on how some surveying went in the system.

'I don't know what to do,' she said, lightly touching the puffy skin on her cheek. She felt as if something heavy were tugging on her eye. 'There are cameras everywhere.'

'You didn't do anything wrong,' Vince said, wincing at the throbbing pain in his shoulder.

Having grown up with an abusive father and few friends, Téa often made poor choices when it came to companionship. In her own mind, the opportunity to marry into the management tier of a mega-corporation was too enticing to pass up, no matter what the risks. She had convinced herself it was necessary for her own survival.

'Jonas,' she said. 'We have to call him.'

'And ask for what?' he snarled. 'He can't cover this up.'

Vince had noticed the bruises from time to time and even confronted her about it directly on a few occasions. She always denied anything was wrong, but it was obvious what was happening.

'We ask to go with him,' she said. 'He made the offer to us, and – *oww!*'

She grabbed at her abdomen, inside of which was a growing fetus. Vince saw blood on the inside of her thighs.

'Oh, no,' he said. 'We have to get you help!'

Breathing heavily, she struggled to Kavon's desk. His terminal was still active. Jonas Varitec was Vince's direct manager in the outpost's ship hangar; he had privately admitted that he was no fan of Lai Dai, and he had approached Vince directly and asked if he wanted a crew position on a frigate he'd bought with his own money.

'I'm sending a message to Jonas,' she said. 'We can't walk back through that office now. Not like this.'

Vince peeked through; the place was empty. He knew it would be: The anonymous note he'd received an hour ago stated that Kavon had sent everyone home for the night and drawn the shades after Téa went into his office. At last, someone's conscience had finally prevailed. Her bruises weren't exactly a well-kept secret. Whenever Vince came down here to visit, everyone avoided eye contact.

'Yes, sir, Mr Giles?' Jonas said, in an eager, ass-kissing tone that made Vince sick.

'It's me, Téa,' she grimaced. 'We need help. . . . I'm sending you security camera footage. . . . Make sure no one's around.'

Vince doubted that security ever looked at these feeds. Kavon Giles could buy off anyone here. Today, Vince just happened to arrive as he was throwing a haymaker at Téa. She was half dressed; what garments remained looked like they'd been ripped. Apparently, she wasn't in the mood, and Kavon had taken exception to that. Then he told Vince he couldn't do shit about it and hit her again.

'Please,' Téa begged. 'We need doctors. . . .'

'Holy *shit*.' Jonas winced, looking away. 'Fuck! Let me think for a minute. . . .'

Vince wasn't feeling well.

'She hasn't done anything wrong,' he said. 'I'm taking her to the medbay.'

'No!' Téa protested, then hunched over in pain. 'Oh, god . . .'

'Don't fight me on this,' Vince said, taking her by the arm. 'C'mon, let's go!'

He made it three steps and then collapsed.

Vince heard his sister panic and wanted to calm her. But he couldn't even speak – and he tasted blood in his mouth. Every movement was a struggle; even his vision was starting to blur.

He knew what was happening and began to panic himself.

Death was coming for him, and he was desperate to escape from it. There was no resignation or acceptance of this outcome; he felt no peace.

Lights faded, then returned. Voices rose, then drifted away.

A violent shock jolted his senses; he saw Jonas above him, who was saying something encouraging. Vince had barely enough strength left to beg him for help.

He felt his heart stop beating. Darkness engulfed him, and Vince was unsure if he was alive or not.

An indeterminate period of time passed before a new voice called out.

'Hey tough guy, wake up,' she said. 'C'mon, you. Snap out of it.'

He opened his eyes and saw an attractive woman staring back at him with a smile.

'You had a scare there,' she said, 'but you're alright now.'

Jonas stepped into view.

'How is he?'

'He'll be fine,' the woman said. 'That shoulder will be sore for a while, but it'll heal.'

'Where am I?' Vince croaked.

'Lorado Station,' Jonas said. 'Nullsec space.'

'The Lai Dai goons can't get you out here,' the woman said. 'You've been unconscious for nearly forty-eight hours.'

'What about Téa . . . ?' he said.

'She's being looked after by another doc,' Jonas said. 'She'll be fine, but she lost the baby. I'm sorry.'

Considering who the father was, Vince wasn't sure how he felt about that.

'How'd you get us out?'

Jonas blew air out of his mouth slowly.

'Well, the short of it is, Kavon Giles wasn't a real popular guy,' he said. 'It didn't cost much to pay some folks to look the other way.'

'Hope you saved some of that cash for me, Joney-boy,' the woman said. 'My services ain't cheap.'

Vince already assumed that this was a one-way trip.

'Don't worry, there's enough left to go around,' Jonas said. 'Vince, this is Doctor Gable Dietrich. She'll be taking care of you until you're ready to join the crew.'

'Hii-i!' she said, with a sarcastic wave. The doctor was a tiny thing: Next to Jonas, she was maybe 150 centimeters tall. Wavy auburn hair fell past her chin, dangling over light green eyes, a supple nose, soft lips, and an irresistible charm.

Then again, he acknowledged this might also be the painkillers talking.

'What crew?' he asked.

'The crew of the *Retford*,' he said with a wink. 'Your new ship. Welcome aboard.'

Jonas left.

'So, handsome,' Gable commented, 'some ground rules about your stay here: One – when I tell you to do something, you do it. You'll heal faster that way. Two – I don't ever want to know how you wound up here. My practice thrives on me not asking patients any more questions than absolutely necessary. The less I know about *circumstances*, the better. Three – and this is most important – you have to say something to make me smile every time I see you. Got it?'

The last rule caught him off guard.

'What?' he said, unable to help himself grin.

'See? It works,' she said, flashing a beautiful smile of her own. 'But you'll have to think of something better next time.'

VINCE, LYING ON THE GROUND on Pike's Landing, was marveling at the comfort he found in Gable's smile, when the Architect spoke again.

You could have achieved harmony with this person, it said. *How could you forget her?*

The serpent's angry black eyes returned, and time was slowly accelerating again. His hand began darting out to meet the threat head on.

Instructor Muros called out from his memory: 'Tell me your creed . . . .'

'I am a Templar,' he had said. 'I am eternally devoted to our faith;

I am the holy sword of the righteous, and I will defend Amarr with all my might.'

No, the Architect said. *Your name is Vince Barabin.*

He remembered now.

I shouldn't know these things, the Architect said. *I don't know who or what you are. I fear the end has already happened.*

Vince's hand smashed into the creature's neck as time resumed full speed.

One of its fangs dug deep into his wrist and latched on. His other hand reflexively drew his combat knife, slashing forward as the reptile attempted to wrap its coils around him. The knife plunged in deep; the grip on his wrist loosened slightly. Vince withdrew and slashed again, this time aiming below the jaw. He connected and pushed the blade all the way through; its body fell away in a flaying death spasm.

The head remained attached to his arm, its angry black eyes gazing at him.

Vince Barabin.

He ripped the creature's head off. His Templar anatomy protected him from the venom coursing through his veins.

Lord Victor was screaming on the TACNET, demanding to know why he hadn't reported the Federation gunships that had overflown his position.

Instead of answering, he keyed the general broadcast channel and said a phrase in a dialect that was thousands of years old.

Only the Templars would understand its meaning.

'Remember that,' he then said, in his usual speech. 'You're not what they say you are.'

Switching the TACNET off, he reached for a flare.

With the signaling device in one hand and his rifle in the other, he stood up slowly. The assassin was staring right at him, purposefully making her way up the ridge with a weapon pointed his way.

Vince raised his hands so she could see them clearly.

Then he set off the flare, holding it as high as he could.

HEIMATAR REGION – HED CONSTELLATION
AMAMAKE SYSTEM – PLANET II: PIKE'S LANDING
CORE FREEDOM COLONY
SOVEREIGNTY OF THE AMARR EMPIRE

'Damn it!' Lord Victor cursed, speeding past a checkpoint and flooring the accelerator toward the nearest armor hangar.

Every Paladin, from noncommissioned infantry through the entire command hierarchy of the Heimatar Regional Task Force, had heard the words of Templar One.

Victor plugged into the channel directly.

'Those are the words of a traitor!' he said. 'Remember your creed! We are brothers in arms and faith! Let no one break—'

A spectacularly bright flash suddenly lashed out from the sky; for an instant, it transformed the land from night into day. Victor was utterly blinded; he had the composure to release the accelerator and brake lightly, but he was going too fast, and the vehicle began to drift off the road.

Striking a rock embankment, the truck began to flip. The helpless eternity that passed between the awareness of calamity in progress and its pending consequence was filled with a mental cry of *No-no-no-no!* It flipped once, twice, and then he lost count. As he was smashed from side to side, Victor knew he had just seen an orbital strike, fired from a Revelations-class dreadnought.

Its placement was in the direction of the Templar CRU farm, five kilometers to the northwest.

The vehicle finally came to rest upside down.

One of Amarr's greatest immortal Paladins lay battered, bloodied, and ruined inside. The physical pain was shocking ... humbling ... something Victor was completely unaccustomed to.

Grand Admiral Sundara's gentle but forceful voice passed through his ears.

'I'm sorry,' he heard him say, 'but I cannot allow this to go on.'

HEIMATAR REGION – HED CONSTELLATION
AMAMAKE SYSTEM – PLANET II: PIKE'S LANDING
THE GFS *PASSAIC* CARRIER GROUP

Admiral Freeman blinked a few times to make sure he wasn't seeing things.

'Eagle One, can you confirm sky-fire impact on the colony?' he asked.

'Confirmed,' the radio said. 'It hit something inside the perimeter.'

Holy shit, he thought.

'Copy that, Eagle One,' he said. 'Be advised, two unidentified gunships have just entered your sector. Transferring overwatch to Stalker-Two for coverage.'

'Roger that. Eagle One out.'

Admiral Freeman manipulated the display layers, extracting the command channel HUD.

'Get me the President, FLASH priority,' he ordered.

'I'm listening, Admiral,' Jacus Roden said. 'Go ahead.'

'The Imperial Navy just bombarded the colony,' Admiral Freeman reported. 'One strike only.'

'What was the target?' the President asked.

Real-time imagery of the blast site provided by Stalker-Two appeared.

'It looks like the HAZMAT truck farm in the vicinity,' he said. 'Tight-beam strike, long exposure.'

'Damage assessment?'

'It's completely gone,' Admiral Freeman said. There were thirteen puddles of molten slag among a field of glass where the truck farm once was. 'Vaporized. No secondary explosions, limited thermal damage to surrounding infrastructure. Pinpoint strike.'

'I've just been informed that Imperial military chatter all the way up the chain of command spiked drastically just a few moments ago,' the President said. 'It seems this was an executive decision.'

Stalker-Two focused its cameras even closer: Armored vehicles were approaching the blast site, stopping a safe distance from the smoldering crater. Soldiers stepped out with their weapons drawn, as a gunship patrolled overhead.

Are they looking for survivors? Admiral Freeman thought. *Or making sure there aren't any?*

'Theories, Admiral?' the President asked.

'They didn't care if we saw what they hit,' he answered. 'They could have tried to drive us away first.'

'Implies a certain urgency, doesn't it?' President Roden mused.

'Like something was down there they don't want us or anyone else learning about,' the Admiral said.

'Yes,' Jacus said. 'Understanding what made them do this is very much a national security concern of the Gallente Federation.'

'Agreed.' Admiral Freeman knew what was coming.

'Send in the rest of what you have,' Jacus ordered. 'You know what to look for. Skirmish them. Don't breach the colony perimeter – not yet.'

'Yes, sir, Mr President.'

'One more thing,' Jacus added. 'The rules of diplomacy stipulate that I can only offer additional support to cover a retreat. Be careful.'

Translation: You're on your own, Admiral Freeman thought.

'Understood, Mr President.'

He keyed a general fleet broadcast.

'Fleet, this is command,' he said. 'We're sending all remaining ground forces to the surface. Your deployment trajectories *must track east of the badlands*. We do not have air superiority. Repeat: red skies west of the badlands—'

'Command, Stalker-Two,' the radio interrupted. 'Republic Fleet bombers just uncloaked near my position—'

There were twelve of them, all vectoring directly toward the same low-orbit Imperial Revelations-class dreadnought that attacked the colony.

By itself, that wasn't a concern, except that Stalker-Two was within ten kilometers of the same dreadnought when the bombers released their deadly ordnance. Admiral Freeman watched helplessly as a dozen blossoms of fire engulfed the dreadnought and Stalker-Two disappeared from his display.

There was no time to mourn him, as more than sixty new contacts – all Republic Fleet warships – warped into view at point-blank range to the Imperial ships surrounding the space elevator.

The first artillery shells were slamming into the golden hulls of the Imperial Navy when Eagle One added to the confusion.

'Command, got eyes on two foot mobiles, possible HVIs,' he said. 'You're not going to believe this, but one just lit off a flare!'

GENESIS REGION – SANCTUM CONSTELLATION
THE YULAI SYSTEM – INNER CIRCLE TRIBUNAL STATION
SOVEREIGNTY OF THE CONCORD ASSEMBLY

'Why would they fire at the surface?' Inner Circle Director Irhes Angireh demanded. 'What did they target?'

Their minds were linked, sharing the latest data from THANATOS. The space above them was a volumetric maelstrom of speculative theories and imagery from the agent's perspective on Pike's Landing.

'We don't know,' Tashin answered. 'But regardless, it implies something unexpected or uncontrollable has happened.'

'Let's assume both, and that the target was immortal technology,' Irhes said. 'Then what?'

'Then the one that's following THANATOS right now could be unique, perhaps spared for some reason,' Esoutte said. 'His isolation from the group also suggests a possible rogue scenario.'

'All the more reason to capture him intact,' Irhes said. 'This is a precious opportunity we can't waste. And, it makes the case for direct intervention even stronger.'

'What do you mean, stronger?' Tara asked.

The Inner Director's visual construct transformed to those of CONCORD battleships.

'I propose that we send in our own forces,' she said, 'and confiscate or destroy any more evidence we find.'

There was silence as everyone else's projected mental imagery froze and then disappeared – as usually happened whenever anyone suggested something preposterous.

'Irhes, that's a little much, don't you think?' Tashin finally said.

'The mandate gives us the authority to do it—' Irhes started, surprised that her staunchest intellectual ally disagreed.

'We know about the mandate,' Esoutte snapped. 'But you're starting to worry me.'

But the defiance only made Irhes more determined.

'The Imperial Navy just fired on their own troops!' she insisted. 'That alone gives us good reason to investigate. There is no clearer message of urgency. If they cannot contain their situation, they may even ask our assistance.'

'Then let's offer it,' Tashin suggested. 'See how they respond.'

'And in the wild chance they accept, then what?' Esoutte asked.

'Order the Federation ships to leave Amamake and secure the colony,' Irhes said.

'And violate the whole reason the mandate was created in the first place?' Tara said. 'Are you insane?'

'I am a defender of humanity who takes her job very seriously—'

'You have no boundaries, do you?' Tara said. 'Did you forget that we already have blood on our hands?'

'We've been through this—' Irhes began. But Tara would have none of it.

'That agent is surrounded by Federation troops,' she argued. 'If she's captured or killed—'

'There is nothing identifying her or her equipment as originating from CONCORD,' Tashin interjected.

'Mordu knows who she is!' Tara roared. 'She sat in his bloody office! Or have you forgotten that as well!'

'But he's not on Pike's Landing now, is he?' Irhes said. 'Your point is irrelevant. To be quite frank, Tara, I'm beginning to question whether or not you've got the spine for this responsibility.'

'And I'm beginning to question if you've got the ethics, Director.'

'My ethics are aligned with the mandate,' Irhes growled. 'Practicing them requires having the courage to make difficult choices, which, clearly, you do not.'

'Well, that makes this arrangement academic then, doesn't it?' Tara said.

Her mind link with the group abruptly terminated. The physical attachment to her neuro-interface socket detached and retracted.

'I hereby tender my resignation, effective immediately,' Tara said, using her voice for a change. 'My security clearance will be void the moment I walk through that door. I'll show myself out. Thank you so much, Irhes. You're an inspiration to us all.'

The echo of her angry words reverberated through the spherical chamber as a live feed from THANATOS appeared suddenly: The immortal soldier she was tracking stood just a few meters in front of her, holding a flare overhead that could be seen for kilometers, as a Federation gunship hovered in the background.

I have been compromised, the agent reported.

'Well . . .' Tara said. 'You're about to find out if your technology works as advertised.'

HEIMATAR REGION – HED CONSTELLATION
AMAMAKE SYSTEM – PLANET II: PIKE'S LANDING
TWENTY-FIVE KILOMETERS SOUTHEAST OF CORE FREEDOM COLONY – BADLANDS GRID
SOVEREIGNTY OF THE AMARR EMPIRE

Vince knew exactly what he wanted to do. He just wasn't sure how. But there were two independent instincts within him now, and both were aligned.

Survive. Find Gable Dietrich. The path to harmony.

Lowering the flare, he took inventory of his surroundings. He knew which direction the Paladins were approaching from, and he had successfully drawn the attention of Federation troops.

The assassin continued her steady advance, navigating up the ledge leading to his position with unnatural ease.

Everything about her physical appearance was designed to trick her prey into underestimating her. She was dangerously unassuming; *pure* might have been the word Vince would use to describe her features, in spite of witnessing what she was capable of. Given her abilities, it was probable she had known he was following her for some time; if this was true, it was also likely he was being led into an ambush – though not necessarily to kill him. There had been plenty of opportunities for that already.

Vince reasoned that she had plans for him. That was fine. He intended to draw a big audience for whatever she had in store, increasing the odds that an opportunity to escape would present itself.

He ejected the cartridge in his rifle, cleared the chamber, and tossed the components aside. Then he unholstered his sidearm and did the same. Both weapons went over the ledge.

The Federation gunship was circling overhead, training a spotlight on them.

His adversary didn't seem concerned or angry as she approached to within three meters. She seemed at peace – completely confident – and quietly determined.

Vince carefully set the flare on the ground and checked his TACNET again. Two Imperial Vex-class gunships were racing toward them.

'You're coming with me,' she said, still leveling the weapon – assuming that's what it was. Separating her from it was his first priority.

'No,' he said. 'So you're just going to have to end my life.'

'I don't want that,' she said, squinting as the spotlight passed over them. 'Besides . . . would you even die?'

'Yes, I would,' he said, pointing his chin in the direction of the Federation gunship. The mission cameras were rolling. 'Just like those Federation commandos you killed.'

'I'm here to protect you from them,' she said, 'for your own good.'

'I saw where you hid their bodies,' he said, trying to keep his face pointed toward the gunship. 'Using the riverbed was smart. Probably lots of caves nearby. Did you stow your ship in one?'

She smiled reassuringly.

'Just relax,' she said. 'This doesn't have to be unpleasant.'

Vince mentally switched the TACNET off; he willed himself to wait, wait, wait . . . .

The Blackjack's engine suddenly revved higher, as if the pilot was reacting to something.

That was the warning, and he began shifting his weight, dropping his hips to generate power.

Three pulse beams, all fired within the span of a second, slammed into the gunship's starboard aft section; the engine cowling vaporized in a torrent of white-hot molten fuselage. A long flame began jetting out of the hole where the engine once was; the rear of the craft caught fire as it dropped beneath the ledge, spinning out of control.

The dazzle of fragments were still flying through the air when Vince propelled himself at THANATOS with all his might: The distraction of the explosions overhead had granted just enough time for him to dive beneath the weapon and plow his shoulder into her midsection.

Vince heard it discharge. But whatever it fired had missed him, and they were both now tumbling down the face of the ledge.

HEIMATAR REGION – HED CONSTELLATION
AMAMAKE SYSTEM – PLANET II: PIKE'S LANDING
THE GFS *PASSAIC* CARRIER GROUP

'. . . *Mayday mayday mayday! We are going down in badlands sector nine-one-lima. Mayday . . .*'

'Fuck,' Admiral Freeman cursed. 'Mr President, we have to escalate; the Amarrians just shot down one of our birds.'

'Do it,' Roden said. 'Can you keep eyes on those persons of interest?'

'Negative. Eagle-Two had to break contact to evade those gunships.'

'Understood. Resume track as soon as you can.'

'Please inform the Minmatar government that we're moving in to defend our people.'

'Consider it done. Good luck, Admiral.'

Eagle One broke through on the channel again.

'Command, we're still alive,' he said, coughing. 'We're on the ground, with casualties, but some of us can still fight. . . . We're redirecting mobile fire teams to our position. . . . Your persons of interest are within sight of us.'

'Solid copy, Eagle One. Hang in there; the cavalry is inbound, ETA six minutes.'

The GFS *Passaic* Carrier Group was composed of forty ships: A third of those were battleships; the rest mostly support vessels and heavy assault cruisers. The *Passaic* was the flagship, a Nyx-class supercarrier whose squadrons of fighters, bombers, and dropships made her the primary force projector of the group. Four Moros-class dreadnoughts were also part of the fleet, each carrying regiment-strength troop components. Admiral Freeman checked his instruments; all told, his officers were directing a division-size force of mechanized infantry to Pike's Landing. To avoid getting blown out of the sky by Core Freedom's defenses, though, the MTACs, tanks, APCs, and even fighter aircraft were all taking the scenic route to reach the surface.

For all intents and purposes, this was a full-fledged surface invasion of a sovereign Minmatar Republic world. At least, that's how it would look to anyone from the outside. There was enough hardware going in to make a serious bid at seizing the colony and its precious space elevator.

President Roden is going to have a hell of a time explaining this, Admiral Freeman thought. *But I'll give him this: The guy probably needs a freighter to haul his own balls around.*

'Fleet, this is command,' he announced. 'The Amarrians just shot down one of our gunships, and we've taken casualties. Well, they just kicked a hornet's nest, because we're going to establish position overhead and get our soldiers out. We will blink-warp across this field and engage Imperial ships from close range. Stalker-One is your beacon. Watch your fire: Do *not* attack Republic Fleet ships, and make sure you avoid damaging that space elevator.'

He scanned the battlefield. From this range, the carnage looked almost serene: The savage twinkle of burning starships and explosions masked how much hatred there was between these two adversaries. But it appeared that the Minmatar surprise attack had faltered, and the fight was starting to shift in Amarr's favor.

In a sense, that was good. It was time to warn them.

'Republic Fleet Commander, this is Admiral Freeman, Federation Navy,' he said. 'Imperial forces have just attacked our marine assets on the surface. We are not sitting this one out. In thirty seconds, my task force is warping into your field of engagement to attack Amarrian targets. If you call primaries, we will comply. The ground action is well east of your colony, and that's where we're going.'

He couldn't believe his eyes, but about twelve Republic Fleet battleships broke off from the main group and started heading directly toward the *Passaic*.

That's just plain stupid or stubborn, Admiral Freeman thought.

A contact only identifying himself as 'Minmatar Nation Command' replied.

'Attention Federation forces,' he said. 'We cannot verify your intentions. Do not approach this position or we will fire on you. We will send help for your fallen comrades.'

That the Minmatar commander didn't even bother to state his name showed how far the two erstwhile allies had drifted apart. More tellingly, several Republic Fleet ships in the main group were clearly in trouble and starting to drift out of control; their flagship, a Hel-class carrier, was taking a horrible pounding.

Time was wasting.

'With all due respect, Commander, it doesn't look that way from here,' Admiral Freeman said, looking away from his screen momentarily. 'We're coming whether you like it or not.'

When he looked back, a second Imperial task force – about 120 warships in all – warped into view, directly between him and the Republic Fleet ships.

According to his HUD, Grand Admiral Kezti Sundara himself had just joined the field, at the helm of an Avatar-class titan. . . .

VINCE WASN'T KNOCKED OUT COMPLETELY, and he had enough wits about him to know that whoever got up first was probably going to win this fight. By the time he managed to push himself up onto his knees, he realized his chances didn't look good.

Grabbed by his own vest collar, Vince was hurled across several meters of open silt into the rock face of the ledge they had just tumbled down.

He was peripherally aware that the Blackjack had crashed just sixty meters from here, and that Federation soldiers were starting to crawl out from the wreckage.

His head whiplashed off the stone, and his stomach exploded with pain; the air was expelled from his lungs as she unleashed a flurry of incapacitating body blows. Her fists felt like they were made of cement, so fast that, even with his augmented reflexes, he couldn't react to them in time.

Unable to retaliate, she threw him facedown into the gravel. Vince glanced up for a moment and saw six Katmai speed bikes pull up to the wreckage; their drivers and passengers quickly disembarked and began assembling weapons.

Three of them were arming shoulder-mounted surface-to-air missile launchers, and all had their eyes on him.

Vince felt the assailant's knees drive into his side and neck. He winced as his wrist was twisted over and pushed high up his back.

'You are my prisoner,' she said, forcing him up to his feet. 'Do not resist again.'

The warm downwash of a gunship's ion turbines kicked up a plume of silt; an unrecognizable craft uncloaked right above them, gently landing a few meters away and blocking his line of sight to the Federation troops.

Then the pulse tracers rained down.

A dashed line of reddish white streaks fell across the idling gunship and presumably the Blackjack wreck behind it. He couldn't see if they found their mark, but there were strange glows where the rounds impacted the assassin's craft. Other than some thermal scarring, there was no apparent structural damage.

The assassin hurried Vince farther toward the ramp that had lowered as the craft idled. He tried falling to stall their progress, but he was yanked up by his immobilized arm so hard that both of his feet came off the ground.

Arching his back in anguish, he saw the bluish white plasma contrails from three antiaircraft missiles as they streaked upward and veered abruptly in the direction the pulse fire came from.

Vince and the assassin were flattened by a deafening explosion; he lost consciousness.

The wretched smell of burning flesh awakened him. His leg was covered in smoldering debris; in fact, he was surrounded by an inferno. The crackle of automatic-weapon fire raised his senses to full awareness; the nanites in his bloodstream were doing their part to keep him alive.

The assassin's limp body lay on top of him; it rolled off as Vince pulled himself upright. She had been shredded by fragments; ironically, her body had shielded him from the worst of it. There was no blood – instead, a whitish gray viscous substance was frothing at the edge of her wounds.

Her expression remained disturbingly pleasant. Whatever she was, Vince hoped he never ran into one like her again.

There were now three downed gunships within one hundred meters of each other. The Vex had clipped the assassin's gunship as it crashed; a secondary explosion after impact had blown both crafts apart. Several dead soldiers lay strewn about in the wreckage.

Peering around the corner of a twisted fuselage, Vince saw a vicious firefight under way. Paladins were advancing on the downed Blackjack. Survivors in the wreckage were returning fire – though not as many as before.

One of the Katmai bikes was lying on its side just twenty meters away but exposed to gunfire from both sides. The Federation soldier who had been riding it was badly wounded and was attempting to crawl back toward cover.

Vince ripped one of the nanite canisters from his vest and plunged it into his leg.

Hyper-rejuvenated, he sprinted toward the speed bike and slid for the last two meters. Every object in his vision turned white at the edges; he felt as though he were moving twice as fast as usual.

Vince hoisted the Federation soldier in a fireman's carry, then lifted the speed bike upright. Its ion turbofan roared to life and the vehicle rose several centimeters off the ground in a sustained hover.

Had he still believed in God, he would have thanked Him.

He launched himself and the bike forward in one frictionless heave, just as Paladin beam fire began tracking him. He circled behind the Federation wreck, leaving the wounded soldier close to his comrades.

Then he pushed the throttle as far as it would go, accelerating to two hundred kilometers per hour in less than a second, racing west toward Core Freedom.

33

THE BATTLE OF PIKE'S LANDING

Muryia Mordu was no stranger to killing.

During the span of his origins as a soldier to leading the most recognized mercenary corporation in New Eden, many souls had died at his hand. Strangling, stabbing, shooting, smothering, detonating – whatever the method, they all elicited the same primal rush. Nothing else came close to making him feel so alive as mortal combat. He was not proud of this fact, even if he could admit that such brutal enthusiasm earned him a successful career.

His thirst for combat continued when he became a capsuleer. Mordu, presently suspended in the viscous fluid of a starship pod, conceded that the immortality afforded by this arcane technology marginalized the 'thrill of the kill'; after all, nothing could ever replace watching the life leave someone's eyes. But the thrill of the *verge* of combat – when one knew it was coming, as it was right now, remained exhilarating. This was the moment that all fighters lived for, when everything hangs in the balance, and history is as yet unwritten.

In this fraction of a second, tunneling through the fabric of spacetime in the belly of a Wyvern-class supercarrier accompanied by an entire fleet of machines capable of untold destruction, Mordu was in his element. The significance of what they were doing was immaterial; there was only the joy of charging into battle, of jumping into the unknown with a band of warrior brothers and an invincible heart.

And as always, he was unafraid to let his peculiar brand of humor show during the most perilous of times.

Pardon the intrusion, you Amarrian cunts! he declared on the command broadcast. *This won't hurt a bit.*

Mordu's pulse accelerated as the warp cone began to disappear, and Pike's Landing grew until it occluded the Amamake sun completely – and then, instead of just the Core Freedom space elevator, as he had expected, something else sprung into view that shouldn't have been there at all: an Avatar-class titan perched over a sea of gold-hulled warships.

His excitement quickly transformed into dread.

In naval combat doctrines, the Avatar was grossly understated as a 'supercapital' vessel. At fourteen kilometers long from bow to stern, the Avatar was built for the express purpose of swiftly decapitating opposing fleets with its colossal beam weapon, aptly called 'Judgment.' The ship was literally engineered and built around this technology: It could destroy a capital ship with a single blast.

Mordu and his fleet were about to emerge from warp directly in front of one; and to make matters worse, the Imperial fleet at Pike's Landing was clearly much larger than their intelligence had shown. But this observation was a mere footnote to the more pressing concern of maneuvering his own ship out of harm's way. By the time the sublight engines of the Wyvern finally engaged, the Avatar's golden armor was less than a kilometer away. Collision alarms screamed over the comm channels, as the shields of the two capital ships began to interact in a brilliant, pulsing coruscation; epic bursts of electrostatic arcs leaping from both vessels as they soared past each other.

The Wyvern was strong enough to withstand it. He knew that a good portion of his fleet wouldn't be so lucky.

Six Legion heavy assault cruisers slammed into the Avatar's powerful shields, each vanishing in a fiery bubble of plasma. The white-hot fragments that made it through impacted the goliath vessel's armor and scattered away like so much junk.

This was not the first time he'd jumped into a tactically unfavorable situation.

But he never expected to see the warships of three different nations at once.

As beam fire erupted all around the Wyvern, Mordu took stock of Republic Fleet and Federation Navy ships all in the same battlefield – and as far as he could tell, all attacking the Imperial Navy. The Legion had just jumped into the middle of a huge naval engagement whose political calculus he just couldn't process.

Before he could determine if he was in any danger of being shot at, the Avatar's Judgment beam lashed out and incinerated a Republic Fleet carrier. The pack of Legion interceptors who happened to emerge from warp directly in front of the titan as it fired simply disappeared.

If not for the Federation Navy and Republic Fleet ships, he would have ordered a retreat immediately. But despite the slow start, he still liked his odds.

'Hawkeye, you're warping in hot,' he warned, as a pack of Amarrian fighters descended on the Wyvern. 'Korvin, I'm sorry, but there are Federation ships here. We're going ahead as planned.'

KORVIN LEARS WAS APPROACHING Pike's Landing from a different direction and briefly considered the possibility that the Federation was there for the same reason as Mordu's Legion. That was certainly easier to accept than the notion that they'd sent an entire task force just to collect the bounty on his head.

Either way, it didn't change anything.

'Copy that, Mordu. We're a go,' he said, as Pike's Landing rushed into view.

The Moros emerged from warp so low to the surface – just 145 kilometers up – that mountaintops and thick cloud formations would have dominated Korvin's perspective of the planet if it weren't night down below. The occasional flash of lightning broke what was otherwise a vast, black surface framed by a backdrop of stars. The *Morse*, five of the Longbow dropships, and its ring of destroyers emerged from warp behind him, perfectly arranged in formation.

The gigantic Avatar, portions of its length lit by intermittent flashes of space combat, was clearly visible a thousand kilometers overhead. The Federation task force, with its flagship Nyx-class supercarrier, was just two hundred kilometers to his right.

Surface-missile radar bands swept over the ship. It was time to focus.

'Radar track,' Miles warned. 'Stackfire launch! Three vampires; intercept course; ETA four minutes.'

'Roger,' Korvin said. For the time being, he was leaving his life in the hands of the *Morse* crew – which under different circumstances he might have considered insane. He turned his attention to the planet's surface, where the lights of Core Freedom were just breaking the horizon. As braking systems slowed the dreadnought's speed, high-resolution tracking cameras on board were already picking up surface targets in thermal imaging.

People – soldiers, Korvin assumed – could be seen clearly, even from this range. The demons that had haunted him for so long returned, because he was about to murder by numbers once again.

'Stand by for surface bombardment,' he announced. 'Fire mission target designation one through four, proximity-fuse plasma charges. Fire.'

The Moros shuddered as four magnetically accelerated slugs erupted from their siege cannons at nearly fifteen kilometers per second.

'Impact in ten seconds,' he said. 'Longbow, stand by.'

Korvin saw the dropship bay doors on the *Morse* slide open; then the battlecruiser rolled gently onto its side.

'Solid track on incoming vampires. Guns guns guns!' Miles shouted.

The Catalyst-class destroyers, with eight railgun turrets apiece, spat out a wall of lead charges.

Three silent bursts of light blossomed twenty kilometers in front of them.

'Targets neutralized,' Miles said.

Korvin smiled, tracking the progress of his own shells. The colony's Cloudburst antiair defenses couldn't catch the rounds in time; their velocity was just too fast.

'Surface impact in three, two, one . . . mark.'

Several milliseconds before impact, the shells began their catastrophic conversion from solid-state to plasma. The spherical antiair batteries surrounding Core Freedom – along with the soldiers seen patrolling outside of them – vanished in fireballs two hundred meters in diameter.

'I confirm four direct hits,' Korvin announced, scanning the damage wrought by the bombardment. The crater at each impact site was more than ten meters deep; the Cloudburst battery destroyed in the mountainside started a massive avalanche.

The Core Freedom elevator platform was visible now; the Avatar was just above it, still surrounded by intermittent pulses of light. A pack of Imperial fighters had broken away from the main fleet and was vectoring toward their position like a swarm of angry wasps.

'Longbow, you're clear to start your descent,' Korvin said. 'Try to keep those elevator cables between you and the colony for as long as you can. There are mobile AA sites tracking down there.'

The five gunships began pitching downward slightly as they aligned their approach.

'Roger that, Korvin. Nice shooting,' Jonas said. 'We're starting our run now.'

THE PANTHER-CLASS GUNSHIP aboard the *Morse* was painted in the same blackish red hues as the surface of Pike's Landing, with the seal of Mordu's Legion prominently displayed on each of its three tail fins, though with its adaptive camouflage fuselage, it was doubtful that anyone on the ground would notice. The craft was carrying enough solid-state fuel to power her twin Roden Shipyards 'Vectorex' plasma engines for the trip to the surface, a trip back into orbit, and about twenty minutes of hard atmospheric maneuvering in between.

For an orbital gunship, the Panther was small – much more so than the other gunships of Longbow squadron, with a span of twenty meters. A 30mm cannon mounted beneath the nose was the craft's main armament; two 20mm turret cannons were mounted beneath each wing. The current cargo configuration was for three passengers; the rest of the hold was occupied by a CRU and just about every conceivable piece of medical equipment Gable would need to keep Vince alive.

The overhead section of the cockpit canopy was a transparent polymer alloy so pilots could see what was above them when docking in hangar bays or maneuvering during combat.

Unfortunately, this feature had Gable on the brink of chunk-spewing nausea, since directly above her head were the dark cloud peaks of Pike's Landing. The *Morse* had flipped completely over to position the Panther for atmospheric entry, and Gable's entire perception of up versus down was completely askew.

Gable's first serious problem of the evening began as she felt herself 'falling' upward.

'Blake, we're clear,' Jonas radioed, as the Panther slipped out of the *Morse*'s hangar bay. 'Take care of her for me.'

'I'll be fine, thanks for asking,' Miles interrupted. 'You guys just hurry up down there.'

'The *Morse* is in good hands,' Blake reaffirmed. 'Good luck, Captain.'

Gable shut her eyes, struggling to control the sensation of her stomach rising up to her throat.

'Rotating alignment for entry,' Jonas said, flipping the Panther over and orienting its belly with the wide horizon below. The blackness of space was already turning deep blue; for all intents and purposes, they were now free-falling, and everything that wasn't secured was starting to float.

When she reopened her eyes, Mack was staring at her with a childlike grin; two of his toy soldiers were drifting in front of him. He gave one a gentle flick, sending it tumbling end over end through the cabin.

Gable's hands barely covered her mouth in time, and the imperfect seal allowed streams of vomit to spew out from between her fingers.

Some of the projectiles collided with the somersaulting toy, making Mack break into a wheezing guffaw that, if one didn't know about his disfigurement, could only seem a medical emergency.

'Oh, man, you didn't take the pills I asked you to?' Jonas grimaced, glancing over his shoulder to see if any of the gunk was on him. 'Where'd all that land, anyway?'

Gable was too miserable to answer. The cockpit was bathed in a reddish white glow; they were now burning through the upper reaches of the atmosphere.

'You okay?' Mack asked.

'I'm fine,' she muttered, fidgeting with her tactical vest. The body armor didn't fit properly and was extremely uncomfortable. Pockets filled with equipment lined her belt, chest, and shoulders, and she had no idea what any of it was.

'Water,' Mack said, offering a container. 'Drink.'

As the plasma arc in front of the Panther's shields dissipated, scratchy radio transmissions began coming in.

'*— day, this is Longbow Five,*' the radio screamed. '*We're not going to make it to the surface. The intel was fucked; there's too much AA—*'

Warnings sounded off in the cockpit; they were being tracked by powerful radars on the surface.

'Korvin!' Jonas shouted. 'Can you do something about these radar sites?'

From hundreds of kilometers away, Core Freedom was taking shape ahead; blocks of light were forming crisp boundaries against the black terrain. Rising toward the sky like a massive altar, the backlit ground terminus of the space elevator dominated the view. The sky was filled with the streaks of missile exhausts; fiery spots on the ground far below marked where Longbows Four and Five had been shot out of the sky.

'Working on it,' Korvin said. 'Mobile SAMs are taking them down. Get low, Jonas; use the terminus as cover! They won't risk hitting it!'

'Mack, Gable, hold on!' Jonas shouted.

Braking the craft's descent just enough for the fluidic surface control systems to catch air, Jonas engaged the Vectorex engines and put the craft in a steep dive, angling directly for the elevator base.

Gable felt herself lift up against the harness again as Mack howled in delight; her vision was turning red, as negative G's forced blood from her lower extremities to her head.

'— strike in five seconds,' she heard Korvin say. They were much closer to the ground now, and the terminus towered ahead like a mountain.

'Pull your visors down,' Jonas warned.

Mack leaned back and slapped gently at her helmet; the tinted shield folded down over her eyes just in time, as four brilliant streaks illuminated the landscape ahead.

'IMPACTS,' MILES DECLARED, monitoring the flight path of Longbow One as it streaked past the elevator terminus and veered to northwest. 'Direct hits, no more fixed radars, but lots of mobile frequencies.'

'Way more than we thought there'd be,' Blake grumbled.

'Copy, Miles; we're following the flight plan,' Jonas said. 'Who's with us down here?'

'No one,' Miles said, sneaking a glance at Blake. 'Longbows Three through Five are gone; Two crash-landed, but no one's answering. We have eyes on the wreck; if we see movement, we'll inform.'

'Damn,' Jonas muttered. 'Guess we're doing this on our own then.'

'Three minutes until those fighters are in range,' Blake warned, tracking the angry red blob diving at them from the direction of the battle above them. 'Odd, they're not blink-warping to us—'

'Ah, wait a minute,' Miles interrupted. 'Korvin, can you verify all Stackfire batteries were destroyed?'

'Confirmed,' Korvin said. 'Core Freedom has no antiship capabilities remaining.'

Miles was no longer brimming with confidence.

'What's wrong?' Blake asked.

'Umm, can you get eyes on that southwestern grid,' he said, leaning back and resting his hands on his head. 'Two-two-five, primary mission objective.'

It took a second longer for him to answer than usual.

'Oh, man,' Korvin said.

Checking his displays for the fifth time, Miles was staring at the location where the CRU farm was supposed to be.

'Blake?' he asked. 'Do you see this?'

Her face turned pale.

'I don't believe it,' she said. 'Let Mordu know.'

'Command, this is the *Morse*,' Miles said. 'The CRU farm is gone; repeat, the primary objective is vaporized; over.'

'Wha – Say again, Miles?' Jonas said. 'What do you mean, "*gone*"? Did we hit it?'

'Negative,' Korvin said. 'None of my rounds landed anywhere near there.'

Mordu's voice came through on the radio, and he sounded anything but his usual flippant self.

'Are you absolutely certain?' he asked.

'Yes, sir,' Korvin answered. 'The objective is a glass crater. Damage is consistent with a large beam weapon strike. The Amarrians must have hit it themselves. Couldn't even begin to explain why.'

'Then the mission is over,' Mordu said. 'Return to HQ immediately.'

'No!' Jonas protested. 'We've come all this way. We have to try!'

'Try *what*, Jonas?' Mordu growled. 'We're losing this fight, and there's nothing to gain by staying in it!'

'Vince could be alive!' Jonas shouted. 'We don't know where he was when the beam hit!'

'You don't know where he is right *now*, which is all that matters,' Mordu said, and then paused briefly. 'You know what? Go ahead and look for him, because our fleet can't withdraw without getting killed anyway. You may as well join in.'

CROUCHING LOW AGAINST THE Katmai as it raced across the steppes, Vince blinked ghost images away as his eyes readjusted to darkness following the latest orbital strikes. Two had set off massive fireballs and secondary explosions; he guessed that these were the remaining Stackfire batteries.

Even while speeding at two hundred kilometers per hour, his hyper-enhanced awareness remained fixated on the details of the land: Wild grasses and silt parted behind the bike as it raced, and swarms of bioluminescent insects streaked by like a meteor shower. His fascination was shattered as a fighter scorched overhead, so impossibly low that there was no question it was following him. The swept-wing craft veered upward far in front of him, then turned abruptly, as a stream of flares and reflective foil canisters erupted behind it; a missile contrail appeared soon after from the direction of the colony.

The ship turned gracefully back toward him and blasted by again, now followed by the missile.

Whatever it was that had drawn the Federation to Pike's Landing had also given them reason to bombard it. It occurred to him they were here for him – for the Templars. Like the assassin, they had had numerous opportunities to kill him. But they hadn't – which in turn gave him hope that there was a way off this world.

Then he could find Gable Dietrich.

Core Freedom had four spaceports: three for commercial transports, and a large industrial port where the Paladins serviced their own fleet of Vex gunships and its larger 'Starlifter' cousin. The latter was his only option if he wanted to get off the planet and actually warp ... somewhere. A station, perhaps another planet. He didn't know.

But anywhere was better than here.

As the colony perimeter appeared on the horizon, his body alerted him to danger:

>BIOSYS ALERT<

>BODY TEMP 41 C, BP 95/65<

>ELEVATED RECOVERY MODE<

>SYSDIAG: VASCULAR NANITE SUPPLY DEPLETED TO CRITICAL LEVELS.<

>RECOMMENDED ACTION: MANUALLY CLOSE OPEN DEFECTS. REPLENISH NANITE SUPPLY ASAP.<

There were holes in him – injuries he didn't even know he had. Nanotechnology was keeping him alive. Replenishing the microscopic machines clotting his wounds was paramount: He wouldn't make it much farther without them. The supply he needed was on the colony, assuming it wasn't destroyed. Getting to it would be difficult, perhaps even impossible. But there was no other way.

A searing hot *vssssh* sound snapped over his head, followed by another shot way off the mark. Several Paladins were guarding a breach in the damaged fortifications ahead; they were firing at him from an elevated position.

The Katmai was already pushing its top speed, and the fastest way into the colony was directly through them.

Vince kicked the compression jets to maximum output, and the bike rose more than a meter off the ground. At this speed, its battery would be depleted shortly, so there was only one chance to get through – and hopefully, there wouldn't be more troops immediately behind them.

The Katmai was armed with a 12mm antipersonnel phase cannon; with a flip of a switch, the bike's targeting system started picking up Vince's eye movements. The turret began to swivel as he moved his eyes around; the weapon system lit up after a moment, indicating it was ready to fire, just as three more beams reached out ahead of him.

Holding his gaze on his targets, he slowed the bike abruptly and squeezed the trigger; the bike jolted as the turret spit chunks of plasma at the Paladins from a range of one hundred meters. As the rounds impacted the concrete barriers and exploded, he turned the bike and accelerated, following his own shots directly toward them.

From twenty-five meters away, Vince pulled the trigger again, but the weapon jammed. Begging the Katmai for one last burst of acceleration, he pointed the nose at his targets and gunned the throttle just as both Paladins began recovering their aim.

The Katmai bolted forward; he power-slid the bike horizontally into both soldiers. Letting go of the handles an instant before the point of impact, he slid a short distance on his hip and tumbled once before coming to rest.

There was no time to check himself for more damage, let alone to see whether the Paladins were dead or not.

As the engine fluttered to a halt, he sprinted toward a building, checking just once to see if he was being followed. For now, there was no one else around. But they would come looking for him soon enough.

He knew he would never reach the spaceport without some serious firepower. Fortunately, he knew exactly where to find it.

MORDU COULD ONLY DO SO MUCH to thwart the merciless Imperial counterattack.

The battlefield was a massive cube in space that began 145 kilometers over the surface of Pike's Landing and went all the way up to the space elevator platform nineteen hundred kilometers above. On the bottom side of the cube were the *Morse* and the Federation Navy elements shadowing it; a thousand kilometers across from them, Imperial warships were pounding the remnants of a Republic fleet that the Federation task force was attempting to protect.

The entire upper portion of the cube was where the main Imperial and Republic fleets were slugging it out. Mordu's fleet was stuck squarely in between them, trapped in a powerful warp-drive-inhibitor field.

Beam after beam struck the Wyvern, reaching deeper into the shields protecting Mordu and his crew of thousands. He considered the possibility that his hatred of the Amarr Empire was actually envy. Their faith afforded them an aura of invincibility. If not for the Joves, they might have become the most powerful empire in the history of civilization.

As it was, the Amarr were not only fending off three navies right now, but winning.

Mordu had done his fair share of mercenary work both for and against the Gallente Federation. This was an opportunity to make amends.

'Attention Federation Navy Nyx commander,' Mordu said. 'This is Muryia Mordu of the Legion. This is quite a predicament, yes?'

The Nyx supercarrier was under fire from several Apocalypse-class battleships. Its fighters were chewing through them one by one; for now it was holding its own. But if the main fleet that Mordu was currently tied up with broke off to assist, that Nyx would have much bigger problems to contend with.

'Commander Mordu, this is Admiral Elijah Freeman,' the reply came. 'State your intentions or stay off this channel.'

'My intent is to form an alliance,' Mordu said. 'Coordinating our efforts would be advantageous.'

'Commander, your fleet is harboring a Federation traitor,' the voice said. 'I'm not inclined to cooperate.'

'You must be referring to Korvin Lears,' Mordu said. 'He's one of the finest officers I've ever met. Sounds to me like he had good reason to disobey orders.'

'You're entitled to your opinion,' Admiral Freeman said.

'Aren't we all,' Mordu said. 'You know what a Moros dreadnought can do, and he's within firing range of your surface troops. If he had any hard feelings, you'd have known about it—'

Before he could finish his sentence, the Avatar's Judgment beam lashed out, obliterating one of his dreadnoughts in a terrifying flash, and with it some four thousand souls.

The beast then began aligning itself with the planet's surface, pointing its mammoth bow toward the Admiral's fleet.

'That'll be one of yours next,' Mordu warned. 'Whatever it is you came here for, you're not going to get it unless we cooperate.'

'Sincerest condolences on your loss, Commander,' Admiral Freeman said. 'We don't have enough firepower to take that titan down, but we can hit her supporting ships.'

'Now you're being sensible,' Mordu said. 'Can you spare a fighter wing? If our bombers focus on their logistical fleet, our capital weapons will be much more effective.'

'I'll give you two fighter wings, plus a few drone carriers if I can get them in range,' Admiral Freeman said. 'You can call primaries and assign wings to escorts, but they'll confirm the order with me.'

Mordu's tactical display erupted with more chatter – above and beyond the cries for help in his own fleet – as nearly three hundred new contacts warped into the field, almost directly on top of Admiral Freeman's fleet.

Every single one had a Caldari State IDENT signature.

*

'*WHAT THE FUCK!?*' Admiral Freeman shouted, as collision alarms sounded throughout the bridge.

His immediate thought was that Mordu had somehow betrayed him; this was quickly discounted when he realized these were all Caldari ships.

He next believed this new fleet was the Caldari Navy coming to the assistance of the Amarr. But instead of targeting him, the armada charged directly past, blasting through the Imperial ships in the way and rushing forward to establish position over the colony.

The fleet, he finally realized, was comprised entirely of Ishukone Watch ships. Sixteen Wyvern-class supercarriers were now in the battle.

One of them began hailing him, as the glow of its six engines passed over the Nyx's forward runways.

'GFS *Passaic*, this is Chief Executive Officer Mens Reppola of Ishukone,' the voice said. 'We have no quarrel with the Federation Navy or the Gallente Federation; we are acting independently of the Caldari State, Tibus Heth, and the Caldari Navy. You are in no danger from us. I repeat: You are blue to our fleet. To demonstrate our goodwill, we're going to assist your operations against the Imperial Navy.'

A barrage of directed railgun fire obliterated an Imperial Abaddon-class battleship trading long-range fire with the *Passaic;* a second volley annihilated its cruiser escorts.

'I do have one request, though,' Mens said.

Admiral Freeman saw a pair of Phoenix-class dreadnoughts warp into the gauntlet, not one hundred kilometers from where the Mordu's Legion battlecruiser *Morse* was positioned.

'Please do not interfere with our surface operations,' Mens continued. 'We're aware that Federation troops are on the ground. They must not enter the Core Freedom perimeter: Doing so could cause confusion that leads to unnecessary casualties.'

The Phoenixes began deploying fleets of dropships.

Ishukone Watch was invading Pike's Landing.

'Mens, thank you for the assist,' Admiral Freeman said. He had to buy time somehow. 'You've certainly given us a lot to think about. Stand by.'

He noticed that Eagle One was frantically trying to reach him, and switched channels.

'Go ahead, Eagle One; make it fast,' he said.

'Commander, we're with the Three-eighty-eighth division moving west toward Core Freedom. We have high assurance that the HVI we spotted earlier is your target.'

'How do you know?'

'Because there's no way a man walks away from the carnage we saw,' he said. 'The whole thing was caught on gun camera; you have the footage on WARCOM to see for yourself. Immortal or not, those HVIs were using the toughest biotech I've ever seen.'

'Do you know where he is?'

'He just breached the colony perimeter,' he said. 'We've got fast movers tracking him, but they're busy dodging SAMs.'

'Keep your eyes on him but slow your advance west,' he said. 'Ishukone Watch is dropping two divisions onto the elevator terminus.'

'*Who?*'

MACK LAUGHED AS THE WHITE-HOT ROUNDS of the Panther's cannon intersected with the gold-plated armor of a Paladin, sending chunks of the man hurtling in several directions at once.

Then the sound of small-arms fire peppering the fuselage sobered the mood.

'Shit,' Jonas muttered, wrenching the craft over and pushing it past the cover of several buildings. At times they were flying as low as a few meters over the ground, weaving in and out of the colony's outpost structures while taking shots at ground forces and the occasional mobile SAM site.

But they were starting to get desperate.

'What the hell are we doing here?' Jonas cursed, as the nose gun spat out some more rounds into a building. 'For all we know, the last guy you gibbed might have been him!'

'We're hoping for a miracle,' Gable said.

'Well, you better hope a little harder, because things are looking pretty fucking bleak,' Jonas said.

'Bad feeling,' Mack admitted. 'Gut says we should go.'

'How much fuel is left?' Gable asked.

'At this rate, less than ten minutes' worth,' Jonas answered.

'You said it yourself,' she said. 'We've sacrificed so much. I say we keep looking for another ten minutes, and then we can leave with a clear conscience.'

'And drag everyone else through mud?' Jonas said. 'The fleet is getting hammered!'

'That didn't matter to you before we got into this,' Gable said.

ESSENCE REGION – VIERES CONSTELLATION
THE LADISTIER SYSTEM – PLANET IV, MOON 4: RÉNEALT
PRESIDENTIAL BUREAU STATION
SOVEREIGNTY OF THE GALLENTE FEDERATION

Jacus concluded his press briefing and left the podium, exiting through a hallway leading from Federation Hall to the Ready Room. Grand Admiral Ranchel was waiting for him inside, along with Directors Orviegnoure and Blaque, all of them having followed his communications with Admiral Freeman.

They all erupted at once.

'Why the hell did you send down the entire division?' Admiral Ranchel roared. 'Could you be any less discreet about this?'

'You let both suspects in the disappearance of my men go free!' Director Blaque said.

'And you're assuming too much from entirely circumstantial evidence,' Director Orviegnoure moaned. 'You've committed us to war on a personal whim and broken the most delicate foreign policy we have!'

Jacus glared at each of them for a moment and then cleared his throat.

'All of you, leave the room,' he said. *'Now.'*

'What is this?' Admiral Ranchel blustered. 'Some kind of joke?'

'Admiral, either get into a ship and protect this nation's borders or send me your resignation,' Roden snapped. 'While you're deciding, get out of my Ready Room. Same for all of you. *Out.*'

Roden's eyes glowed green, staring each of them down.

Ariel was the last to leave, shaking her head as she did. When the door shut behind her, he keyed the fleetcomm TACNET.

'Admiral Freeman,' he said, pacing back and forth. 'Please ask Mordu and Mens Reppola if they'll join me for a conference. Tell them it's personal.'

'Stand by.'

Jacus waited, mindful of the fact that everyone in the office was staring at his cabinet members arguing outside the Ready Room.

'Alright, Mr President, we have Commanders Reppola and Mordu listening,' the Admiral said.

'Thank you,' Jacus started. 'Gentlemen, we have a history of shared interests. The Federation is here because we recognized a threat to our national security. So it's time to come clean about our reasons for coming to Pike's Landing – just among us, no one else.'

There was silence at first, which Jacus saw as dangerous given they were all in a firefight.

'We can contribute to each other's goals,' he continued. 'So I'll speak first: We have reason to believe the Amarr have deployed immortal soldier technology on Pike's Landing. We lost contact with a team sent in to investigate, then sent more troops to recover them. During this operation we made contact with a prototype and are actively tracking its movements as we speak.'

'Mr President,' Mens Reppola said. 'You are aware that I'm acting independently. Tibus Heth has nothing to do with this.'

'Yes, I understand,' Jacus said.

'I have detailed schematics of the tech,' Mens said. 'We haven't had time to analyze it yet, but the source is reliable. We're here because we need a prototype to help reverse-engineer it. Doing so in the shortest timeframe possible is of utmost urgency to Ishukone. We have no intention of profiting from it.'

'Understood,' Jacus said. 'Now, why is the Legion here?'

'We made contact with a prototype,' Mordu said. 'One of our

mercs knows the man personally. We're attempting to recover him right now, with the intent of developing the technology ourselves.'

'So we're all here for the same thing,' Jacus said. 'But to what end? Deterrence or aggression?'

'Amarr has done enough to leave its mark on history,' Mordu said. 'I won't let them paint our future in gold.'

'Heth will destroy Ishukone,' Mens said. 'I need this technology to defend it from him.'

'And I can help both of you,' Jacus said. 'If my government objects ... then I'll bring the assets of Roden Shipyards to bear on this matter.'

'So then how do we help each other right now?' Mens asked.

'Simple,' Roden said. 'You have the blueprints. I know where the prototype is, and Mordu has the best chance of capturing him alive.'

'If we get him,' Mordu asked, 'what happens then?'

'We start the research,' Mens said. 'I own a facility in nullsec. It's secure. Including me there are three people alive who know where it is. I can make arrangements to have your personnel brought there to participate in research, on the condition its location remains a secret.'

'I agree to those terms,' Roden said. 'So we have a joint venture now?'

'How do we know that everyone will honor their word?' Mordu asked.

'We don't,' Roden said. 'But we have no reason to distrust each other now.'

'Fair point,' Mordu said. 'I'm in.'

'Done,' Mens said. 'Where's the prototype?'

'Admiral Freeman is now authorized to disseminate that information,' Roden said, glaring at his incompetent cabinet through the glass. 'I'll leave the tactical collaboration to you. Work together, gentlemen. You need to be your best right now. Good luck.'

34

MORE SMALL-ARMS FIRE PEPPERED the underside of the Panther as it raced through the colony, hugging the terrain to avoid the deadly SAM sites located throughout.

In the back of his mind, Jonas had known all along that he was in over his head.

With no formal military training as a dropship pilot, Jonas had picked up his skills mostly on his own money from commercial flight schools in the Caldari State. Flying and ship captaining were hobbies long before they became the enduring profession of his life.

As it was, commercial schools did little to teach pilots some of the more crucial aspects of military flight, like learning how to avoid surface-to-air-missile fire. Granted, automated electronic countermeasures and stealth systems – the Panther was well equipped with both – did more to neutralize attacks than human reflex did, especially at high velocities.

Military academies taught students that flying low and fast were advantageous if the objective was to hide from opposing gunships and radar installations. However, this tactic was not advisable when the antiaircraft system was designed to strike targets from above.

The Viziam AV-11 'Block' antivehicle missile had two acquisition modes: 'direct optical,' in which the operator pointed the weapon at a target manually and waited for the guidance system to lock its image into memory; and 'seeker' mode, in which the user selected from a list of known vehicle types and fired blindly. Not only was the Block's targeting software smart enough to recognize the shapes of different aircraft, but it could also recognize their heat signatures, meaning it could defeat adaptive camouflage systems. If the guidance system spotted the designated target within its sensor cone, its 4.5 kilogram shaped-charge warhead was hurled toward the target at speeds that made it all but impossible to evade.

Once the warhead cleared the launcher, it traveled straight upward, tipped over, and sought its prey from above. There were no active targeting systems, and thus little to warn recipients that trouble was imminent.

An inexperienced pilot could easily mistake its signature vertical contrail as an errantly fired missile. And by now, enough Paladins had seen the Panther skirting in and out of cover around the colony to tell the weapon exactly what to look for.

As such, a Block missile rocketed off a rooftop that Jonas saw clearly but ignored, and slammed into one of the Panther's Vectorex engines from above.

The craft pitched and spun wildly, sideswiping buildings twice as it lost power. To his credit, Jonas held on to the stick and made a commendable effort to control the craft's final descent.

But the landing was going to be violent no matter who was flying it.

'JONAS IS DOWN!' Miles yelled. 'Korvin, can you see him?'

'Affirmative. I see them,' he responded. 'There's movement; stand by. . . .'

The Panther crashed into the rubble mound of a partially collapsed building; the entire wing with the destroyed engine had broken off on impact and tumbled a short distance to the bottom, where it continued to smolder. Though listing to one side, the craft was resting on its stomach and, other than the gaping hole in the fuselage where the wing once hung, was surprisingly intact.

Korvin saw the rear ramp open partially and jam; then he saw the sparks of plasma torches erupt from the seams. When the door fell away a few seconds later, the craft's six-legged Rantula sentry drone emerged. Standing at nearly two meters tall, the machine began circling the wreck, gracefully navigating over rubble and debris, searching out its surroundings for hostile targets.

Mack hurried out next, clawing his way to the top of the Panther's intact wing, where he tore open a service hatch and plunged his hands into the cowling.

'*Morse*, we're alive,' Jonas said. 'Ah ... is there a way out of this mess?'

'Jonas, stand by, we're working on getting you air support,' Blake said.

'Right,' he said. 'Korvin, what's your recommendation?'

'Dig in and get ready for a fight,' he answered. 'About two dozen foot mobiles are approaching your position, and a pair of tanks is within three klicks.'

'Tanks?' Jonas asked.

Mack had pulled the gun turret out of its housing and set it down; he was now frantically pulling out belts of 20mm-charge ammunition.

'How bad is Gable hurt?' Miles asked.

'I'll live,' she said, obviously in pain. 'Jonas can't fly worth shit.'

Blake saw something terrible unfold on her display and froze. The Avatar had just blink-warped across seven hundred kilometers of space, positioning itself within firing range of their group. The fighters were now escorting the titan as it prepared to fire its Judgment weapon.

The shrill alarms sounding off on the bridge alerted everyone to the danger.

'Korvin!' Blake exclaimed.

'I know,' he said. 'There's nothing we can do about it. Blake, get the *Morse* at least thirty klicks away from me and take that destroyer ring with you.'

Korvin activated an automated warning for his crew to abandon ship.

'What's going on up there?' Jonas asked.

'Tell Mack to set that cannon up facing the northwest; that's the direction six of the bad guys are coming in from,' Korvin said. 'I'm going to bombard those tanks. Pay attention to my countdown; you're outside the blast radius, but you better be behind cover when the hate comes down.'

'Korvin, it's targeting you,' Miles warned. 'Wait a second – what are you doing?'

Life pods began ejecting from the Moros; the siege-door bays had retracted, and dozens of shuttles and dropships were pouring out. Korvin began losing control of the ship: It was now stuck in its present orbit with its propulsion systems disabled.

The only equipment that worked were his camera drones, surface optics, and siege cannons.

'You guys are in charge of picking up my crew,' Korvin said. 'Now get out of here!'

GABLE WAS WONDERING if her back was broken.

'Are you hurt?' Jonas asked, looking her up and down. 'I don't see any injuries . . .'

She reached inside her vest and pulled out the pendant.

'Mack, overwatch,' Korvin said. 'Six tangos approaching from the northwest, sixty meters out. Two from the east at forty meters.'

'Gable, we're in deep shit,' Jonas said. 'Can you walk?'

She took Jonas's outstretched arms and attempted to get out of the seat, but she felt incredible pain radiate from her lower spine through her hips and legs.

That was actually a good sign, she knew, even though she screamed.

'Alright, well . . . this is going to sting a little,' he said, as she felt a needle plunge into her neck. A furious adrenaline rush made the pain fade – somewhat.

As she gasped for air, he pressed a rifle into her hands; she tried to refuse it.

'You have to fight!' Jonas said, pointing her toward the open hatch in the rear of the craft. He pulled up a collapsible blast shield in the deck and let it fold over onto its back. 'Stay behind this, rest the barrel on top, and shoot anything that moves.'

Mack lumbered past the open hatch, dragging several coils of

20mm ammunition with him; his enlarged cybernetic arm was hoisting the enormous cannon like a bag of luggage.

'Get ready,' he said.

'I'll be right up front,' Jonas said, now looking scared. He was out of his element; this was not his game. 'Yell if you need me.'

Hurrying through the twisted cabin, he made his way toward the gaping hole where the wing used to be. He braced himself against the fuselage and pointed a rifle through.

The Rantula suddenly took off, bounding down the rubble hill and stopping midway; a 40mm shell was fired with a *thoomp* from its weapon mount into the third-story window of the building across the street.

Jonas saw two men blown out of the wall in the resulting explosion as the drone scurried back toward the rear of the craft where Gable was and stopped, its multifaceted head swiveling about, scanning for more danger.

Beam fire lanced out at it from the northwest; one struck the drone in a flash of sparks. Damaged but not incapacitated, the Rantula began moving away from Gable's position, drawing more beam fire.

Then Mack unleashed the 20mm cannon.

Gable was deafened by the sound as it thundered in the same direction that the drone was now firing. Its rounds cast an eerie strobe in the night as they passed over the rubble and silt.

'Good hits, good hits,' she heard Korvin say. 'Mack, the roof of the building at your twelve o'clock . . . Wait until he gets to the edge. . . . Now!'

She saw the rounds streak up until they hit the top of the structure; Mack howled in triumph as the material exploded and a sniper fell four stories in a hail of debris.

'Strike coming down in ten seconds!' Korvin yelled. 'Three targets approaching from the south! Gable, that's your line of fire!'

The Rantula darted back toward the front of the craft to help Jonas, who was now shooting into the darkness. She looked through the thermal optic scope of her weapon and saw the bright white heat signatures of several Paladins sprinting toward her from more than a hundred meters away.

'Five seconds,' Korvin warned. 'Gable, you have to shoot.'

One of the figures fired; the pulse beams were off target but hit the fuselage nearby.

'No,' she said, caressing the Amarr symbol around her neck. 'I won't do it.'

'Lifegiver, please!' Mack shouted. 'Shoot!'

The sky brightened; streaks of lightning lashed out of the clouds as a bluish white beam erupted from a vortex in the sky. A clap of thunder slapped at them nearly the same time as the sound of the explosion itself.

'Heads down!' Mack warned, too late.

A bubbling wall of dust nearly as tall as the buildings rushed over their position; all three of them started coughing.

'Gable, listen to me,' Korvin said gently. 'No matter what you believe in, if you don't defend yourself, they'll kill you.'

She looked through the viewfinder; two of the Paladins were getting back up to their feet. Jonas began firing again; the Rantula was wreaking havoc farther down the street.

'I don't kill,' she said. 'I'm sorry.'

'That's admirable,' Korvin said. 'I wish more people had your strength.'

Mack was the only one who could see it: A bright star in the sky, so bright it could be seen through the dust cloud swirling around them, suddenly went nova as a beam of light impaled it.

Grabbing the remaining 20mm rounds, he leapt down to where Gable was.

'Jonas!' he shouted. 'Time to move!'

KORVIN SAW THE BEAM hit his ship from the outside perspective of his camera drones; then the imagery shook and went black as his pod mechanism attempted to activate.

He was dead by the time he realized it wouldn't have made a difference anyway. The Judgment beam was too powerful, melting through the dreadnought's shields, armor, and hull in an instant.

But that realization happened inside the mind of a clone – not inside the mind that had just been vaporized over Pike's Landing.

There was an incoherent darkness that lasted for a few moments.

'Good morning pilot,' a woman's voice said. 'Try to relax. Your vital signs are excellent. Do you know what your name is?'

Having been through this a few times already, Korvin knew he was inside a CRU.

'Korvin Alexander Lears,' he answered.

The screen in front of him retracted. Two Federation MPs and a spindly looking officer in a Navy uniform were standing over him.

'Captain Lears,' the officer said. 'You're under arrest for the charge of treason against the Gallente Federation. Do you understand this charge?'

Korvin remembered everything that had happened to him since the last time he died.

'Yes,' he said, thinking of Mordu. 'Yes I do.'

VINCE COULDN'T BREATHE, see, or hear anything.

A few moments ago there had been a bright flash immediately followed by the sensation of air being forced out of his lungs, his eardrums collapsing, and his being thrown a considerable distance into a wall.

>BIOSYS WARNING<

>BODY TEMP 42 C, BP 82/50<

>CRITICAL RECOVERY MODE<

>SYSDIAG: VASCULAR NANITE SUPPLY DEPLETED.<

>BIORHYTHM UNSUSTAINABLE.<

He crawled, somehow, for several minutes, looking for a weapon.

A dead Paladin emerged in the fog ahead, a pulse rifle still strapped across his chest. Vince went through the dead man's belongings, retrieving a TACNET interface from the helmet and additional charge packs for the weapon.

Vince was just 800 meters from the armor hangar when the explosion struck. Winding his way through the civilian complex, he had been eyeing a pair of tanks guarding the entrance when they left suddenly, rolling down the street. The last thing he remembered was seizing the opportunity to move toward the hangar entrance.

Before the blast, cries for help were coming in from positions near the western gates; apparently more invaders were dropping in, probably to seize control of the elevator's ground terminus. Several squads had mentioned making contact with Ishukone Watch forces, which was sowing more confusion because it was believed Mordu's Legion had started the attack and that Federation troops were somewhere in the vicinity as well.

It was as if all of New Eden had declared war on the Amarr Empire at once.

Both of his ears started ringing; miraculously, they were beginning to recover.

It was then he noticed that none of the electronic equipment was functioning. The rifle was useless; he tossed it onto the ground. That made him think the blast had been another orbital strike, but with a plasma charge, not a beam. The magnetic field that a charge generated before detonating would incinerate the electronics near the blast area.

There was so much dust in the air from repeated bombardments that it was becoming almost impossible to breathe. Staggering forward, Vince realized that his eyes weren't damaged and that actual visibility was limited to less than three meters.

He was in crippling pain but driven by the will to live.

Regaining his sense of direction, Vince pressed on toward the armor hangar. The wind was beginning to pick up, increasing visibility enough so that he was able to see the lights at the hangar entrance. Scanning the area, he decided there was no one around.

He staggered forward, unsure of what he would find inside that could help him.

Vince was so focused on the sound of his own panting, and then the wind whistling, that he didn't hear the shouting coming from the hangar entrance until it was too late.

A beam lashed out and struck him in the chest armor; the thermal guard and reflective layer within absorbed some of the blast. But what did make it through was strong enough to burn the ceramic plating and half a centimeter of flesh in his sternum.

Vince hit the ground and rolled, but it was pointless. There was no cover. More beams lashed out. He tried to remain a moving target.

Then the firing stopped. Vince was now gasping loudly and feeling faint.

Someone was standing over him, wearing the helmet of a Paladin. The figure removed its mask slowly, and Vince saw burnt, disfigured skin beneath.

It was Templar Nine.

'We don't belong here,' the Templar said, using the ancient language. His disfigured hand reached for a nanite canister.

Vince's vision was starting to fade.

'They mean to kill us,' Templar Nine continued, kneeling. 'The rest are dead.'

The nanite canister plunged into Vince's thigh; he felt the life-saving biotechnology rushing through his system, revitalizing his senses.

Templar Nine offered his hand; Vince took it and was hoisted to his feet.

'What is this language we speak?' Nine asked, leading Vince toward the hangar. 'I believed we were soldiers of God.'

'So did I,' Vince said, as they reached the entrance. Dead Paladins were everywhere. He wondered if they had all died at Nine's hands. 'I don't know the answer.'

'I sacrificed everything, *everything*, to be a part of this,' Nine said. 'It was all a lie. We have been betrayed, and . . . whatever this is inside of us . . . they have been betrayed as well.'

Vince felt a wave of emotion return as he recalled what the Architect had showed him. He felt a strange kinship with this Templar.

'What will you do?' Nine asked.

'Run,' Vince answered, spotting a Guardian-class MTAC that was still docked to its service platform.

'Where will you run to?' Nine asked.

'I don't know,' he said. 'As far away from them as I can.'

'Would you return to our Empress?'

'No,' Vince said. 'She doesn't deserve to live for what she did to us.'

Nine snapped a gun upright and pointed it at Vince's forehead.

'We swore an oath,' he said. 'Your words are treason.'

'Please don't,' Vince said, raising his hands. 'I have a chance.'

'To do what?' Nine demanded. 'Run away? Don't you remember what Six said to us?'

Vince was overwhelmed with guilt as he recalled the ancient words that Templar Six spoke during their drop into Pike's Landing.

'He said this wasn't their war,' Vince answered. 'That we'd all been deceived . . . and that once we learned the truth, we would regret our actions.'

'This isn't what Empress Jamyl wanted,' Nine said. 'This isn't her war, either.'

'Then whose is it?' Vince asked, remembering the creatures with the strange eyes from his visions. 'Who did this to us?'

'Use your chance to find out,' Nine said. 'It may be too late for their world. But it doesn't have to be for ours.'

Vince thought of the city that crumbled into the sea.

'They know we're still alive,' Nine said, tapping his helmet. 'They're telling me that if I kill you, they'll spare my life.'

Vince took a step back as Templar Nine straightened his aim.

'For the Empress,' Nine said, placing the gun to his own temple and squeezing the trigger.

Vince was horrified; the thing inside of him anguished as the body collapsed. But there was no time to mourn him. Nine had three more nanite canisters; Vince grabbed them and then raced up the ladder to reach the Guardian's cockpit.

The spaceport was just on the other side of the apartment complex, less than two kilometers away.

'EAGLE ONE' LEANED OUTSIDE from his perch in the Blackjack-class gunship, braving the wind and dust hitting his face shield to get a glimpse of the murky lights from the colony perimeter ahead.

The Blackjack was flying less than twenty meters above the ground; two Leander-class combat MTACs were hanging from either side of the craft's fuselage by their backs, scanning the terrain below for targets.

Looking out from the open hatch, another Blackjack in the same configuration was just a few wingspans away, and dozens more were forming a huge flying wedge. Armored vehicles were on the ground speeding beneath the formation, and fighters combed the sky high above.

The Essence 388th Mechanized Division was looking to kill some Paladins.

They were close enough to see muffled flashes on the horizon, mostly toward the southern end of the colony. Rumors were swirling that Ishukone Watch troops were dropping in from the south.

'Eagle One, this is Hightower Five,' the radio squawked. 'We lost direct visual contact after the last orbital strike. But two foot mobiles near the blast site entered an armor hangar at grid marker one-one-five; and one MTAC just blasted its way out, moving on a southwestern heading. If your guy is still alive, the only place he can be is inside that walker, because everything else in the area is wasted.'

'Can you get an ID of the pilot?'

'Negative; there's too much debris in the air,' Hightower Five said. 'But your HVI was looking for a ride. This might be him. The spaceport is just two klicks from there.'

'Copy Hightower; can you mark that target as neutral until we can get a poz ID?'

'Wilco; target is marked.'

'Commander, did you get all that?' Eagle One asked.

'Affirmative; good work,' Admiral Freeman said. 'Fleet broadcast coming . . . . All units, this is Command. We are now jointly participating in the op to extract the HVI with the assistance of Ishukone Watch and Mordu's Legion. Their assets have been marked as friendly in your TACNETs.'

Well, there's a surprise, Eagle One thought.

'Ishukone will suppress Imperial targets inside the perimeter,' Admiral Freeman continued. 'Our task is to assist a squad of downed

Mordu's Legion mercenaries and funnel the HVI toward them. We believe this group knows the HVI personally and that he'll cooperate if they can make contact.'

'... Better and better,' Eagle One mumbled to himself.

'Paladins are enemy targets,' Admiral Freeman said. 'Shoot to kill. If Mordu's troops are neutralized before you can reach them, we will try to take the HVI alive ourselves. His probable location is also marked in your TACNET; we believe he is using enemy MTAC armor to move around. Watch your targets. When the HVI is secure, retreat to our extraction points in the badlands and west of the elevator terminus, whichever is closest. Ishukone and Legion dropships are all cooperating; get into the nearest one you can and get the hell out of there.'

Eagle One looked over his shoulder at the tarps covering the corpses of the soldiers who died earlier.

'I don't know who this HVI is,' he said to himself. 'But he better be worth it.'

VINCE WAS SURPRISED at how powerful the Guardian's beam cannons were.

Awash in the blue glare of the MTACs instruments, he steered the machine through the smoldering hole at the rear of the hangar. Confusion reigned on the radio: It seemed Ishukone Watch troops really had landed inside the perimeter walls and were hammering fortified Paladin positions to the south.

That was a mixed blessing. On one hand, Paladin ground forces were so busy fending off the invaders that his chances of reaching the spaceport were fairly good. On the other, they were also in such disarray that there might not be any dropships left by the time he got there.

Vince eased the throttle forward, heading for the apartment complex. The buildings would provide cover from the open spaces to the south, where the heaviest fighting was. Once through, it would be just a short distance to reach the spaceport entrance.

As he marched into the open, an APC whirled from around the

hangar corner; its driver was demanding an explanation as to why the MTAC wasn't in the fight.

Vince answered with a burst from the beam cannon, which seared through the armor and detonated the vehicle's reactor inside. As fragments of the exploding troop carrier peppered the Guardian's cockpit, proximity warnings alerted him that other armored units – currently marked as 'friendly' on the machine's tactical computer – were closing in on his position.

Two small jets – possibly drones – buzzed low overhead; the Guardian's automated shoulder turrets followed their trajectory across the sky. But Vince eased off the trigger. If they were Imperial birds, he would have been dead. They had to be Federation, who again for some reason were showing surprising restraint from attacking him.

He pushed the Guardian into a full march, shaking the ground with each heavy step. Dealing with multiple tanks in the open was suicide. But if they followed him into the urban terrain ahead, he would have the advantage.

GABLE'S HEAD KEPT STRIKING THE BACK of Jonas's armored vest as he ran toward cover.

'Must get off street,' she heard Mack say. 'More patrols nearby.'

Jonas could barely breathe.

'Okay,' he gasped. 'She's . . . getting heavier by the second.'

'This way,' Mack said. Gable felt Jonas make his way up a small mound of rubble.

She saw one of the Rantula's plated legs scoot by.

'In here,' she heard Mack say. Jonas grunted as he knelt; and then she was gently let down onto the floor.

It was pitch black.

'Put your night optics on,' Jonas said.

The room brightened into shades of gray and white; Jonas's eyes were eerie orbs in the enhanced lighting. Mack set the 20mm cannon down and began scouting the area, sniffing the air on occasion.

The Rantula's head peered into the opening where they entered;

it reminded Gable of a lonely pet that wanted to come inside and play.

'Up,' Mack told it. 'Overwatch position.'

With a cheerful chirp, the death machine scurried up the side of the building.

Gable saw children's toys, old furniture, and cooking appliances strewn among the bones of small animals and the carcasses of dead laaknyds. Several walls had been knocked down, revealing the apartments next door; destroyed pipes and twisted support beams were exposed. A hole in the ceiling went straight through to the roof five stories above them.

Her back hurt so much she wanted to cry.

'What the hell happened to this place?' Jonas asked.

'It was abandoned when I arrived,' Gable said, trying to find a more comfortable position. 'More than a hundred thousand people lived here once. Most died during the fighting; others were lucky enough to leave. General Kintreb kept those who remained closer to the barracks.'

'Voices low,' Mack reminded them, lurking about in the shadows.

'Captain Varitec, are you still alive?' the radio blurted.

It was Mordu.

'Yes,' Jonas answered. 'For now anyway.'

Mack's chin suddenly went up; he took a deep sniff of the air.

'Time is short, so I must be brief,' he said. 'Your friend Vince is still alive, and Ishukone Watch and the Gallente Federation have both agreed to help you find him.'

Mack frantically motioned for Jonas to keep his mouth shut, then pointed to his own nose: His augmented olfactive abilities sensed that trouble was coming.

After slowly pulling the vowrtech off his back, he reached up through the hole in the ceiling and quietly pushed the weapon over the edge.

Then he pulled himself up and over the ledge effortlessly, courtesy of his cybernetic arm.

'They're going to try to funnel him toward you in the hope you can persuade him to join us,' Mordu continued. 'We need you to make your way south, toward the spaceport. There's enough room there for a gunship extraction.'

Gable was terrified. The radio was audible only inside the earpieces they were all wearing, but now Jonas tensed up as well, his rifle drawn.

He motioned for her to shut the radio off.

'Jonas, do you copy this?' Mordu asked. 'Jonas!'

Gable did so, and then just listened.

The wind had picked up, passing through the broken building with a ghostly hum. There was a clicking noise, perhaps made by the insects that made their home here; and the distant sound of war, with muffled thumps and explosions carrying through the corridors of buildings outside.

Jonas was backing away from the entrance when a *whoosh-thud* startled her; he fired a burst from his rifle wildly as sparks jumped out from the space where a wall once stood.

A figure uncloaked as it collapsed in the opening; a knife hilt was protruding from his neck.

Gunfire rang out from above them.

Jonas was whirling around looking for something to shoot, when Mack appeared at the room's entrance and fired the vowrtech almost directly at him.

Gable flinched as another soldier uncloaked in midair, pummeled by the weapon's focused overpressure blast. He landed in a heap, white-hot blood foaming from his mouth and ears.

By the time her eyes moved back to the door, Mack had pushed Jonas to the ground and fired the weapon a second time; the round missed whatever he was aiming at and threw several pieces of kitchen furniture into the wall.

A third figure emerged in front of Mack. A gun discharged as he swung his cybernetic arm downward, cracking the man in his shoulder and driving him to his knees.

Mack staggered back once, then stepped forward and swung so hard and fast that the man's head came clean off. It rolled to a halt beside Gable.

'Special Forces,' Mack said. 'Paladin cloaking armor. More approaching. Must move.'

'*Fuck* me,' Jonas said. 'Are you hurt?'

Gable could tell he was; Mack's body armor was shredded in the abdominal plating.

'Come here,' she said. 'Let me see it.'

'No time,' he said, hoisting up the 20mm cannon. 'We go now. Hurry!'

She dreaded the thought of moving, but before she could protest, Jonas injected her with more painkillers.

'Up we go,' he grunted, lifting her up. Mack was leading them through the first floor of the building, using his arm to bash obstacles out of the way.

'Mordu, this is Jonas. We're in direct contact with hostile forces and moving to the southwest, per your instructions.'

'Tank!' Mack screamed. 'Get down!'

A horrible, numbing blast made the wall in front of them vanish; Gable shrieked as she felt herself fall, blasted by a rain of heavy debris.

Gasping for air, she flipped onto her back. Jonas was hurt; he had a dazed look in his eyes.

His helmet was cracked.

'Stay down!' Mack shouted.

She could see the street outside; the tank's beam had obliterated the ground-floor wall. They were completely exposed from this position. The Rantula was scurrying down the street in a zigzag pattern, as a tank about sixty meters away fired at it but missed; the drone leapt onto the tank's turret and began cutting into it with plasma torches.

Mack took aim with the cannon, but it jammed; the feed mechanism for the belt must have been dented during the attack.

As the tank's turret trained on them, Gable felt a rhythmic pounding that shook the crumbling gravel around her. The turret suddenly changed directions just as a bright white beam blew it apart; an MTAC stomped past its flaming wreck, approaching their position.

The Rantula changed targets and began charging after the walking machine; another beam blew the drone to pieces.

She pulled herself behind some rubble, for all the good it would do.

Mack, still defiantly standing out in the open, pointed the cannon in its direction, then threw it down in disgust as the MTAC marched directly toward him and stopped. Its spotlights made everyone shield their eyes.

As Gable shivered, waiting to be killed, the walker turned its lights off.

THE TARGETING RETICLE CENTERED on the scarred man's face. Vince recognized him instantly. His rage returned; the gold-plated arm of the Guardian pointed its tank-shredding cannon his way.

Stop, the Architect pleaded. *He could be dear to the one you seek.*

Vince shook his head.

He can bring you to her! To harmony! Your rage brings nothing but torment.

The scarred man was thinking, he saw. . . . But he stood defiant. He wouldn't move.

As if he was protecting something.

He does as you would, the Architect said. *Protecting the one you love.*

Vince felt a familiar fear descend over him . . . like in the days when he feared coming home to an abusive father, of facing his instructors as a military cadet, and of dying aboard the *Retford.*

Let yourself be vulnerable. Just this one time.

GABLE WAS PRAYING when Mack called out.

'Lifegiver,' he said, 'come forward.'

She tried to move; it hurt so much.

'Do it!' Mack shouted. 'Show yourself!'

The drugs and the adrenaline compelled her to listen.

She pulled herself forward.

Mack hurried over and lifted her up, then walked close enough for her to see that the MTAC had its cockpit hatch open.

'Gable,' Vince called out. 'Can you help me. . . .'

*

ADMIRAL FREEMAN WATCHED HELPLESSLY as another Judgment beam lashed out from the Avatar and destroyed one of his dreadnoughts from 250 kilometers away.

A lot of people died today, and he wasn't sure why.

It was time to test this new alliance.

'Commander Reppola, I just lost half my towing capacity and have a mechanized division stranded on the surface,' he said. 'That titan is murdering anything in low orbit.'

'We'll get them back,' Mens said. 'But it would go faster if we could focus on personnel and abandon the equipment.'

'Whatever it takes,' Admiral Freeman said. 'I'm in your debt.'

'Gentlemen, we have him,' Mordu interrupted. 'My team has made contact, and the HVI is cooperating. We can start pulling back, but they need an extraction, and the LZ is hot. Do either of you have gunships nearby that can assist?'

'Eagle One, do you copy?' Admiral Freeman said.

'Yes, sir, go ahead.'

'Alright, Mordu – where are they?'

'An apartment complex in the southwest of the colony. Two klicks south of that is a spaceport.'

'Yes, it's marked on our maps as grid one-one-five,' Eagle One said.

'The HVI is in a Guardian-class MTAC,' Mordu said. 'Our team marked it *and* themselves with IR strobes, six-flash pulse. Got it?'

'Affirmative,' Eagle One said. 'Can we communicate with them directly?'

'Yes; stand by. Mack?'

'Copy,' Mack said. 'Have two casualties. Need extraction.'

'Mack, this is Eagle One, Federation Marines. Can you make it to the top of any of those buildings?'

'Negative. Building structure unstable.'

Admiral Freeman was directed to his display by more warnings: A huge fleet of Minmatar ships warped onto the battlefield. Six Naglfarclass dreadnoughts were already in the gauntlet, with the rest of the armada 900 kilometers above them.

The Avatar was turning away from the surface.

'We need to hurry,' Mordu warned. 'I don't know what those crazy Minnies are going to shoot. We have to get off the surface or this is going to get ugly.'

'Concur, Mack, this is Eagle One. Stay where you are; we're coming to you. Close air is in your grid.'

'Copy.'

'Command, this is Hightower. If you don't get him now, you're not going to. They're surrounded by foot mobiles, with armor closing in.'

'Those targets will be priority for our own armor,' Eagle One said. 'After we get them, we're fast-tracking south and west to your drop-sites, correct, Watch?'

'That's correct,' Mens said. 'We'll cover your flanks.'

'Mordu, I recommend you start pulling your ships out,' Admiral Freeman suggested. 'You can't do anything else from there.'

'We're not leaving until our team is off the surface,' Mordu said.

'Your call,' Mens said. 'But you need to trust us.'

JONAS FELT A CRUSHING GROGGINESS obscuring his view of the world as it slowly came back into focus.

Someone was screaming into his ear: 'Jonas, talk to us!'

It was Blake. He put his hands in front of his face and saw four of them.

'We can't get you back to the *Morse*, and they're not saying where they're taking you!'

'Who?'

'Ishukone Watch! Jonas, a mega-corporation is hauling you back into Caldari space! You're a wanted felon there!'

Mack came into view.

'Be strong,' he said. 'This over soon.'

'It is?' Jonas asked. 'Who's coming to get us?'

'Federation,' Mack said. 'Ishukone Watch get us off planet.'

'Mack, this is Blake. How could Mordu agree to this? We don't know if we can trust—'

'No choice,' he growled. 'Miracle to leave Pike's Landing at all.'

Jonas stared at his friend, who in the low lighting looked like a monster.

But Mack was *his* monster.

'Stand up,' he said, heaving him up. 'You were right.'

Jonas saw the towering MTAC with Vince sitting in its cockpit.

'Well, I'll be damned. . . .' he said, stumbling toward it as recognition spread across Vince's face.

Sharp explosions rumbled in the background; the sound of AA rockets filled the air.

Tears were streaming down Gable's face.

'She told me you insisted on coming here,' Vince said. 'Thank you.'

'Clearing, just past that building,' Mack said, coughing a little. Jonas thought he saw droplets of blood spray from his mouth. He was pointing to a spot two hundred meters from where they were standing.

'. . . Pickup is there. MTAC provide cover until Feds assist.'

The sound of grinding treads was getting close.

'Legion team, this is Eagle One,' an unfamiliar voice said. 'Enemy units are closing on your position and we're sixty seconds away. Break for the LZ right now! Get out of there or you'll be overrun!'

'Stay close to the buildings,' Vince said as the cockpit hatch began to close. 'I'll draw their fire as best I can.'

Jonas felt numb; his entire head was throbbing in pain. He was watching himself from the back of his mind, wondering if this was how redemption was supposed to feel.

'Miles, Blake,' Mack said, 'get *Morse* away from Pike's Landing.'

'Not until we know where they're going—'

'*Go*!' he shouted, hauling Gable up onto his shoulder. She shrieked in pain as the Guardian took a step backward and swiveled its torso toward the north, where the bulk of trouble was coming for them. 'We be okay. Save the ship.'

'Mack, listen, man,' Jonas said, feeling very woozy. 'I'm a little out of sorts here . . . don't mean to be an anchor. . . .'

The mercenary grabbed a nozzle syringe from Jonas's own flak jacket and slammed it into his neck.

'Wha – *ffffuck!*' Jonas shrieked, his eyes bulging out of his sockets. 'What the fuck . . . was that?'

The Guardian was marching to the middle of the street; several small-caliber beams struck it in the leg. The machine answered with an air-scorching blast of its own.

'Listen!' Mack said. 'You run fast as you can! Stay on my back! Yes?'

'Hell, yeah,' Jonas said. 'I got this.'

'Then go! Run for life!'

Jonas watched himself break into the fastest sprint he could ever remember himself attempting. For every three steps he took, the MTAC in front of him took one.

They were being shot at. The beams left reflections on the ground as they carved through the night; every time the Guardian's cannon fired, the air behind its weapons and torso roiled in expended heat.

It was strange that he could hear himself breathe, but not Gable as she screamed, bouncing over Mack's shoulder as he ran his peculiar skip-stride for dear life. Nor could he hear the rumble of several tons of machine as it crushed the ground with every step; nor the lines of exploding rock and metal as fighters overhead strafed armored targets to their east. . . .

. . . Nor the sound of a tank cannon's blast take an arm off the Guardian as it marched painfully slow in reverse to protect its tiring companions.

Jonas's lungs began to burn; his legs filled with acid. The world was a strobe of hellish images, and time ceased to matter. People were trying to kill him, and that seemed unfair. Vince was his responsibility; he was part of his crew; and this is what good men did for those in their care.

There is no price too high to pay for honor, and this is what he hoped others would do for him.

A violent burst of energy knocked the three of them over.

He tasted a mouthful of dirt.

Looking up, he saw the bluish-white jets of a gunship land just fifty meters away.

The Guardian was still facing away from it, guns blazing despite the fact that it was on fire. The cockpit opened, and Vince jumped down as the machine walked itself into the withering barrage of beam fire.

As it collapsed and exploded, a ramp began to lower on the gunship; masked men emerged with rifles as a pair of turrets spit out streams of plasma into the night.

Mack had made it. He set Gable down inside.

Jonas smiled, thankful that his crew was safe, and let his head fall to the dirt.

But he was yanked upright. He was being carried through hell toward the open ramp.

His legs were no longer working. Turning his head he could see Vince. *My God, what did they do to you?* he wondered. The man barely looked like his old self, with flaps of crimson skin hanging from a face that was ghastly pale and crossed with bluish veins. Turning the other way, he saw Mack. They were both lifting him, an arm over each one's shoulder, and were so close to the ramp's edge, when both men dropped him.

Jonas struck the ground again.

Mack, also prone, was staring at him from just inches away. Blood was flowing out of his nose; his deranged smile remained, but his eyes were filled with sadness.

His mouth moved to say something and then stopped.

The last words Jonas heard belonged to Gable.

'God in heaven, *please*,' she begged. 'I can't save them all. . . .'

EPILOGUE

METROPOLIS REGION – GEDUR CONSTELLATION
THE ILLUIN SYSTEM – PLANET III: KHATAJAN
REPUBLIC PARLIAMENT BUREAU STATION

'Let me make sure I understand this,' Sanmatar Shakor said. 'You bombard one of our worlds, invade one of our colonies, leave most of your weapons behind, and you expect me to keep all this . . . quiet?'

Jacus looked at his counterpart impassively.

'Yes.'

'Just pretend it never happened, and the Federation prisoners I'm holding are just ghosts that no one will miss?' Shakor said.

'I think we can reach an agreement to secure their release quietly as well,' Jacus said.

Shakor, his eyes clouded over in blindness, exhaled forcefully. 'Do you feel that you're negotiating for something here?' he said.

Jacus smiled. 'Have you given any thought as to why I would authorize these actions?' he asked.

'Short of you providing the explanation I'm entitled to, I'm willing to write it off as insanity,' Shakor said. 'But if you think you can bargain with the truth, you're gravely mistaken.'

'In the last century, the Federation has funded the Republic with staggering sums of money,' Jacus said. 'I believe I'm entitled to some knowledge of how you've spent it.'

'Is that so?' Sanmatar Shakor said, his knuckles whitening around the grip of his khumaak. Jacus could see his reflection in the ceremonial weapon's steel spikes.

'In exchange for that transparency, *and* the unconditional release of any Federation or Ishukone Watch prisoners, I offer you, "the truth," ' he said.

'You can read about the invasion in this evening's SCOPE broadcast,' Sanmatar Shakor said, pulling himself off the seat. 'Thank you, Roden, that will be all.'

Jacus didn't move.

'The Skymother Project is in peril,' he said. 'As is your new government.'

Shakor froze.

'The latter I very much want to succeed,' Jacus said. 'But Skymother – not unless I know more about it.'

'You're playing a dangerous game now, Roden.'

'As are you, Sanmatar,' Jacus said. 'You of all people understand there are times when urgency compels action, not discourse. The truth is that I invaded your nation to save it. The action is past, so now, if you're willing, there can be discourse.'

'You sound like an Amarrian now,' Sanmatar Shakor growled. 'Did you get what you wanted from Pike's Landing?'

'Almost,' Jacus said.

HEIMATAR REGION – HED CONSTELLATION
AMAMAKE SYSTEM – PLANET II: PIKE'S LANDING
THIRTY KILOMETERS SOUTHEAST OF CORE FREEDOM COLONY – BADLANDS GRID
SOVEREIGNTY OF THE MINMATAR REPUBLIC

Minmatar Republic soldiers stood about in pairs, glaring at the Federation Navy salvage drones toiling under the Amamake sun. The wreckage was mostly blackened, twisted metal; in most cases it was difficult to determine where the Amarr gunship stopped and the unidentified one began.

But the drones were meticulous, collecting even microscopic bits of debris. A construction barge already filled with evidence was slowly making its way toward an idling Pegasus dropship, which would eventually transport the material to a warehouse owned by Roden Shipyards.

The remnants of the downed Federation Blackjack, a little over a hundred meters away, remained untouched. Bodies of the slain 626 Recon commandos were discovered near a dry riverbed less than two kilometers from the crash site. The Kruk-class gunship that had brought them to Pike's Landing was found intact, located near the bodies in an erosional cave. In some spots, the craft's edges had less than a meter's clearance with the cave walls. The margin of error for a pilot to fly it inside was nearly zero.

Eagle One, now dressed in nondescript civilian clothes and accompanied by two military contractors dispatched by the President himself, found what he was looking for at the base of a rock ledge.

'That's it,' Eagle One said, clearing some silt off the device. 'She dropped it as they fell to the bottom.'

'You say it discharged?' one of the contractors asked, as their Republic soldier escorts leaned in for a closer look.

'Yeah, I think so,' he said. 'I was standing at the jump position when we got hit. As we spun around, I thought I saw something.'

'Did you hear anything?'

Eagle One shook his head.

'Too much shouting going on,' he said.

The other contractor put his case on the ground and began excavating around the weapon, making sure he'd found the edges before picking it up very carefully and setting it inside. As the lid hissed shut, lights on the outside of the container suggested that something dangerous was inside.

'Any chance you could go up there and take a look around?' the contractor asked. 'You know, look for shell casings, maybe a blast mark . . . .'

It was a steep rock face, but only a ten-meter climb or so.

'Give me a few minutes,' Eagle One said, rolling up his sleeves.

Taking a firm grip of a small ledge overhead, he pulled himself up and began working his way to the top.

Along the way, the contractor called out.

'You doing alright?'

'I'm fine,' Eagle One said, gaining purchase in another crevice with his boot. 'But this is one hell of a distance to fall.'

Reaching the top, he pulled himself over and brushed himself off. Hearing reports about the aggressiveness of some local predators in the ecosystem, he checked his sidearm once before waving at the contractors and guards, then turned around.

He blinked several times.

'You guys have to come up here,' he called out over his shoulder.

'Why?' the contractor yelled back up. 'You found something?'

'Just get up here,' Eagle One said. 'You have to see this.'

THE FORGE REGION – ONIRVURA CONSTELLATION
THE POINEN SYSTEM – PLANET IV, MOON 26
INTERNAL SECURITY ASSEMBLY STATION
SOVEREIGNTY OF THE CALDARI STATE

'So it's Khanid technology, eh,' Tibus asked. 'Does it work?'

'If you're not concerned about her well-being, then yes,' the scientist said. His wrists were exposed, prominently displaying the tattoo of the Templis Dragonaurs. 'The Amarr use it to "Reclaim" their inmates. But in the right hands, it can be used to walk into any part of her mind to extract information, usually at the expense of leaving the victim ruined.'

Haatakan, dressed in nothing but undergarments, sat with her arms bound behind her, her head listed to one side, with eyes unfocused and a blank expression on her face.

She hadn't uttered a single word in days.

Heth glared at her for a few moments.

'So you're a masochist now?' he asked. 'You know I'm going to find out everything anyway, right?'

Her eyes remained blank as drops of urine began falling from the chair.

'Fine,' the dictator said. 'The hard way it is.'

He looked at the scientist.

'She's all yours,' he said. 'Keep me posted.'

'Of course,' the scientist said, kneeling in front of her.

'Hello, Haatakan,' he said. 'My name is Doctor Zaan, and I'm going to be your new mind warden.'

He ran his fingers through her hair, grabbing a handful.

'I'm rather looking forward to it,' he said with a smile. 'Aren't you?'

GEMINATE REGION – F-ZNNG CONSTELLATION
SYSTEM UBX-CC – THE MJOLNIR NEBULA
INSORUM PRODUCTION FACTORY

'I'm impressed by what you've built here,' Mordu said. 'If somewhat unsettled.'

Lurking in the shadows, drones were following him everywhere he went, always within striking distance.

And those were just the ones he could see.

'First the Broker, now Heth,' Mens said. 'I trust machines more than people now.'

'You don't really mean that,' Mordu asked. 'Do you?'

Mens flashed a brief smile.

'You can come here whenever you like,' he continued, leading Mordu down a hallway. 'The pickup location is random, never the same twice, and you must always come alone.'

Mordu followed as doors opened in front of the Ishukone CEO. There were windows that showed the space outside, but all he could see was swirling dust.

'A word of caution, though,' Mens added, stopping before the final door and turning to face him. 'If the drone suspects that it's being followed, one of two things can happen: It will either stop wherever it is in space and eject you from the ship, or it will lead you and whoever is following into . . . something unpleasant.'

Mordu looked into Reppola's eyes and, for a brief instant, recognized a much younger and tormented version of himself.

'You saved my son's life,' he said. 'We are with you!'

Mens looked away.

'Thank you,' he said. 'We'll find out soon enough if you really are.'

DOMAIN REGION – THRONE WORLDS CONSTELLATION
THE AMARR SYSTEM – PLANET ORIS
EMPEROR FAMILY ACADEMY STATION
SOVEREIGNTY OF THE AMARR EMPIRE

With perfect recollection, Grand Admiral Kezti Sundara calmly explained all of the events leading to his decision to bombard Pike's Landing.

Despite the indisputable testimony, Empress Jamyl could not accept that the order had been her own.

'I can't remember any of it,' she fumed. 'Nothing.'

'You are the divine embodiment of the eternal struggle between good and evil,' Grand Admiral Sundara said. 'The Demon has many tricks, but you will find a way to persevere.'

She pulled her wavy auburn hair back in frustration.

'And after all this, we lost the colony anyway?'

'I ordered the retreat when the Ishukone fleet arrived,' Admiral Sundara said. 'The Caldari have been an ally, yet they destroyed several of our ships. I was unprepared for that and decided it would be unwise to retaliate without fully understanding the circumstances.'

'I received a personal apology from Tibus Heth, who claimed Ishukone Watch acted alone,' Empress Jamyl said. 'You would have done him a great service by pounding that fleet into dust. Given the circumstances, there was no way for you to know that. But the next time anyone attacks our forces, Grand Admiral, don't think. Just react in kind.'

'Your Majesty,' he said, bowing his head.

'Send Lord Victor in,' she ordered.

The chamber doors were pulled apart by palace guards, and Lord Victor Eliade strode inside. Ignoring the Admiral, he knelt before the Empress, then stood.

'Do we know the fate of Templar One yet?' she asked.

'No, my lady,' Lord Victor said. 'We have not found a body, and his broadcast array stopped transmitting during the Ishukone withdrawal from Pike's Landing.'

'What of his imprint?' she asked. 'Is it still in storage?'

'Yes,' Lord Victor said. 'As with the remaining Templars as well.'

Empress Jamyl took a deep breath.

'He must be found, Victor,' she said. 'Do whatever is necessary.'

'As you wish,' he said. 'It shall be done.'

Alternating glances between both men, she straightened her posture.

'I need both of you,' she said. 'Pike's Landing is my fault. But you must move past it.'

'The blame is not yours,' Grand Admiral Sundara said, 'but with the struggle inside you.'

The Empress began to pace.

'You can't imagine what this is like,' she said. 'Regardless, it's my burden, and I must carry it better.'

'Marcus Jror is dead,' Lord Victor said. 'Whom do you wish to continue his work?'

'I leave it to you to replace him,' she said. 'But choose wisely: These forces are indescribably sinister. I shall rely on you, Victor, and you, Kezti, to be my closest guides as I fight this battle. Set your differences aside; Amarr needs both of you to be strong.'

'I hold no grudge against the Grand Admiral,' Victor said. 'It is an honor to serve beside him.'

'Good,' she said. 'We will persevere, my captains. And I know in my heart that our Templars will lead the way.'

GEMINATE REGION – F-ZNNG CONSTELLATION
SYSTEM UBX-CC – THE MJOLNIR NEBULA
INSORUM PRODUCTION FACTORY

'Mom's gone, isn't she?' Amile asked.

'Yes,' Mens said, holding his daughter's hand.

'I remember boarding a gunship . . . we were supposed to go to . . . Myoklar?'

Mens nodded slowly.

'It was attacked during the approach.'

'By who?'

'Heth.'

'I wish I could remember what we talked about,' she said.

'She loved you very much,' Mens said.

'It was a bad idea,' she said, frowning. 'I knew it then.'

'No, no . . . Amile . . . if anyone's to blame, it's me. Please. Not you.'

'The last memory I'll ever have of Mom is that I didn't stand up to her. If I had, she might still be alive.'

Mens took a deep breath.

'Amile,' he said, 'remember when you told me you wanted a more active role in protecting yourself?'

'Yeah?' Amile said.

'You have it now,' Mens said. 'We're far, far away from Ishukone, someplace where Heth and the Broker can't find us. This is where we're going to make our stand.'

'By hiding from them?'

'By figuring out how to beat them,' Mens said. 'Let me show you something.'

A tiny drone, no larger than a datapad, scurried up the side of Amile's bed and sat on her lap, startling her.

'It's okay,' Mens said, as it playfully flipped onto its back, then righted itself and performed a salute with one of its appendages.

'See? Put your hand out.'

She did so, and the creature reached out with one of its legs and touched her hand then pulled it away. It repeated the act again, as if judging whether it was safe, and then jumped into her palm, spreading out as though lounging on a couch.

'This is VILAMO,' Mens said. 'Rali built him. Don't let his size fool you. He's quite capable, as you'll soon find out.'

'Capable of what?' Amile asked.

'Of teaching you how to protect yourself,' Mens said. 'When

you're feeling better, there's someone else I'm going to introduce you to. But for now—'

'Are you going to be here?' she asked.

Mens took a big swallow.

'Rali will be here a few days a week to continue your education—'

'Dad,' Amile said. 'Are you going to stay here with me?'

'As much as I can,' Mens said.

'DOCTOR DIETRICH,' MENS ASKED, 'how is our patient doing?'

'Stabilized, for now,' Gable said. 'Though I don't know how much I had to do with that. His anatomy is incredibly resilient.'

'Is he cooperating?'

'He trusts me,' Gable said. 'He fully understands that we can't help him until we learn more about him. But there is one concern I have.'

'What's that?'

'His entire hippocampus and thalamus have been replaced with a cybernetic implant I've never seen before,' she said. 'And there's more technology I'm unfamiliar with. For example, I think his entire spinal cord is a transmitter of some kind.'

'It probably is,' Mens said. 'He's a prototype. The technical specifications for his clone type will be here shortly.'

'His normal body temperature is elevated already, and his back is almost hot to the touch,' she said. 'I'm guessing it's still broadcasting.'

'We'll look into it,' Mens said. 'Do you have everything else you need?'

'Yes; the facility is state of the art,' she said. 'But the drones are very intimidating.'

'They're for your protection,' Mens explained. 'You know there are risks.'

'I understand, and I appreciate it,' she said.

'My colleague Rali is very impressed with your background,' Mens commended. 'You two are going to be working closely together.'

'Oh? What's his background?'

'His contributions to Ishukone are too numerous to count, but first and foremost, he's an engineer,' Mens said. 'The best there is.

He can build anything, including the cybernetic technology you might need to save Vince's life.'

'That will come in handy,' Gable said, folding her arms. 'Reverse-engineering him sounds like quite the business opportunity.'

'You're welcome to express your opinions, Doctor,' Mens said. 'But this work is important. Vince isn't the only one here whose life is in danger.'

'WHEN CAN I MEET HER?' Mila asked.

'Soon,' Mens said, staring into the room where Amile was sleeping. 'She needs some time.'

'VILAMO has taken a liking to her,' Mila said, noting the drone sprawled out at the foot of her bed.

'That shouldn't be possible,' Mens said.

'I always thought he was built that way,' Mila said.

'VILAMO was built to learn and to hunt,' Mens said. 'The nurturing behavior is new. I'll have Rali look into it.'

'You're asking a lot of him,' she said.

'I ask a lot of everyone in my life.'

Taking one last look at his daughter, he turned and walked straight past Mila.

'Mens,' she called out. 'I'm sorry about Lor—'

'*Don't* you ever say her name to me again,' he growled.

PURE BLIND REGION – MDM8-J CONSTELLATION
SYSTEM 5ZXX-K – PLANET V, MOON 17
MORDU'S LEGION HQ STATION

Jonas looked up from his work as Miles and Blake appeared in the doorway.

'You wanted to see us, sir?' Blake said.

'Yep, come on in,' Jonas said.

'How're the new stilts doing?' Miles asked.

Jonas lightly kicked one of his metal prostheses against the desk.

'They'll do until my new legs are done growing,' he said. 'I'm not a cybernetic kind of guy. Have a seat.'

As the two officers moved toward the chairs in front of his desk, Miles unleashed a low whistle.

'*Love* what you've done to the place!' he sneered. 'Geez, you'd think a billionaire would spend a few creds on, like . . . a painting. Or something.'

Blake just shook her head.

'I guess the walls in here are a little bare,' Jonas said. 'I admit when it comes to these things, I don't have a clue.'

'You need a lady for those,' Blake said. 'Clues, that is.'

Jonas smiled.

'So I hear,' he said. 'Alright, let's get down to business. First, I've recommended both of you for the Legion Cross. You not only displayed poise and leadership under fire, but your actions at Pike's Landing saved the lives of thousands of crew. I couldn't be prouder of you, and it's an honor to have you aboard the *Morse*. Thanks for bringing her back to me in one piece.'

The officers were beaming.

'Thank you, sir,' Blake said.

'Bam!' Miles said. 'That'll look sharp on my dress blues.'

'Next, regarding your compensation,' Jonas continued. 'Well, let's just say it's a lot of money. It was wired into your accounts just before you arrived, so if you have your datapads with you, you're welcome to check that figure now.'

Blake was trying to act composed, but Miles was on the verge of drooling as they dug into their pockets to retrieve the devices.

Then they turned pale.

'You both received the same amount,' Jonas said, rubbing his eyes. 'The Legion has some really good finance guys you should speak with. There's enough there for you to live *really* comfortably without working another day as long as you live, but only if you're smart about where you invest it. Which brings me to my next and final point—'

'Captain, I don't have the words—' Blake said.

'Oh, I do!' Miles said, slowly standing up. 'And those words are *fuck yeah!* Woo!'

While Miles danced like an idiot, Blake appeared concerned.

'Are you sure about this?' she asked.

'Absolutely,' Jonas said. 'I restructured both your contracts. You're no longer bound to its terms, meaning you're free to leave the *Morse*.'

Miles stopped dancing.

'Huh?'

'As mercenaries, you're no longer obligated to be here,' Jonas said. 'You're free to go right now, if you wish. Start a new life.'

They tried to find some indication that he was kidding, but it just wasn't there.

'Don't get me wrong, the *Morse* wouldn't be the same without you,' he said. 'But in this profession, you never do know how it's going to turn out, so ... I just want to make sure you both had a chance to walk away.'

Miles sat back down.

'Well, to be honest, sir,' he said, 'that's a real buzzkill.'

'You don't have to give me an answer now,' Jonas said. 'In fact, I insist you both take some time off to think about it. The *Morse* isn't leaving port anytime soon.'

Blake rose from her seat.

'I'll do as you asked, sir,' she said, gently placing her hand on Miles's shoulder.

He looked up at her and then stood.

'Well, what are you going to do with your share?' Miles asked.

Jonas forced a weary smile.

'I gave it away.'

Blake closed her eyes in disbelief, then took Miles's hand and began leading him toward the door.

'*All* of it?' Miles asked.

'Yes.'

'C'mon,' Blake said quietly. 'It's time for us to go.'

As they walked out, Miles turned to ask one last question.

'Are you going to be alright, boss?' he asked.

'I'm fine,' Jonas said. 'Thank you for asking.'

When the door closed, Jonas turned the terminal off. Then he shut off all the lights except for one.

He stared at the new addition to his glass trophy case. The toy soldier barely fit inside.

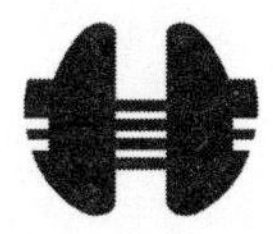

AFTERWORD

JUST OUTSIDE THE BORDERS of Caldari space, hidden in the unremarkable asteroid belts of systems abandoned by prospectors long ago, lurked a series of outposts. The insides of these hardened structures were crammed with highly advanced technical equipment, usually of the sort found in secure Empire stations. Vast datacore centers linking to fluid routers, all still active, sat alongside cloning equipment, including CRUs with clones waiting inside. Curiously, lockers filled with neatly arranged garments of all manner of styles were also present, despite the fact there was none of the more customary creature comforts associated with a common research center.

In each of these outposts, everything was covered in dust.

A sentient life-form chanced upon one during a belt-surveying mission and promptly informed its master.

Within hours, its smaller companions had broken inside, not realizing how lucky they were; a thermonuclear device powerful enough to atomize the asteroid upon which they stood had somehow failed to detonate following the unauthorized breach. Whoever had rigged it had made a mistake.

It was one of many the Broker made toward the end of his physical lives.

AKNOWLEDGMENTS

Whew. The second one was definitely more challenging to write, mostly because I kept letting my worries get in the way of creativity. I learned a great deal from my experience writing *Empyrean Age*, especially from the feedback I received from colleagues and fans alike. This time around, my goal was simply to tell a more human story. Hopefully I've created characters that you would like to read more about.

To those who read *Empyrean Age* and are not using the book as a doorstop, you have my sincerest thanks. *Templar One* would not have been possible without your support. This is all very bizarre to me, thanking strangers. But my development as a writer is influenced in huge part by your enthusiasm for this work. For what it's worth, it means a lot to me. Thank you.

I have the honor of working with great people who may not even realize their contributions to this book. From CCP, first and foremost I have to thank the video team: Greg Kruk, Robin Whitehead, Jói Jónsson, Oliver Nicholson, Sölvi Ingimundarson, Ólafur Haraldsson, and Jói Reynisson. You are all brilliantly talented, and your work is an inspiration to me.

I owe thanks to the entire EVE Content team, especially Nathan Knaack, Nick Blood, Chris Cowger, and Jason Bolte for your creative guidance and support, with special thanks to Scott Holden for going the extra mile in editing the manuscript.

On the DUST 514 team, I would like to thank Gavin Frankle and

Elijah Freeman for helping me navigate through this new IP. My role in helping to shape this game is very small, but you've both made me feel like I was a big part of it.

I owe special thanks to the entire marketing team at CCP, particularly Mike Read and Ned Coker for giving me the kick in the pants I needed to embrace what I am just a little bit more; Elísabet Grétarsdóttir for being the voice of reason in every storm; and Greg Fountain, from whom I have learned so much.

For everyone on the hockey mailing list at CCP: The ha-ha's and trashtalk keep me sane. Thank you. There's a Hanson in every one of us.

And finally special thanks to Hilmar, for leading with your heart, and for giving us all the chance to spread our wings a little further.

From Tor I'd like to thank Eric Raab and Katharine Critchlow, not only for your precious editorial guidance, but also for not sending mercenaries to intimidate me into finishing this draft sooner.

To my lifelong friends Brian, Ron, Mark, Keith, Ken, Darrell, and Will: Thanks for checking in on me every now and then to make sure I was still alive, especially all you new dads. Time flies when you're changing diapers.

To Grandma, Christina, Coco, Teo, Ines, and Angela: Thank you for helping me discover my roots.

To my extended family, George, Catherine, Alainna, Alisa, Joe, Denise, Joe Jr., Michele, Billy, Lou, Sue, Galina, Barbara, and Don: Raising toasts with you brings me happiness. We should do it more often.

To my parents: I couldn't live this wonderful life, let alone raise my daughter, without you. I can never thank you enough.

To my beloved wife: Thank you for your patience and support throughout all of this, especially as we became parents.

And to my daughter: I've never been prouder. I love you.

Tony Gonzales
Twitter: CCP_TonyG